An Unpolished Gem

**Book Two
of the Souls of
the Saintlands**

Tonya Adolfson

Published by Fantastic Journeys Publishing,
Boise, Idaho
PUBLISHING HISTORY
E-Book released through Kindle Jan 2012
Soft Cover trial edition March 2012
Mass market edition April 2013

Cover art created in Gimp 2.6 by John Farmer
Cover Art copyright by Fantastic Journeys Publishing
Content copyright ©Nov 2011 Tonya Adolfson.
Interior art: Map by Suzette Snyder
Edited by William Sparks and Julia Stidolph

Published in the United States of America.

ISBN: 978-0-9832556-3-5

Reviews for An Unpolished Gem

"In a perfect follow through to Thine Enemy's Eyes, Ms. Adolfson continues to illustrate just how sticky the politics and personalities of her world really can be. She never lets go of you, even after the book is done. Just when I think I have a character figured out, they surprise me; I can't even tell how many sides to this story there are. I can't wait for book three!"
Julien McBain, author Ghosts of the Past

"It is difficult for second books in a series to have the same weight as the first. This is the rarer case of the second book surpassing the first."
Christopher Garcia, editor of *the Drink Tank*

"This book is just as captivating as the first book in the series. Again I was so enthralled with the characters, plot twists, and story line that I litterally couldn't put it down and finished reading it in one day..."
Chalyse Padigimus, Amazon Review

"I love her writing style. She creates this world that becomes real to its readers. Oh and then there are these great characters with such richness and depth you cannot help but to love and in some cases hate them! She has written it in such a way you have no idea where or who, if anyone, the main character will end up with. There is such a depth in the story you just cannot put it down. I read it in a matter of hours. I know these are books I am going to read again and again throughout the years. It has to be a great book for it to have that kind of status on my bookshelf."
Maryanne Durant, Amazon Review

"Love the way the characters grow and mature. Can't wait for the next book!"
Shelley Wolf, Amazon Review

Dedicated to the original Black Sparrow,
Sgt. Jeffery Ross Shaver
Persian Gulf, Iraq
Purple Heart, Bronze Star, Combat Medic
10-22-1977 to 5-12-2004
"Love and Live with Passion!"

Acknowledgments:

First and foremost, I'd like to thank all the people who were inspirations for this book:

Gwen, for Gwen; Erik, for Dom; Brady for Markus; Jeff for James; Jared for Draethen; Dave for Octavius, Aaron for Duncan, John for Myrgen and Jennifer for Ce'Nedra. Without each of them, these characters could never have the depth they do.

I'd also like to thank Alice, Tammy, Paul and Hannah for their feedback and assistance editing. Alpha Readers Unite!

I'd also like to thank Gwen J. and John F. for endless hours of inspiration and consultation. Thank you guys!

Thanks to Shannon Galarneau for being my agent and helping me fulfill the dream of Fantastic Journeys Publishing

And finally, to my wonderful family: Morgan and Misha, for being so tolerant of Mommy's work; to my Daddy, Ray Lamar Manley, for inspiring me to tell stories for the sheer pleasure of my audience; to my Mom, Rosemary Virginia Manley, for reading historical romances; and to the Great and Powerful Todd, for being everything a Prince needs to be.

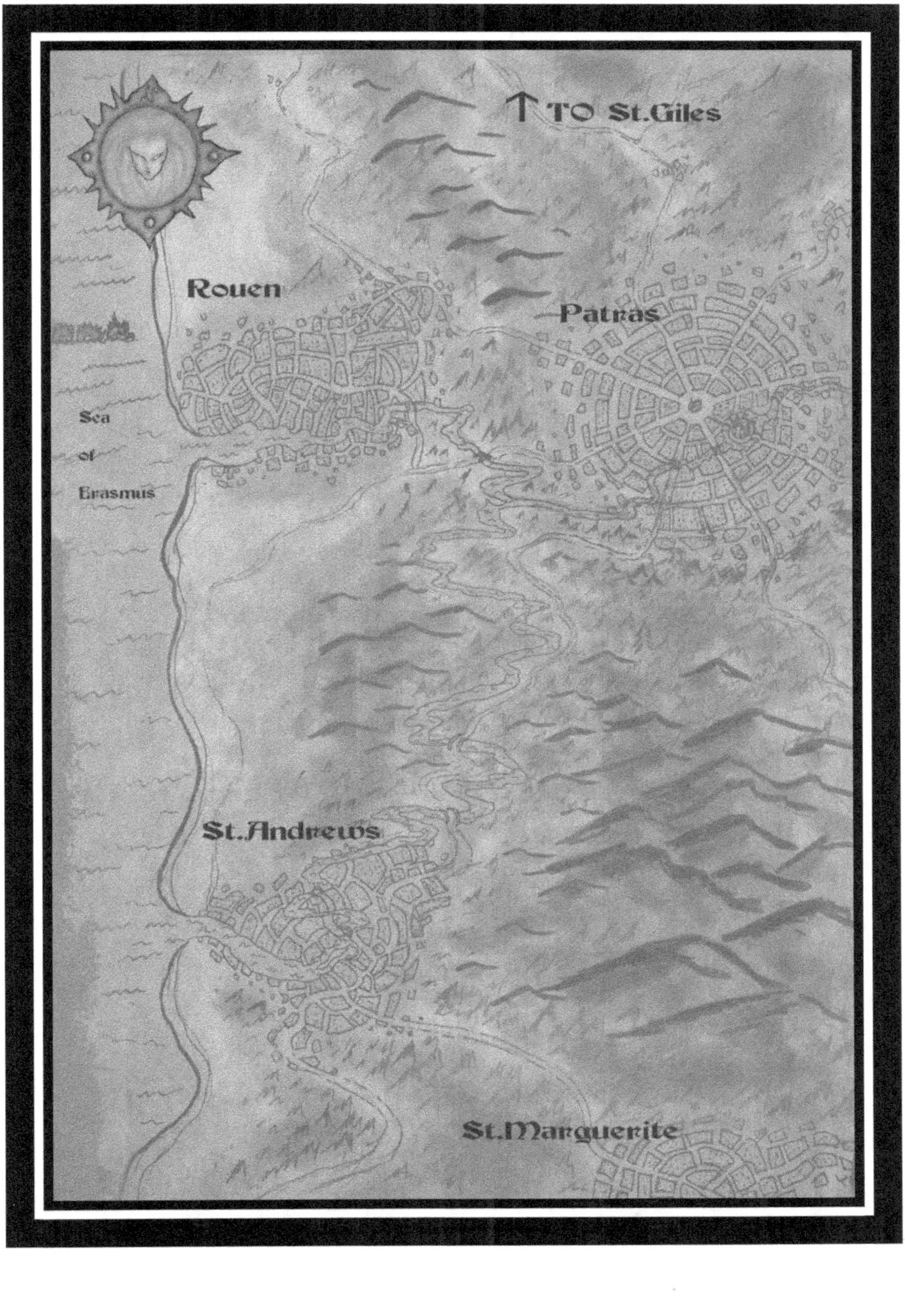

TO St.Giles
Rouen
Patras
Sea
of
Erasmus
St.Andrews
St.Marguerite

Tasty Tidbits from the Wise Wench! Monique Delorme, proprietress of the Wise Wench Tavern in St. Giles, is known for her good advice and tasty treats. One of her patrons from Krakte wrote down her best recipes and witticisms and now, you can have a copy too!

Look for the *Wise Wench's Tavern Book* from a bookseller in Patras near you!

Book One

"A gem cannot be polished without friction, nor a
man perfected without trials."
The Wise Wench's Tavern Book

"Make no judgments where you have no
compassion."
Anne McCaffrey

One

"The first point to know while owning a tavern is who the true servants are."
The Wise Wench's Tavern Book

"His Holiness will see you now."

The man in the hooded coat stood and walked into the giant office in the cathedral. The carved doors opened for him and closed for the conversation. He knelt before the man in the lavish silk robes and mitre.

The Archbishop Alonzo de Patrone acknowledged the man on one knee before him, his covered head bowed in respect, and smiled. Alonzo had been listening to confessions personally since he had been given the Archbishopric of Patras ten years ago and was the secret leader of the Patrasian Underground, the network through which unsavory types got their assignments. As the confessor of every thief, cutthroat, and con artist in the capital city, he was kept well-informed of who was the best candidate for which assignment. The man before him was one of his favorites.

This was evidenced by the fact that he was allowed a face-to-face confession instead of the way confessions usually worked.

"Duncan. I take it by your presence back in Patras that the Writ has been carried out?"

"Yes, Your Excellency."

"Good," he waved his hand in the sign of Absolution. "There's someone who wishes to speak to you. Rise, my son."

Alonzo rose from his receiving chair, a beautifully carved creature with a high back and wide seat. The Archbishop had grown large before taking this post. He needed the heavy oak chair to support his massive weight. However, the bishops underneath him had felt he needed exercise to keep him sharp and healthy. They had started him on a regimen of diet and activity. At first he had protested, of course, but then he started to feel the effects in increased stamina. Now, he was far more fit than he ever had been, even in his youth. The only drawback to this was the excess flesh from his over three hundred pound body, which kept a bit of bulk on his body in sagging bags, now that he was half that weight. His furniture was never replaced, at his request, to remind him of his change in life.

The loose folds of his cassock hid this bulk nicely and the mitre on his head added height to counter the weight. The white and red he wore was complemented by gold filigree embroidery in ancient crosses all over the fabric. Alonzo had decided to grow a beard to cover the excess flesh of his chins. After the weight was gone, he decided he was too accustomed to the look to get rid of it now. He worried he was slowly working his way through the entire list of deadly sins; Pride, Sloth, and Gluttony already covered.

Alonzo stepped before a large gold mirror that hung over a basin of matching design set into a mahogany cabinet. He took a ewer from the cabinet top and blessed the water before pouring it into the basin. As he poured the water, the mirror's surface wavered like the surface of the water in the basin. When he stopped pouring, it took a moment for the surface to settle into a flat reflection again. When it did, it showed not the Archbishop's reflection, but that of a small, venerable man.

"Yes, Alonzo. What news have you?"

"I have the one I spoke of, Your Holiness. Duncan McVryce."

The Pope nodded and Bishop Alonzo stepped aside to permit the other man to be seen. Duncan pushed back his hood and revealed himself to the dignified man who was Heaven's Representative on Earth. Duncan was very tall, his head shaved completely bald with a black patch of hair framing his mouth. Hazel eyes were constantly shifting colors, like shadows chasing the bright points away from the light. He bowed his head in deference, his voice crisp and hiding a cheerful lilt behind a somber expression.

"I understand you asked for me, Your Holiness."

"Yes. Bishop Alonzo has stated you might be interested in a particular assignment, one that involves great danger. I need you to rescue a lady in distress."

"I'm much better at putting ladies *in* distress, Your Holiness."

"I see. However, His Excellency insisted you would be more inclined to this task than the other task I needed accomplished."

"Perhaps if you offered me both, I could decide for myself."

"Very well. The first task is to stop the King of Mervolingia from getting engaged to a Catriona Moriarity. It should be fairly simple. I understand the woman is married."

"Moriarity? I'm afraid that man is dead. He was killed earlier today in a street fight with the King."

"I see. Your sovereign is quite insistent about securing this woman."

"It appears so. What is the other job?"

"To rescue the Honorable Lady Tanglwyst de Holloway and get her safely to the Papal City where she will be under my protection."

Duncan grew still. "You were right, Your Holiness. I shall indeed take the second job and make it my priority."

"Good. It is mine as well. The other task can be handled later, possibly by someone else. This one, I was assured, was best left to your abilities."

"It will not be a problem. Where is she being held?"

"Under house arrest, at her Patras estate."

"Thank you, Your Holiness. It will be done according to Heaven's Will."

"Saints and angels protect you, my son."

Duncan stepped away from the mirror. It went back to reflecting the Archbishop's visage. "Will this be a problem for you, my son?"

Duncan shook his head. "I serve Heaven first, then the Crown of Mervolingia, according to the Oath of Fealty I swore."

Alonzo nodded. "I'm satisfied this will work out according to Heaven's will." He put his hand upon Duncan's shoulder and glanced at the centuries old amulet on Duncan's neck. It was one of only three remaining from a holy war that resulted in the purging of Fae and arcane practice from the Saintlands. "You are in Heaven's hands."

Tanglwyst sat in her study overlooking the alleyway where her husband had been murdered, twirling her long, auburn hair. Her injuries from the catacombs were gone now, thanks to the healing herbs the Prince gave her, but the brutal loss of her best friend and Queen, Elizabeth, was overwhelming. For all his kindness, Alexander apparently had a vicious side to him as well. He'd stabbed Elizabeth through the stomach, then had her dragged away to be impaled and hung to finish dying outside the city. Tanglwyst saw a peasant girl wearing the Queen's gown walk past her window an hour ago, the blood and rips barely washed away, the final indignity for Tanglwyst's best friend. *By the Saints, I hope there are no necrophiliacs in Patras. That would be Alexander's ultimate victory.* She found her ability to cry no longer accompanied her. Now she simply sat and watched the world mock her in the streets with its lively step and the music of the marketplace.

She shifted on the window seat. The stained glass figures of the window casting blue and orange shimmers on the small wrinkles near her eyes. The bruises on her face and body from the fight with Catriona had faded within the day and she faced her imprisonment the way she faced all her other challenges; with elegance and opulence. She was dressed in a long robe of Mandian design, the brocade several shades of green to complement her envy-colored eyes. Her hair was unbound, a luxury she reveled in since she wasn't allowed out of the house. Usually, her hair was caught up in several different braids, some hers, some from a young woman down on her luck who sold her hair for just such an occasion. Small shoes and stockings kept her feet comfortable. She almost neglected the fire in the fireplace chasing away what discomfort did get in. She wondered where Nicolai was and why he had not yet come to rescue her.

She was under house arrest until the new King returned. Elizabeth's execution for the murder of Charles, and Myrgen's inexplicable escape from prison left only her with whom to be dealt. The wait was as bad as the news of Elizabeth's death. It had only been by intervention of her grandfather Pope Gregory that she was not swinging from a crow's cage at that moment. Alexander's disappearance after Myrgen's escape was the final stroke of luck but she didn't expect to survive his return. Moreover, she doubted Myrgen would survive his absence. She let out a sigh that threatened to call the tears back after all.

A small sound at the door drew her attention. She slowly turned her mournful gaze at whatever servant was bringing her whatever meal. She blinked and straightened when she saw the tall, bald man standing in the doorway, feet spread and gloved hands balled into fists, one holding a swept-hilt rapier. His forearms were on the doorjamb and his head lowered, but he raised his eyes to meet hers.

"Tangl."

Tanglwyst stood. "Duncan?" She saw the blood dripping from his gloves and the handle of his rapier.

"I think it would be wise for us to go now." His tone left no discussion points available. Duncan looked over his shoulder, inspecting the stairs behind him as she rushed into her bedroom and untied her robe. "Darlin', I don't think now's the time for that."

She looked up and saw Duncan glancing about the room he frequented so often in the past few months.

Tanglwyst tossed her robe onto the floor and pulled on a shirt over her substantial uncorsetted chest. "We're going to be running, yes?"

Duncan glanced over his shoulder again, then back to the better view. "Oh, quite a bit."

"I can't do that dressed like a lady."

Duncan pursed his lips and nodded, sheathing his sword and stepping into the room. "Good point." He tilted his head and she turned her back to him and pulled on riding breeches over her rear. He always loved it when she did that, and this was no different. She smiled to herself, reassured again of her attractiveness. She flipped her hair out of her shirt and pulled a doublet from the wardrobe, tossing it onto the bed. She pulled some high boots out of a chest and he blatantly admired her breasts as she bounced into the boots. By the time she was clothed and ready to leave, she had Duncan more than ready to make her reverse the process.

"Come, I have money in a chest here."

Duncan grinned. "I wouldn't mind exploring that chest."

Tanglwyst smiled at him and kissed him on her way by. "You get me out of here, and I have every intention of letting you do just that."

"Your horse awaits, my lady."

Tanglwyst grabbed the chest with the money in it and handed it to Duncan. He recovered his senses and started towards the stairs and the numerous exits the main floor offered. As they got to the bottom of the stairs, the front door opened and two more guards from the grounds entered the room. They saw the bloody bodies on the floor and drew steel on Duncan. Duncan handed the chest to Tanglwyst and drew steel as well, putting himself between the guards and his lady. "Gentlemen, your comrades have already fallen before my blade. Let us be on our way, and you'll live to tell the tale."

The men at the door charged Duncan. He drew a breath and took them on. A parry with the right sword pushed the second attacker away while his main gauche stopped the first guard's blade from finding purchase in his flesh. Duncan shoved them into each other, pushing them back a bit. The opening allowed him to move to a better angle, and caused them to circle to the unsteady ground of the blood pool left by the fallen guards. He feigned a move. As hoped, one of the men slipped a tiny bit. Duncan plunged his sword through the guard, spraying the other guard with his partner's vitae.

The other guard shook his head and dodged to the side as Duncan spun his partner off his sword. The other guard saw Duncan's mistake at the same time Duncan did, and he, too, took the opportunity. He grabbed Tanglwyst and drew her before him, his sword at her throat.

Duncan saw the blood drip from the guard's chin, his sleeve sullying the woman Duncan loved. Tanglwyst's eyes watched Duncan carefully. He saw she was not scared. He squinted, his breath low and silent. The guard was breathing heavier. He seemed to be waiting for Duncan to make his move. Tanglwyst's rescuer watched the man, waiting for the right moment. The guard blinked. His hand was on her upper arm. His breathing slowed as he relaxed a bit. Duncan could smell her pheromones exuding from her. The guard was right beside her ear. The guard glanced for a second at the lady's ample bosom and Tanglwyst closed her eyes, and fainted.

Her body suddenly slack, the guard looked down at her, then up just as Duncan's sword pierced him through the eye. He pushed the dead man off his sword and knelt beside the lady. "Angel?"

Tanglwyst's eyes opened. She winked at her rescuer. "Nice move."

He lifted her to her feet. "Were it not dangerous to do so, I would make love to you right now."

"Isn't that precisely why you want to?" She looked out the front door and then toward the kitchen. "Are their horses in back?"

"Yes, in the stables."

"They're using *my* stables for their horses while I'm under house arrest? Bastards." She ran towards the back door and let Duncan take the lead. She grabbed two keys and some papers out of a drawer in the dining room and tucked them into her doublet. Duncan peered out into the garden.

He swore. "There are four of them out there. One of them is a lieutenant. I've run across him before."

9

"How did you do?"

"Well, we're both still alive. I doubt that will happen a second time." He looked back at the front door.

"He's that good?"

"Yes and there's no wagon load of chickens." He looked at her as she stared at him, eyebrows raised. "Long story. Come on."

The couple crept to the front door again and looked outside. They didn't see anyone in the street in uniform, but it was only a matter of time before the guards on break in the back would be walking the perimeter again. Tanglwyst nodded to the alleyway and took off running. Duncan closed the door behind them and followed. He stopped in the shadows of the alley and watched to see if anyone had noticed their exit.

He seemed to find himself in this alley a lot. It was the same alley where he had first met this lady, and first realized he loved her. It was the alley where he held on to her to keep her from running while his other partners slit her monstrous husband's throat. It was the alley where he had watched her entire mansion being built, where he took his breaks from posing as a worker putting in the carpentry. He'd planted the roses in her garden out back, each one hand-picked by him to complement her hazel eyes and auburn hair.

This was the alley where Guillaume de la Rapier stumbled, cut by his own hands as a ruse to find himself in the lady's bed, under her care. Duncan had watched it all from this alley. He turned to look at Tanglwyst, checking her for damage, and then checked himself.

"Where are we going?" She was worried, but excited. Her voice revealed everything to him.

"I don't know yet. I just need to get you out of Patras before the King returns."

Her eyes grew wide. "Am I to be... like Elizabeth?"

He reached over and caught her head in his hand, fingers slipping quickly into her hair. "Not if I can help it, my love." He kissed her, the first of thousands of kisses he planned to give her.

The sound of shouts interrupted them and he took her hand. "This way." They ran through the alleys dodging the shouts of the following guards. Suddenly, Duncan turned a corner and he saw the gendarme at the end, entering the alley. They saw the pair and pointed. Duncan retreated, putting himself between the guards and Tanglwyst. They turned the corner, retreating. There, blocking their escape, was Lt. Gomez de Santander drawing his sword and grinning.

"Ah, Duncan McVryce. And with a suspected traitor as well, one trying to escape. And not a chicken in sight."

"I can see one." Duncan's voice was cruel and sharp as his blades, and twice as bloody. He put Tanglwyst behind him, seeing the lieutenant as the real threat but she tapped him on the shoulder.

"Duncan, there are five behind us. What do you want to do?"

Duncan watched four more guards join Gomez at this end of the alley and swallowed. He had one choice to get her out of this alive. He knew he was willing to sacrifice himself for her, but he couldn't warn her, not if he wanted the maneuver to succeed. *Forgive me, my Angel. I have no other way.*

He grabbed Tanglwyst and held her close to him as Gomez seemed to sense something was up. "I love you," he whispered. She looked at him, fright intensifying her eyes so they practically glowed. With a gasp from the woman he loved and a shout from the man he hated, Duncan closed his eyes and fell backwards into the shadow of the building. In a flash of light and the faint scent of lemons, they were gone.

Two

"Always trust a Caratian farmer. They speak to
the Land and know of the Fae."
The Wise Wench's Tavern Book

Myrgen de Sablonierres leaned on the railing of the black ship, the *Enigma*, head down, watching the small waves lap between the dock and the hull in the rising moonlight. He was starting to feel fatigued. After all that had happened in the past couple of days, he was impressed it took this long to hit him. His clothes still had some of the splendor with which they began the adventure. The blue of his long, loose court coat still complemented his eyes, his best feature if he had to put one out there. The coat showed signs of the struggle with the guards, blue vomit (both his *and* the former king Charles') from poisoned bread, blood from being interrogated by the late Nicolai Moriarity, dirt from the underground catacombs used in the escape, the stink of horse from fleeing the capital city of Patras, and even a long black hair from the woman upon whose ship he was now a guest. The shirt was a bit less filthy.

It had been a long two days.

He reached down to dust off some of the filth, but it proved more persistent than he anticipated. He extracted the hair from his thigh, and it caught just a little as he pulled. Her hair was black as shadow and had a natural wave to it. There were women all over Patras that spent hours to achieve what this woman was graced with naturally. Her dark skin had been tanned from a life in the high seas, yet was still somehow supple and only barely showing age. Her viridian green eyes could cut through a person's soul and spell out for her all their sins. Her figure was honed by pulling on flooded ropes and commanding a ship of men in the trials of the sea. Although he had been told she was incredibly dangerous, he was unprepared for the real truth behind the rumors.

He could still smell the fire on his clothes from burning the bodies; a sick, sweet stench now mostly dissipated by the torrents of rain which had started to lessen just an hour ago. He couldn't imagine how Catriona felt at this point. Her husband and first love had died in the muddy street. His back and arms snapped from the convulsions caused by a swift poison, while she clawed at her crew to get to him. Their restraints saved her life but she was not a woman accustomed to being powerless.

Myrgen contemplated for a moment how he and the captain had both lost their lovers, murdered before their eyes, in the past few days. The main difference between them was that Catriona wanted to save Nicolai. Myrgen had been more than happy to see Elizabeth's blood drain onto the flagstones.

That first night, the storm had raged around them, threatening the fire with every gust. . Myrgen and Thessius, a seasoned sailor from the crew, had fought to keep it going and hot enough to incinerate the bodies. Oilcloths were brought in and set up to protect the fire and try to keep the heat on the bodies, but all they did was smoke the flesh. This morning, Catriona herself came to tend the fire just as several crates arrived at the pit.

Catriona had told Thessius and Myrgen to return to the ship to eat and rest. At first, he had not wanted to leave, his tending of the body the least he could do for the woman who spared his life. Myrgen had fallen to the sailor's superstitions in the night. He envisioned Nicolai's soul haunting the person torching his body.

13

Thessius pointed out that he was starting to shake and one of the other men said they were willing to take the risk. Only Thessius' cryptic urgings managed to sway him to leave his post.

Myrgen was still mystified by Nicolai's attack, and Catriona's strange sense of honor. Even after Nicolai had snuck on board her ship and tried to kill her, she was merciful. *"Leave Nicolai,"* she had said. *"Don't seek me out and don't bother me again. Just take Tanglwyst and go. I'll leave here and we'll be dead to each other again."*

He looked at her. "What about him?" He nodded towards Alexander, who was being helped to his feet by Myrgen and Octavius, her First Mate. Myrgen looked up as he heard the conversation. The sound came to him not through the air, but almost as if through the ground. He glanced about to see if anyone else heard it, but they seemed oblivious.

"Don't you worry about him. I'll deal with that. Just go."

Nicolai looked around and then nodded. "I see. If you marry him, you'll never sail again. You won't be able to. If you're his subject, then he can command you to stay. And you never have been one to do as you're told."

But her mercy had been for naught. Now, his body was ash and she had turned to stone to cope. Her voice when she told them to return to the ship to rest had lost its sensuality, instead rasping through a throat brutalized by crying. She limped on sore muscles taxed by sorrow and wear. He didn't know what the crates that arrived at the burn site held, but they were obviously something for the pyre.

Movement on the street near the mooring caught his attention. He saw the crew members returning, their bedraggled Captain punctuating their arrival behind them. Her face was smudged from her vigil at the fire. Catriona dropped to a knee and touched the ground where Nicolai had fallen as the last of the crew came back to the ship.

Her Quartermaster came down to her side as she knelt on the street. She spoke to him as she stood. Against the urgings of her entire crew, she had gone to the fire pit to tend the pyre. Many of the sailors had been willing to risk a haunting so she wouldn't have to, but in the end, she refused to allow them to weather a danger she herself would not risk. As such, her crew insisted on attending her, even though, from what he had determined, they all believed the ship would be haunted as a result. It was quite a feat to be able to override a sailor's superstition.

Myrgen turned to Alexander. "She's coming."

Alexander, Sovereign of Mervolingia, the largest country in the Saintlands, looked up from his seat on a crate on deck. He didn't look quite as tired as the rest of them, though his ordeal had been no less trying. Between losing his brother one day and losing his freedom the next, Alexander was dealing with more emotional stress than nearly any of them, not the least of which was the weight of executing his brother's treasonous queen, Elizabeth, personally. Myrgen was certain Alexander had never taken a life before, being dedicated to the healing arts. Still, if anyone who didn't know him had seen the viciousness with which he ran the sword through the former queen, they would have believed he not only was proficient, but that he'd *enjoyed* it.

Alexander stood and walked over to the railing by the top of the gangplank. "Do you think it worked?"

Myrgen nodded. "I doubt she'd return if it didn't. I think she feels responsible, somehow."

Alexander watched her movements carefully. "She looks exhausted."

"She has a right to."

Alexander nodded and stepped down the walkway to meet her halfway, extending his hand to her. Tears still streaked her face through the soot, though they showed signs of being wiped away, small traces in the dirt on her cheeks looking smeared. Her eyes were still red, but the puffiness from crying had faded. The lines in her face were deep around her mouth and eyes. She looked dehydrated and defeated as she stepped onto her ship.

Myrgen asked, "How are you doing?"

"How do I look?"

"Beautiful," Alexander said instantly. Myrgen glanced down at the deck, not sure if that was what she was looking for in an answer. Then again, Alexander was deeply in love with the woman, and rightly so. She probably expected no less.

Myrgen had no such expectations on him. "Exhausted."

15

She looked at him and nodded, a very weak smile of gratitude revealing her thanks at his honesty. "Rather like I assume you two are. Thank you for staying with me. I fear I have stranded you in a storm though, Alexander. It would be unpleasant to try and make it back to Patras in this."

"It's fine. Thank you for putting my men in the cabins with beds."

"I could hardly let them try to heal in hanging nets. How are they doing?"

"I have seen to their wounds and I'm sure they will recover just fine. But thank you all the same for your consideration. *I'm* sorry I've held you here as they healed."

"They were injured protecting me. It's the least I can do. It's not like we can take off in this weather anyway." She looked at Myrgen. "We'll find a place for you as well."

"I can stay on land, at an inn. I don't want to impose."

"And what do you plan to use for money, Myrgen? I didn't exactly allow you to stop by your house and pick up a bag."

Alexander raised his hands a little. "Well, money isn't an issue, Catriona. I can put us all up in the finest inn here in Rouen. It wouldn't be a problem."

"No, thank you, Alexander. I've been off ship long enough. There are preparations to make for setting sail as soon as we can and I need to get my sea legs back before we take to the waves."

"You can come back every day. But I've missed you all winter. Let me enjoy your legs as they are before you sail away from me again. Please." He took her hands in both of his. "Let me do at least this."

She looked at Myrgen, who tried his best to be supportive with just a look. *It's up to you, though you look like you could use the rest.*

"I'll tell you what: this storm looks to be a lingering one. Let me stay on board and get some work done. Tomorrow, we'll go into town and give the crew a proper send off. How's that?"

Alexander straightened and gave a crisp bow. "If that is what you offer, that is what I'll accept. Do you have any suggestions as to a place for me to stay?"

She nodded. "Of course. I understand the King's Table is quite elegant. Run by a former cook from your own kitchens in Patras, if I recall correctly."

"I'll have to see if that's true. Good night, Captain. I look forward to tomorrow's festivities."

"As do I."

Alexander kissed her hand and left the ship.

Myrgen stepped over to her. "Can I get you anything?"

She shook her head. "I suppose I should have had him take you with him to the Inn. His guard is in the quarters I had set aside for you."

Myrgen looked to the sky, which was threatening rain again. "I don't want to seem rude, but frankly, I don't think having Alexander put me up at an inn when I was responsible for the past few days chaos would be wise."

She turned sad but clear eyes on Myrgen. "You aren't responsible for the past few days. Elizabeth played you. She played everyone. I think even Tangl was impaired."

"Tangl was impaired?"

She nodded, frowning and started walking back to her cabin. "Yes. I got the impression she was fully behind everything, but she seemed too easily molded. At the time, I was too upset to care, but thinking about it now, and I think she might have been drugged or something to make her uninhibited." She waved a hand and shook her head. "Doesn't matter now. I'm going to lie down."

Myrgen bowed and let her go. He was likewise exhausted, but had no idea what to do next. Octavius walked over to him, watching the Captain go. "You are the one that took the body and burned it, right?"

Myrgen looked at Octavius. "Yes. Yes, Sir."

Octavius smiled, bright blue eyes shining in a face accustomed to life at sea. They betrayed his status as First Mate by revealing his competence. The man had some power to his body as well, though it was moderate enough in appearance. However, the way he held Catriona back from running to Nicolai's aid meant he had more under his loose clothing than just winter fat. "Sir, huh? Interesting. Judging from your clothes, you were a pretty important person on the ground."

Myrgen blinked, not sure if that was a snide remark or just an observation. He decided to treat it as the latter. "Was. Past tense. I was the Chancellor of Mervolingia."

Octavius whistled. "Not bad work if you can get it."

Myrgen snorted a laugh. "No, but getting it is the hard part."

"Seems a shame to leave all that behind."

Myrgen shook his head. "Not when faced with the alternative."

"Still, we should give you something to do here. Idle hands, you know."

Myrgen nodded. "Yeah. I do."

"Tell you what. Thessius has said you can use his bunk. He's on duty for the next six hours. Why don't you get some rest and we'll talk later."

"I'm a little worried if I lay down, I won't wake up for a tenday."

"Oh, I doubt Thessius will let you take his bunk for that long. Come this way."

Octavius turned towards the stairs going below decks and Myrgen followed. He realized this man might know the answer to something. "Excuse me, but crates arrived just as the Captain came to the fire pit. I didn't see them return with her. Do you know what they were?"

Octavius took a deep breath. "Lye, in powder form. The other crates were bottles of water. With the weather fighting the fire, the body was never going to be properly consumed. The Captain had lye brought in and put the crates of it on top of the bodies, then once the crates released their powder, she dowsed the flames with water. The mixture destroyed them to the last bone in a matter of hours."

"And she stayed there and watched that?"

"She had to. If the gusts blew that foul mixture onto anyone there, they'd be scarred for life. She contained it just fine though. She knows how to do things like that. Saved depleting further the stacks of wood by the campsite. She had half the crew cutting wood and dead-fall to restock it while she took care of the bodies, mostly to keep us safe."

"Wouldn't the water just boil inside the bottles?"

"Not if you break them with the right size rock." Octavius gestured to a hanging net attached to the wall. "Here's Thessius' bunk. Have a good rest."

"Thank you." Myrgen eyed the net and sat back into it. It took a couple tries to figure out how to get his feet in it without flipping out of it, but eventually he sussed it out. Within a couple sways of the hammock, he was asleep.

Catriona closed her door and leaned against it. She was actually glad Alexander had left instead of deciding to accompany her into her cabin. He had always been so patient, but perhaps the toils of the winter months caused him to alter his pattern. She couldn't really blame him. To have the woman he'd pursued for several years so close to committing, only to have her stolen away by a man she thought was dead would have to be incredibly depressing. She knew her own moods had been colored by that fact.

She let out a long held breath. She could barely stand, the ride all day culminating in the fight with Nicolai and the slow, day-long destruction by fire of the only man she had ever truly loved had worn her to her core. Alexander had graciously dealt with the city officials regarding the cremation. She kept all poison from entering the soil, allowing the fire to devour it utterly. It had not been easy. She had built an oven from the stone around to contain the flames and shelter the fire. It had been the only way to destroy the bodies of her husband and the ill-fated dog that licked his face.

Whatever this poison, it was persistent and completely invasive. By the time she'd arrived, there was no part of the body that wasn't fouled with the stuff. Nicolai's soul was doomed from the moment the dart had hit his skin. Her men had filed through as well, each offering prayers and purifying rituals as per their own faith, in an attempt to set his spirit to rest. She hoped they'd succeeded.

With Nicolai settled, her thoughts now turned to Alexander. Here was the chance she, and he, it turned out, had dreamt of all winter. Now that it was here, she found it difficult to concentrate on the possibility. She knew she cared deeply for Alexander, but by comparison, it was tough to hold a candle to her affection for Nicolai.

No, that wasn't true. It wasn't tough to hold a candle to her love for Nicolai. It was impossible to hold a candle to her *memory* of her love for him. They had loved each other purely and deeply, even after they thought the other was dead. But this last winter, she and Nicolai had been together every day, and she found he changed too much, or she had. They were left with even the memories being ruined. In the end, she sat, night after night, looking out her window at the palace. She thought about it now and wondered if she had really given their relationship a chance, or if she deliberately sabotaged it in favor of one with Alexander.

She moved away from the door, pulling off her gloves and untying her hair. *No point worrying about it. What's done is done. I can't save him. I can't save either of them now.* She was so tired. She wanted to lie down and stay there for a while. She felt guilt at letting Nicolai die, despite the fact it would have killed her too. The way that poison acted, he was dead before she could have pulled it from his body. Alan would be an orphan instead of just fatherless. Her crew had done the right thing in stopping her.

She sat down on her bed and looked at her boots. There were still dots of Nicolai's blood on them from when she had cut him. She wanted to rub them off, remove them, but she couldn't lift her arms to do it. She couldn't convince her eyes to let her cry again. She was so dehydrated, she couldn't even muster spit, and the water skin on her desk was too far away. Instead, she threw her legs onto the bed and laid back, her head sinking into her buckwheat pillow. She barely had time to think about how nice it felt before she was gone.

"Hey! Wake up."

Myrgen opened his eyes, fairly certain his rescue from prison had been a dream. Only prison could be this dark or smell this bad. "Yeah?"

"Octavius wants you on deck."

Myrgen nodded to the young man with the dark hair, and then realized how bad an idea that was. When he had climbed into the net bed, he had felt very comfortable. Now that he had slept in it for a while, he was far less enamored with the idea of a suspended bed with no support. Every part of his body ached like he had run from Patras on foot. He sat up and bumped his head on the bulkhead. "Ow."

He rubbed his head and tried to put his legs out of the hammock, thinking to slip onto the floor that way. His boot tip snagged on the netting and his overbalance flipped him onto the floor.

The sailor in front of him reached down and helped him to his feet. "Yeah, that happens to all of us the first time."

"I feel like I've been beaten with a brick," Myrgen rubbed his back. He could feel the mesh marks embedded in his skin beneath his shirt.

The young sailor narrowed an eye. "You kinda look like you have as well. C'mon." He started for the stairs.

Myrgen followed, his body begging for his fair and legal execution. He climbed the stairs and determined this was *almost* as bad an idea as getting out of the hammock had been. While he was *in* the hammock, it hadn't been a bad idea. It was clearly the decision to *leave* said hammock that was the problem here. He limped before the First Mate and straightened up with effort and a groan. The weather had not changed in the few hours he had slept and it was dark out. A light drizzle drenched the already soaked crew.

Octavius looked at Myrgen and, without so much as an acknowledgment to his tender and tragic condition, nodded greeting. "How long have you known the Captain?"

Myrgen cocked his head in curiosity. He realized he might not be able to return it to an upright position. "Um, personally? A few days, but I have known her name for some time now. Why?"

"She's asking for you."

"Oh." Myrgen stretched his neck.

"She's in her cabin."

Myrgen nodded, testing his muscles.

"We can't wake her."

Myrgen stopped, his attention fully on Octavius. "Excuse me?"

"She's been asleep for over a day. You both have."

Myrgen's eyebrows rose. *"Over a day?* I thought you said Thessius wouldn't let me sleep that long."

Octavius barely blinked. "We're in port. He got a better offer."

Myrgen realized Thessius could have gotten mugged in an alley and suffered a severe head blow and still would have been more comfortable than Myrgen was right now. *Bloody hammocks.* "I see. Is the Captain still on board?"

Octavius motioned to the rear of the ship. "Yes. We didn't want to move her. This way."

The Captain's room was dark, barely lit by the port illumination seeping through a stained glass window in her wall. Myrgen stepped over to a bed behind a screen that was bolted into the floor and looked on her. She was fighting against something, from the look on her face and her hand movements. She was speaking a foreign language. He strained to listen, trying to understand her words. "I think she's speaking an ancient form of Caratian. The sentence structure is strange."

Octavius turned his head to listen. "You understand ancient Caratian?"

Myrgen shook his head. "Not conversationally. I read three hundred year old texts from the time of the First Dûcesa at the university."

She mumbled something and then said his name. "...Myrgen..."

"Yes, Catriona, I'm here."

Her eyes flung open at the sound of his voice and she said something that didn't make sense. Her face was marked with fear and surprise and she raised her hand to strike out. Without thinking, his own hand shot up to catch hers, his eyes never leaving hers. Their fingers intertwined, extracting the violence of the dream. She blinked, confused. "Myrgen?"

He set their hands on her stomach, noting her shaking. "Yes. It's me. Are you all right?"

She sat up on her elbows, looking around the room. "What happened?"

"Octavius said you were asking for me in your sleep. No one could wake you."

"How long have I been asleep?"

"Apparently a day."

She looked out the porthole as a flash of lightning cast aside the shadows. "The weather doesn't look any better."

Octavius stepped over to the bed. "No, not yet, but the ship seems to feel the storm will pass tonight or tomorrow."

Myrgen released her hand, politely stepping away to give her First Mate access and turned to the door. A silhouette filled it and a flash of lightning revealed a worried Alexander. "Is she awake?"

Myrgen approached, nodding. "Yes. I don't know what was in her dreams, but it seems to have lost its hold on her now."

"And *you* got her to wake up?"

Myrgen blinked, trying to stay calm in the face of the threatening tone in Alexander's voice. "Don't read too much into it. I was just present in the dream at the right time. She actually tried to claw me."

Alexander nodded, his jaw set in an ugly way. "Did you understand what she said there at the end?"

Myrgen decided it was unwise to take his eyes off Alexander. "Not really."

"She said, 'Don't kill me, Myrgen.' I think that's a wise suggestion. I also think that's probably more like what will happen if she stays in your company."

Myrgen realized Alexander must have tried to wake her himself. He was offended that Myrgen's presence had been the trigger to pull her from her sleep. *This is a power struggle for him. He sees me as some sort of rival or interloper.* "Your Majesty let me assure you, I have no designs upon your beloved."

"Good. Then you'll have no problem leaving now and returning to Patras to stand proper trial, correct?"

Myrgen straightened, waiting.

Alexander looked over at the screen protecting her sleeping area. "Except I can't do that, Myrgen. That woman has put you under her protection. I can't raise a finger against you." He looked Myrgen in the eyes, the power of his sovereignty full in his voice. "But if you cross her, hurt her, threaten her or in any other way cause her or allow her to come to harm, I will flay your skin and make you eat it. Are we clear?"

Myrgen nodded, keeping his expression very carefully neutral. "Very." He turned to leave as Alexander stepped further into the room to attend the Captain. Myrgen watched the king approach her. She shied from him at first, and then settled into wakefulness. Alexander's threat didn't disturb him. It was to be expected, truth be told. What disturbed him was the thing Catriona did say. It wasn't "Don't kill me, Myrgen."

It was, *"Don't let them kill me again."*

"Hey there."

Alexander sat on the edge of Catriona's bed and touched her hair. She still felt the vestiges of the dream where someone was chasing her and throwing things, heavy things, at her. It felt very recent and still very long ago. He seemed too close and his hand on her hair put her off. But as she grew more alert, she reined in the knee-jerk response and settled her nerves.

"Hello."

"You've been gone for a while." Alexander nodded to Octavius. "We were getting pretty worried."

She looked at him, rubbing her face. "Have we really been asleep for a day?"

"Over a day. We tried to wake you earlier but couldn't bring you around. Octavius said there was no need to move you, that you'd wake up on your own. It appears he was right."

Octavius smiled. "Lucky thing, too. Grymalkin here would have had my skin if you took much longer." He patted Alexander on the shoulder. "I'll leave you two to talk."

Catriona watched him get to the door, then thought of something. "Is Myrgen all right, Octavius?"

Octavius opened the door, looking at his captain. "Yeah, he's fine. He was asleep almost as long as you. You two must have been through a lot."

"Yes." She blinked away from a sudden memory of her dream. The vague images were unidentifiable at best and unrecognizable at worst. Regardless, they made no sense. Her destination while unconscious was usually a sanctum, an ancient church. To be hunted in her dreams was unheard of. "Yes, we have."

Alexander rubbed her palm with his thumb, bringing her back to him. "So, how are you feeling?"

She looked down at their hands, and then smiled to reassure him. "Better. I'm sorry I frightened you."

"It's over now. Octavius felt it was just the ride and the fight and the smoke, all of it together."

Catriona dismissed the image of Nicolai's bones on fire as she had come upon them at the cremation site. She understood the premise behind the burning. Myrgen had explained the reason well so she felt no need to dwell upon that aspect. It truly was the right thing to do. When it was done, she had returned the ashes to the ground, leaving the camp site unmarred by their existence. It was the only thing she could do. Nicolai had been raised to believe the Sea Goddess Callista would refuse to accept a body touched by flame, having been spurned by the King of Volcanoes. However, it was neither her belief nor Alexander's and she was grateful no such fears would be associated with their deaths.

She sat up, nodding. "That's probably it. Could you excuse me?"

Alexander frowned. "Excuse you?"

"Yes. I need a few minutes of privacy, if you don't mind. To change."

"You look fine. I'll get your brush." He stood and she kicked her feet to the side of the bed.

"Well, I've been sleeping in these for a day and they smell like it. Let me take a few minutes to freshen up a bit."

"Well, if you're going to change, let me help you. It's not like I haven't seen you naked. And we'll go to dinner afterward."

She looked at Alexander, hands at her side. "I would like to use the facilities, Alexander, and I'll not do so in front of you."

He looked at her and then realized what she meant. "Of course. Forgive me." Reluctantly, he left and she was finally able to empty her bladder in the chamber pot in the corner. She opened her stained glass window and emptied it off the stern. The storm had quieted a bit, no rain or thunder at that moment, but heavy clouds protected the stars from viewing by mortal eyes. The breeze spirited away the urine smell in favor of the scent of sea air, damp from the sky as well as the sea. She closed her eyes, letting it refresh her. The grogginess of sleep left her, evacuated on the wind, easing her mind from Alexander's insensitive clinging. She had caught herself feeling less than enamored with him twice now. It was unsettling her. She was having trouble figuring out what was wrong with her.

She had left home at least once a tenday all winter to spend it at Gweneviere's because at least there, she could talk about Alexander without risking ruining his life. She felt loss over her choice to separate from him that autumn and it was made all the more maddening by the knowledge he was living right there in Patras. She could see the palace from her home. She had chosen that flat because she knew that, from her son's window, she could see Alexander's. She had watched him walk in front of the window every night, sometimes staying up as long as he did. She imagined he knew she was out there because he would also spend hours just sitting at his window and watching the city.

She had been intimate with Nicolai only once all winter, and in so doing, she discovered he had wanted her to do something physically that would help his fantasy that she was Tanglwyst. She had been livid. She had left the house with Alan and went straight to Gwen's. She never told Gwen why she had come that night, but she had asked to leave Alan with her while she went for a walk in the new snow. She had walked to the woods and found herself just a few yards away from the back door to the palace's kitchen. At that moment, Alexander had entered the doorway, nibbling on a mince tart. She had watched him as he spoke at length to a cook named Lawrence but in the end, she had turned her back on the man, her heart heavy with longing, and returned to Gwen's house.

She stood from her perch on the ship, closing her stained glass windows to keep the table and upholstery on the window seat dry. She went to her sea chest and looked through the folded clothing, settling on a Caratian long coat with a series of ten buttons down the front. She set it aside and poured water from a pewter ewer onto a cloth and washed her face. She was saddened by the residual ash that came off with the water. What she needed was a bath, not a wipe down, but she didn't have time for a proper dousing. She checked her polished silver mirror, the only kind durable enough to handle life on Callista's Realm, and scrubbed off the tenacious bits of grime. Then she brushed her hair, disgusted that it seemed greasy at the roots. She didn't mind the stray hints of silver that were finding their way into her hair. She felt she earned each and every one. She did mind that the activities of the last few days had robbed her of their shimmer. She bound it into a braid, hiding most of the unpleasantness in the folds, and then walked over to her long coat.

Alexander was waiting for her out on deck, wanting to dine with her and she found she was disinterested in doing so, at least alone. He may be asking to have dinner, but what he *wanted* was a repeat of the night they had last year at the cabin she owned on the cliffs above St. Giles. Her memory of their lovemaking had haunted her all winter, and now, as she changed her clothes from something comfortable to sleep in to something difficult to remove, she tried to determine why she no longer seemed to care for Alexander.

She pulled on the coat, focusing upon the multiple buttons, and let out a sigh. No, she did care for Alexander, far more than she had cared for Nicolai all winter. It wasn't that. It was something else. She felt pulled in different directions when she thought of him. She wanted to be with him, yes. However, she *didn't* want to be with him *more* than she wanted to be home, or more than she wanted to be at sea or more than she wanted to be there for her crew. If she could just figure out a way to abandon all that, she could go with him without looking back. All it would take was to remove her soul.

A knock at the door caused her to jump and her heart became explosively loud. "Yes?"

Alexander opened the door and leaned in. "Do you need any help with anything?"

She looked down at her hands as they did up the last two buttons on her coat. "No, I think I have this."

"I was thinking, since you're in port, that maybe I could get you a room at the local inn. It might be the last night you spend on land for months."

She finished the buttons as she tried to figure out what to say. "I don't think I can. Many of the men have been staying on board for a tenday now and it would be inappropriate for me to sleep in a fancy inn when they are stuck in hammocks."

Alexander looked down at the floorboards, trying to figure a way to counter her argument. His eyes got a glint to them and offered, "Well, then I guess I'll just have to put them all up in the inn as well."

She blinked, stunned by his proposal and his determination to be with her tonight. "That would be rather expensive."

"I'm the King of Mervolingia. Since Rouen is *part* of Mervolingia, I can look at this one of two ways: First, I can decide that, since I'm Sovereign, all that is here already belongs to me and therefore, I should have no more trouble nor expense securing lodgings for any and every one I please or, second, I can decide to support the economy and livelihood of my subjects by returning a portion of their hard earned tax money back into their pockets. Regardless, I can afford to put your entire crew up at the inn."

"Well," she smiled at his generosity, "it will do naught if they go there hungry. The season has not yet started, so none of them have money for food either."

"Then I shall feed them as well." Alexander made the offer without thinking, which was exactly what she wanted.

She walked over to him and kissed his cheek. "Thank you. I appreciate your kindness. I'll tell the crew." She slipped past him and went on deck before he could retract the statement.

She walked over to Octavius and nodded. "Alexander has graciously offered to put anyone who wishes it to stay in an inn here. Any recommendations?"

"Food too?"

Catriona nodded. "Never been to an inn that didn't have the meal included."

"I hear the King's Table is a good one, Captain."

"Octavius, some days it's like you're the one who reads minds. Please alert the men." She glanced over as some movement caught her eye. She saw Myrgen emerging from the hold, his hair pulled back in a ponytail low on his neck. It looked as if he, too, were disgusted at his unkempt appearance. She smiled and waved him over as Alexander waited near the gangplank for her. She turned to Octavius. "I take it the wounded guards are in the guest quarters, as planned?"

"Yes Captain."

"Good." She turned to Myrgen as he came to her side. "Myrgen, Alexander has graciously offered to put all the crew up for the night at a local inn and buy them dinner. Care to join us?"

"A real bed and dinner that isn't hard tack and salted fish? Dare I?" Myrgen smiled, and then glanced at Alexander, remembering his comment before. "Then again, maybe I should stay put."

"Why do you say that?"

Myrgen was about to answer when Michael came out of the galley and saw him. "Myrgen!"

Myrgen looked and broke into a smile. He walked over to embrace his friend. Catriona and Octavius followed. "Michael! So this is where you ended up?"

"Yes." Michael gestured to Catriona. "This fine lady offered me passage on her ship to wherever I needed to go."

"She has made me the same offer, my friend." He turned and looked at Catriona. "Are you in the habit, My Lady, of picking up strays?"

She smiled. "Apparently so. Michael, we are leaving the ship. Please, accompany us."

"Where are we going, if I may ask?"

Alexander stepped up to the group, abandoning his post by the gangplank. "The best inn in Rouen. I'll buy."

Michael looked at Myrgen, questioning. Myrgen nodded, returning a different look. Catriona read them both and saw that

Alexander had threatened Myrgen when they were talking at her doorway. She found herself extremely irritated at him, and extremely grateful that Myrgen was around to reveal these little indiscretions. She nodded to Octavius.

"My First Mate tells me the King's Table is the crew's choice."

Alexander clapped his hands together. "Having eaten and stayed there myself last night, I can attest to its quality. Turns out, the cook really *did* work at the palace. I remembered him from my childhood. Please, Octavius assemble the men and send them to us in shifts or whatever it takes to get them all fed. Make sure they know of the offer for a room at the inn as well, would you?"

Octavius nodded and Alexander offered his arm to Catriona. "Shall we, my Love?"

She nodded consent and they left the ship.

Three

"Always offer a meal with your rooms. Your customers will either want one coming or going, but they'll usually pay for the other one too."
The Wise Wench's Tavern Book

Michael waited until the King was seated and the entire restaurant was fawning over him and his requests before he broached the subject. "Myrgen, what happened?"

"Oh, you mean to get me here or between me and Alexander?"

"Pick one."

Myrgen smiled. "Because I made sure her son was saved, she rescued me."

"That's what she said?"

"Well, that and a little speech I made to Nicolai that she happened to overhear, through solid rock walls..." He looked sideways at Catriona as this thought dawned on him.

"Did she tell you about our talk?"

"Wha..? Uh, no. You two talked?"

"Yes, when we carried Tanglwyst to the stables."

"'We?' You carried my sister to the stables?"

Michael rubbed the back of his neck, his face belying his discomfort at the subject matter. "Well, Catriona seemed like she might have trouble managing on her own. I thought it would be nice to help her out."

Myrgen blinked at him, several times. "Did she at least say thank you?"

Michael spread his hands, gesturing at the crowded room.

Myrgen shook his head and smiled. "She must not have wanted to get you in trouble. All I knew was that she sent you on ahead. I suspected it was for my benefit. And frankly, my friend, I'm glad you're here."

Myrgen glanced down the table at Alexander who was speaking privately to Catriona, their heads together. Myrgen couldn't decipher what he was saying to her but her eyes wandered up to Myrgen's in the din of the room. She seemed to notice him looking at her. She looked away, caught. Myrgen blinked and sat back a bit.

"What?" Michael picked up the tankard the waitress set before him.

Myrgen glanced at his friend and then back at Catriona. She was keeping her eyes to herself now, but Myrgen remembered her waking plea. He felt of all the people in her life, he was the most likely to make that mistake. Yet he found himself, especially at that moment, very protective of her. Moreover, he felt the need to protect her from the man at her side right now.

"Nothing," he said into the cup.

Alexander looked into Catriona's eyes in the moonlight. He managed to get her out of the common room and alone on the balcony of the second floor, which had taken quite a bit of doing between both of their sycophants. He knew she loved her crew, but that many men keeping track of her every move was annoying. It was like trying to date a girl with one hundred brothers. "Ah, quiet."

She smiled and leaned on the balcony railing. "It can get a bit loud, I must admit, but you wanted to buy dinner."

"That I did, and I'd do it again if it meant I could spend a moment alone with you." He leaned next to her and took her hand again, a common thing throughout the night. "How are you doing?"

She took a breath. "I think I'm getting my second wind." She laughed a little. "Or maybe my fifth."

"I know what you mean. So, what do you plan to do now?"

"Go home. Where I belong."

"I could make you belong here."

"But you would have to *make* me belong here. There, I already belong."

"I can't lose you Catriona. I won't. Not now, not after all this."

She put her hand on his. "You're not losing me, any more than you've lost me any other season for the last six years."

"Yes, but now I can't haunt the dock taverns and harbormasters for word of you."

"I know." She looked away. "I know."

He watched her a moment then reached out to touch her hair. "Stay with me tonight."

She looked up at him, eyes concerned. "Alexander…"

"No, don't think about it. Do it." He kissed her, pulling her to him to embrace her with his whole body. He felt her will eroding as she responded to him. She was very responsive when she gave in to their desires, but very reserved all other times. He wanted to break through that and hear her cry out in passion, to shake the rafters. His room was ten steps away. They could be together all night.

The sound of someone coming out of the inn below them tore her away from him. He looked down, scowling at the intruders. It was Myrgen and Michael, talking about the day's events. Nothing important, but it broke the mood and gave her a chance to escape. *Saint's Blood!* He looked at her again but he could see it was too late. The gold flecks in her vivid green eyes had lost that shimmer and gone cold again. He would be starting from scratch to get her to give in now.

Myrgen was now, quite firmly, on Alexander's bad side.

Myrgen shrugged. "I don't know, Michael. I can't return to Patras and I have no idea where to go. Maybe I'll go back to Yantap. The culture in Yndia is so relaxed. I miss it there. In the end, I suppose I'll need to ask the Lady what she has in mind for me. She has given me my freedom and I have been informed by His Majesty that he will not tolerate any harm to her. It's enough to make me feel that maybe I need to leave her company as soon as possible."

"She offered to return me to Nubia."

"I have never been to Nubia."

"That is wise."

Myrgen stopped and looked at his companion. "Ah. Saintlanders aren't taken well there, I assume?"

"You would be correct. Even with my protection, many tribes will kill you rather than listen to you. The others who have come before have always been a bane to my people."

Myrgen leaned against a wall. Michael did likewise across from him. "I'm sorry about that old friend."

"I know. Truly, Myrgen, you have long since proven yourself to be my friend. I would stand between you and any danger."

"Thank you. I would do the same for you, even more so now." Myrgen glanced back at the inn and noticed the couple on the balcony overlooking the door.

Michael looked over to see what caught his attention. He saw Alexander take Catriona's hand and ask her something. He attempted to draw her down the hall. She appeared to be politely resisting and he looked to be politely insisting. Finally, she put her hand to his face and said something that seemed to make the difference. He straightened up and bowed, offered his arm to her, and escorted her to a door down the hall. He opened the door for her and she took the key he used from him. After a kiss on the hand from him, she disappeared inside. He stood at the door a moment. He seemed to be chastising himself for something.

Myrgen stepped back a bit to the shadows, watching Alexander's response. He went to the door across from hers and opened it, entering quietly with one last look at her door.

"You know," Michael observed, "I think that man is very regal and I don't think he could choose a better woman to pursue, but I think perhaps he is mishandling this situation."

"You're very observant, Michael," Myrgen kept his attention on the doors. "I don't know how likely it is that they'll end up together though. If he doesn't deal with her in the right manner, he'll alienate her. Why don't you head back to the ship? I'm going to stick around here for a little while."

Michael did not question. He nodded and left. After a few minutes, Catriona's door opened and she stepped out. She looked at Alexander's door like she was trying to figure something out. She shook her head and went downstairs. A few minutes later, she came out the front door and glanced around. As she began to walk down the street, Alexander's threat came to Myrgen's mind. He stepped out of the shadows and hurried to catch her. "Captain!"

She turned and stopped. "Myrgen? I thought you left with Michael."

"Not quite. What are you doing out on the streets at this hour, unescorted?"

"I can handle myself, Myrgen. I don't need a guard."

"I didn't mean to imply that you did. Perhaps I am the one who needs guarding." She smiled, taking the edge off her comment. He relaxed a bit. "So, where are you off to? Back to the ship?"

"Actually, no. I'm going to take a bath."

"A… bath? At this hour?"

"I happen to know a place. I just feel the need to…"

"Get the smell of smoke out of your hair?"

She looked at him, amazed. "Yes. That's it exactly."

"Well, I might have need of a bath myself." He gestured to the clothes he was wearing, "Though I might hold off until I can at least replace these."

She smiled at him. "Thank you Myrgen. I would love the company."

Myrgen looked at her, a little stunned. "Was I that transparent?"

"To me? Yes. Almost everyone is."

"But not Alexander." He gestured in the direction she had been traveling and they began walking again.

"No, not Alexander. I'm sorry he threatened you."

Myrgen glanced down at the street, then up ahead at the occasional pedestrian. "He had every right to. The man who conspired to kill his brother is now in the company of the woman he loves. I would expect no less. I can't say I wouldn't do the same. So, how did you come to know the King and Prince of Mervolingia?"

Catriona smiled. "Ah yes. I imagine you would want to know that."

"Well, it did end up being my foil."

"Ten years ago, I got in a fight with Nicolai about the business he ran. His father had left him a couple ships as a merchant business and he had just lost one, fully laden. I told him we needed to seek investors but he refused, saying he didn't want any outsiders telling him what to do with his father's company. So, the next morning, after he left for the docks, I slipped away and decided to petition the richest man in the area, Marco Giovanni, for help."

"That name... he's related to Dominic, isn't he? You killed him."

"Yes."

"Was that when you met them? Charles and Alexander?"

"No. I met them when I escaped."

"Escaped? Apparently, I missed something."

"Yes, Giovanni brought me into his home on Cheryb, via one of his own ships, and asked me to tell him my proposal. He listened very intently and when he found out no one knew I had come to see him, he invited me to stay for dinner. Next thing I remember, I awoke in his bed, restrained and in the middle of a rather unpleasant act. He held me there as a prisoner for four months. I fought him every chance I got. Then, the priest who tended my wounds after the sessions informed me I was pregnant.

"At first, I was horrified this monster had done that to me, but then Father Benjamin told me I was too far along for that to be the case, that I was pregnant when I came there. That took the fight right out of me. I was too afraid of hurting the baby to fight Giovanni anymore. Once I stopped fighting, he lost interest. He forgot about me, but the priest did not. When Alan was born, he helped me escape that night. We got to the small village outside Giovanni's estate and rested in the church there. I was still exhausted from the birth.

"Unfortunately, Giovanni found out and came after us. His guards set fire to the church and we fought him. Benjamin was killed and Giovanni decided he was going to take me back. I grabbed a sword and blinded his right eye. The results so shocked me, I stopped and he managed to grab me and bear me to the ground, where he... well, let's just say his interest was renewed." She shuddered a bit and Myrgen put a hand on her shoulder, which made her jump. He removed his hand like she was a hot stove. "Sorry. The memory still unsettles me."

"I didn't mean to bring up such a painful thought."

"No, it's good for me to talk about it. I never really have, not even to Nicolai when we found each other again. I think Gwen knows because Alexander told her."

"And he knows because?"

"He and Charles witnessed it. Not all of it, but the aftermath. They came upon me after Giovanni finished with me and left me for dead. I remember Alexander healing me, channeling energy from his own body to stop my bleeding. Most of that was from the birth, but the brutality of my captivity was a shock to them both. Seeing me like that inspired Alex and Charles to rescue all the captives Giovanni had in the dungeon, including the midwife who tended to my son, and the family of Gomez de Santander."

"*Gomez?* I didn't realize he had been with the royal family so long."

"Ten years. He had no loyalty to Giovanni, having just started his position as a guard the year before, but Giovanni threatened the life of his family and told him he would put his new wife through the same paces he put me through. She had been pregnant when he was hired and Gomez rightfully feared for the lives of his wife and child. We managed, with his help, to rescue the entire group and get them to safety in St. Marguerite."

"That's quite impressive. No wonder you two are so close."

She nodded. "It went a long way towards healing me, as much as the healing he gave me to save my life."

"Alexander healed you by channeling his energy?"

"Yes. I think it was just because of the situation as he's never been able to do it since. He's had a lot of opportunities."

"He has?" Myrgen thought a moment. "Ah. So you're the reason he kept disappearing."

"I'm afraid so."

"He seems to be a good man."

She stopped outside a well-lit building. "He is." She gestured to the building. "This is it."

Myrgen looked at it. The sign swinging from a fancy worked-iron hook said "The Open Lotus". Myrgen looked at Catriona. "This is a bath house?"

"The finest in Mervolingia. Come on. I'll buy you a bath."

Alexander sat on the bed in his own room, looked out the window, and thought about the Lady across the hall. He would not intrude upon her privacy tonight. He kicked himself for being so insensitive. Her boots still carried the splashes of blood from her fight with her husband. He believed she needed time alone to heal her unseen wounds as well as her external ones.

His own wounds were healed now, thanks to his healing kit on the *Enigma,* where he kept some Cyprian herb salve, a special mixture which healed his leg wound overnight. Alexander could not remember a time where his room did not house several pots of this herb, just in case. He was taught from an early age by the Royal Physician that his royal blood enhanced the inherent powers of the plant, which was specifically engineered over a hundred years to preserve the lives of those who rule.

He got up and went to the window. The inn was tall enough to have several rooms with unobstructed views and this was one of them. It showed the city laid out in sparkling splendor. He knew Catriona's actually looked all the way to the docks and her ship. He was glad he didn't spend money on a room for Myrgen. Having that man too close made Alexander's skin crawl. He couldn't understand why she would be interested in helping him after he had taken her son, but he didn't dare move against the man at present. He had seen her powers of observation for himself several times over the years. He had also seen her cold wrath a time or two. She would not take kindly to interference right now.

He had rushed to her side so many times, he practically had a uniform. His noble and recognizable features had to be covered but hats were impractical and masks were obvious. A hood pulled up over a simple hunting doublet and breeches in grays and browns with no real decoration, went further to camouflage his status as Prince than any disguise. Alexander hadn't even been crowned yet, so there was no widespread minting of fresh coins bearing his visage. Brown eyes and barely blonde hair couldn't be translated into metal anyway, so he always had that anonymity. His facial hair was distinctive enough but was luckily the current trend, so it made no difference. Not many other men could grow the small beard and mustache right around the mouth and not look ridiculous, which unfortunately didn't stop them from trying, but Catriona liked beards. People rarely looked at the money anymore anyway, as long as it spent.

His brother Charles was gone now, tucked safely away on a ship taking him to a distant and remote island where he could live out his days with the woman he loved, literally dead to the world. Now, with the Rite of Sovereignty performed a few days ago, Alexander had to shoulder the power and responsibility that went with being King. His one and only focus for the next four months before his official Coronation ceremony would be to get Catriona to be his queen.

He stepped out on to his private balcony to look out over his domain. It was very different from hers. The *Enigma* was her flagship, her crew hand-picked by Catriona herself. A Caratian carrack, the *Enigma* was one hundred feet of ebony livelihood for a hundred sailors and officers. She was capable of carrying one hundred fifty tons of cargo, had forty oars and thirty guns. Her boards were sealed with a special pitch from an ancient forest on the Latian isles. The pitch protected the ship as well as gave it the black color for which the *Enigma* was famous. No other ship that sailed the trade ways of the Sea of Saint Erasmus sported this color. On any other ship, the color seemed to fade within a season at sea, where Catriona had never had to paint her ship. The three masts gave her the speed necessary to get where she needed to go, while the shimmer of electrum fittings displayed the duality of a silver glint in the moonlight and a golden homage during the day. She flew no flag, for the ship itself was distinctive enough to need no heraldry, although the flag of Caratia was kept in her sea chest near her bed.

Alexander had never met Drake and Anika, rulers of Caratia, but Gwen had and spoke highly of them. They were good folk, decent and strong and had adopted Catriona as their own daughter. He knew nothing of her childhood or anything about her before she'd married Nicolai. Sometimes, it seemed as if she hadn't existed before she'd walked into the small Latian fishing village. When Alexander met her in the terror of the fire of the church outside Cheryb, she could already see into other men's souls, though she admitted she could never see into Alexander's. She believed it was because of her life debt to him, but it didn't matter. Catriona trusted him, and he trusted her. They had no need for mind tricks.

He watched the city and thought about his future. Traditionally, the King was crowned and wed at the same time, the first day of the month of Franco, endowing his Queen with the Mantle of State. However, Alexander had already decided he would marry no woman but Catriona. Charles married the Queen Mother Catherine's choice, but had loved another woman with all his heart. His brother had lacked the strength to stand up for his beliefs and eventually paid for it with his soul. Alexander did not want to fall prey to the same fate. If he married, it would be for love. As King, he could choose that path. If he had to rule alone, he would rather do so than wed a broodmare for the sake of the family line. It was unnecessary. Charles already had a son. The Angloume line was secure, at least for the next generation.

He didn't need the Coronation ceremony to rule the country. The Rite of Sovereignty had cemented his right to rule. Coronation was for the public swearing of fealty by the nobles, a practice required by the Church for their support. Long ago, the church had merely received word of the current ruler of a kingdom in the Saintlands, but then a war three hundred years ago changed everything. Now, they demanded direct involvement and public oaths to prevent usurpers from plotting against the Crowns. The practice may have saved hundreds from assassination attempts and the civil wars which follow, but there was truly no way to tell.

The only drawback to stepping up before securing his bride would be the endless favor-currying and social climbing from the nobles. Every family would have a woman's name to put in the pot, hoping to be the one chosen. He felt certain Elizabeth had been chosen for Charles by drawing her name from a jar of potentials. He had stopped his mother from doing that for him by embarrassing the family the last time. The mere thought of the look on the Queen of York's face always brought a smile to his.

He had no doubt he would be inundated with offers by the time he returned to Patras. Thank the Saints Gwen was on his side. She would be able to inform Dominic not to entertain any of them. With Nicolai out of the way and the Writ commanding his assassination destroyed, very little stood in Alexander's way. If he could get her to acknowledge his sovereignty, he might be able to command Catriona to be his wife.

He shook his head. *What am I thinking? Is that truly what I want? A mindlessly devoted subject?* No. He knew her irrepressible will was why he fell in love with her in the first place. To steal that from her would make her no different from the hundred other sycophants vying for his attention at court. He'd loved her since he had first seen her, covered in blood and crawling to save the life of her son from being smothered under the body of a decapitated priest. Charles had rushed to the body, hearing the infant's muffled cries, as had a man and his wife also arriving on the scene. They had pried the large man off the child, his body elevated by a rock large enough to spare the infant, but smooth enough to be mostly hidden by his considerable bulk. Had the monk fallen a couple finger widths further forward, the child's head would have been

41

crushed between the rock and the monk, but the placement of the stone had allowed a great deal of protection.

Once her son was safe, she collapsed; a battered, bloody, and broken mess. Alexander had put his hands upon her, willing his own life's blood into her body to save her. Her breathing had stabilized and her bruises disappeared, and he carried her to the couple's home while Charles carried the baby. The woman, the village midwife, inspected her after that and found no lasting, or even apparent, damage. He never forgot the feeling he had when her wounds mended beneath his fingers. It was like he had been touched by Heaven to save her life.

He remembered taking the baby from Charles as he left to deal with the guards they had ditched. The midwife had asked him the child's name. He looked at Catriona, unconscious on the recovery bed, and at the baby and named him Alan, after Alexander and Charles' grandfather. The midwife and her husband had assumed he was the father and he said nothing to dissuade them. He always wondered why Catriona never gave the boy a different name but she never told him. He always took it as a sign that they were meant to be together, that she must have been in love with him as well when he healed her, or she surely would have changed the name to mirror Nicolai's.

Alexander felt his eyes tear up as he thought about it now, and his heart grew heavy as he thought of a future without her. She had been the impetus for the first truly heroic act he and his brother had ever done, and probably the only heroic act Charles ever did. They were on Giovanni lands to meet a potential wife for Charles when they rescued Catriona. Once Alexander had healed her and she had rested, Catriona told them about the other captives in Giovanni's estate. Charles and Alexander had arranged for a ship to take them away to St. Marguerite in Mervolingia, and then followed Catriona to the route she had used to escape.

The way back in had been blocked by a newly installed gate and was guarded by a man Catriona seemed to recognize from the battle before. His family was being threatened by Giovanni and he begged them to wait until the next time he was on shift at this gate before they tried the rescue, so his family could be saved as well. Catriona vouched for him and they held off for a couple days.

When they went in, they rescued the entire dungeon and the guard's family. They, along with Catriona, her son, the midwife, and the midwife's family, set sail before Giovanni even knew they were gone. That guard's name was Gomez de Santander.

Catriona and the baby had disappeared not long after the incident, apparently pursued by Giovanni's men. The midwife and her husband were slain in the attack. Although Alexander tried to forget the damaged damsel he had healed, he found her always there, slumbering in the nighttime reaches of his consciousness. He had dreamt of her for years before he saw her again.

Once he did, every emotion for her resurfaced as if it were brand new. He escaped the palace and the pettiness it afforded for the open road and the open sea most days out of the year in the hopes of running into her again. Charles knew what Alexander was doing. He lived vicariously through Alexander, escaping his own prison. Catriona and Alexander became close friends as he healed her with the herbs and hearth wisdom he had learned, but he always hoped he would be able to heal her spontaneously like before. She had politely rebuffed his every advance, no matter what the occasion. Gwen had explained to him that Catriona was a widow and dared not release her heart from her grief lest she lose someone else she loved.

Then, one amazing night, she kissed him. She told him she had mourned long enough and they gave in to their passion at last. He had never been happier. He had returned home and Charles knew instantly. They made arrangements to meet again and spend the winter together, but when Alexander arrived at the meeting place, Catriona was there with Gwen and would not be alone with him. Nicolai, it seemed, was not dead after all. He was working for the Lady Tanglwyst as well. Catriona and her husband were going to spend the winter together and try to restore their marriage. Alexander had been willing to fight Heaven itself to save their relationship, but he could not raise so much as a protest before her considerable will. She had walked out of his life.

He had not even begun to heal when he had to sign a pay voucher for Nicolai Moriarity, a new guard hired at the request of the Queen. Alexander found out that Catriona lived there in Patras. He followed Nicolai home once to see where she was, perhaps to get a glimpse of her. Instead, the man went to a tavern and Alexander never found out where she stayed, but he had a general idea after that. Had he known her location, he would have put Nicolai on constant duty and gone to her. He probably could have gotten her away from him too. Gwen had told him Catriona spent at least one night a tenday away at her house because she wanted to see Alexander.

Had he done that, there would have been no reason for the Writ against Nicolai. As it stood, thanks to the few minutes alone in Charles' room after he realized he was to be King, he had freed them both of Nicolai's poisonous presence. Thank the Saints for Duncan McVryce. *And thank the Saints she can't read me*, he thought. If she knew he had put out a Writ of Destruction on Nicolai, he would never win her for his own. But he had needed to free her from Nicolai's grasp. If he hadn't, they couldn't possibly be together. She was even running to him to take him back when Duncan killed him. He *knew* it. She was never going to walk away from him, so he had to kill the man. He had to be strong for them both. Maybe if she *could* read him, she would see he did it for them.

Alexander yawned, finally feeling tired. With all that had happened, he was surprised it took this long to wear him down. Between killing Elizabeth when she tried to steal the Power of Sovereignty, and watching Nicolai die, the past few days had been rife with death and rebirth. Charles had a new life, and now, so did Alexander. Now he just needed to convince his beloved to abandon her old life for one with him.

"Catriona! Welcome, welcome. What can I get you fine people?" The beautiful lady in the entry room smelled of sandalwood and cedar. Her dark features were complemented by the sunset colored silk of the sari she wore. She bowed and gestured to the elaborate furnishings in the sitting area.

Myrgen swallowed, unable to tear his eyes from her. She was stunning. Her eyes were rimmed in kohl and her skin was caramel, smooth and sweet smelling. She wore golden lip color and eye shadow. The clothes she wore showed her bare midriff, a short tight top coupled with a low, long skirt with pleats folded into the waist at her left hip. Her bare arms moved like a dancer's and sparkled with several bangles at the wrists.

"Xannu, I am so pleased to see you working tonight. Xannu, this is Myrgen."

Xannu curtsied, her large, soft eyes drinking in the former Chancellor. He looked at Catriona in panic, pulling the filthy coat he was wearing around him self-consciously. "Myrgen, is it? You look uncomfortable. Please, let me take this for you."

"I don't need you to… oh well, alright…" He relinquished his schaub and stood there in his slightly less smelly but equally roughed up shirt and pants, still highly aware of himself. He hunched his shoulders and folded his arms.

"Xannu, we are in desperate need of a bath and laundry. Perhaps a room for the night?"

Myrgen looked at Catriona, the panic in his eyes getting bigger.

"Together or separate?"

"Separate, thank you, but within talking range."

"Attendants?"

"Please."

"Same or opposite?"

"Same for me, opposite for him, I think."

"Relax a moment and I will make the arrangements." Xannu curtsied again and went upstairs.

Myrgen leaned over to Catriona. "Same or opposite what?"

"Sex."

Myrgen's eyes narrowed. "This is because I kissed you, isn't it?"

Catriona just smiled. "Are you worried you won't know what to do?"

"I'm not inept, Catriona. I'm just… not ready to be seen by a woman, that's all. Too soon."

Catriona looked at him a moment and he felt her invade his soul again. She stood and went to the top of the stairs and called for their hostess. After a few whispers, she returned. "Problem solved."

"Thank you." Myrgen sat down on the brocade couch and leaned back, closing his eyes. "That's actually a handy skill you have there. Saves a lot of time."

"You don't mind?"

He opened his eyes. "Not at all. I've spent quite a while walking in the darkness, Catriona. It's about time I walked in the light. You'll keep me honest, at least until you send me on my way." He laid his head back again. "Hopefully, it will be a new habit by then."

The smell of sandalwood and cedar caressed his face. He looked upside down over the back of the couch at Xannu. The angle here was just as striking. He was surrounded by the most beautiful women in the world. Somehow, he was having a very difficult time feeling he was paying penance for his crimes.

Four

"Choose carefully what entertainments you offer, as well as the ones you refuse."
The Wise Wench's Tavern Book

Xannu led Myrgen to a room in the upper floor and opened the door. Three more exotic women and three rather impressively sized men stood in the room surrounded by fragrant towels and velvet curtains. The room was lavishly decorated. Myrgen recognized it as Yndian. He had spent a bit of time in the capital city of Yantap as a guest of the ruler of that city, the Rhamidhal. He suddenly realized what this really was and why Catriona would be here.

"This is an Incense House." He turned to Xannu. "Isn't it?"

"Yes. You are familiar with the Incense House?"

"Indeed. I have a book about them at home." He looked around the room. "Lots of illustrations." He turned to Catriona. "This explains everything. I couldn't figure out why you, of all people, would come to a brothel. Now I realize this isn't a brothel."

"Why would you think it was a brothel?"

He looked at Xannu, at the other women, at Catriona and swallowed embarrassed. Yes, he was *quite* familiar with the difference between an incense house and a brothel. "Wishful thinking. So!" He clapped his hands together. "Let's get soapy." He walked over to the shelves and tried to ignore the quiet snickers exchanged between the women. The assortment of soaps and oils was impressive and he felt he could hardly choose. He turned to Xannu and Catriona who were still standing by the door, talking quietly. Their eyes were still on Myrgen, but their looks were more serious than jesting.

Catriona nodded and walked over behind a standing screen accompanied by their hostess. A few moments later, the coat Catriona had been wearing was in Xannu's hands and the garments just continued to pile up. Once she had everything, including the boots, Xannu handed them to one of the male attendants who left the room with them. Myrgen focused on the scented soaps, giving the lady her privacy, despite her lack of need for it. He read the names on all the jars of creams, and tried to determine what he would want to smell like for the next couple of days. One of the jars was unmarked and he picked it up. The scent was spice and musk and a little floral and smelled very familiar. He could definitely enjoy that scent all over him.

"Thank you." A hand reached past him taking the jar from him. He looked at Catriona who was now dressed in a silk robe of shimmering black, her hair tickling the opening in the front that revealed her clavicle. He looked at the jar and saw it was indeed labeled on the other side. It said "Catriona".

"I thought that smelled familiar. This is where you get your perfumes?"

"And soaps and towels. It is amazing. They have an alchemist here who creates scents for you. They could do the same for you. Make a new man out of you."

She turned to Xannu and the three women left with them, with Xannu promising to return. Myrgen realized what Catriona meant when she said she took care of the problem. The men were to be his attendants. He admitted to being a little disappointed, but also a bit less self-conscious as well. He looked through the jars and found one that he liked just as Xannu returned a few minutes later. "You are ready, Master Myrgen?"

"Please, just Myrgen. Titles are inappropriate here."

"They are indeed. That doesn't stop some people from wanting them used." She led him out of the towel room and into a room steaming with hot bathwater. A large tiled tub about ten feet square and three feet deep showcased the room, drapes and flowers everywhere. She took the jar and sprinkled a good dose of the scented powder into the tub and waved towards it for him to test the temperature. He dipped a hand in and found it to be a bit hot, but probably exactly what he needed. "Thank you, My Lady."

"I thought titles were inappropriate here?" She granted him comfort with her smile and he accepted it graciously. "Can I get you some refreshment?"

"I suppose this is the place where I say only if I may drink in you." She arched an eyebrow, impressed and he shook his head. "No, thank you, My... Xannu." He looked around for a moment and touched his shirt. "Where do I...?"

"Ah, here, give them to Amman before you get in the bath. Catriona requested them be laundered."

"Bless her, yes. Thank you."

Xannu bowed and left the room. Myrgen got to work removing his clothes and found his back hurt near the belt line. He carefully removed his breeches and felt the area. In addition to a nasty bruise, it appeared he had a gash that was in bad shape. His breeches waistband was bloody and smelled rather bad. He was worried it was worse than he thought and he thought it was probably on its way to turning septic.

His outfit had started much better. He had worn blue, because Elizabeth had requested it, to match his eyes. The doublet and shirt were bloodstained and ripped now. Myrgen was afraid there might be a bit of poisonous vomit somewhere on his breeches and boots too. Unfortunately, the poison was also blue, and the ornate pattern of the fabric would require sniffing to find the offensive areas. Well, if he were to be on the ship for any length of time, he would take a needle and thread and try to repair the damage. It might help heal his own wounds as well.

He finished disrobing and handed the clothes to Amman, who left with them. He asked one of the other two left, "Um, what is it you are supposed to do, exactly?"

"Help with washing you, get refreshments, extra towels."

"I don't need help with any of that, but I would appreciate some way to get the filth off me before stepping into that nice water."

"This way, sir." The man led him to a curtain which he pulled aside. There was a bunch of reed plants in this room, surrounded by soft candles tucked in behind. From the wall, a large reed protruded plugged with a large cork. Amman removed it and warm water flowed from it into a drain in the floor. Myrgen shook his head, amazed. "Thank you."

The man bowed and left, dropping the curtain back in place. Myrgen went over to the reed and let the water flow onto his head. He had no idea how much his hair hurt until that moment and he turned around and leaned against the wall, moving so the water went to the spot right above the injured area. He let the water flush it out and relaxed.

Although Myrgen's cheek bore the covert signs of brutality, the soreness he felt alternated in severity between the pain from his captivity and the pain from his betrayal. He marveled again at his willingness to trust Catriona, what with her being a woman and all. Most men lamenting a broken heart would have condemned the sex. Myrgen still didn't know why he didn't.

Maybe it meant he knew all along Elizabeth would betray him. After years of being blind to her flaws, he was shocked at the clarity with which he was seeing things. Hindsight, he supposed. He never saw it coming. Their initial chords of emotion were as pure as he had felt as a young boy for his first love. He truly didn't see the signs that would have heralded his downfall, and now he was looking for them. In the end, he knew he could not have known what Fate had in mind for him. Perhaps he needed an augury to better prepare him in the future.

Myrgen reached back and carefully rubbed the gash he had received from Nicolai's interrogation. He wanted to keep an eye on that particular wound. Even with bandages to protect it from chafing, he would have to be vigilant. His facial wounds were more obvious. If anything started to go wrong there, he was certain someone would notice. The back wound was another story. It was covered much of the time and his breeches rubbed it, making it sore. The reopening wound could have problems at sea, where wounds could turn gangrenous in a matter of days. Its location made it possible that Myrgen might not be able to tell. Maybe he should ask Alexander for something to heal it.

Sure, as if he would jump at the chance to help me. Three days ago, I was the reason his brother was dead. I'll try my own way first. If for some reason that fails, then I'll seek outside help.

Myrgen didn't foresee Alexander as being too concerned for his welfare, especially after what he had said on the ship. He tried to put himself in Alexander's place. Brother gone and having to assume a throne he's never wanted, the woman he loves married to another, though, granted, that last part was no longer an obstacle. Myrgen leaned both hands against the wall on either side of the water pipe.

By Saint Martin, that was a horrible encounter. He had seen Catriona and Alexander being circled by Nicolai, whose blades were already bloody. He had ridden to aid them, knocking Nicolai into the water and allowing Catriona to get to her ship. Alexander had been wounded in the leg and he had rushed over to the man, their previous differences forgotten in the heat of battle. Octavius had come over to help get the King off the street and away from the horse who was responding to the smell of blood.

The horse had moved and he had seen Nicolai come up behind Catriona, swords about to run her through. But before he could strike true, Catriona bent and dodged, her swords disarming him of his off-hand weapon and knocking aside his sword like a horse swats a fly. Another movement and she had her blade at his eye. He gave up. If only it had ended there, but no. Even after her speech to Nicolai to leave and take the prize of Myrgen's sister, she must have decided she needed something from him. He stopped in the street and a dart came from nowhere, poisoning the man, killing him almost instantly. Catriona had been devastated.

Myrgen had heard screaming like that from a woman only once before, and he never wanted to hear it again.

Myrgen breathed deep, settling his pain. He had studied the Fusion of Flesh technique in Yndia, where holy men still practiced hearth magic of a far different sort from the familiar Mervol medicinal remedies. In spite of the medical advances made in the Saintlands through herb research, these people explored a spiritual magic unknown in his occidental homelands. Myrgen discovered it could be learned, if one took the time to learn it. Unlike certain Mervolingian magic, Yndian practices were not dependent upon bloodlines. The oriental way of life was very different from that of his childhood, but he preferred it in many ways.

He pulled his mind into his body and focused on the pain in his back. He felt the fire of the fever there and focused on the healing energies his body was trying to summon. Myrgen took the energy from his neck and chest, pulling it towards the gash on his back. He envisioned maggots eating away the dead flesh, then leeches pulling out the bad blood around the wound, taking the pain and inflammation away. Destroyed in the process, the leeches and maggots dissipated and the wound began to scab. The scabbing flesh pulled the torn skin together, closing the wound to the elements and protecting it from further infection. Myrgen took another deep breath, returning the energy from his wound to his chest and neck.

He raised his head and stood away from the wall, sore from the effort. After a few stretches, he felt the muscles snap back into place. He rubbed his hand across the wound on his back. It was still sore, but nothing like it had been before. He felt much better. He could feel the flesh restored, though there might be a bit of a scar to tell the tale.

He felt parched so he drank some of the water from the reed, letting it splash off his face as well. The process of healing was taxing, though much less than if he had tried to do it for someone else. He knew he could never muster the power that Alexander had displayed. To heal another person, you gave them part of your soul. Myrgen didn't feel he really had much of that left. He had forfeited so much of it in intrigues and lust for another man's wife. Now came the penance for his sins.

He rested like that a few minutes, and then realized he was getting a little cold. He went to work rinsing off the bulk of the filth. There was a bar of soap hidden near the reeds and he used it to clean away the captivity of the palace.

When he was done, he stepped back into the main room and went over to the tub. The water was still hot. In fact, it was as hot as it had been when he checked it before. He wasn't sure how they managed it, but regardless, a bath that didn't get cold was a brilliant idea. The fragrant water soothed him and he closed his eyes and sighed. His old life was gone but he found this new one more than adequate. He knew a hard three tendays awaited him on the ship starting tomorrow, but for now, he was suspended in a womb of comfort. This thought drifted with him into slumber and he was soon snoring.

Five

Catriona took the lantern. Suddenly, Myrgen seemed to touch a thousand centers of pleasure in a single movement so fluid, she was encompassed in it before she knew it was happening. He placed a hand behind her head, stroking the nape of her neck as he slipped into the unbound beauty of her ebony hair. His other hand went to the small of her back and he kissed her. Yet to say he kissed her is akin to comparing the sun to a candle glow. Her skin tingled, her fingers trembled, and her thighs seemed to burst into flame. She could feel every heartbeat, every breath, and every ounce of vitae in her being, and, more importantly, she felt him embrace her very soul with his kiss. The feel of his lips sent shocks through her and she dropped the lantern.

The lantern sparked a fire in the burnt out church beneath the Mervolingian Palace. The two were instantly surrounded by a *fervent tempest which mirrored their passion for each other. Catriona gave herself over to the emotion she felt, the emotion she craved. He knew her. He knew her body like he'd been with her for years, his hands and lips working magic upon her skin. More than this, she needed him. She needed to feel him inside her, physically as well as spiritually.*

She fell to her knees with him, her fingers questing for his flesh and finally ripping his shirt to get to him. He moaned as she kissed his chest. He grabbed her and brought her lips to his, consuming her as the flames consumed the edges of her vision...

Catriona sat up in her bed, sweat clothing her as the dream burst around her. The images were fresh in her mind, lingering. She could smell the fire and taste Myrgen's lips as if he were in the room with her right then. She lit a lamp and checked quickly but he was not there and nothing was afire except her. Her heart was pounding and adrenaline chased her blood around her veins like a swarm of bees. Never before had she had such a vivid dream, not while sleeping. It was as if she had flayed open someone's soul and that was the scene she was shown.

She looked around, trying to orient herself. She was in one of the beds at the Open Lotus, and she was still alone. She breathed in and out for a moment to calm her heart, but her mind and body were still reacting to the dream. She got up and went over to one of the mirrors to see if the ministrations of the Incense House had rejuvenated her as she had hoped. Her hair was snarled from laying on it wet and she grabbed a silver brush in an absent gesture. The rhythm of the strokes let her mind wander and she thought about the dream. The vivacity of it surprised her. She was used to having visions like that when she read someone but she'd never experienced it from the receiving end. She wondered if it meant something. She wondered if it meant nothing.

Alexander would be leaving the city in a few days and she noticed she missed him. Usually, when they were in the same town, he couldn't be pried away from her side. Of course, usually when they saw each other, she was injured. This was not the sort of place she would want Alexander to be watching over her. This, in fact, was the sort of setting that would be her downfall. To be with him in this very romantic and lavish place would seal her fate as his wife with deadly certainty. She could barely resist him now.

She was especially grateful for his absence after that dream. He doubtless would have asked her what woke her. She had not told him about the kiss in the catacombs and she wasn't sure she would, especially after the threat he issued to Myrgen. Granted, she had not realized the kiss would ever cross her mind again, seeing it as merely an odd encounter, singular in nature. Their initial meeting would never have belied an occasion for her to know what it was like to be kissed by him, but there was no doubt the man was skilled. The way he brushed her neck in just the right way, how his arm felt around her waist...

She shook off the thread of thought. *Down that path lies madness.*

Catriona put the brush back on the vanity and pulled on the silk robe from earlier. She had been land bound for too long, but the activities of the past couple days now made her need to be at sea pressing. She looked like a husk most of the winter. Today, though, after sleeping in the bed she usually slept in before setting sail from Rouen, it was as if her body knew, and was celebrating.

She opened the door and went out to the balcony that looked over at the harbor. After she spoke to Xannu about the business end of things, she intended to go to the ship, if only to commune with the *Enigma* for a while. Her arrival and subsequent collapse into unconsciousness had not given her time to reacquaint herself with her old friend. She felt the void this left. Callista still ruled the seas, according to the sailors, and she was a jealous goddess who insisted homage be paid. She was glad to pay it. That ship had given her purpose when she had none and was her life as much as her home. She felt positive about the new faces on the ship and hoped Myrgen could handle the seasickness. From what she could see by his clothes, his stomach had been through enough.

A door opened down the hall and she turned to see who it was. Myrgen limped out of the room, easing the door closed behind him. There were red marks on his face and he seemed to be in great pain. "Myrgen?"

He looked up at her and waved, turning towards her with great difficulty. She moved to him to see what had happened. "Did someone hurt you?"

"No, just me. I fell asleep in the tub."

Now that she was closer, she could see the marks on his cheek were the grout from the tile tub, making a large lattice on his face.

"Here, come with me." She walked him down the hall to her room and admitted him. "Lie down."

He did as commanded. "Oh... ooohhhh, yes... This is *amazing!* This is the most comfortable bed I've ever been on."

"That's why I stay here when I come to Rouen. It's very rejuvenating. I'm surprised Xannu let you fall asleep in the tub."

"Well, it's not like she stayed there with me."

"She didn't?"

He looked at her. "Of course not. I was here to take a bath. I was far too rancid to want a woman to see me like that. The bruises alone were enough to deter any intimacy." He sat up, leaning on his elbows. "You really expected her to stay?"

"Of course. You're a very attractive man. She usually takes care of those personally." The lines on his face were fading and she walked over to him, looking at the differences from the day before. She knelt beside him and reached over to touch his face. His eyes watched hers as she inspected the place where the wound from his interrogation had been threatening to scar. "Your wound looks much better. In fact, it looks three tendays healed. Did Alexander give you something for it?"

Myrgen looked into her eyes a moment longer, then at the bed. "Uh, no. That's not the kind of relationship we have."

"Then how?" She moved her fingers over the mark on his cheek, examining the progress from the night before. The gash he had sported during the rescue was now all but a memory. He fidgeted under her touch, glancing around the room in discomfort. She noticed and withdrew her hand, a little surprised at her uncharacteristic intrusion on another's personal space. She stood up and stepped back a bit to a more respectful distance.

"I... did it myself," Myrgen revealed, sitting up, self-conscious of both her closeness and the surroundings. "It's a flesh mending technique I learned in my travels before coming back to Mervolingia."

Catriona arched her eyebrow. "Really?" She looked closer at the wound, keeping her hands near but not touching, then saw the discomfort in his eyes again, and released him from her scrutiny, stepping back. "Well, I should like to know this technique of yours. It seems to have done the job. It would be nice to take care of things like that myself rather than to rely so often upon Alexander's proximity."

Myrgen nodded. "Certainly. I'm sure you could master it. We have a couple tendays at sea after we leave here. I'll teach it to you then."

Catriona smiled. "Thank you."

She turned to the vanity and saw her clean clothes hanging near the mirror. Her boots were cleaned and everything smelled like her favorite scent. It was beginning to get light out. She felt a strong pull to get to the ship before Alexander woke up and found she hadn't used her room at the inn. He might get angry and she just couldn't process how to handle that right now. She was still trying to process things that happened in this room, and all she did was sleep here.

"You don't like having him around, do you?"

Catriona glanced over her shoulder. "It's not that. Things are different now." She stepped over to her Caratian coat and touched the two winged lions embroidered in black on the black fabric.

"Because he's King?"

"Yes." She turned back to him and walked over to the bed, sitting on the end, facing him. "Before, I could dream of us traveling together, being together out on the sea or bringing him to Drake and Anika to dance at one of the Balls that are so common back home. But when he took that power from Charles, Myrgen, I almost felt compelled to bend my knee to him and swear fealty."

"I know what you mean. Even as a traitor to this land, when he stood there, he commanded those people. Even Catherine acknowledged his Sovereignty. I don't know if she ever did that to Charles."

She looked down at her hands, remembering his speech to Catherine about his choice for his queen. If he had known they were standing there... It bothered her to be so vulnerable.

Myrgen moved to sit up closer to her. "You're thinking about what he said to her, aren't you?"

She nodded. "He's always had a gift for saying the eloquent thing. I've only known him to be speechless once."

"When was that?"

"The first time I kissed him." She looked at him and was suddenly very aware of everything around her, more so than she had ever been. She could feel the duvet on the bed, its silk and velvet lotus appliqués luxurious beneath her fingers. She felt the silk on her skin from the robe and loose pants they provided for her. The smell of her favorite perfumes blended with another scent, one of spice and musk, merged with her own like they were made for that purpose. His eyes were intensely blue. The dream gave her images of incredible passion under his touch, passion she had never known in all her years.

"That must have been some kiss."

She almost moved to kiss him then, without thinking about it. The romantic setting of all this was too right for such a situation and she was too exposed right now. Her body and mind needed the reassurance that she was alive and not someone else's possession. Doing this with Myrgen here, now, would prove both those things. Her dream fueled the need for that contact, revealed it to her. She wondered if she was revealing it to him as they spoke. She blinked and read him.

He was aware of her authority over his life, and was happy to give it after all he had put her through. He felt she deserved to get some control back in her life. He was truly sorry he allowed her son to remain a prisoner of the plot to do away with Charles. He was at her mercy, awaiting his fair judgment. He was completely oblivious to the impact he had on her with that kiss. He respected her, and was not thinking of her like that at all, even now, in this setting, with the subject of kissing as the crux of the discussion. She felt like a fool for assuming he would be fawning over her like the other men she had met.

She looked away from him and stood.

"It was a long time coming. He had been coming to my medical rescue for years at that point, in love with me all along. For him, it was his dream come true."

"And for you?"

"For me, it was the release of years of mourning and self-loathing. I had abandoned Nicolai and waited two years to return to him, only to find he had died because there was no one to take care of him. I carried that weight, that *guilt* for over five years. It was Alexander that caused me to give it up."

"And that's why he can't give you up."

"Yes."

"When did you find out Nicolai was alive?"

"I walked into a meeting in St. Giles right before I was to come down here to see Alexander, and Nicolai was sitting at that table alongside Tanglwyst. It was like the guilt had left to go get friends. I talked to Nicolai about what had happened to him, a bit about what had happened to me and how I had been chased by Giovanni's men ever since my escape. Nicolai told me he forgave me, but it turns out he never forgave me for interfering with his relationship with your sister. Once he started that up again a couple months ago, I just couldn't stand to be with him anymore."

"So you went to Alexander?"

"No. I didn't. That would have been betraying Nicolai."

Myrgen sat forward, confused. "But he was already betraying you."

"That wouldn't have made it right."

Myrgen looked at her and she could feel his scrutiny on her as surely as he would have felt hers. It was just as disconcerting as she had been told. Myrgen stood up and took her hand.

"I stand here alive, right now, because of your bizarre sense of what is right and wrong. Who am I to question?" He kissed her hand and released it. "As much as that bed is incredibly comfortable, it would be inappropriate for me to be found in it by anyone, nor to be seen with you like this. It's only starting to get light out so there's still time to sleep off some of this soreness. I'll leave you to the rest of your ministrations."

"Thank you, Myrgen."

He bowed and left the room.

Alexander awoke to the need to pee. Pity *that* didn't disappear with the Power of Sovereignty. He used the chamber pot and looked in the mirror. His hair was a tousled mess. Someone could mistake this for a wild night with a passionate woman, and he was reminded that Catriona was actually right across the hall, very accessible. He couldn't go to her like this though. She deserved better than to have the first thing she saw be this bedraggled monstrosity. He got dressed and wet his hair from a pitcher over a basin before combing it. He washed his hands and face and cleaned his teeth, using a touch of clove oil to take the taste of sleep away. Once he had made himself respectable, he opened the door and went across the hall.

Noises from inside caught his attention before he knocked, the sounds of a man and a woman coupling. Fury erupted from within, driven by the image of who would have the audacity to touch Catriona. His first thought was that Myrgen was raping her. He slammed open the door, the assailant forgetting to lock it in his haste, and caught her on top of him, naked and bouncing. The blonde woman screamed. Alexander blinked, embarrassed beyond belief and closed the door quickly.

He looked over at his room, then at this one. He knew this was the one he bought her. He knocked on the door. A moment later, Ambrois, the cook from the *Enigma*, opened the door in sailor's breeches. "Yes, Alexander?"

"I'm very sorry to bother you, Ambrois, but, isn't this the Captain's room?"

"Yes. She gave it to us when she saw my wife had come to town to see me off. She said it was inappropriate to spend the last night on shore with the love of my life in a crewman's bunk. Since both guest quarters were taken…"

Alexander nodded. "Yes, of course. No, she's right. Do you know where she went then?"

"Where she always stays when we're in Rouen. The Open Lotus, down the street."

"When did she leave for that place?"

"I'm afraid it was rather late. I was a little concerned, in fact, about her walking to the Lotus alone, but when we got up here, we saw she was being escorted, so we went to bed."

"Escorted, at that hour? By whom?"

"I think it was that Myrgen fellow."

The fire in Alexander's heart grew dark and cold and his voice reflected the change. "Thank you, Ambrois." He turned and left the Inn.

Catriona came down from her room, dressed for the day and ready to go. The sunrise had been splendid to watch, the world and city refreshed from the rain. It simply sealed her desire to be at sea. She saw Myrgen, also dressed, sitting at a table drinking something and chatting with Xannu. They were going over ledgers and books and seemed quite delighted with the idea.

Myrgen looked up as she descended the stairs. "Ah, Catriona! Good morning!"

"Good morning, Myrgen. What are you two up to?"

Xannu stood, prompting Myrgen to stand as well. "I was explaining your unique system of recording your journeys. We use it here as well."

Myrgen nodded. "It would take some time with the inventor of it, but I think I understand the principal. I didn't know Xannu was your chief bookkeeper."

"Yes. We are owners in this Incense House. She comes from Yantap."

"So she told me."

Xannu nodded to Myrgen. "Catriona, I must say I am most impressed with this gentleman. His alacrity with numbers is astounding! He's better than me."

Myrgen wagged a chastising finger at Xannu. "That is a bold-faced lie in an attempt to flatter me into doing something. This woman is the smartest creature I've ever met."

Catriona folded her arms across her chest. "Let me see if I understand things correctly: You had the chance to spend the night with a beautiful, exotic, intelligent woman, and you talked about accounting?"

"Don't say it like that," Myrgen grinned. "You make it sound so sinful."

Catriona laughed, and then glanced at Xannu. The two women nodded. "Well, I am in need of a Chancellor for the Zara office. Would you be interested, Myrgen?"

His smile dimmed a little with confusion and he looked at Xannu for confirmation that Catriona was kidding. She didn't appear to be.

Xannu nodded. "It's true. I can't travel anymore. This business is taking all my time and I think you would be a good person to have in that position."

Myrgen glanced at the floor, his face becoming serious. He stepped over to Catriona with a small bow to Xannu. "Captain Moriarity, I may have made a good impression on this lovely woman, but you and I know, from our own first encounter, what I'm really like."

"Yes, Myrgen, I do. You are a man recently burned by a corrupt person who drugged your sister to get her support. She manipulated your infatuation to feed your anger at losing someone very close to you. I also know you gave up your own chance at freedom to save my son. Xannu thinks you are a good choice, and I believe in her ability to see the balance in people."

The bell on the front door announced a customer in the other room and Xannu excused herself, giving them privacy.

He sighed. "She just met me last night. She doesn't know me."

"Just because she met you last night doesn't mean she doesn't know you. It simply means you don't know yourself."

"And that fact alone should make you rethink this. Look, Catriona, I'm not *accustomed* to trusting people in the life I've chosen, any more than you do. Your little trick with reading people demonstrates a strong distrust of those around you. So you can understand my unease at this prospect. I may be capable of this job you recommend, but you need someone you can trust."

"In the last tenday, you have given my son a puppy to help ease his captivity, insured his rescue when he was threatened, attacked a man endangering me *with a horse*, destroyed a toxic corpse despite the possibility of being haunted and escorted me through the streets of a port town, where an assassination attempt occurred, after dark. I can think of no safer place than in your company."

He looked into her eyes and found something he needed. He took her hand and raised it to his lips. "Then I will do my best to remain at your side."

"Find another position, de Sablonierres." The edge in Alexander's voice was enough to carve bone. They both turned to see him, his eyes raging with fire. "That's *my* place."

Six

"Flies never visit an egg that has no crack."
The Wise Wench's Tavern Book

Catriona stepped outside the Open Lotus and Alexander closed the door behind her, his fury barely contained enough to keep from slamming the door. The audacity of Myrgen to say something like that to his intended was bad enough, but to do so in such a setting as this? He needed to find a way to keep that man grounded while Catriona set sail. Then he could deal with Myrgen himself. Perhaps another Writ was in order.

She turned to him and waited. He found he needed to pace but he knew that would make him appear weak in front of her, so he steadied himself and tried to calm his anger. He knew she couldn't read his innermost secrets, but he could certainly vouch for her ability to understand even the slightest change in his voice or demeanor. "Catriona, what happened? Why didn't you stay at the Inn?"

"Because the beds here are more comfortable, Alexander. I know the owner as well. I happen to stay here every time I am in Rouen."

"But *I* was at the Inn. Why not bring me to this place instead?"

"It would have been inappropriate for you to be seen here. You are the King of Mervolingia."

A gasp came from a couple passing on the street, and they bowed immediately upon recognizing Alexander. He acknowledged their bows and thanked them. The couple rushed off down the street and Alexander cast about for a more shielded area to talk.

"Please, walk with me." He nodded in the general direction of an alleyway behind the incense house and out of earshot of the general street. Catriona stopped where she could see both ends of the alley and waited.

"I understand that I may be the King, but I am as interested in *your* reputation as you are in mine. I don't want the future Queen of Mervolingia to be seen in such a place any more than you want me seen there."

Catriona folded her arms across her chest. "You make a lot of assumptions, Alexander."

"Yes, I do." He took her hand and looked in her eyes. "I love you. I can't think of anything else when I'm away from you except finding a way to be by your side. But I can't run off to search the ports for you anymore, so I need to find a way to keep you here, with me. You are the best thing in the world, essential as my next breath. What I voice here is a hope, a dream that we can be together."

Catriona relaxed and Alexander took heart. He could always melt her with an eloquent speech. She offered a small smile.

"It does not change things between us, Alexander. I still care for you. Yesterday's battle... Like I said last night on the balcony, I..." She exhaled. Alexander caught a bit of pain in her face and body.

"Let's not talk of that. Let the dead rest. If I may ask, what would prompt Myrgen to make such a statement?"

Catriona blinked and swallowed past the previous subject. "I... Xannu suggested he would make a fine chancellor for my Zara office. I agree with her."

"You mean for your shipping business? How can you possibly consider such a thing?"

"He is more than adept at accounting. In fact, I think I can safely say he'd rather talk accounting than romance a beautiful woman."

"That just makes him an idiot. Not to mention that he was clearly thinking of romance when he made that statement."

"He didn't mean it like that, Alexander."

"Didn't he? Did you flay his soul and discern that? Or are you the one making assumptions now?"

A man in royal livery came out of the side door, escorted by Xannu. They looked around and saw Catriona and Alexander standing near the end of the alley. The man thanked Xannu with a nod and moved with haste down the alleyway. He bowed at ten paces and awaited acknowledgment from Alexander, who glanced at Catriona, then nodded to the man. He bowed and approached.

"Your Majesty, I have important news." He handed the king a messenger's tube with a special stamp in the side. The locking mechanism was keyed to the royal signet ring. Alexander realized he had left it in a pouch in his saddlebags back at the Inn.

He nodded to the messenger. "Thank you. I will read this presently." He turned back to Catriona. "I fear I must investigate this. May I talk with you later?"

Catriona blinked slowly, her way of buying time to think. She was quite brilliant, and could process all sorts of information in the span of a blink. Blinking slowly was her way of thinking things over. He had seen this before and wasn't sure if she was thinking good or ill at the moment, but her taking the time to process it felt like it was more inclined to go in his favor.

"Certainly, Your Majesty. I'll be on the ship, getting it ready. You know where to find me." She bowed and left him with the messenger in the alley. Alexander noted her formality and tried not to be offended by it. She was very mindful of the appearance of things, which made this infraction so blatant. He had a hard time understanding what would cause her to allow the appearance that she was entertained at a brothel with a man who is a fugitive and a traitor.

Alexander left the alleyway and returned to the Inn, going into his room. It was as he had left it not twenty minutes before. It was amazing how much could happen in so little time. The sun's position had barely changed. He went to his saddlebags and found the signet ring hidden in a secret pocket. He pulled it out and put it on.

The lock on the scroll tube was designed not to work unless the ring was worn by the rightful King of Mervolingia, a safety precaution hundreds of years old. He unlocked the lid and pulled out the message.

"Your Majesty,

I regret to inform You that the Honorable Lady Tanglwyst has escaped house arrest. She was aided in her escape by Duncan McVryce, who killed four guards before managing to leave the premises.

I and my remaining men gave chase. We managed to steer him into a trap and caught them in an alley in central Patras. As we approached him, he grabbed her to his chest and stepped into the shadows, which then enveloped him, leaving behind thick air and a stink of sulfur. I stabbed the shadows with my rapier, but the two fugitives were gone.

Dark magic is at play here, My Liege. Be careful.

Grande Guarde Gomez de Santander"

"Damn," he whispered. *Why would Duncan rescue Tanglwyst? He just killed her lover.* Then it occurred to him exactly why Nicolai had fallen so quickly. Duncan wanted Tanglwyst for himself. The Saints only knew what he had in mind for her. Having the man who had carried out the Writ of Destruction calling for Nicolai's death, who knew Alexander was the one who put out the contract, enamored of a woman accused of treason, was too dangerous to let slide.

Alexander needed to find Duncan McVryce before he told Tanglwyst anything.

Tanglwyst awoke to a room very dimly lit, the stink of sulfur still in her nose. Her hair was matted with sweat and her clothes felt almost stiff, like she had sweated out a fever. A soft glow in the room, barely making a dent in the dark, was enough to see the table it sat upon and still allow sleep. She traced the glow with her eyes and saw it was a pattern, some sort of symbol in the stone. The room was small and there were no windows or doors. Duncan was asleep next to her and she felt him stir as she moved on the bed. The furnishings were good, but old from the look and sound of the things. Her sitting up and moving to the edge caused the frame to creak in the silence like a church bell in the room.

"Angel?"

Tanglwyst put her hand on Duncan's shoulder. "I'm here, Duncan."

He rolled over and opened his eyes. "Forgive me, my Lady. I'm afraid my escape was probably rather frightening to you."

She looked around. "Where *are* we?"

"In a sacred hiding place. We're safe. We can't be found here."

"There are no doors or windows. How did we get in here?"

Duncan sat up and glanced at the symbol on the floor and walls. They glowed brighter, like right before dawn.

Tanglwyst drew back. "Witchcraft."

"No. It's a holy artifact. This place was set up by the Church centuries ago." He gestured to the symbol in the room. "I was invested with an office which is associated with this symbol. It was laid down by a scholar centuries ago who was tasked with the protection of the Church."

"And this office, what is it?"

"I... don't think I can tell you the specifics. Suffice it to say you are safe here and Gomez won't be able to find you. We'll stay here a few days so we can't be found, then we'll find someplace better for you."

"*Better* for me? Why am I here?"

"I think you know why you're here, my Angel."

She put her lips together to deny it, and then realized what he meant. Her grandfather was the Pope. She let out a breath. "I see. I must have really been in danger."

He touched her cheek. "Yes, I'm afraid you were. You could have been executed before His Holiness could have requested your release. I'm to see about getting you to the Papal City."

"How did you get me here?"

He opened his shirt. An amulet with symbols on it similar to the one in the room lay upon his neck. She instinctively felt nauseated and the scent of sulfur became stronger. Duncan touched it. "This. It was given to me by an agent of the Church, for doing business and protecting the king."

"The *Church* gave you this?"

He looked at her. "Yes."

"And that thing is connected to this room?" She looked around, now suspicious of the rune set in the baseboard.

"Well, yes. It's a safe place to hide, to be protected. The office I hold is designed to protect."

"And how do we get out?" Tanglwyst looked around. "I notice there's no food here."

"We'll get out the same way we got in. I have another place nearby. This place is just untraceable. It's probably been a night. We could leave in an hour or so."

"And what did you have in mind to do until then?"

Duncan smiled, bouncing his eyebrows, suggesting sex. She felt uncomfortable in these surroundings, especially since he didn't seem to recognize the darkness swirling in his eyes. She frowned. "I'm afraid my stomach did not care for the travel here as much as you did. And the smell still lingers in my nose."

Duncan sniffed the air. "Ah, the lemons. You are unfamiliar with them, aren't you?"

"Lemons? You mean the fruit? I know that smell. Is that what you smell here now?"

"Yes, of course. It's part of the process to use this amulet, it causes a flash of light and the smell of lemons. And it brings me to this place. I can use it to go anywhere I've been before. I can also use the amulet to attach a thread to those about whom I care deeply. Unfortunately, you and I parted ways before I got this

70

amulet and I never got the chance to place a thread on you. There's one now."

She looked at herself, suddenly feeling a web on her. She brushed at it, but it remained, like a hair on her skin that she couldn't quite locate. "Get it off!"

Duncan's brow furrowed. "It's perfectly safe, my dear. I wouldn't let you be harmed."

"But if you can track me, someone might be able to use that against us. How many of these are there? These amulets?"

Duncan looked down at his chest. "I don't know that there are *any* others."

"You *don't know* if there are any others, which means you don't know if anyone else could use them."

Duncan blinked several times, frowning, but sorting through the wisdom of her words. She felt her will push against him, and felt him fold. "I see what you mean. Who knows what could happen? I'll remove the thread."

He waved his hand, caught something and rolled it up and put it against his amulet. It flared with dark fire for a second and the sulfur smell returned. He breathed it in. "Lemons. You can't smell that?"

She smiled, apparently convincingly, and nodded. He hugged her and kissed her forehead. She closed her eyes, grateful she had managed to stifle the shudder that threatened to reveal her disgust.

Seven

"Have a wit like a kitchen knife, but don't sharpen it on your heart."
The Wise Wench's Tavern Book

Catriona stepped onto the ship and the entire crew smiled at her presence. She felt at home once again, free from the strife that dominated her time on land. The only thing better would be putting to sail. She walked over to Ambrois and nodded good morning.

"Captain! Good to have you back on board."

"How are the guardsmen doing?"

"Not well, I'm afraid. They have suffered quite a series of wounds. That one belly wound looks especially bad. He might take a tenday to perish."

Catriona frowned at the news, blinking in contemplation. Finally, she took a breath, making a judgment. "Nicolai's taken enough from Alexander. I'll not let him have these men as well."

Ambrois exhaled slowly and nodded, understanding. "Aye Captain. I'll inform the crew." His tone indicated he did not approve but would comply.

Catriona turned and went to her cabin. She was going to need a drink for this. She stepped into her familiar surroundings and reveled in the imagery greeting her. The chart table properly covered in maps dominated the room, complemented by an upholstered bench with a map motif that had been woven just for her. Above that, inviting the sun to entertain the inhabitants was a custom-designed stained glass window of a satyr chasing a nymph around her tree, a beautiful tower gracing the background and the barest hint of a ship in a port beyond it. The other side of the tower showed wolves running through a forest where scholars studied on the slopes of the surrounding hillside. The caption declared its name was Galadorn.

The pitch that sealed the ship came from the woods around the Galadorn Covenant, where lived a Fae Lord who had befriended Catriona years ago. It was infused with the blessings and protection of the Midsummer King. It was also responsible for the sleek black appearance of the ship and its timeless elegance. She missed that place sometimes, but she knew she would. That was why she had this window made when the ship was built. Perhaps she would return there, now that she was free.

She went to her desk and retrieved a bottle of wine from the series of upright pigeon holes designed for holding bottles and goblets. She poured some of the wine into a goblet and returned it to the hole out of habit, her gaze already escaping the thoughts of what she had determined to do. Healing required giving up a piece of her soul and right then, it was feeling a bit ragged. Between watching her first love die on the flagstone street and the pressure Alexander was putting on her to commit, she was in desperate need of restoring herself at sea. At least on the ship the effort of healing seemed easier, like she had more energy to draw from here.

Her bed was behind a screened wall, giving her a modicum of privacy from the doorway. She opened the lid to her sea chest and saw it had been put back in order, probably by Octavius. She was so grateful for his foresight. This particular part of the journey was going to be especially difficult. Dealing with the guardsmen's wounds would make putting to sail a serious threat, and she would have to pull rank on Octavius in order to get them out of the harbor.

A knock on the door made her adrenaline spark and she downed the last of the wine and replaced the goblet before opening the door. The blond man at the door had shed his scholarly pudge in the years since she had first met him in Galadorn. He was now a bit more chiseled in his shape and but his face was still round, though now she realized that was just the shape of his face. His scholastica was still reflected in his eyes, sharp blue disks that could define the ship's position by the stars or show excitement over the latest debate about religion or state politics.

Octavius blocked her path, arms folded. "No."

"Excuse me?"

"You're not healing them."

Catriona folded her arms as well, already having anticipated this conversation. "Odd, I thought *I* was the Captain here."

"Only until you die and frankly, I'm not ready to take on the Captaincy of the *Enigma* just yet. I've seen those wounds, Captain. I'm not going to let you do this."

"They need to be helped."

He pointed behind him. "They're strangers! I could see it if they were family or crew, but they're not. They'll heal just fine if they are given time. You don't need to do this."

She put her hand on his arm. "Yes, I do. Those men were injured because of Nicolai and the fight between us. I'm partially responsible, and I'm not going to have their families go through what I went through for seven years. And, according to Ambrois, they will die without this help. Now let me pass." The two stood, facing off, and then Octavius shook his head.

"I want it on the record that I object to this."

"Duly noted."

"And I'm going to be right next to you. If I think you're taking on too much, I'll tear you off them, I swear it. This crew can't lose you."

"It won't. Thank you, Octavius. Are they ready?"

Octavius pursed his lips and nodded. She stepped past him and went down the hallway to the room on the right. Two crewmen were in there and they had carefully exposed the man's wounds. She took a deep breath and looked at the injury. It was the other man, the one with the chest and arm wounds. They were bad, but healable. She stepped up to the side of the bed and looked at the crewmen.

"Hold him."

The crewmen put their hands on either side of him and looked at her. The guard opened his eyes slowly and she looked into them. "This is going to hurt a bit, but it will make you better, okay?" She ignored the confused look on his face and put her hands on the chest wound.

The fever in the wound was hot and she drew energy from the surrounding air to cool it. She felt it working and the man moaned under her fingers. Octavius stepped up behind her as she took in a breath to relax herself for the next part. She exhaled and then pulled. The wound on his chest grew wet and the blood splashed up on her hands. The man screamed as the pain from the wound was ripped from his body like a bandage removed quickly. Catriona's head snapped back, her entire body rigid and she absorbed the wound into her own chest. Her doublet front bloomed crimson, like the wound was fresh, but the gash beneath her fingers disappeared.

She staggered a bit and Octavius held her shoulders. "Stop, Captain. He's fine now."

"He won't be able to use that arm again if I don't do something. It's going septic."

"Captain…"

But he was too late. She put her hands on the guard's arm and pulled. The lesion erupted on her own arm as the man cried out. He arched, the pain in his chest too fresh a memory coupling with this new agony from the arm. She gritted her teeth and breathed between them, trying to slow the frequency as she tried to get the throbbing under control. Octavius pulled her to a chair in the room next to a desk. He moved around to the front of her and called for a cloth. One of the crewmen handed him one. Octavius wiped the blood from her face and hands.

"Captain, can you hear me?"

"Yes... yes Octavius... I can... hear you..." She closed her eyes and exhaled, trying to funnel the pain out on the breath. She focused on the wound on her chest and the wound healed a bit. Octavius saw the cut close a bit across her clavicle and looked at the younger crewman.

"Johannes, get Grymalkin. He's at the Inn from last night."

"No," Catriona grabbed his arm. "Not yet."

Octavius frowned. "By the time he gets here, you will have healed the other guard. I just want him here as soon as you're done." He looked at Johannes. "Go!"

Johannes ran onto the deck and down the gangplank as Myrgen stepped onto the pier. The intense look on the crewman's face caught Myrgen's attention and he grabbed the man as he passed. "What's wrong?"

"The captain's injured. I need to fetch Grymalkin." Johannes took his arm back and ran towards the Inn. Myrgen looked up at the ship and ran up the gangplank to the deck. Octavius was helping her out of the guard's room and they were walking towards the other end of the ship. Myrgen saw the front of her doublet glisten and there was an ugly scar fresh across her upper chest. "What the hell happened?"

Octavius looked at Myrgen. "She healed the guard."

Myrgen took the other side of her and supported her. "How?"

"She takes on the wound herself. This one's bad, but not as bad as the other one will be. That man is going to die."

Catriona gripped Myrgen's shoulder. "Not if I can help it."

"Myrgen, help me stop her. She'll die if she does this."

Myrgen looked at his savior and back at Octavius. "Has she done this before?"

"All the time for crewmen, but these guys..."

"And she's survived it every time?"

"Well, yes, but..."

Myrgen shouldered her weight. "Then I trust her. Where's the other guard?"

Alexander put the saddlebag on his horse and tightened the straps holding them in place. He was going to need to return to Patras and investigate Tanglwyst's escape personally. Because of his previous dealings with Duncan, he felt he might have some insight he could lend this investigation, but he couldn't do it by messenger. He needed to see the evidence himself. He would have liked to have Catriona's eyes on this, but that was too risky. If the same poison that killed Nicolai was used on those four guards, she might suspect. And if she laid eyes upon Duncan McVryce, she would know Alexander's part in that. He needed to kill Duncan in order to keep his secret from ever getting out.

The Innkeeper came through the doors with one of Catriona's crewmen, a Krakten fellow named Johannes and pointed to Alexander. "Johannes, what is it?"

"The Captain's hurt. She needs you, sir."

Alexander nodded and stepped into the stirrup of his saddle. He ducked his head to keep from hitting the doorway as he spurred his mount through it. Johannes and the Innkeeper got out of the way. *Catriona's hurt? How? Could it be that Duncan has returned to avenge Tanglwyst's injuries at her hands?* The thought scared Alexander as he pictured her body thrashing about enough to break her back as she died. He turned his fear into fury and kicked the horse, speed becoming his ally. The hooves thundered through the streets and people jumped from his path as they heard him coming. He turned into the docks area and charged down the docks to where the *Enigma* was moored.

He dismounted and grabbed the travel physician's kit that he always kept in his bags. He also drew his sword, preparing for trouble. He stormed up the gangplank, eyes flicking back and forth into the small shadows, looking for threats. He heard a scream from the aft cabin area and ran in that direction, recognizing Catriona's voice. He came into the hall and saw the door to the guest cabin was closed. He threw it open in his rush to rescue her.

Myrgen was pulling her to the ground, her limp body falling into his arms. Her doublet was wet and the pain on her face was fading as she passed into unconsciousness. Alexander leveled his sword at Myrgen, death in his voice.

"I warned you."

Catriona felt the pain of the wound split her like a piece of wood under an axe. She knew she could not take on the whole wound. Octavius was right, that would kill her, but she could take on half the wound, lessening the blow to his body's own ability to recover. She did so and immediately felt the folly of such a decision. Yes, the man might now live, but the pain he was being forced to endure might also kill him. What was just as bad was that this wound, coupled with the other two she'd healed from the first guard, might still claim her life. Once again, she was glad someone had sent for Alexander.

She felt someone catch her as she fell back, strong arms that were as supportive as the earth. She fell into blackness, and then she was lying on the ground on her back, a bright light falling down upon her. She opened her eyes and saw a brilliant, beautiful light from a large open set of doors. She rolled over and got to her feet, her chest, stomach and arm showing no signs of the damage her physical body endured. She was grateful for the respite from the pain.

She stepped up to the doors before her. The ancient church welcoming and peaceful. A priest was coming toward her down the aisle, a concerned smile on his face as he saw her. She only came to this place when she was unconscious but she also found advice and spiritual healing here as well. She stepped towards the doorway, steeling herself for the impact of entry when she suddenly heard shouting and smelled blood. The priest looked at the stained glass windows on the side of the church and Catriona walked around the side of the building.

Alexander had a sword at Myrgen's throat. The whole room was still as everyone tried to assess what to do. A small line of blood was trickling down Myrgen's neck from the point of the blade and it was coming uncomfortably close to Myrgen's jugular. Catriona ran for the men, the memory of her wounds gone in the heat of battle.

Her eyes flew open and she pressed backwards while she kicked the blade away from Myrgen's neck, moving him aside as it was swept around. The effort saved Myrgen from Alexander's blade but she felt the wounds she had suffered gush from the movement. Alexander looked at her, surprise crossing his features.

"Drop the weapon, Alex. You'll not spill blood on my ship."

"Catriona…" He sheathed his sword, eyes on Myrgen who righted himself.

"Myrgen had nothing to do with this decision. It was mine. You needed to have your…guards…" She felt light-headed and the room started spinning. She put her hands down to steady herself. "Swear you'll leave him be."

"Catriona, you're hurt…"

"Swear it!"

Alexander looked at Myrgen, then back at her. "I swear. He's safe from harm by me on this ship."

Catriona felt a flood of energy enter into and out of her as the oath was spoken and she closed her eyes a moment as she tried to gather it, redirecting it to the wounds. It worked somewhat, but she didn't harness the energy efficiently and lost most of it. At least it stopped the bleeding and she opened her eyes as Alexander put his hands on her to examine the cuts.

"Alright then, de Sablonierres, make yourself useful and help me get her to her cabin." Alexander stood up and Myrgen shifted so he was on a knee before he scooped her up. The crew cleared the way as Myrgen carried her to her cabin. Alexander directed him to her bed behind the screen. As Myrgen laid her down, Alexander set his kit down on a table by the bed and opened it. The table was specially made for her by a master carpenter and remained level in all but the roughest seas due to being on a swivel. This was especially helpful when he was setting out his kit. She stirred at the clunk of the ceramic vials as he set them on the wood. She opened her eyes and watched the men helping her.

Myrgen stood and stepped back out of Alexander's way as he went to work. He started to open her doublet to inspect the wounds and Myrgen bowed to her and ducked around to the other side of the screen. "Will you need anything else, Your Majesty?"

Alexander smiled as he looked at the wound on her chest. "I might need you to get something from my horse."

Catriona caught the death threat in Alexander's voice and frowned. "Myrgen, I need you to talk to Octavius. Please, see him." Her breath caught as Alexander slowly pulled the fabric away from the drying blood covering the wounds.

"Y... Yes Captain."

She heard the door close and she looked at Alexander. "That wasn't nice."

He looked into her eyes. "I never claimed to be." He returned his gaze to her chest wound. "Damn." He picked one of the vials from his kit and a cloth and poured the contents onto the wound, catching the spills with the cloth and wiping them towards the injury. Catriona felt the fever in the wound dissipate like smoke before a breeze and her breathing became easier. "Better?"

She nodded. "Yes. That's helped a lot."

"Well, I enjoy this scenery too much to let it be scorched by a careless fire." He winked at her, and then focused on his work. "So, tell me, why are you letting him stay?"

"Myrgen? He saved Alan."

Alexander flicked his gaze to her eyes, then back to her wound as he inspected the healing that had taken place. "Did he? I thought he was the reason Alan was in danger in the first place. That pretty much excludes him from any grace I might have towards him for saving the boy."

"He wasn't the one who took him. That was Tanglwyst's choice. He rebelled against the idea. When she did it against his will, he didn't want to endanger the plan by releasing him."

"The plan to murder my brother, his king? That plan?"

She looked away. "I understand your anger. But I did my best to save Charles, not damn him."

"And damned me instead, by freeing him and making me king. However shall I repay such an act of kindness?"

She kept her gaze from his and he watched the progress on the healing liquid. It was an extract from a Mervolingian herb similar to the Cyprian, a hybrid that did not take the will of the patient but still improved their healing. He always made certain he kept the Cyprian separate, in his own kit for his own wounds, but he realized the two acted in identical ways. An onlooker would never be able to tell the difference, even if the onlooker was a patient like this one.

He glanced at her a moment, then blinked the thought away. *This is foolish thinking; there are no other patients like this one. If there were, I wouldn't love her so much.* He exhaled, deciding to make peace instead of allowing any further wedges between them.

"Still, I guess I was a bit harder on him than I needed to be. He saved someone precious to both of us, despite his involvement in setting up the situation."

Catriona exhaled through the extinguishing pain. "Yes, he did. See now why I put him under my protection?"

He looked at her and nodded. "Yes. Yes I do." He took her hand and pressed it to his lips. "Forgive me, my Lady. I spoke in haste. Your wisdom is beyond my limits to comprehend, but I do trust it. I am your servant."

Her look softened at his words and she reached up and pulled him to her to kiss him. The effort pulled at the stomach wound and she cried out at the unexpected pain. Alexander swore and the door to her room opened. Octavius' voice asked, "Is she all right?"

"Yes, yes, she's fine. This is a nasty belly wound is all. Go on." The door closed and he smiled at her. "Sorry. I should make sure you're up to such activity before I allow it."

"Probably best." She smiled and he moved on to the rest of her injuries.

Myrgen looked out from the aft deck at the city. He was mulling over the incident below in the guard's cabin, and Catriona's movement, even as hurt as she was. He was impressed. He realized he was alive now only because of her willing it so.

Anyone who could take on the pain of another and still stop a sword at someone else's throat was beyond impressive. *That* was legendary. Still, he was certain she was paying for it now.

Movement on the main deck caught his attention as Octavius emerged from the area behind the stairs going to the Captain's cabin. He looked around and saw Myrgen above him, then climbed the stairs to join the former Mervol Chancellor. "Time we made this official, I think. Myrgen, wasn't it?"

"Yes. And you're Octavius, the First Mate." Myrgen nodded greeting and nudged his chin in the direction of the steps. "How is she doing?"

"Grymalkin is an expert healer. She'll be fine. She's irrepressible anyway, and being on the ship will help her heal faster."

"Why would being on the ship matter?"

Octavius shrugged and leaned on the railing overlooking the city. "Don't you know the legends? The sea has healing properties, according to the Clerics of Callista." He looked at Myrgen's neck. "You might want to keep an eye on that. Wounds on the sea can turn septic."

"If Callista feels the subject should suffer?" Myrgen reached up and touched the graze. "It will be fine. I'll take care of it later."

"For a man who just had the King's own sword at his throat, you're handling this very well."

Myrgen smiled at the man's observation. "I guess I've had enough violent contact in the past two days that I'm getting used to it. Seems I can't turn a corner without some incredibly intense situation playing out around me."

"Ah. So this is all *your* fault." Octavius returned his gaze to the city. "That's a relief. I was afraid I was going to have to dock Ambrois' pay again."

Myrgen chuckled at the joke.

Octavius smiled. "Eh, you needn't have worried. Grymalkin's a healer, not a killer. I don't think he could bring himself to actually *take* a life."

Myrgen's eyes fluttered at the memory of Alexander running his sword through the former queen when she tried to steal the Power of Sovereignty from her husband's corpse. With the Power, she could have commanded the people of Mervolingia to eat themselves and any citizen would have done so. Myrgen still felt it was the best course after she went insane.

"Well, he might have a surprise or two still in him." He looked at the First Mate. "Any idea when we'll set sail?"

"As soon as those land monkeys are off ship. That's why she took on those wounds in the first place. To get under weigh."

"And where will we go once that happens?"

"Probably Caratia. Captain's due to make a stop at home. That's about a month or so at sea, weather permitting." He looked at Myrgen. "You ever put to sea before?"

"Oh yes. On my sister's ships all the time, for trips to Mande. Spent a while in Yndia studying. There were ships in and out of there every day."

"Well, let's hope you are as useful as your friend Michael. He's pitched right in since he came on board a couple days ago."

"He's a good man."

"He's a ruthless bastard. I've never seen a man give a beating like he gave the three crewmen he was playing with last night! Luckily, he can take a beating as well and still have a good humor."

Myrgen was startled to hear Michael had been in a fight and, more impressively, that he had not killed anyone. "Er, you have any idea where he is?"

"Oh yeah, in the galley."

"Thanks. Excuse me." He nodded to Octavius. He went down the stairs to the main deck, then further on to the galley. Michael was, unexpectedly, washing dishes in the sink. Myrgen looked at him but saw no signs of brutality. "So, what's this? Punishment for the beatings you gave and took last night?"

Michael turned, his Nubian skin glistening with sweat that simply enhanced his large muscles and dark color. He smiled and waved a foamy hand. "Greetings, Myrgen," he said in Mervolingian. "Yes, it turns out I am not as good at throwing dice as I am at playing cards." He gestured toward the sinks of dishes. "This is what happens when I get bored winning and try another game."

Myrgen blinked, confused. "Cards? Dice? You mean the beatings you took were in gambling?"

"Of course. You don't think I would start a fight with the crew of the woman who saved me? That would be ungracious."

"That it would, my friend. That it would." Myrgen smiled and grabbed a stack of clean dishes. A gesture from Michael and he put them away in the right cupboard. "Did you run out of money?"

"In a way. The currency on board is chore duty. Some chores are desirable, some not. In order to play, I had to be willing to take certain undesirable chores and give up desirable ones."

"What constitutes a desirable chore?" Myrgen put another stack of dishes away, clearing the counter for more.

"Captain's laundry. I guess she must have good soap."

Myrgen pursed his lips, remembering the soaps and perfumes from the Open Lotus. "Yes, I'm certain that's the draw. I shudder to think what your currency could have been."

"Actually, cleaning and restocking your cabin once you get settled in and we get under way, or 'weigh' I guess is the right term, spelling it properly in my head. You know, 'weighing anchor' so they get under weigh, it's like learning a whole new language!"

Myrgen smiled at the man's mental exercises. "I see. Why would they want to restock my cabin?"

"Some of the men are quite curious. A new face on board the *Enigma?* Apparently, that's pretty rare these days. They also were interested in cleaning and sharpening my weapons. Apparently, they wanted to know what sort of steel the Mervol Palace carried."

"Interesting. It sounds a bit naïve to think these salty dogs would gamble with chores. I've been around sailors, Michael. That's unnatural, what you speak of."

"I must admit, I thought it odd as well. However, the Captain, I'm told, doesn't tolerate gambling for money or drink. If the men want a game of chance to turn interesting, they gamble chores. Apparently, it's a lot more common than not. Money doesn't spend at sea. In port, they gamble for money, but not at sea or prepping for sea, at least on other ships. Not this one, though." He glanced back down at his sinks and pulled a clean dish from the water to set it on the counter in the drying rack.

"She forbids gambling with money? And they adhere to that? I find that hard to believe."

"I was assured that these men would rather sail under her flag than any other ship in the sea. They adhere to her rules without fail. I understand several of them have been rescued by her as well. They also told me she pays better than any ship on the oceans."

"Well, if these men understand a good thing when they see it, then adherence to such rules must not chafe too badly or they wouldn't stay."

"None of these men would even tolerate the thought of leaving this ship. I can see their point of view, though. The woman I met under the palace was someone I would follow into battle."

"Well, let's hope it won't come to that." Myrgen picked up a towel and started drying the dishes in the rack. He liked Michael. He was a good friend, and although he allowed himself to be seen as Myrgen's slave, Myrgen considered him his own man. He had hoped Michael could, someday, become a landowner so he could have rights under the Mervolingian laws. Perhaps Catriona could make a request upon the Dûce of Caratia. Caratia had regular dealings with Nubia due to sharing the Bloody Sea between them. Myrgen had never been there, but he supposed Caratia did not ostracize Nubians since Catriona appeared to be half-Nubian herself.

"Did you also gamble?"

Myrgen snapped out of his thought process. "Huh?" Michael nodded and glanced at the dish in Myrgen's hand. Myrgen looked at it and shook his head. "No. I'm just giving them some time."

"The Captain and the Prince?"

Myrgen nodded, looking out the open door. "King, actually. We saw him invoke the Rite of Sovereignty."

Michael put his hand upon Myrgen's shoulder, soaking it with suds. "Be careful. Alexander is a man with great focus and stamina. If he chooses to go after you, he will not stop until he gets you or dies trying."

"I'll keep that in mind." The sound of boots coming down the stairs into the well-lit galley stopped the conversation's progress. Alexander emerged from the stairway.

"Myrgen. She wants to see you."

"About what?"

"I didn't ask. She didn't offer."

Myrgen put the towel next to the sink and walked over to the stairs as Alexander returned to the deck. The King escorted him to the Captain's door and bedside, offering a sweeping gesture to the area behind the screen. Myrgen stepped behind the screen to Catriona's bedside and was surprised to see her sitting up, dressed and looking like she had never been hurt. She was wearing a clean doublet and pants. Her boots were different from the ones she had worn before. She was pulling on her gloves when he came into view.

"Ah, Myrgen. Alexander, would you see to your men and make sure they are ready to travel?"

Alexander looked at Myrgen, then at Catriona before bowing. "Of course, My Lady."

She waited until the door closed and she stood up. Her efforts caused a small grimace to flash across her face and Myrgen stepped over, offering a hand. "Are you sure you should be out of bed?"

"I'll be fine. It is inappropriate for you to be in my bedroom."

"You didn't seem to mind last night."

Catriona looked at him as if shocked he would bring up such a thing. Myrgen swallowed, embarrassed. "Sorry. That...didn't come out right."

"I'm not squeamish about your presence in my sleeping area as much as I intend to discuss business and it is not something that should be done in a place of solace and refuge."

"Ah. My apologies, Captain. I did not understand. Charles, when he was King, conducted business from his bedroom more often than not." He stepped out into the main room, releasing her hand as soon as he felt she was stable. He knitted them together behind his back as she went to her desk. "I would also like to apologize for all the trouble I've caused. That incident with Alexander was..."

"Not your fault. It was likewise not his. He is very protective of me and my son. He feels you are a threat to me and does not want to let you think he won't dispose of you. I understand the machismo at work here, Myrgen. I'm on a ship with a hundred men." She poured some wine into the goblet there and offered some to Myrgen with a gesture. He politely refused. "However, he is well trusted by this crew and you are a stranger. As such, I would like to keep you close to deter any of my crew from getting ideas about removing you from the ship while we're at sea. There's a cabin right there," she nodded to the one housing the first guard. "I would like you to take it as soon as that guard is gone."

"That close? Would Alexander approve of such proximity?"

"Alexander got a very important message this morning. Special seal. Whatever was in that missive was urgent enough for me to believe he'll return to Patras right away. That's why I healed the guards. Thus, he isn't going to be on ship when you move in to the cabin."

"I see. And why is this going to be a deterrent for the crew?"

"I'll be able to hear if they try to attack you."

"Ah. What reason are you going to give them? They're bound to ask why you want me so close."

"I will explain to them that I will be going over the books with my new Chancellor and having you nearby means I can work you harder."

Myrgen smiled. "So, you still want to go through with that? Even after Alexander's threat a little while ago?"

Catriona looked at Myrgen. "Yes. Are you still interested in taking the position?"

"Most definitely."

"Then the deal is struck. I'll draw up the contracts in the next couple days. Now," she set the goblet in the pigeon hole, "do you think you could expedite the removal of those guards from my ship?"

Myrgen smiled and bowed. "Again, most definitely." He turned and left the room.

Eight

"Don't allow gamblers or goblins within your walls.
They will leave a stench that drives away luck."
The Wise Wench's Tavern Book

Catriona let her breath out in a rush after Myrgen closed her door. The pain was now bearable, thanks to Alexander's ministrations, but it was still there. She was glad Alexander had somewhere else to go. The fact she had almost kissed him, even while wounded, said he was still too much in control of her emotions. She took a drink of her wine to take the edge off the pain. *Is that really so bad, caring for him like I do?*

Yes, it is. I still have far too many duties and responsibilities to take care of to let myself be swept into his arms. She could still smell the lingering smoke in the air from where they destroyed her husband's body. Yes, it was incredibly inappropriate and irresponsible for her to be craving that human contact. To have such a thing with Alexander would merely seal her fate as Queen of Mervolingia and that was not her place in the world. She was a citizen of Caratia, a servant of the Land. To split her loyalties would mean neither country got her best. She was not the sort of person one chose for a royal marriage. Her role in Caratia was not royal. It was as Champion. It carried no land or nobility since it was a title earned and granted, not the product of birth. For all his adoration of Catriona, Alexander had never bothered to learn much of her home or their customs. Their worlds could be no more joined by a marriage than he could own the sea by buying a fish.

As much as she cared for Alexander, it was not meant to be between them. When Nicolai had accepted her apology, she realized Karma was against a union between her and the Mervol noble. She had put the thought of being with him out of her mind as courting the impossible. But with Nicolai gone, that was no longer as impossible as it had been before. As callous as it seemed, she had mourned Nicolai for seven years. She truly felt she had no more tears to shed for him. Alexander had released her from her guilt over her abandonment of her husband and it was clear she still felt that gratitude.

Damn Elizabeth! Had the woman not decided to try and steal the Power of Sovereignty for herself, Alexander would not be the King. Catriona had already made up her mind to leave Nicolai at the beginning of this season. She had a letter written in her mind, asking Alexander to meet her in St. Andrew later this month so she could tell him. There had been a chance for them, but once again, Karma interfered. Why was it so wrong for them to be together?

She didn't know, and she was too unwilling to try and find out. In a couple months, she would be back in Caratia and in between then and now, she would be at sea. It would take time for it to fade, but she knew it would. It had been stifled all winter. Distance was the best thing for both of them right now. Without her close by, he would be able to move on and that was essential. Political marriages, despite Alexander's protestations, were best for the country. She couldn't allow personal feelings to interfere with the well-being of thousands.

She finished her wine and braced herself for what would probably be the last time she would ever see Alexander.

Myrgen watched as Ambrois and Thessius helped the guard onto his horse. Alexander had offered for Myrgen to step off the ship earlier. Myrgen wasn't certain the King wouldn't utilize such an opportunity to behead him and ask forgiveness later. A door opened to his right. Catriona stepped out of her cabin and came over to him.

"I see our charges are on their way." She leaned on the railing overlooking the dock.

"Yes. They are both well enough to ride, so long as Alexander doesn't push them too hard." He looked at her. "You said he got a message in a specially sealed envelope?"

"A message tube, actually. It had a mark on the side about the size of a signet ring."

Myrgen narrowed his eyes. "Gold tube, about this long?" He held his fingers on his hands apart about a foot, keeping the gesture subtle while he watched the men and horses.

"Yes. You know of it?"

"Yes. That's a tube from the head of the Grande Guard, Gomez de Santander."

"What does that mean?"

"It means he's been alerted to the escape of a prisoner. Since that's probably me, I doubt you needed to injure yourself healing the guards. He won't be in any hurry."

"That's not the impression I got. See his horse?" She nodded towards the animals. "The saddlebags are on it. If he wasn't planning on leaving to deal with this, that horse would be barely saddled. As it stands, it's ready to go."

Myrgen blinked, again impressed with the insight she possessed. It also bothered him because she was right. The appearance of a casual gathering to make sure his men were healing was now marred by Myrgen's awareness of Alexander's intentions. Alexander's nods to his men as he watched them mount their own horses alerted Myrgen to the likelihood that the King would soon be coming to say his farewells to the Captain. After the threats and tension from earlier, Myrgen wanted no part of this scene. When Alexander glanced up at Catriona and started coming towards them, Myrgen pushed away from the railing. "I'm going to give you two a few moment's privacy."

Catriona nodded and Myrgen slipped away to the galley. "Michael. Can I speak to you a moment?"

Michael put away the last of the dishes then closed and latched the cupboard. "Of course." He turned to face his employer.

"Alexander is leaving right now to take care of something back in Patras. He got a message tube from Gomez."

"Really?" Michael folded his arms. "It's probably about you."

"I don't think so. Alexander is returning to Patras to deal with it. He mounted his men already and his horse is ready to travel."

"I see. So whatever it is, it's urgent business."

"Yes. Do you think you can follow him? Find out what's wrong?"

"Of course but why?"

"Because Tanglwyst is still in Patras, and Alexander cut Elizabeth down without batting an eye. You're not a fugitive, but she might be now. I just want to make sure she's safe."

"Your sister betrayed you, Myrgen. She's a viper in green brocade. How can you want to save her?"

"First of all, she didn't betray me, she manipulated me. There's a subtle yet important difference. I can far better handle her manipulations, especially since she thought she was giving me what I wanted, than I am handling the betrayal by Elizabeth. And second, for all her machinations, she's still my sister. Our family, especially our grandfather, would have issue with me if I didn't make sure she was safe." There were, of course, the older stirrings, but he pushed those aside. "Regardless, be careful. She's still, as you said, a viper in green brocade. I would beware her bite and I'm her brother."

Michael breathed in and out deeply. "Alright, but you'll be responsible for my debts to this crew."

"Gladly. It will give me something to do so I don't feel useless."

"That it will. I'll get my things." He patted Myrgen on the shoulder and left the room.

Alexander stepped up to Catriona and took her hand. "It looks like we're about ready to leave."

"I saw. How are they doing?"

"Good. Your efforts really helped them. The one wouldn't have survived without your generosity."

Catriona glanced down. "I was glad to help."

"How are you feeling?"

"Sore, but once again, your healing gifts have saved me."

"Then I thank the Saints I was given them. You're continued existence in the world makes my life worth living."

She smiled, falling prey to his charm once again. She wanted more than anything at that moment to ask him to make love to her one last time. *Please, Alexander, get on your way before I ask you to stay. I have no idea what could be pulling you from my side at this moment, but I dare not ask. If you rethink your decision, I'm lost.*

"I wish we had been able to spend more time together." His words echoed her own feelings and she nodded in response, not trusting her own voice. "This new business is something I can't ignore."

He reached over and took her head into his hand, drawing her in for a kiss. For the first time on her ship, she did not protest. She blended with him, giving all she had to this one last moment together. The passion took his breath from him and she breathed her own into his mouth. He accepted her gift and let the kiss trickle out. He put his forehead to hers, still holding her to him. "I love you, Catriona. I can't bear the thought of another day without you in my sight." Before she could say anything, he touched her lips with his, quieting the protest he obviously expected her to give.

She ignored her standard admonishment and gave in, for a moment, to his will. *Go ahead. Ask me, Alex. Ask me anything and I'll do it, for you.*

"I have something I wish to discuss with you, next time I see you. Will you let me?"

"Of course. I can't deny you anything, it seems."

"From your lips to the Saints ears. Then 'til next we meet." He kissed her again, fully and completely, then turned and left her. Once he mounted his horse, he looked at her again. He nodded to her, and spurred his horse to run, the guardsmen right behind him.

Myrgen stepped out of the galley as Alexander rode off to the east, towards Patras. Catriona kept her eyes on him until he turned a street corner and was gone, then lowered her gaze, at a loss. The pain from his parting melted into pain from the wounds she had taken on. She put her hands on the railing, aware that her crew was watching her closely. Myrgen's voice came from right next to her. "Are you okay?"

She looked up at him, surprised he had managed to get so close without her realizing it. She swallowed and nodded, looking around the ship. "Yes, I'll be fine. I'm just a little… spent, you might say."

Anyone at any distance would see she was leaning casually on the railing, the wind taking her hair across her face, but she couldn't lift her hand to brush it aside without unlocking her elbows, and right then, that was the only thing holding her upright. She felt the color drain from her skin as the pain drew her strength. She suddenly had no idea how she was going to get back to her cabin under her own power. She turned to look at Myrgen. His gaze skated across the hollows of her eyes and her skin, which was starting to pale. The wind blowing her hair concealed this fact to anyone else, but she had just shown it to him.

Myrgen's visage changed immediately, realizing he had been slow in his appraisal of the situation. "St. Andrew's blood, Catriona, let's get you back to your cabin so you can sit down. Why didn't you say something earlier?" He glanced around at the crew and offered his arm, as if from courtesy.

"Don't berate yourself, Myrgen." She took his arm automatically, and steadying herself with it. "I needed to see him off. Chances are very good I'll never see him again." She turned to Octavius as he approached for orders, willing the color into her face. "Set course for St. Andrew, if you please. I want to give the crew some sea time. Mr. Lioncourt has the helm. Octavius, you have the bridge. I need to tend to the charts, and Myrgen is going to be learning the books so he is going to accompany me."

"Aye, Captain." Octavius nodded. As she turned away from him, she saw Octavius look at Myrgen, impressed.

Myrgen nodded to the man and escorted Catriona from the deck. He opened the door to her cabin, leading her in just as she was starting to lean on him pretty heavily. Sitting her on her bed, he knelt down in front of her and looked at her doublet for indication of seeping or bleeding. The lightweight shirt she was wearing was loose in the sleeves but tight at the cuffs, so she couldn't even pull up her sleeve to check her arm.

"Catriona, you were starting to lean on me when we got in here. Be honest. How bad is it?"

"I'm not sure what's wrong. It's usually better than this." She unbuttoned her doublet and revealed bandages wrapping her entire torso. There weren't any signs of seepage but she was still very uncomfortable from the unexpected return of the pain. "He makes a poultice that takes away the soreness, something I've never been able to reproduce."

"He's always had a gift for that sort of thing, I've been told. Trained with a midwife in Cheryb for a couple years, I hear. This time, though, I guess the wound is deeper." Myrgen leaned back from examining the wound. He looked up at her eyes, then blinked away. "How are you doing otherwise?"

Catriona understood what he was asking without having to read him. "You mean, with the fact I watched my first love get murdered in the street?"

Myrgen nodded, his lips tightening.

"I don't know yet." She cocked her head and squinted her eyes a bit, confused at her own answer. "I have spent the last seven years mourning his death, only to find him alive seven months ago. It has been one thing after another since then."

"Did you love him?"

"Originally? Yes. Near the end though..." She looked down at her hands. She realized she was sitting there exposed and started buttoning her doublet again. It was unusual how comfortable she was with Myrgen. Between her invitation for him to sit in her room last night and her willingness to trust him with her level of pain just now, it seemed he was the confidant she had always needed. She even lacked her common sense of modesty with him, easily unbuttoning her doublet as if he were her protégé Gwen or her son Alan.

"If I may ask, what were you going to say there, when you stopped him in the street?"

"What was I going to say? I have no idea. I just knew I couldn't allow it to end like that. We had been everything to each other once. It was because I was carrying his child that I stopped fighting Giovanni and thus survived for Alan to be born. The memory of his love haunted me for five years after I was told he had died. After all we had lost, to let him leave like that..." She shook her head. "I just couldn't..."

He stood and poured her some wine from a bottle on her desk. "And Alexander's advances? How do they figure into this?"

She rolled her eyes. "That's an entirely different problem. Last night, he wanted to come into my room at the Inn, to spend the night. With all that had just happened, I couldn't... it would feel like I was betraying Nicolai's memory by lying with another man while the stench of his burning flesh was still in my hair. I lay down on the bed at the Inn and I could smell it, clinging to me." She shuddered as he brought the goblet to her.

"That's why you left. To try and get rid of the disasters of the day."

She nodded, drinking a bit of the wine. "Had I fallen asleep with that on my skin, I would have awoken screaming from the nightmares."

"But you didn't."

Catriona looked at Myrgen's questioning storm grey eyes. Their color was intense and stood out from the soft brown hair he wore pulled back into a ponytail at the base of his neck. She could just see the hair on his chest peeking out of the opening of his shirt at the neck and she was glad to see the laundry at the Open Lotus had gotten the stains out that had threatened to be a constant reminder of his brutal captivity. He was appealing and she caught herself thinking briefly of the kiss and the dream it caused. She blinked and lowered her eyes back to her goblet. "No, I didn't."

"I'm glad to hear that. I was actually quite worried this would linger, adding to your difficulty."

Shouts from the crew outside brought their attention to the imminent sailing of the ship. Myrgen looked up, and then back at Catriona. "I should go. Are you in need of anything?"

She shook her head, grateful for the chance to be alone with her thoughts. "I'm good. Thank you, Myrgen."

He bowed briefly. "At your service, Captain." He left the room as the sound of the anchor being weighed thumped the internals of her ship.

Myrgen closed the door behind him and went on deck, looking for Michael. The large man was standing on the entryway to the gangplank, shouldering his bag. "You ready?"

Michael nodded.

"Good. Let me know when you discover something. We're setting sail for St. Andrew first. After that, all I know is we're headed for Caratia."

"Octavius gave me a run-down of the regular stops on the way to Zara and the time frames. I'll send word as soon as I can."

Myrgen nodded and Michael stepped onto the gangplank. As soon as he was on the dock, two deckhands pulled the plank up and stowed it along the railing, securing it to hooks put there for that purpose. Michael turned back and gave Myrgen a wave, then went in the direction of the Inn, knowing there was a stable there. Myrgen exhaled, trying to dispel the feeling he was losing his friend forever, then looked around the ship. He went over to Octavius and asked, "What do you need me to do?"

Octavius looked surprised to see Myrgen offering to help. "Um, you and the Captain finished already?"

"I'm tough to take in large doses. I figured I'd give her a break and see about getting this ship on the ocean."

Octavius smiled, nodding. "Well, then, get on that rope there and start hauling. We'll need to get the main sheet unfurled to get us out of the harbor."

Myrgen nodded and went to where he was directed. He did as he was instructed by the other crewmen, It didn't take long for his bookkeeper's hands to feel the rending of the hemp ropes. He stopped when they had a moment and discreetly healed them, allowing him to keep up with the other crewmen until the ship was well under weigh. Once they were navigating the bay, Octavius came over and greeted him.

"I'm impressed, Myrgen. For a noble accountant, I figured you for a tender handed fellow, but you stayed on those ropes like you've done this all your life."

"Oh, don't be fooled. It tore me up pretty good." The healing had given Myrgen some calluses to spare his hands and he knew those would fade with subsequent efforts but, at least for now, they accomplished his purposes.

"Ah. Next time, wear gloves, like the rest of us do."

Myrgen looked around and saw that, indeed, the other crewmen were either wearing gloves or putting them away now that the need for them had passed. Myrgen arched an eyebrow at Octavius.

"It's tough to truly enjoy the feel of soft skin if your fingers are desensitized." Octavius winked and Myrgen laughed.

"Very true. However, I suppose I don't figure that's in my immediate future. A little too sore from the last encounter."

"Aren't we all, my man? Aren't we all? Ah, speaking of fine ladies and soft skin, here comes the Captain. Captain on deck!"

Catriona strode over to her First Mate, her hair billowing out behind her like a gathering storm. Her crewmen snapped to attention, awaiting her orders. "Octavius. Myrgen."

"Captain," both men said at once.

Catriona smiled at the unity Myrgen was already displaying and looked around the ship. "Any trouble, Octavius?"

"None at all, Captain. Myrgen here threw in on the main sail and we got her up just fine. He's not as bad as I thought he would be at this."

Myrgen frowned and shot his eyes at Octavius but kept himself facing Catriona.

"Really?" Her eyebrows arched. "There may be hope for you yet, Chancellor. Carry on."

The men nodded and the rest of the crew returned to their business at hand. Octavius called Myrgen over to help him with the helm while Catriona talked to the Quartermaster, Mr. Lioncourt. "So, this is pretty different from life at the palace, eh?"

"Yes, but much safer nowadays. I'm glad to be getting away from there."

"Why?"

Myrgen looked at the man. "Um, do you not know what's been going on?"

"Not really. The Captain sent word with your friend Michael that there would be passengers. Then you came along. When I saw Grymalkin, I rather expected he would be joining us. I guess not, though."

"He's got a lot on his mind right now."

"Yes, I saw the kiss."

Myrgen blinked. "Kiss?"

"Grymalkin. And the Captain." He nodded to the area where the gangplank had been. "Right before he left ship."

"Oh. I was below deck, in the galley. Talking to... Michael... He kissed her? Right here?"

"Yes. Rather surprised me she allowed such a thing. She's usually pretty guarded about such intimacies." Octavius leaned on the *whipstaff* of the ship, dangling his arms. A sizable piece of heavy, dark wood, it connected to the rudder and steered the ship. "I'm not sure I approve, I must say. If he has his way, he'll be asking her a question before too long."

Myrgen looked at Catriona and said, "A question? What...." He realized Octavius meant Alexander was probably planning to propose to her. Myrgen had an unexpected feeling of concern insinuate itself upon him. It wasn't so much concern that Alexander was going to make a lasting mistake in asking. *No, this was different. Not concern over him asking her, but over her reply.* "Do you mean marriage?"

"Aye. He's been in love with her for years. With Nicolai out of the picture, she's available. I never liked that man she married anyway. You should have seen the way he treated her in front of us. He's lucky he lived as long as he did."

"Well, she'll make a fine Queen, if he does ask. He won't need to invoke the Power of Sovereignty to get the people to love her."

"Ah yes. I had heard he was actually King now. Glad to hear it, really. He'll do well I think. Though I will miss the Captain if she marries the man."

"Excuse me, but heard from whom?"

Octavius looked at Myrgen, eyes wide. "Huh?"

"Heard from whom that he was King now? Since he travels under the name Grymalkin, I figured his true identity was not known."

"Oh, well, um, I'm First Mate on the *Enigma*. She lets me know things."

"Catriona?"

"Her too."

Myrgen blinked out his confusion.

Octavius bowed his head, laughing. "The *Enigma* is as much a living entity as she is a form of transport, Myrgen. You'll learn that as you sail on her."

"I... see."

"So, you know the King, right?"

Myrgen folded his arms across his chest and nodded.

"Do you think he'll ask her? Propose, I mean."

"If he loves her? Oh yes. Alexander has never liked arranged marriages, probably because of what he saw his brother Charles go through. I don't think he'd pass up the chance to have her on that throne next to him just to get a wool treaty with York." He looked at her, a slight smile stuck in his throat. "Besides, Catherine already tried to arrange a marriage with York's Queen Elizabeth and Alexander put her off so badly, it ruined any future negotiations on his behalf. It could have ended free trade between the two countries."

"How?"

"He brought a dress for her and wore it instead of giving it to her."

Octavius' eyes grew wide in disbelief and he stared at Myrgen, who laughed at his response. "He did what? Why?"

"Can you think of a better way to make sure your mother doesn't try to arrange any more marriages for you?" Octavius shook his head, snorting a small laugh. "Besides," Myrgen continued, "I think it had something to do with making sure he stayed available. To be honest, I didn't properly interpret the gesture at the time. I thought he preferred the company of men. I believe Catherine did as well. Now, of course, I can see that he merely had his heart set on someone else."

"Oh quite. He's haunted her for years. I think she was planning on joining with him this winter, until that chum bucket Nicolai showed up."

"You really didn't care for him, did you?"

"Oh no. That man was every kind of person the Captain avoids in a crew member. I found it appalling she would allow someone like that near her son, even if he is the boy's father. I felt even stronger that she should have gone with Grymalkin after meeting her husband. She's always been so careful regarding this crew, taking care our needs are met over her own. Taking care of a nation must be so much more of that same type of work for someone like Grymalkin. He needs to watch himself though. He can't put the fate of a nation into second place over his heart."

Myrgen leaned on a barrel as Octavius straightened up, leaning less on the wheel. "I don't think that's what he's doing, Octavius. I think he's trying to make sure he has a strong, loyal supporter right next to him, someone who won't arrange his assassination so she can rule in his stead, or put her own son on the throne. These are fairly common ends for kings who have arranged marriages. Look at what happened to Charles. His Queen tried to have him murdered, then she tried to steal the Power of Sovereignty from his corpse."

"Jeesh! People actually do things like that? What happened?"

"Alexander killed her as a traitor."

"Grymalkin killed someone? A woman? Personally?"

Myrgen realized these men had a very different point of view when it came to Alexander. "Yes, he did."

Octavius pursed his lips. "I didn't think he had it in him. Maybe the Captain should give a bit more thought to this, if he does try to propose, maybe try considering it after all. Then again, there might be other unions that would be a better choice."

Myrgen's gaze fell upon Catriona. The wind generated from the ship's progress tossed her hair about like a dancer. He spoke his heart without thinking. "I can't think of any."

Octavius looked at Myrgen, then slowly nodded at the Chancellor's assessment. "So you think she should do it? You think she should marry him?"

Myrgen felt that strange dread fill him again and he noted it this time. Octavius watched Myrgen, waiting as if his own fate hung on the answer. Myrgen said, "I don't feel that's advice I can give, to her or him. I definitely won't marry for anything except love, I'll tell you that, but I'm not in charge of a major country either. My decisions are inconsequential to the lives of thousands of people." Myrgen looked at Octavius, who nodded slightly and hid a smile.

"Well, I can vouch for her decision-making abilities. I trust her with my life, and so does every man on board, save maybe you."

"No, you're wrong, Octavius. *Every* man on board trusts her, *especially* me."

Duncan opened the door to the small shack behind the church above the secret room. The shack was left locked from the inside so there was no chance of someone being inside the building. He touched the lock and it glowed. With a click, it secured the door again once it was closed. They stepped out into a quiet churchyard, a thin sliver of moon being the only real light.

"Where are we?" Tanglwyst looked around for some landmarks but found none.

"A small but very old church outside St. Augustine. It's fairly central. We can go anywhere from here and it is unlikely the gendarme will find you now. Where we are is out of the range of where Gomez would believe we could have gotten in the amount of time we've had. As the word goes out about your escape, they will spread the net wider to catch you, but we will keep ahead of them as we ride because we are already two days farther away from Patras than they believe we could be. You're safe now."

"So where do we go from here?"

"I'm to get you to the Papal City."

"I suppose that is the safest place to be. Which way is that from here?"

"Four days east. We'll get some horses from an inn here and head out immediately." Duncan put his hand on hers. "If you feel up to it."

"I can't spend another hour in that tiny room. I'll start screaming and no one will hear me."

Duncan smiled and kissed her hand. "Well, I wanted to get you to scream for the past hour, but you were queasy."

"You cad. You remind me of another young rogue with whom I am most familiar."

"A pirate?"

Tanglwyst shook her head. "My brother." She glanced around. "We should get horses for the trip. Do you still have my money?"

"Of course." He fondled the amulet for a second. She worried he might use it to take her to her Grandfather. Then he shook his head.

Tanglwyst drew her eyes back to his face. "What?"

"I thought about using the amulet to take you to the Papal City, but I can't." He looked at her. "Never been there. I think we are about as close as I can get us."

Tanglwyst exhaled, smiling. "Well, I need the fresh air anyway. Let's go."

Nine

"If you want to know the road to Patras, ask the
Church's messenger."
The Wise Wench's Tavern Book

Michael entered the gates of the city and pulled in his reins, trying to decide where to go next. Alexander and his men had stopped at an Inn halfway to Patras, probably to give the injured men a chance to rest, but judging from the way the King was driving the horses, Michael wasn't at all sure he would let them rest for long. He was ahead of them, but just by an hour or less. His first concern was for Tanglwyst, so he decided to go to her manor house.

The clacking of the horse's hooves on the cobblestones jarred his ears like the force of them striking the ground jarred his body. The city sometimes bothered him because it was so structured, but he liked the gardens of the palace. Even though they were groomed, at least there was some nature there. Tanglwyst's house had manicured gardens as well, but her home always felt to him like a predator's hunting ground. After spending time with her in the catacombs during her "capture", he felt even more so.

He was glad Catriona rescued Myrgen like she had promised she would. He liked her, and he felt a kinship to her that he had not felt in another person, save Myrgen. Myrgen had earned that from the beginning with Michael. Michael had stayed attached to Myrgen as his slave to keep his freedom, as ironic as that sounded. With Myrgen, he had the status and ability to move about at will. Had he been set free, as Myrgen had often offered for the price of a single silver piece, he would have been captured as soon as he was out of the country and the whole ordeal would have begun again.

The manse on Fleur Street came into view at the same time the scent from her gardens reached him. There was a bit of activity around the front door, more than he expected of a lady. It felt like something had happened to her, and the guards out front were wearing the King's livery, not hers. Michael got off the horse and tethered him to a pole outside a shop. He slipped into the alleyway that crossed the street from her front door and let the sound of things funnel to him. He could almost make out the discussions the guards were having and he moved a little closer, keeping to the shadows and letting his dark skin hide him.

He was well known to both the guards on duty and the guards in her house so he didn't think it wise to show his face at this time. He was far too distinctive to escape notice or memory. He had managed to get himself into a good position when the sound of arriving horses caught the attention of the milling sentries. They snapped to attention and Michael knew Alexander had arrived.

A shout went through the men and the front door was opened. One of the guards poked his head in and shouted for the Lieutenant and a moment later, Gomez de Santander stepped out as Alexander strode over to him, removing his riding gloves. "Lieutenant," Alexander said with a nod.

"Your Majesty. Thank you for coming so quickly."

"This seemed to need my personal attention. I have a request, before we go into the details though." He turned to his guards on the horses behind him. "These men have suffered injuries and need to be relieved. I need two volunteers to return them to the palace and two volunteers to take their places."

Gomez saluted. "I volunteer to take the place of one of the guards. Fernando, will you do likewise?"

A tall, buff guard with wavy hair and a distinct lack of beard nodded, his blue eyes dancing merrily. "Certainly, sir."

Gomez turned to two of the other men guarding the door. "You two, escort the guards to their respite. See to their wounds." The men saluted and moved immediately to their task.

Alexander turned to Gomez and nodded. "Thank you. Now, your report. You said you thought you knew who rescued the Lady?"

"Yes, Your Majesty. I believe the fugitive to be in the company of Duncan McVryce, a known pirate and cutthroat."

"Did you get a look at the man?"

"Yes, though I do not know how he escaped. He merely fell backward into a shadow and was gone."

"What did Tanglwyst do?"

"They seemed to know each other. I would say they were probably intimate from the way he held her. I also believe I heard him tell her he loved her, right before he took her into the shadows."

Alexander blinked, shifting his gaze to the street around them. Some people went by at the cross street but no one came down towards the King in traveling leathers or his accomplished sentinels. "Did you hear him or her say anything else?"

"No, your Majesty. I did not."

"And when did this happen?"

"Two days ago, mid-morning."

"So they've had days to get far from here."

"I'm afraid so, Your Majesty. They could, quite literally, be anywhere."

Alexander shot his gaze at the alley and then at the house door. "Did she take anything with her?"

"They seemed to be carrying a chest."

"Let me see where she was kept."

"Yes, Sire. This way." He opened the door and the three men went into the manse.

Michael nodded and went to gather the horse again. He needed to get this information to Myrgen right away. He didn't know who this Duncan person was but he might and would know if his sister was safe in his care. The trouble would come in trying to determine how best to get this information to his master. Riding to St. Andrew would take time away from investigating this further. He opened his doublet and pulled out the itinerary of the *Enigma*. It would take them a tenday to get to St. Andrew. A rider could do it in four days, changing horses and riding hard. Now he just needed to find the rider.

Gweneviere Kelly looked at the door, wiping her hands on her apron. She was covered in flour from making shortbread and the trail of dust from her impeding long blond braid followed her to answer the knock that had seized her attention. She wiped the flour from her face with the backs of her worker's hands, which successfully smeared it under her robin's egg blue eyes like woad war paint. She was expecting Dominic sometime today, but not right now, and wasn't sure who might be visiting at this time. It was still a bit early for him.

She opened the door to find a tall, black man dressed in brown riding leathers, a horse tossing its head behind him, tied to a fence around her property. He looked familiar and it took a moment for her to realize he was Myrgen's servant. Her eyes grew wide as she realized he might not know Catriona had saved Myrgen and might be planning something sinister to find out this information. She stepped back and tried to prepare herself for a fight.

"Forgive me, my Lady. I am hoping your fiancée is available. I am in need of his services." Michael bowed, lowering his eyes in respect.

Gwen stood down, but stayed wary. "What do you want Dominic for?"

"He knows the Captain Catriona Moriarity and I need to get word to her. I hoped he could suggest a messenger."

"Aren't you the one who dumped her into my well a tenday ago?"

"Yes. I'm afraid I am that man."

"She was hurt. You hurt her. You're lucky I didn't catch you then. I'd have thrown you down there next to her and let her deal with you herself."

"She has since seen fit to let me go. I left her ship this morning to get here before the King."

Gwen didn't know where this was going, but she definitely didn't want this conversation overheard by any passersby. She looked at the horse. "Bring the animal around the back and come in there. I don't want everyone to know I'm having dealings with the companion of a traitor." He nodded. She closed the door, making sure she saw no watchers. Her house was actually a bit out of town due to her choice to raise five sheep from her family's stock for her own use. This gave her the luxury of her own well and some privacy from having neighbors attached to her walls on either side. She walked to the hearth and made sure it was stoked well. It was getting on toward evening and the chill of night was already starting to show itself.

Michael's knock at the back door before opening it brought out her more domestic nature and she asked, "Would you like some tea, or wine to warm you?"

Michael looked around the room, brow furrowing. "If you are having something, I would gladly partake, but please don't go to any trouble on my account."

Gwen realized this man was more than capable of taking down a woman her size but his manners and his command of Mervolingian language was impressive. Myrgen had taught him well how to get heard in a society where his requests could go unnoticed. She nodded and got some wine and a bag of mulling spices out of the cupboard. "So, why did you need to be here before the King? Are you still in his employ?"

"I am still in Myrgen's employ, my Lady, if that is what you mean."

"Then you know where he is."

"It would be inappropriate for me to say."

Gwen sat back. One of the things she had learned in her time with Catriona is that one never knew who was an agent of the woman. She was a master at getting people's respect. She had gotten Dominic's in the span of a few hours, and he was loyal to himself above all. Catriona had said she was going to rescue Myrgen, and he turned up the next morning. Most of the palace figured Nicolai had taken him away and was disposing of the body since he had disappeared too. She wondered what Michael knew about that, if anything.

"But he's safe?"

"Yes."

"Is Nicolai there?"

"Nicolai is dead, I'm afraid. He engaged in a fight with first the King and then with Captain Catriona herself. She released him, but an assassin shot him with a poisoned dart from the shadows. He did not survive the encounter."

"Nicolai's dead? Are you sure?"

"The King ordered the body destroyed by fire where it lay to avoid anyone else suffering from the poison. The man's death was immediate and painful. Both he and the Captain said it was best to destroy it, although the Captain did express concern for the man's religious beliefs."

"Yes, Nicolai was Latian. Catriona told me that they believe the wounds to the body carry over to the soul when they die, impairing their ability to journey to the afterlife. If their body is destroyed utterly, their soul is trapped here." Gwen stared at her lap, trying to process what this would mean. Nicolai was dead. *Catriona was free!*

Gwen realized this could cause as many problems as it cleared away but she couldn't help but be happy about it. It bothered her for a moment to be delighting in someone else's misfortune, but she really hated Nicolai for what he had done to her friend. Gwen had even performed a charm a couple months ago to strip away any facades Nicolai was putting up so she could see the kind of person he truly was. She didn't know if it had worked or not, but Catriona *had* come to stay at her house, Alan in tow, for a tenday afterward. Now, it was over. Gwen was relieved Catriona had not been the source of his demise. That would have scarred her forever, especially when she had to tell Alan.

She looked at Michael. "I don't know when Dominic will be by, but I don't think he'll like you being here. You're the companion of a known traitor. Who knows what kind of price is on your head, nor what kind of punishment will be dealt to anyone who associates with you? That fact you know where Myrgen is might be a problem for you."

"I understand I am putting you at great risk. However, I know the King is currently at Tanglwyst's manor. He is busy investigating her disappearance."

"Tanglwyst is missing?"

"Yes. The Grande Guarde Lt. de Santander was saying he had an idea about how and who. From the sounds of things, the King will have plenty to distract him looking into this situation. Since this is the reason he left the Captain's side, I imagine his attention will be focused upon this problem in order for it to be resolved so he can return to her."

Gwen realized Michael knew Alexander and Catriona had feelings for each other. That was odd because they had kept their affections very private and very secret. "Why do you say that?"

"He was quite demonstrative during the time they were together in Rouen. It was clear he cared deeply for her."

"Demonstrative?"

Michael related an account of the fight, Alexander protecting her, his attention during dinner at the Inn and his affection on the balcony before Michael left Myrgen to return to the ship. Gwen sat back, exhaling. He had shown to her crew and everyone in Rouen, effectively, that he was in love with her and she had let him. *Now is the time to strike!*

"I see." She rubbed her palm with her thumb. "This message you wanted to send, where did it need to go?"

"That is something I would rather discuss with only the messenger, if you don't mind. I would not want to put you in danger by giving you knowledge of the whereabouts of a known traitor."

A voice from the doorjamb of the foyer said, "Then maybe you should explain why you're here talking with my fiancée."

Dominic stepped outside the back door of Gwen's house with Michael and closed the door after them. Gwen was offering dinner to them both and her puttering always felt very servant-like to Dominic. He preferred not to think of himself as marrying a servant, but he did like her cooking. "Now, why have you come here looking for me?"

Michael bowed respectfully. "Lord Dominic, I apologize for this inconvenience. I came here because I need to get sensitive information to someone on Captain Catriona's ship and I need a messenger that can be trusted. Since all the messengers I am associated with are cut off from me now, I came to find you. After all, you are one of her associates."

Dominic straightened up. He had never been an "associate" of Catriona's before, being Tanglwyst's most trusted companion, but the incidents of the past tenday had shown him the true pirate was most definitely Tanglwyst, and not Catriona as he had been led to believe. He had always enjoyed the brutal business nature of his employer, but her part in the plot to overthrow the Mervolingian throne had put him off. Luckily, it had also gotten him his appointment as Acting Chancellor for the entire kingdom, a position which he was striving to make permanent.

"And why should I jeopardize my entire career and future and quite possibly my life by helping you?"

"Because I have information that is not common knowledge just yet, but if you act quickly, you can be prepared for this and show how adept you are at getting information and dealing with it properly."

Dominic realized Michael had been Myrgen's slave for years. The man had obviously picked up on how to sell a point. "Well, if you are looking for a messenger, I know the best one for this mission. They know where Catriona can be found at this time of the year, can anticipate trouble and is illiterate, so your message won't be read."

"That is perfect."

"Good. Let's get you back inside. I have supplies here for writing letters and things and a private room where you may do so. I can get your message to your charge in very short order."

"Thank you, Lord Dominic."

The two men stepped inside. The smell of the food was charming. Michael looked like he had not eaten in a day the way he responded. It turned out he hadn't. Gwen's mutton stew was filling and hearty and Dominic could never finish an entire bowl personally, but Michael had three. Gwen was quite impressed. When the meal was over, Dominic took Michael to the room he used for drafting notes at her house, leaving Gwen to tidy up and plot her next move. She needed, first and foremost, to get rid of these men. Her ritual would take all night and the sooner she could get started, the sooner it would start working. She cleaned the dishes quickly and swept up while Michael did whatever it was he was doing. When the two men finally returned to the main room, she worried she was going to have to concentrate to keep from seeming shrewish.

Dominic took Michael to the back door and said, "Gwen, I told Michael he could leave his horse here for the night." Michael nodded his thanks and left the room. Dominic stayed and Gwen started worrying he was planning on staying the night. She need not have worried. "After he takes care of the animal, I'm going to take him to a place I know where he can hide. I'm probably going to stay at the palace tonight because I want to have my whereabouts accountable, in case he's captured. Gwen," he lowered his voice to a whisper, "I want you to take the message to Catriona's ship. She'll get it to Myrgen from there. Michael says the ship is going to St. Andrew first and St. Marguerite after that."

Gwen nodded. "Ah. When did she leave?"

"Yesterday."

"St. Andrew is a four day ride from Patras overland. She'll be there a tenday to conduct business. St. Marguerite is a lot farther. It would be quicker to go to Zara overland from Patras."

"Well, I doubt you'll have to worry about that. He's already written the letter." He handed her the missive, a simple parchment folded for easy hiding and transport. It wasn't thick so Michael clearly didn't have a lot he needed to convey. The extra time it took was probably Dominic hovering, telling him how to spell things. "It's ready to go. You can leave now."

"After dark? Are you insane?"

Dominic looked a bit surprised she was not just leaping at the opportunity to rush right off. "Well, I just figured you'd want to set out as soon as possible."

"I'm not foolish enough to rush off to be bait for bandits. A woman traveling after dark? Alone?"

"Well, it's not like you look like a woman…"

"Excuse me?" She leveled a cold stare at him, something she had learned he hated because it felt to him like an apparition was touching the back of his neck. He often tried to get her to act shrewish, and this was her counter.

He seemed to realize he was in dangerous waters. "I mean, you wouldn't be foolish enough to *dress* like a woman while traveling and you're stronger than most men I know…"

Gwen put her teeth together. "Dominic…"

The back door opened. Dominic looked gratefully at Michael as if he were his saint and savior. "Michael! Let's get you to your safe house!" He moved like a hurricane was chasing him. To be honest, Gwen qualified at that moment.

She closed her eyes, seething at his attitude. *By the Fae! What do I see in him again?* She centered herself and remembered why she wanted him gone the first time. The Cleansing Heart Ritual. She had done it once before and it had worked perfectly. She looked around and started gathering the things she would need. She pulled a satchel from a hook by the back door and pulled certain herbs and items from her cupboards and drawers. A metal bowl, a crystal bowl, candles that smelled of elderberries and vanilla, a mandrake root, mistletoe. She put them all in the satchel and then put on her wool plaid Caratian coat Catriona had made for her. It would keep her warm at least until she got to the clearing in the woods.

She stepped out into the night air and was gratified by the fact it wasn't nearly as cold as it had been a couple nights ago. She was going to have to chant all night to send off a beacon for the Fae and it would be clearer if she could do it from the sanctity of the woods. The last time it had been easier because she had sea spirits nearby. However, the presence of a city made it harder for the Fae to hear her call. Even going into the woods, she couldn't be sure she would get a benevolent answer.

She remembered the last time she worked the Ritual. It was after Catriona had been hurt badly in Cheryb, fighting a Red Hand contract holder. The Red Hand engaged in, among other unsavory practices, slavery and the wife of one of her crewmen, Ambrois, had been captured. Catriona had managed to track them down and was seriously hurt in the process of saving her. Gwen had seen Alexander in town earlier and fetched him to patch Catriona up.

The recovery time was going to be longer than they had ever done before and staying in Cheryb while this occurred was unsafe. There was a cabin on a cliff near the port town of St. Marguerite that Catriona used when the crew wanted shore time there. It was private and unknown, even by the majority of her crew. They sailed there quickly, with Alexander never leaving her side.

By the time they actually got to the cabin, her wound was healed but she was tired as was Alexander. She spoke to Gwen before they landed and asked her to go to the cabin and prepare it for inhabitance for a few days. Gwen realized Catriona meant to *spiritually* prepare it and she knew exactly the ritual to use to do so. She went quickly to the cabin while Catriona and Alexander spent time in town getting supplies for the ship and goods for trade. She used the herbs and bowls and candles to call forth Fae to cleanse Catriona's heart of the pain and sorrow she had been harboring for all these years, preparing her for love again.

It had worked too. Catriona and Alexander had arrived at the cabin and he had not returned to the ship that night. In fact, they had not returned to the ship for three days. When Gwen had visited to bring food and wine, Alexander answered the door wrapped in a blanket, thanking her for her consideration. He looked freshly bathed and smelled of the vanilla musk soaps Catriona had bought him as a gift. Gwen had heard Catriona calling to him and the sound of splashing, making them both smile before he closed the door.

The following tenday had been the happiest Gwen had ever seen her Mistress. It was marked especially by the complete turnaround a tenday later. Catriona had gone into a meeting in St.

Giles with Tanglwyst at the company vineyard manor house. When she had returned, she was dark and quiet, the opposite of how she had been all month. She all but whispered orders to Octavius and then asked Gwen very politely to join her in her cabin. The difference frightened everyone on board.

Alone, Catriona told her that Nicolai was alive and working for Tanglwyst as a captain of one of her flagships and her tactical advisor. They had both been invited to the meeting and his presence had shocked her. They were going to be meeting alone for dinner to talk. Gwen had asked what that meant for her and Alexander and Catriona told her she didn't know. The mere fact she had been with Alexander was a betrayal of her marriage vows, but Gwen had protested firmly, talking her away from that line of thinking. If Catriona believed herself to owe Nicolai something, she would sacrifice everything she had to make amends.

Unfortunately, that was exactly what happened. Catriona returned from dinner very, very late and told Gwen that they were going to live together as a family this winter, as was proper. Gwen had to stand by in the room while Catriona told Alexander they couldn't be together. She hadn't wanted to be alone with him, for fear she would have betrayed Nicolai again.

Now, Nicolai wasn't a problem. Gwen wasn't going to be denied this time. If it took all night, Gwen was going to get a love spirit to heal the wounded heart on that ship.

Ten

"Beware a Glarren woman with free time."
The Wise Wench's Tavern Book

Alexander was exhausted. His fatigue after riding all day from Rouen with only the short break to rest his men was amplified by the frustration of the investigation at Tanglwyst's manor. Gomez had been very clear in his directions to his men: don't go near the Lady, don't be alone with the Lady, don't talk to the Lady. Duncan had come out of one of the closed areas of the manor, fought the guards in the main room by the stairs, and got Tanglwyst out through the front door. Lots of signs of battle, no trace of the final escape. The only knowledge to come from this was that Duncan could take someone with him when he stepped into the shadows.

He proceeded up the stairs to the third floor where the Royal Family kept quarters. No one was in the hallways save a couple guards patrolling. Alexander nodded hello but did not engage the men. He opened his door, grateful for the chance to rest.

The fireplace held banked coals in the hearth. Alexander looked around. He had been gone for more than two days. There should have been no coals, no fire, no occupants of this room. Heracles, his giant wolfhound, raised his head from his perch on the large bed and his movement caused a small noise to come from the expensive covers on the bed. Alexander stepped over to the bed. He was not concerned because Heracles would not have let a stranger into Alexander's room. Sure enough, it was not a stranger at all, but someone Alexander loved.

The Princess Marie-Elizabeth snuggled under the covers, her tawny hair splaying across the pillow, long eyelashes caressing her cheeks. She had perfect, delicate lips. One of her tiny hands gripped the case on the pillow while the other rubbed her upper lip. She didn't suck her thumb like many three years olds but instead found comfort in stroking her lip, a quirk Alexander found very endearing. He reached down and caressed her hair. His exhaustion bled out of him as he knelt by the bed.

Her presence here meant that she either didn't know he was responsible for her mother's death, or that she didn't understand what that meant, but Alexander knew. He had, with a single stroke of his sword, effectively made her an orphan. He looked down at his knees, dreading the time when he was going to have to tell her. He removed his hand and started to stand when he heard her small voice.

"Hi, Unca Awex."

"Hello, Dear One. What are you doing in my room?"

"I wanted to wait fow you. Awe you cwying?"

Alexander reached up and wiped his hand across his eye, noticing the moisture for the first time. "I guess I am, sweetie."

"Is it because Muvver was bad?"

Alexander's brow furrowed at her precision. Leave it to a child to be able to see what adults tried to hide. "Yes, honey. I'm sorry."

"I sowwy too, Awex."

"Do you want me to take you to your room?"

"No."

Alexander stroked her hair again. Heracles crawled forward to try and get in on this attention shower. Alexander smiled and

116

rubbed his ears too. He stood and said, "All right, you two. Scooch over."

Marie-Elizabeth bounced over to give him room on the huge bed and he climbed on, boots and all. He put his arm under her head and she snuggled into his chest. He worried that she would hate him when she grew older for killing her mother, but right now, she loved him. Her affection made him feel the blood of his sins wash away as if Heaven itself had absolved them. He closed his eyes and fell asleep.

Catherine D'Medici stepped out into the garden and slipped into the patch of plants that grew under the window to Alexander's room. She checked the plants there, gathering the flowers that were blooming in the dark. *Cyprian Herb. Fully viable. This is good.* She used the basket, lined in silk dyed with rosemary leaves, and took the stamen from the flowers. It was vital she take the female part of the flower for this part, for the herb had already been synched with the male. This mixture was specifically designed to be given to their mate. She had to be careful not to destroy the flower for this herb was more valuable than any other item in the Kingdom. She wanted to make sure her King was properly mated.

Catherine had planted these flowers in this patch back when Alexander was first born. She had followed the instructions of the herbalist who gave it to her and used Alexander's own urine to water the plant, making it distinctly his. The leaves were used to heal him, for since it was introduced to him at his birth, the plants had grown and changed with their young host, adapting to his particular chemistry. They knew how he was supposed to be and as such, aided healing

Because she had used the petals of the flowers in his bath, his ability to resist sickness or serious injury was far above any other person in the kingdom, especially now that he had assumed the Power of Sovereignty. Using the leaves to make a poultice stopped any poisons or infections and made him heal three times faster than he would without them. The roots made his bones and muscles strong enough to weather a fall from his third floor window and walk away.

But the stamens were special. Because they came from the sexual part of the flower, they could be used in an infusion which would make the woman who used them better able to get pregnant, carry the child to term, and survive the birth. It also made the child stronger, better able to survive the first four years of life. They were also said to enhance the pleasure of lovemaking.

Catherine picked the stamens and placed them carefully in the basket. When she had gathered twenty, she stood. She took the basket with her. *Twenty should be enough.* She turned and made her way towards the entrance she had used to enter the garden. She went upstairs to the room she inhabited and walked over to her wardrobe. Opening the doors, she pulled a small chest from the top shelf. She took the box and basket over to a table next to her desk and set them both down on a cloth. She opened the box and pulled out a mortar and pestle and several small bags of herbs.

She removed some gauze from her desk drawer and spread it out on the table. She put the contents of the basket onto the mantle over the fireplace, spreading them out to let the heat dry them. As they dried, she took one of the other herbs and put it into the mortar and used the pestle to grind it into a powder. She dumped that onto a small plate and did the same with two other herbs, making powder each time. She opened the remaining bags of herbs and laid them on the gauze in layers.

She checked the stamens of the Cyprian Herb and found them to be sufficiently dry to add to the mix. She was already weary and it was taking effort to keep focused on her goal. Had she needed to wait for the stamens, she surely would have fallen asleep. She took the stamens and ground them up in the mortar. They were a tiny bit pasty but when she added the other three powders, it dried out completely. Finally, she sprinkled the powder mixture on the herbs, distributing them with precision in an even layer.

The process took a while, but when she was done, she had an infusion that could be used either as a tea or as a poultice for healing. Either way, the effect would be the same. All he would need to do is give this to his intended and bed the woman and she would fetch with child that night. Catherine sat back, tired.

Now, I just need to convince him to use them.

Gwen knelt in the middle of the clearing, the woolen coat discarded on the ground. The heat generated from her ritual was causing her to sweat and she didn't need the distraction of temperature. The movements she made through the ether were fluid and sweeping. She was doing her best to send the right ripples through the air to find the spirits of her homeland. She would have used the ones that were local, but she did not know their language. The Glarren Fae, she understood and could speak to them regarding her wishes. Her attempts to communicate with even the simple hearth spirits in town had proven difficult. She still found her offerings to the house spirits overturned as often as she found them accepted.

It was nothing like the time she had cleansed the cabin on the cliffs for Catriona. There, the spirits of the sea had come to her call. Those spirits were well traveled and spoke several different languages. Since the cabin had overlooked the sea, the reply was almost instantaneous. She had asked those spirits to cleanse the cabin of lingering memories and prepare the place for the warmth of love. She had wanted her Mistress and Alexander to finally have their chance together, and it had worked.

The spirits had lingered and cleansed Catriona's heart of the pain and guilt of her marriage and the loss of her husband. Gwen had met her after Nicolai's death, or rather, before they found out he was actually still alive. Gwen hadn't known at the time what caused her Mistress to be so sorrowful, but she had decided it must be a broken heart. She had turned out to be right, of course. Matters of the heart were her forte. After all, her meddling brought Catriona and Alex together at the cabin on the cliffs. She felt confident she was doing the right thing here too.

She performed a ritual that called the spirits and sent them to Catriona's house to reveal the lies and deceit. The spirits that had responded were local. That was when Gwen first realized they didn't understand her. She was able to communicate her intentions, however. The next day, Catriona and Alan had shown up on Gwen's doorstep, tearful and sullen. Although she never told Gwen what had brought her to the home of her friend, Gwen knew Nicolai had been lying and was caught.

Gwen's eye caught on movement in the shadows and she focused her attention in that area. Slowly, a green, glowing wisp of cloud slipped into the clearing. It wavered and moved, like milk in tea, revealing and covering the trees behind it. She felt in her head an answering of her call.

Good friend, I welcome you to this glade. Can you understand my speech?

The billowing mist sent an affirmative emotion her way.

Good. My friend travels this night on the sea, on the Caratian ship, the Enigma. *I need you to go to that ship and cleanse the broken heart there, preparing it for love again. Find the one who was betrayed and heal that soul, if you would.*

The spirit again emoted an affirmative and floated up into the sky, looking like a cloud that looked like a whale. Gwen smiled and got dressed.

Eleven

"The white cap mushroom may look safe, but it's still the child of nightshade."
The Wise Wench's Tavern Book

Alexander awoke when Marie-Elizabeth climbed out of bed. She toddled off to the door, opened it and crept out, holding her crotch and heading for the privy. He rolled onto his back and realized two things: his arm was numb and he tasted and smelled like a horse that had drunk a lot of wine, then peed in his mouth. He lifted his arm and sat up, the pins-and-needles feeling just starting. He desperately needed a bath and a clean set of clothes, ones that didn't reek of horse.

He sat up and swung his legs over the side of the bed. He shook his arm as the feeling returned. He wanted to think about what he was doing here in Patras, what his next move was. Eventually, the circulation in his arm grew tired of torturing him and he could concentrate again. No one knew where Duncan had taken Tanglwyst, and Alexander was at a loss as to where to look next. He was more than a little curious as to what had prompted that action, romance or duty, but he felt he had nowhere near enough intelligence on the topic to even venture a guess. Whenever Charles had needed unsavory information to be found out, he always gave the assignment to Myrgen. Alexander didn't have that luxury.

He *did*, however, have the next best thing: a D'Medici. Two of them actually, though he didn't want to become beholden to his Mother over this. Dominic was still young enough in the Chancellor's position that he might still be gullible. How could he know what Charles had done during his reign? Myrgen had been far too secretive to have told his protégé everything he did. With a few well-placed words, Dominic could be sent to figure this out none the wiser.

Alexander stepped out into the hall and found his valet, Gabriel. Gabriel was a tall man, sturdily built, with golden hair and failing eyes. His position as the King's Valet afforded him spectacles for any close work he needed to do, which luckily wasn't much. Alexander was quite self-sufficient and often absent, of late. He wasn't sure how much that would change now that he was king. "Gabriel, there you are. What are the chances a bath is ready?"

"At this hour, Your Majesty? Quite good."

"Thank the Saints. I am in desperate need of one."

"I shall bring your clothes presently. Any preference, sire?"

Alexander waved his hand and started towards the bath room. "Something functional. Leave the doublets and fancy things for court. I have things to do."

Gabriel nodded and entered Alexander's chambers. The King opened the door to the bathing room and found it peacefully empty. It was good because it meant he could take time to think. A word from him and Gabriel would ensure no one disturbed him while he was in here. He began undressing and set his road-weary things by a bench near the giant tiled pool. The bottom of the bath was decorated with a mosaic of a great battle from long ago against giant dragons and other monsters. It even showed a few griffins flying around. Griffins were his favorite creature. He had always said he would have had griffins on his personal arms, had he ever been allowed them. Now that he was King, that prospect was impossible. He and the Kingdom were one. That was evidenced in the bearing of the Mervol Arms by him from now on.

He eased into the water and found it to be the perfect temperature. How the servants accomplished this evaded him, but he was grateful and quite tempted to seek out this information so he could knight the person responsible. He eased under the water and let his hair rinse in the soothing liquid. He turned and swam to the other side, the bath being deep enough to just barely pull this off. He raised his head out of the water and saw a basket of soaps and sponges on the ledge. He looked in and the soaps were decorated with the arms of Mervolingia with different colored soap creating intricate detail in the pattern. He remembered his mother always telling him that those were for their father because he needed to be "adorned in the beauty of the kingdom" even while bathing. The end result was that he had always believed those soaps were sacred. Even now, he couldn't bring himself to use them.

He rummaged through the basket for a simple bar and found nothing else, so he picked up one of the fancy bars and made a mental note to request some useful soaps. The scent was nice though, woodlands and musk.

He soaped up, scrubbing the travel and blood from his skin from the previous days' activities. He splashed back in the water to rinse. He floated on his back and let his hair billow around him. He rested, listening to the sound of the water against his eardrums and pretending it was the sound of the ocean against the hull of the *Enigma*. He opened his eyes and caught a tall, black figure next to one of the pillars in the room. He spun in the water and stood, glaring in that direction, heart thumping. When he saw who it was, he exhaled and dropped back into the water.

"Mother. What are you doing in here?"

"Your brother and I often met in here. He said he did his best thinking here."

"I'm not Charles, Mother. If I'm in here, it is not to conduct business."

Catherine sat on a bench in the room, spreading her skirts out and averting her eyes. Her graying blonde hair was caught up under a highly decorated snood, adorned with pearls and silver threads. The silver accentuated her hair like the dark blue taffeta gown accentuated her skin tone. Her delicate gloves of matching blue leather were undoubtedly suffering in the humid room. Alexander decided he didn't care. If this was a ritual with her and Charles, she was obviously aware of the surroundings.

"Did your trip turn productive?" she pursed her lips which made her look like she was nibbling on lemons. "You left here with a purpose, did you not?"

"Yes, I did. I made my intentions known to the Lady in question."

"And did she reciprocate these intentions?"

"I believe she did, though I did not get an answer from her at the time. Something came up."

"I see." She stood and Alexander was worried for a moment that she would slip on the damp tiles. "I will see you later, after your bath. I have something to give you to assist in this endeavor." She did not wait for a dismissal, which was fine with Alexander because he rather felt like dismissing her the moment he saw her in the first place. After the Massacre of two years ago, he didn't trust his mother in any way. Still, it would be interesting to see what she was planning to offer. Perhaps a family heirloom to give to Catriona.

He watched her leave and lay back in the water again as the door closed behind her. He listened to the imaginary sea again and let out a sigh, sinking beneath the water's edge again as the air in his lungs ceased to keep him afloat. He was finally starting to relax when a flutter of papers snapped him upright again. "Saint's *blood,* Mother! What does it take to get some privacy around here?"

Dominic coughed into his hand and bowed to the naked King. "Your Majesty. I... I apologize. Master Myrgen always came in here to talk to Charles after the Queen Mother left. I... I thought..."

"Just exactly how many more people should I expect to interrupt my bath today?"

"Um..."

Alexander waved his hand, dismissing the subject, small droplets flying about in a display of irritation. "Never mind.

Explain to the rest of them that I am not my brother and do not wish to be disturbed when taking a bath. No wonder my brother farted whenever he felt like it. It was a satirical statement I never understood before." He looked at Dominic. "Is the business you have in your hands so vital it can't wait until I'm finished?"

"I doubt it, Sire."

"Then leave. I'll meet you in my brother's room when I'm ready. Wait for me there."

Dominic bowed and left at a brisk walk. Alexander saw three other officials outside the door and caught Dominic waving them away as the door closed. Alexander nodded in satisfaction. The man might last here after all. It baffled Alexander that Charles conducted business in such a manner. It explained why he never seemed very busy during the day. Clearly, he took care of everything first thing. Alexander leaned on the edge of the bath and let his legs float. Maybe this was how Charles got through the ugly things he had to deal with every day. By having the vultures come in during his bath, maybe he felt he could leave behind the unsavory sensation of what he did. If bathing here had the power to cleanse guilt, then he might end up following Charles' patterns after all.

Alexander thought about the reason why he was back in Patras now. Duncan's association with Tanglwyst was worrisome. He suspected Duncan wanted this notorious man-trap for himself, but it occurred to Alexander now that this might be his own romantic situation with Catriona coloring his view. It was possible there was another reason entirely, one unrelated to matters of the heart, that was the impetus for the rescue. Perhaps Tanglwyst paid him, or Myrgen did. Perhaps Dominic did. That made a bit more sense, for a D'Medici to remove a past employer who could impugn his reputation and hurt his new position. After all, Alexander's mother was a D'Medici. He understood the type.

He thought about how Duncan had gotten the Writ. One second it was there on the desk in the King's Bedchamber, the next it was gone. No trace of how he got in or how he left. Alexander wondered if he used the secret passages like Catriona had. He was starting to believe everyone knew those passages at least as well as he did, like they had grown up in them as well. What he ought to do is ask Duncan himself. Speculation was foolish in this situation. He would retrace his steps and see what he did. Duncan seemed able to step into a shadow or walk out of sight and disappear. Maybe he could do likewise in reverse.

The biggest problem with this whole thing was the uncertainty. He had hired Duncan to destroy Nicolai for a reason. He had seen and heard every day the surliness and drunken disfavor of the man. Every day, he had wanted to follow him home to find Catriona and see if she wanted to leave. He never did, out of respect for her request, but he was certain if the man was that distasteful at the palace, he would be equally or more unpleasant at home. The thought of Catriona and Alan being in that sort of environment for this last winter angered him. That he had waited this long to do something about it shamed him. But would she thank him for it, or condemn him?

He got out of the bath and dried off with one of the large, fluffy towels in the room. He knew of only one person he could ask, who would be sure to tell him what he wanted to know. With any luck, she would see him. Alexander wrapped up in the towel and left the room for his own.

Dominic puttered around the King's Bedchamber, a giant room where Charles had spent his last days. There were cobwebs in the corners of the rafters but that was not unexpected. Spiders went everywhere with impunity. He looked around. The portrait of the Queen had been removed and burned, as well as the one in Myrgen's study. The portrait of the Princess had been repaired. Myrgen's gift with paint and canvas was astounding. In the light of the morning, Dominic felt the picture practically breathed. There was no portrait of the former king here. Instead, it hung in the study downstairs, hiding a small vault set in the wall, disguised as a rock. That vault had been the downfall of the former Queen. He wondered if Alexander was going to utilize that again.

The door opened and Lieutenant Gomez de Santander entered, carrying a report in his hands. He looked up from the report and said, "Ah. Excuse me, Lord Chancellor. I was not expecting anyone to be here."

Dominic frowned. "You often wander into the King's Bedchamber when you expect it to empty?"

"Well, yes. I leave the reports regarding the guards and active investigations here for His Majesty to peruse at his leisure. Everyone knows he doesn't use this place to sleep."

"*Everyone knows?* The man just became King three days ago."

Gomez arched an eyebrow and looked around. The gigantic bed could hold five people, ten if half of them slept with their heads to the foot. The entire room was decorated in royal blue and red with the Mervolingian fleurs-de-lis in gold. Intricately carved wood adorned every chair and table leg, following the fleur motif. Every piece of furniture was the size of a monarch's ego. The only place this wasn't unnecessary was the desk, which held papers, reports, writs, decrees and laws in all stages of composition. "My mistake. This place has Alexander in every corner."

Dominic gave Gomez a prissy frown, but he recognized the man's powers of observation. The Chancellor didn't know Alexander really, but he knew that Alexander had always taken a powerful interest in the guards and their activities. He had seen the King and Gomez together daily going over the reports. Dominic thought about dressing the man down, establishing himself as the dominant power here in the palace staff, but Gomez' competence intimidated him so he decided upon a different approach.

"You know him pretty well, don't you, Lieutenant?"

Dominic was pleased to see Gomez' eyes flutter in surprise. Clearly he expected a confrontation like Dominic had entertained. Gomez set the reports in the massive desk and folded his arms, nodding. "You might say I've gotten a feel for how he thinks over the past winter."

"And how *does* he think?"

Gomez glanced at the elaborate bed and surroundings. "Simply and clearly. He's not fussy or over-pretentious. This place offends him. Depending upon who he ends up marrying, this room may never be used again as a bedchamber. It could merely be as a meeting place or study."

"How will who I marry factor into this, Gomez?"

Both men turned to see Alexander had joined them in the doorway, the door still ajar from Gomez' entry. The Lieutenant bowed, as did Dominic. "If the woman you choose as your queen prefers this room, you will accommodate her, Your Majesty."

Alexander nodded and glanced around. "That's true, but thankfully unlikely. What do you have for me?"

Gomez glanced at Dominic and proceeded. "There's still no sign of where Duncan McVryce might have taken the Lady Tanglwyst. No one has reported seeing them in the past day. I'm afraid I've lost them, Sire."

Dominic swallowed. *Tanglwyst has been taken by Duncan?* In all the excitement of the past few days, he had neglected to go check on her this tenday. Duncan had been her lover to ease her pain of losing Nicolai to Catriona. If Duncan had taken her, it might have been to make her suffer for jilting him when Nicolai came crawling back. He looked at Gomez, who continued talking with the King.

Alexander took the report Gomez had brought in and glanced over it. "What are the chances he's killed her by now?"

"Not a chance in hell, Sire. The woman's power over men is undeniable. Once she's had one, he cannot betray her. I've seen it over and over again. That's why I instructed my men to not be alone with her at any time and to not let her touch them under any circumstances."

Dominic leaned over to see what the report Alexander was reading detailed, but stood upright again when Alexander looked at him.

Alexander closed the report and turned a baleful eye on Dominic. "You were in her service for years, were you not, Lord Dominic?"

"Yes, Sire."

"Do you concur with the Lieutenant's findings?"

"Undoubtedly, Sire."

"So I should trust you why?"

Dominic looked directly at the King. "Because Catriona does. Sire."

Alexander did not look at Gomez, but he certainly was aware of the man's puzzled look, as was Dominic, who also did not include him in the conversation. The King said, "Gomez, I think you might consult with Dominic here about where his former employer might be found, where she might run to hide. Chancellor, I expect your full cooperation on this investigation. I will leave you to it." He turned to Gomez. "You may use this room, if you like."

Dominic swallowed as the King left the room and closed the door.

Alexander closed the door behind him and smiled. The look of shock that flashed through Dominic's eyes indicated he didn't know that Duncan had taken Tanglwyst so that meant there were other factors at play here if she was rescued. It hardly mattered. Dominic had walked right into his plans. Gomez would get every movement the Lady made in a year from the Mandian, leaving Alexander free to go see Gwen. If anyone would know if Nicolai had mistreated his beloved or her son, it would be Gwen. He went off to his room to leave via the secret catacomb passage in his prayer nave. There was a leg of the passages that put him near the King's Woods, which bordered Gwen's small farm. He could go see her and none would be the wiser.

He opened up his door and found his mother waiting for him. She was holding a small basket of egg-shaped herb packages. "Mother. What are you doing here?"

"I made something for you, Dear, to help you with your courting of your queen."

Alexander frowned, distrusting of her efforts *or* her intentions. "In what way?"

She stepped forward and closed the door behind her son. "These poultices are made from the Cyprian herb that grows in the garden beneath your window. They are similar to the ones used upon you when you are injured. They are the reason you are never sick, have never had a disease, regardless of your travels." Apparently, the thought of him traveling caused a foul taste in her mouth for she frowned and quickly went on. "If you use these on the woman you plan to engage, she will be very receptive to your endeavors."

She picked one up and handed it to Alexander. The wrapping was very fine cotton cheesecloth, almost like gauze the way it was wrapped. He couldn't see what was inside. "You expect me to injure the woman I want to marry in order to put one of these on her?"

"Well, granted, it is better if it is used as an infusion upon a wound, but you can make a tea from it as well with a similar effect, though there will be side effects in either case."

"Side effects? Like death?"

"No, Dear. These are life *savers* not life takers. They will make her more attuned to you, to your needs and desires. They will make her stronger, and more importantly, better able to bear your children and survive the process." Alexander looked down at the poultices as Catherine placed one of them in his hand. "Don't you want your Queen to bear you a son?"

Alexander thought of the passion with which he and Catriona had made love at that cabin, how she would look pregnant and what their child would look like. He might be expected to have a boy, but a daughter who carried her mother's eyes and features was just as desirable. *By the Saints, I love her.* He blinked away from this line of thought and discussion. He didn't have time for this now. He looked at his mother and thought of an evil comment to make.

"What makes you think she hasn't already?"

Catherine's look of sly coercion turned quickly to one of panic. "A bastard? Out in the world? Alexander, how could you?"

He tossed the poultice back into the basket. "He's only a bastard if I *don't* acknowledge him, Mother. But thank you for the kind gift. I'm sure your apothecary worked very hard to make these."

Catherine drew up to her full six foot height and placed the basket deliberately on the desk. "These herbs are not for just anyone to harvest, Alexander. They are poisonous if gathered or worked by someone to whom they are not attuned. I raised these herbs, with your fluids. When it comes to working with these in their raw form, only one of us can do so. Those herbs are very special, Alexander. Don't dismiss their use." She glared at him and gave him a sharp-edged curtsy before storming out of the room.

Alexander smiled and locked the door against further intrusions. He picked up one of the infusions and inspected it. Several herbs were dangerous to work with when fresh but once they dried out, were safe, even if reconstituted. He knew the herbs he used to treat his wounds came from a special plant and that they didn't work on anyone else. In fact, if they were put on someone else's skin, they caused burns. He learned that when he tried to heal one of Catriona's sailors long ago. After that, he didn't let anyone else touch them.

When Tanglwyst was recovering after being beaten after her capture, he saw that her blood was tainted with a poison. He suspected Cyprian herb that was unattuned. He remembered a new servant woman who worked the garden and how she fell very sick, very fast on her first day. The Royal Physician had Alexander put leeches on her, suspecting she had been accidentally poisoned. Alexander later heard the Physician tell his mother he thought she might have touched the Cyprian Herb. His mother's comment was that at least the girl would be very susceptible to suggestion.

So, this is yet anther attempt by Mother to control the throne. Could she really be trying to make Catriona susceptible to suggestion?

It seemed likely. He had no love lost on his mother after the St. Michael's Day Massacre, and no trust lost either. Unfortunately, he could also tell she wasn't lying about the effects. That troubled him. His old experiences warred with this new one. He looked at the poultice and made a decision.

He realized didn't know enough about this herb but he knew someone who might. He was on his way to see her anyway. He pocketed the poultice and slipped off into the catacombs.

As he entered the crossroads area, he stopped. Here was the perfect place to try something. He took a deep breath. "Duncan. Come to me." A mark under his skin flared light through his shirt, outlined in a dark flame he almost missed. Suddenly, the bald man was moving in front of him. He knelt before Alexander, then looked around, confused.

"Sire?"

Tanglwyst heard Duncan's horse turn into the woods behind her and canter off. She likewise turned her horse and went into the woods, fearing he had suddenly heard or seen something. They had been traveling at night and resting during the day, but the sound of horses this morning on the road stopped them from making camp. The horses had been gendarme on road patrol. Although Duncan had reassured her they couldn't be looking for her this far away, he still decided to play it safe and take them into the woods. He had just mentioned they might head deeper and then camp. Apparently, he had meant a bit farther away than she thought.

She saw his horse ahead of her a bit, slowing. She pulled around the heavy trees. It took her a minute to realize something was wrong. The horse was rider less. She turned to look for him behind her, sneaking, fighting, or unconscious. She turned back around just in time to feel the full brunt of the low hanging tree branch right across her chin. She crumpled off the back of the horse and hit the ground unconscious.

Alexander blinked. He hadn't quite expected Duncan to appear instantly from nowhere and he stepped back, on guard. A flash of light lit the room, a golden glow that caused Duncan to shy away for a moment. Alexander looked around. *By the Saints, what is this? It seems to be coming from me!*

Duncan looked at Alexander. "Sire? What need have you of me?"

Alexander thought Duncan looked nervous and watchful. "What's the matter, Duncan? Is this the first time this has happened?"

"To be summoned out of the air like this? Yes. The Oath of Fealty citizens give, allows them to be summoned by their

Sovereign. My own oath has a… *different* availability. I've always figured it could be invoked in an emergency. I've just never had someone do it." He looked around again, shielding his eyes from the glow of the king. "And this light…"

Alexander realized it must be the Power of Sovereignty. The glow was similar to that which he took from Charles a tenday before. It pulsed a bit in rhythm with his heartbeat. He breathed in and out slowly to calm himself. The glow subsided, leaving them alone in the dim lamplight. "Sorry about that."

"I am at your service, Sire, if you would be so kind as to give me your request."

Alexander tilted his head at his assassin. "In a hurry to be somewhere? Or are you worried about leaving the Lady Tanglwyst alone?"

Duncan straightened his back, though he did not stand.

"Yes, I know you spirited her away. What I want to know is why. Why would you, the King's own Assassin, rescue a traitor to that crown? I should set a Writ against her, since you know right where she is. I should make you kill her personally."

"With all due respect to the Crown, my Liege, I fear I would not be able to carry out such an order."

Alexander had a moment of arrogance flare behind his eyes, strange to his senses. He had noticed its touch before, at the Inn in Rouen and at the bath house when Myrgen had spoken with such familiarity to Catriona. Then, as he reined in the arrogance, he realized he was below the palace, quite possibly with a traitor, one who could kill him without even touching him, like he killed Nicolai. He felt the glow begin again as his fear started to unsettle him. "Because you love her?"

"Because I serve Heaven, the Church, and the Crown of Mervolingia, in that order, Sire. There is only one power on Earth that could override the will of the Crown."

Alexander frowned, thinking. "Why would the Church choose to save her?"

"Begging your pardon, Sire, but she donates quite heavily to the Church. I can tell you she shows signs of withdrawal from some sort of herbal agent. It's mostly out of her system now, but it is an extract of an herb from Cyprus. It renders the mind easier to manipulate. Judging from the time it took her to get it clear of her body, she might have been under its effects for a month or more. She said she lost a lot of blood."

Alexander remembered the mess on the sheets when he treated Tanglwyst. He had assumed she had a miscarriage but now he wasn't so sure. "Cyprian herb? How do you know about Cyprian herbs?"

"How do you think the Church insured my loyalty? There's a lingering effect as long as the person who administered it still lives. I only recently laid eyes upon the man who holds that loyalty and I knew instantly that I could refuse him nothing."

Alexander got a look of horror. "And they did this to you?"

"No. They taught me about the herb, had me process it myself. I was told of the after effects and what would happen when the Donor passed away. That's how I know about the lemon smell. They were right. It smells exactly like lemons, a whole room full of them. Anyway, I was told about it, taught the effects, then offered the option to take it. I chose to take it."

"And you believe this has been introduced to her system?"

"I do, Sire."

"But with Elizabeth dead, she's lost the connection."

"Indeed, Sire. The blessing is that Elizabeth was a woman. It is used in Mande and Cheryb to insure a woman's fidelity because the connection is maintained between her and any child she has with the man to whom she is bound."

Alexander's eyes narrowed. *Giovanni. That's how he had so many servants who never spoke against him, and why his wife never protested his activities.* He closed his eyes, shaking his head. *If he had given that to Catriona...* "Well, you should see to your charge then. And Duncan, how secure is the knowledge of our previous arrangement?"

"I serve Heaven, the Church, and the Crown, in that order. She is none of these, Sire. My oaths preclude me from telling her anything. Just as I would be unable to tell you who asked me to rescue her."

Alexander examined the man before him. If he served the Church before the Crown, did that mean an archbishop or a lowly priest outranked Alexander? Or could it be that only the embodiment of the Church, as he was the embodiment of the Crown, was able deliver that order? He thought about pressing the question, but then he realized he had something better to do. "Thank you for your discretion. You may go."

The symbol on his arm flashed again, this time without the dark flame, and Duncan was gone. Alexander looked at the mark, trying to decide if he had truly seen the dark flame before, then proceeded out of the crossroads towards the outside.

Duncan returned to the section of woods where he had been when the King summoned him. He was horseless, missing his charge, and without supplies. He hoped she was nearby. He looked around, trying to see signs of the horses. He listened for the nickering of the animals or the sound of hooves, even the whisper of his name as she tried to call out to him. He heard nothing. Then he heard the sound of horses on the road through the woods, the barding announcing the return of the gendarme. He moved to the bushes nearby and squinted through the brush to see them pass. He saw a something pale flutter from one of the horses, landing on the ground behind them. The riders didn't seem to notice, though all he saw was horses, the foliage hiding the riders. They rode off towards the nearby town of Bordeaux.

After they were well away, he went up to the road. The pale piece of silk, embroidered with tulips and emblazoned with a purple lioness stretching looked up at him from the cobblestones. He picked it up and went after the riders.

Gwen packed the last of the road biscuits into the saddlebags, chewing the one in her mouth she had tasted to ensure they were good fodder for the road. They were made from chick peas and had the benefit of being road rations for both herself and her horse to supplement the grain for the trip. She planned to go more as the crow flew than to keep to the King's Highway. There were inns and wagons on the highway which would slow her progress. It also meandered to get folks to other towns like Rouen and St. Marguerite. She could cut cross country to St. Andrew in half the time it took to go by road. She closed the pack and headed for the door.

She opened the door and found Alexander standing on her back doorstep. She swallowed the bite of biscuit almost whole, then went into a coughing fit as the crumbs dropped down the wrong pipe. A few minutes later, after Alexander got her some wine and made sure she wasn't going to die on him, she finally choked out, "What are you doing here?"

"Good morning to you too, Gwen," he beamed, his eyes still showing concern. "I hope this isn't the face of things to come. I don't want to lose my populace simply by visiting them."

Gwen waved her hand at him. "It isn't that, Your Majesty. I was trying to figure out a way to get a meeting with you but I'm no one important so I couldn't figure out how to reach you." She nodded to the wine. "Thank you, by the way. I don't know what I would have done if you hadn't been here."

"Not choked in the first place?"

Gwen nodded and smiled through a final cough. "Good point." She drank a bit of wine to quell the final bastions of irritation in her throat. "My question still stands. The King of Mervolingia is in my house. There must be a reason, unless some unexplainable force led you here. Dreams perhaps?"

Alexander shook his head. "Not really. I was wondering if you have seen Catriona recently."

"Um, recently? You mean since you last saw her?"

"Well, um, I saw her early yesterday. Nicolai's dead." He watched her eyes for reaction and she maintained her gaze. "You don't seem surprised."

"Good news travels fast."

Alexander's eyebrows raised. "So it's good news. Good. I was worried."

"Why?"

"Just the way she reacted." He shrugged and looked at Gwen's mug of wine. "Could I get some of that? It smells wonderful."

Gwen rolled her eyes. "Where are my manners? Of course, Your Majesty."

"Gwen," he said. He followed her movements as she got a mug for him as well. "you've known me as Grymalkin or Alex longer than you've known me as King. Please, use my name."

"Are you sure, Your... Alex?"

"Quite."

"I'll go with Grymalkin then. I've always liked that name. It smacks of magic."

Alexander smiled. "You know, just hearing you say it brings back memories. Thank you, Gwen." He took the offered mug of spiced wine and sipped it. He seemed to have something on his mind, but Gwen had learned patience dealing with Fae so she settled in and waited for him to be ready to talk. He reached into his pocket and pulled out an egg. "Could you look at this for me?"

She took the item and discovered it was a poultice, wrapped well in expensive gauze. This was no commoner's dressing. She stood and went over to the counter. "Certainly. Where did you get it?"

"My mother. She said she made it for me. I don't know when. I'm a little hesitant to use it and I thought I'd bring it to the finest herbalist in the Kingdom to have a look."

"Thank you!" She beamed at him and turned, glowing, back to her task. "What can you tell me about it?"

"It's made from a *Cyprian* herb that grows beneath my window. I never knew the name of that plant, only that none of the gardeners were allowed to touch it. However, I know about this herb. It's Mandian in origin, used for centuries now to preserve the line of kings. Mother said it was only workable by me or her."

Gwen looked at the bundle. "I've never heard of a plant that was selectively poisonous."

"I have. If you build up a tolerance to the poisons, you can work with them. It's common among apothecaries to be immune to the poisons they make for household pests."

Gwen looked at Alexander, shaking her head. Working with Fae to keep pests from the house and yard was so much easier. "What do you want me to do?"

Alexander sighed. "Well, she said this mixture was for Catriona."

Gwen's gaze grew wary.

Alexander nodded. "Trust me. I'm right there with you. Her claim is that it's beneficial to my wife. It will make her stronger and more likely to survive childbirth. It would also make the baby stronger."

Gwen smiled. "I rather like the idea of you and Catriona having babies."

He laughed. "Well, so do I, to be honest." His smile faded. "However, Mother used Catriona against me before, to manipulate me into making that St. Michael's Day mess happen. I just want to make sure she isn't trying something like that again." He glanced at the poultice. "Besides, I think a friend of mine might have been exposed to some of it and I need to make sure she's not in any danger."

Gwen turned to the poultice, but her mind caught on his last statement. *She? Was there another woman already?*

She took a deep breath, dismissing the idea. Alexander had always been loyal to Catriona. He would never even consider another woman.

She set the hammer down and picked up a knife instead. She carefully cut the housing away from the herbs and started strewing them on the counter. She saw several high quality herbs used for healing and carrying healing properties through the body. Certain herbs were better if made into a tea, others if applied to a wound. The content of both indicated it was safe to ingest. She looked at the stamens of the herbs in the center and watched them closely. She saw a small wisp of movement and realized this herb had a spirit associated with it. She tried to sense it better but she couldn't. It was too tiny. She leaned back.

"It's fine. Nothing dangerous here."

Alexander exhaled and took a drink of the wine. "Thank the Saints. It seems mother is not immune to the Power of Sovereignty like I first suspected. That will be important someday, I'm sure. So," he placed the mug on the hearth table, "you don't seem to mind that Nicolai was killed in the street."

Gwen shook her head and walked over to the chairs by the hearth. "No. As inappropriate as it is for me to go against my Captain's wishes, I despised that man, Grymalkin. He always reeked of rum and bad wine and he treated her like she was expendable, in my opinion."

"Expendable?"

"You always made her feel like she was important in your life. Essential, I think Dom would say. But when she would come to visit with me, it was as if she had been beaten down by him."

"What?!" Alexander gripped the arms of the chair and half-stood. Gwen shook her head.

"I don't mean like he ever raised a hand to her or Alan. He would never have survived that."

"I agree."

"More like she regretted her choice. Like she knew it would never work, but she had committed to the decision and already made the sacrifices." She looked down at her mug, unsure how to say what she wanted to say. She decided to just say it. "Alex, I told her at the time, and I maintain that her decision to break with you was the wrong one. She deserves better than what she returned to. She deserves you."

Alexander smiled, a slight touch of sadness to his eyes. "Thank you Gwen. I'm hoping for that end myself." He set his nearly empty mug on the small table and stood, prompting Gwen to rise as well. "I will go then. Please let me know if you see her. I would like to speak with her again, if I may."

Gwen thought about telling him that she planned a trip to St. Andrew, but she didn't want to mention Myrgen right then. Besides, the poultice had given her an idea. "I will. Please feel free to visit, should you need to."

"I will. You have a standing invitation to the palace anytime you want to visit and you have access to me should you need it. So say I, King Alexander, sovereign of Mervolingia." A spiritual pulse went out from him and Gwen felt certain that anyone who needed to know that in the entire kingdom had that information. She smiled. He said, "I love that. I need to do that for my baths, I think." He hugged her and went to the door. "Thank you."

"Thank *you,* Alexander."

He started to walk away, but turned back. "Gwen, if someone were exposed to this herb, one that wasn't attuned to a single person, what would happen?"

"Well, depending upon the dosage, they might build up that immunity you mentioned before."

He straightened, and a hint of light entered his features. "Really? You think that's possible? To be immune to this stuff?"

Gwen shrugged. "It's an herbal remedy. I don't see why not."

His mouth got a smile Gwen wasn't sure she'd ever seen before, like he had a weight lifted he didn't know he carried. "Thank you again."

He left and Gwen noted his step was a little lighter as well. He closed the door behind him. She looked over at the counter, smiled and rubbed her hands together. She was *not* about to leave their love vulnerable again.

A shadow fell across Tanglwyst as she lay motionless on the forest floor. A small beetle crawled near her hair, oblivious to the creatures above or beside it. A second shadow stepped from the other one and the boot wearing it crossed to the other side. The male stooped in his dirt colored leathers, the dags on the edges of his mantle resembling oak leaves in mid-spring. His shirt was straight sleeved and his vest was embroidered with leaves that shimmered as if turning in a spring breeze. His hair was a soft, rich chestnut. His eyes were a wicked quicksilver. He poked the beetle with a stick, hurrying it away, and stood.

"Uh, okay. Who's she?"

The woman beside Tanglwyst looked up at the man. "I don't know. What did you ask of the spell?"

"To bring to me a major player in this forthcoming drama, but look at her! She's hardly impressive." The man folded his arms across his chest.

"We may have to put her back on her path and watch her to see what happens. It's not like she's the Emissary of the Last Child."

"No doubt." He turned Tanglwyst's head with his boot, looking her over. "At least she's fair."

The woman moved aside the hair on Tanglwyst's face. "Hey! I know her! I gave her the Love Touch after that nasty business with the woman and the boy in Patras."

"You mean the Massacre? What prompted you to do that?"

"I saw her about to be attacked. I could see she had already endured a lot of pain. After that other business, I couldn't stomach more atrocities."

"And how, pray tell, did giving this woman ultimate power over the emotions of men help her? Did she use it to escape the attackers?"

"No, they were just rabble. They moved past her as soon as she invoked the Saints to protect her."

"Then what did it do?"

The woman didn't look up from the woman on the ground. "It helped me. After being powerless to stop the murder of that woman's son, it helped *me* to be able to empower another woman to control her own destiny."

The man studied his companion. Her silver hair flowed past her shoulders, moving like spider silk in the light forest breeze. Her eyes were also silver, but not by birth, but by proximity. Her clothes were doeskin, soft and black. She made no noise at all when she moved. The only skin showing was her face, all the rest was covered so as to hide her better. Centuries ago, she had pledged her service to the Fae Lord Embertwist Apocraphix and he never chose to release her. If he were to do so now, she would turn to dust in the space of a whisper. The look on her face was hard, showing the centuries of her service to the King of the Vernal Equinox, the finest thief in the world. She was the Sinister Glove of Embertwist, his second in all things. The only thief more skilled than this woman was the man beside her.

"You know, Glove, sometimes, I forget you're a woman."

She stood, straightening to her full height and leveled a powerful look at her master. "What in the Shadow of Sovereignlumen would make you think that could *ever* be the *right* thing to say?" The Sinister Glove turned from him and leapt away into the trees.

Embertwist paused, eyes wide. When she was gone, he let out his held breath. "Reminder acknowledged and noted. You *are* a woman, and all the random hostility that includes." He looked again at Tanglwyst. "And what of you, young miss? How do you factor into this?" He crouched again, looking at her face. He frowned at the branch-shaped bruise forming there. He touched her face and a sprinkling of dew appeared where he willed it. The dew covered the bruise and he blew on it to dry it. The bruise became flaky, like old paint. When he blew a second time, it fluttered away in the breeze caused by his breath. He smiled. Behind him, he heard the sound of people coming through the woods. One of them called out something about horses and Embertwist stood, looking down at his charge.

"Time to put you back on your path, my lady."

A man came through the underbrush and saw the lady on the ground next to a large chestnut stallion seemingly standing guard. The horse nickered softly, then nudged Tanglwyst's foot. The man came over, tipping back his ranger's hood.

"Well, now, what have we here?"

Twelve

"The hardest step is over the threshold."
The Wise Wench's Tavern Book

A knock heralded Myrgen's entrance. He brought lunch in with him, bowls of chowder and a small loaf of bread tucked under his elbow.

"Are you ready for this?" Catriona asked. She had laid out the merchant logs for the company on the huge charting table and she stood up from where she had been leaning on the table, perusing the charts beneath.

Myrgen caught a glimpse of cleavage before she stood and he blinked to banish the thought. *Please. It hasn't been that long since Elizabeth.* Myrgen brought the bowls of chowder with him to the table. "As ready as I'll ever be."

"Up or down?"

Myrgen blinked, the image of her cleavage popping by again to say hello. "Excuse me?"

"Sit or stand?"

Myrgen said, "Ah. Thought you meant... never mind. Sitting would be better for keeping track of the soup, I think."

He set the bowl on the table before her, retaining his own brimming bowl. He pulled the bread from under his arm and set it between them. Catriona tore it in half and sopped up some of the chowder. She poured some red wine while chewing and offered some to Myrgen, who accepted with a nod. They ate while they talked. Catriona pointed out the codes for the journal notes, Myrgen was impressed that he understood it. The logs were kept quite regularly by Catriona and she had her own system. Myrgen had spent the last two days on this ship becoming familiar with it. As long as Myrgen could decipher it, he was fine. The system wasn't the best, but he knew from experience that few people could handle having years' worth of work suddenly replaced by a new system. Change would require patience on Myrgen's part and that was something he had in abundance.

They worked on the books for hours. She explained what the different entries meant and what trade routes the *Enigma* traveled. Conversational tangents and stories of seedy ports and court intrigues populated the studies. Myrgen recommended a couple changes to the travel routes which would enhance the financial aspects by going from least to most lucrative in regards to the financial exchange rates.

Catriona looked up from the work they were doing and noticed the settling twilight. She stretched. "Augh! I have to get out of this room. I can't focus on my own door and my muscles are screaming to be off this bench. You fancy a walk?"

Myrgen crept from behind the table, his left foot limp and unresponsive. He almost fell, catching himself on the table.

"Are you alright?" Catriona turned towards him at the sound of his collapse.

He leaned back, shaking the foot into spiny wakefulness and wincing at the results. "No... Ish! My foot is numb. I hate that."

Catriona smiled and stepped back to him. "Shoulder?"

"No, just give me a moment." Myrgen shook his foot, then cringed as the feeling returned. Myrgen limped as they left the cabin and made their way on deck, the wakening nerves losing their edge as he climbed the stairs to the upper deck. He had recovered fully by the time they made it to the railing to overlook the sea. Myrgen put both hands on the rail as Catriona stretched her arms behind her. She leaned on the rail, shifting her weight and stretching her calves. She turned to Myrgen.

"Help me here, would you?"

"What do you need?"

"Hang onto my coat to steady me. I'm going to stretch out my neck."

"Huh? How?"

She stepped to the rail. "I'm going to dangle off the edge and let my body weight stretch out my neck, but I need to make sure I don't go over the rail."

Myrgen blinked. "You're going to what?"

She put his hand on the strap across the back of her Caratian coat. "Just don't let me fall."

As she bent over, Myrgen braced himself, wrapping his fingers around the strap and steadying himself with a foot against the hull. Catriona hung almost upside down, dangling her arms over her head. She bounced a bit, relaxing.

"Does that actually do anything or do you do this to torment people?" Myrgen's vantage was enviable, and this was not lost on him. He could see the form of her body beneath her fitted coat and the top of her rear pressed against his hands. His forethought to brace himself in victory over gravity was threatened by her bouncing, as was his peace of mind.

"Yes. It works. I'll do it for you next. Pull me up." He helped her back to a standing position, and she stretched a bit more as she regained her footing. Myrgen moved back, releasing her. "Now, switch places with me."

"I don't know if I'm ready for this."

"Don't you trust me?" Catriona walked behind Myrgen to face the sea.

"Should I?" He smiled and leaned up against the railing. "Now, what do I do?"

"I'll hold onto you and you just let yourself hang."

"You. You're going to support me?"

"Yes." She took hold of his waistband and braced her foot on the hull between his legs.

"How's your arm?" There was doubt in his voice.

"Just bend."

Myrgen leaned over, wavering in his trust of her. His arms went above his head but he held off taking his eyes off her.

"Relax your upper body. Let your head dangle."

Myrgen dropped his head down and let himself relax. He felt a couple things pop and snap. The underside of his arms felt a little itchy from the stretch. He felt his hair wisp across his eyes, coming partially undone from its restraints. He reached up with his hands and pulled the tie from it, letting the hair fall towards the waterline. His eyes closed, he felt the stresses of the day abandon him. He wasn't sure why this was working but it certainly seemed to be.

Catriona gasped. "Myrgen, look!"

Myrgen opened his eyes and raised his head in time to see a mist on the sea in the distance. He pulled up and wiped his hair away to look at it. "What was it?"

"A whale. I saw it spout just now." Her voice illustrated her excitement at the discovery and the gold flecks sparked in her eyes.

"A whale? Here? Isn't that unusual?"

"I know. Either it's off course or we are. Did you see it?"

"Not exactly. Where?"

She pointed. "Over there. Watch."

He looked but saw nothing. "Where? There?" He pointed.

She corrected him, sighting where she suspected the whale would surface again. "No. There. It surfaced there, so it should come up about here."

Myrgen stepped in close and sighted along her arm. She turned a little sideways so he could get a better vantage to see where she was pointing and they waited. The sea stirred a breeze which tossed Catriona's hair around Myrgen's face. He noticed the smell of her hair and her perfume from the Open Lotus, designed just for her. Her body seemed suddenly warm and he realized how close they were, her hand on his shoulder. He fought the urge to wrap his arm around her waist, to pull her into his arms. As it stood, if she were to turn her head, they could be in a kiss before they knew it. It felt familiar, being this close to her, and he

146

remembered the kiss he gave her in the catacombs under the palace. He remembered her response and wondered if she would do that again if he kissed her now. He watched her as she went on seeking out the elusive whale and when it surfaced again, he found he really didn't care.

"There. Did you see it?" Catriona turned to look at Myrgen and met his gaze unexpectedly. At first, she didn't seem to understand what he was looking at. In a blink, she caught on but she didn't pull away. Instead, the gold flecks in her eyes seemed to shimmer, as if on fire. His hand twitched slightly, will and desire were vying for control. He felt a massive war within his body fighting between what was proper and clutching her to him. It would be so easy; a nudge of her hip and his arms would engulf her like they did in the catacombs. His muscles under her fingertips were tense, ready to spring at the subtlest of hints that she wanted him too. They could be making love on the deck by the next swell.

He reached up to touch her face with his seaward hand, caught in the moment as much as she seemed to be. His thumb brushed her jaw line as it moved to the base of her skull, and he felt her shudder in anticipation. She closed her eyes and he knew he could kiss her, right then, right there, with The Saints and the entire crew as their witness, and she wouldn't care.

At least not right then.

The sound of footsteps up the stairs startled them both out of the moment, unrequited. The two broke apart, stepping back to a more appropriate distance. Catriona looked disquieted, and more than a little bit unsettled by the incident. Myrgen looked at his hand as it retreated to his side, as if accusing it of treachery. The deck commanded his eyes for the intervening moments, keeping him from actually lingering on its captain. He looked around but the whale was gone. A whale? A *whale*...? This felt simultaneously perfectly right and more than a little contrived. *Is there a charm on the breeze?*

"I believe I have things to do," Catriona said. "Perhaps we should call it a night on the books." A look of regret at a missed opportunity cloaked her. She blinked it away, but not before Myrgen caught it.

He took a deep, calming breath, trying to assess why he had just acted without thinking. He thought about trying to apologize, but he noticed one of the crewmen standing at the top of the stairs, watching them. He wasn't sure how much the man had seen and thought better of drawing attention to the indiscretion. "Yes. That would probably be best. Well, good night Captain." Myrgen bowed slightly, then left for his cabin. As he passed the crewman, he nodded greeting. The crewman's gaze never left Myrgen's, a silent threat telling Myrgen the man had seen enough. Myrgen met the man's glare, letting him know Myrgen was willing to be confronted about what just happened, but not right now.

The crewman watched him go, then turned to his Captain. At the bottom of the stairs, Myrgen dared a glance at the woman he had almost kissed. She crossed her arms and turned back to the sea, as if looking for answers in the waves. The whale was gone, Myrgen noticed, and with it, the insanity of the moment. The crewman came up behind her. She didn't turn to face him when he spoke. "Captain, are you okay?"

"Yes, Liam. I'm fine."

"That fella wasn't botherin' you, was he? He looked a little too close, ta me."

"No, Liam, he wasn't bothering me. Are you here to take the crow's nest for the night?"

"Yes Cap'n."

"Then I shall leave you to it."

Liam appeared to get the hint that Catriona wasn't in the mood to talk to him about what he had seen and Myrgen was grateful. He still needed to suss it out himself. He continued down the hallway to the cabin she had given him. He was suddenly very aware of exactly how close by she truly was. They didn't exactly share a wall on their bedrooms, her main room being along his wall, but her room was open. He wanted to be certain he didn't say or do anything stupid that would call her sharp attention to him through those walls.

He took off his shirt and hung it on the peg. He hadn't noticed his injury all day but suddenly now, it was reminding him of its presence. He reached back and felt the cut. It was sore but not seeping, he didn't think, but he could use a bit of healing to stop that from happening again. He had no idea if he was going to be in that room for hours again, talking, laughing…

He closed his eyes and shook his head. *What's wrong with me? Is my heart truly so fickle? I have lost all respect for Elizabeth, it's true, but have I healed so quickly from the pain of her betrayal? It must be just the situation. She rescued me from certain death, gave me a new life, and brought me into her most intimate home. I need put this into perspective.*

He looked at the small desk in the room and noticed a bottle of wine in one of the pigeon holes. He didn't remember bringing one in. It was sealed and he needed a drink right then. Thank the Saints Catriona had stayed on deck. He doubted he could face her at that moment.

Catriona passed the door to Myrgen's quarters. The light was on and she found she wanted to knock on the door, to talk with him. She tried to analyze it on deck, figure out what had happened. There was no denying she was attracted to Myrgen, not now. Her dreams belied that truth whether she ignored it or not. Now, she could push it aside no longer. They had almost kissed, she was sure of it, and the dynamic of their relationship had suddenly changed. It bothered her. She wanted the company Myrgen offered, but suspected leaving things like they were right now would jeopardize that.

She knocked and heard the rustle of breeches and the echo of boots on the flooring. Myrgen opened the door, shirtless, a goblet of red wine in his hand. He seemed a bit surprised to see her and stood back. "C, Captain. I thought you were staying on deck."

"I, I did, but I wanted…" She frowned, not sure why she was here or why she needed to talk to him right now. Her mind seemed to be having trouble focusing with him half-naked. He was surprisingly well developed. His clothing hid the musculature and definition of his chest. She suddenly realized his thighs and arms were also quite well developed. She fought with her stoic nature and a strange yet powerful passion to complete the task they had avoided on deck.

Myrgen gestured suddenly, offering her entry. "Would you like to come in?"

"Thank you." She stepped in and got her emotions under control, thankfully. She was commander of this ship. She didn't have time for such frivolity. "I seem to have caught you preparing for bed." She stood by the desk in the room, glancing around to keep her eyes from lingering.

Myrgen shook his head and crossed in front of her to set his goblet in the upright pigeonhole on the desk. "Actually, I was going to examine my injuries." He reached for his shirt.

"Oh. Please, don't let me interrupt then. I can come back." She realized that sounded a bit like she meant she could come back later, tonight, and the implications of this comment smacked her like a gale-force wind. She blinked and tried to recover. "I mean, I can see you tomorrow, if you need to be alone."

"No, I don't need to be alone. I'm not really sure there's any reason to worry about it, really. The wound, I mean. Not... never mind."

"I could look at it for you, just to make sure."

"Are you..." He licked his lips, as if trying to recover himself. "If you're sure it isn't an inconvenience."

"No, it's no inconvenience, Myrgen. I don't want anything to happen to you out here." Catriona swallowed, desire from the whale encounter following in the wake of that gale force implication, complicating matters. She was suddenly worried her hands were cold.

Myrgen turned to face the wall and leaned on it, exposing the wound by his waistband. Catriona rubbed her hands together to warm them and pulled the waistband down, noting the reddened area rubbed by the fabric.

Myrgen cleared his throat. "About what happened tonight, on deck just now, I wanted to apologize. I don't have an excuse."

Catriona touched the area on his back and she felt his heart jump again. "I'm sorry if my hands are cold."

"Oh believe me, it isn't that they're cold. It's... well, up on deck... Saint's blood, what's wrong with me?"

"I was thinking the same thing, Myrgen, but about myself, to be honest. I don't know what happened either. This looks good. You still need to show me how to do that sometime."

"Yes." He stood up, putting his shirt back on before turning to face her. He went to his desk and offered her a drink with a gesture.

Catriona nodded. "Myrgen, do you think I'm unwise for wanting you in service to this company?"

"That's not really my call, Captain. I would feel horrible if my indiscretion on deck caused a rift between us, but I would also understand completely. That was incredibly inappropriate. First I was looking for the whale, then, well…."

Catriona glanced at her goblet as Myrgen handed it to her. *Stop this now,* she thought. *Don't be alone with him. You're still too vulnerable, too empty, too curious. And definitely don't ask him…*

"Yes…"

Do not ask him that!

"Myrgen, I've been wondering something for several days now."

DO NOT ASK…

"The other night, under the palace, why did you kiss me?"

Thirteen

"The delicacy of the feast is the well-traveled guest."
The Wise Wench's Tavern Book

Myrgen arched an eyebrow. "Are you sure you want to know this?"

"If you like, I can read you and tell you why you did what you did. I just think I'd rather see if you know." She squinted at him then stood. "Do you mind if I light another lantern?" Myrgen shook his head.

"Thank you for that courtesy, Captain." He looked into his wine, as if calling forth visions of his own soul in the dark liquid. "You're right. As convenient as that is, I think I should explore this undercurrent myself. I think I kissed you before just to see if I could, because it seemed like a good idea at the time. I can't say I regret it. I have studied the human instrument for years, rather like you have. I learn what drives people, then use that information to my advantage. It's easy to believe a weak person would want to be strong and dominant, but just as common is the strong-willed person's desire to be dominated. These usually come out in intimate situations with someone a person trusts."

The lantern flared, brightening the room with extra firelight. She moved past him and took a seat in the chair that complemented the desk, right across from the bed. He looked at her viridian eyes, interested in his musings. The firelight dancing on her features reminded him of the kiss beneath the palace and he used that memory to narrate why he had kissed her, hoping to discover why he tried to do it again.

"Catriona, you are a strong, enrapturing woman. I will admit that the thought had not crossed my mind upon our first meeting, but when that wall to my cell opened and I practically fell on you? I had that thought bouncing around in my mind like a child's ball pretty regularly after that. I suspected you would like to be kissed with strength, but not with power. You want to be enveloped, but not smothered. I believed I could do that. You were the ultimate test for all those years of study."

Catriona dropped her gaze to the floor, a blush defeating her cool exterior. Myrgen politely looked away and pretended not to notice. He downed the remainder of his wine, then stood and refreshed his goblet, offering more to his Captain with a gesture. It was refused with another. "Do you miss Elizabeth?"

"You mean the crazy woman cackling in the royal crypts, promoting corpses?" He shook his head. "No. Not really."

"I am truly sorry for your betrayal at her hands, Myrgen. You didn't deserve that."

"Well, we both know that isn't true." He looked at her, nodding to her eyes. "That soul vision you have took away all my secrets, thankfully. Would that you had used it on her when I first took you."

"Believe it or not, I don't like using it on you."

"I don't mind at all. Like I said back in Rouen, it keeps me honest. I mean, isn't that why you came in here, just now? To keep things honest between us?"

"And as I said before, I'm not the only one who sees the truth in things. I believe I will have a hard time keeping things from you as well."

He stretched, smiling. "Well, I don't read women well enough to keep me on shore. Hopefully, I'll stay ahead of things enough to keep me at sea, since I can't fly."

Catriona looked at her wine, the easy sway of the ship rocking the fluid and making patterns with her reflection. "You think you should have known she was doing it? Elizabeth, I mean." Catriona leaned on her knees, her own goblet suspended in her hands between them.

"Yes." His voice was soft, distant. "I should have seen through her. I'm smarter than that."

Her eyes narrowed, like she was trying to focus on something distant. "We don't always see what is right in front of us, Myrgen. Nicolai once asked me, during our only intimate coupling the entire winter, to try something he had heard about. I tried it and then read him secretly, to see if I was doing it right. It turned out it was something Tanglwyst frequently did when they were together and he had been wanting me to do it so he could fantasize he was with her. When I discovered this, I found I couldn't resolve my disgust." She stood and walked over to the edge of the desk, setting the goblet down in the holder. "I felt I, I should have *known* he wasn't thinking about me at that time, that maybe his touch changed or his eyes closed or something." Even with her back to him, she failed to hide the salty edge of tears in her voice. "After that, I couldn't bear having him touch me again."

Myrgen didn't ignore the emotion in her voice like he had the blush on her face. "I guess we've both had our fill of betrayals of late." He watched the ripples in his wine dance back and forth across the surface of the liquid. "You know, I spent so much time, years in fact, studying the human animal in order to use them to my advantage, but I don't seem to have a problem with the fact that I was used that same way. I don't know what's wrong with me." He took a drink of his wine.

Catriona glanced at him. "Maybe it means you felt you deserved it."

He raised his eyes to hers. "Then what did I do to deserve you?"

He watched her eyes, aware that he asked something that was intimate, considering the incident they had just avoided on deck.

He didn't know why he was not maintaining an appropriate distance with her, outside of how comfortable he felt just being with her.

"I don't know." She tilted her head, watching him. "I really don't. Why do you trust me?"

He looked at his goblet, swirling his wine. "Because, of all the players in this drama, you have never lied to me." He looked at her again, noting her interest in the body language she displayed. "You made it very clear you would rip my lungs out when we first laid eyes upon each other, and I must say when my cell opened, it was a real possibility that you were going to do that very thing."

Catriona folded her arms, smiling. "I probably should have."

"Probably." He pointed at her, returning her smile. "But you didn't. You have treated me with respect and honor that I frankly don't think I've deserved. I have no idea what you want from me, but I feel completely safe in saying, whatever it is, if I have it to give, it's yours. If I can obtain it, through fair means or foul, you only need speak your desire." He raised his goblet in salute to her. "Much, I imagine, like everyone else on this ship." He took a drink. "So the question begs to be asked: Why do *you* trust *me*?"

"That *is* the question, isn't it?" She rested her hands on the desk, leaning back and opening herself up to him. "Because my instinct tells me to. I have guardians around me on all sides, every day. People who watch me, who heal me, who guide me, who make sure no foul magics come my way. Every one of them has a place, doing what they have decided to do for me because of something I have done for them. But you," she nibbled on her lips, "you're different. You have some dirt on you, Myrgen. You've been through a darker place than I've ever traveled, and no one I know has been where you have. Something tells me, I'm going to need a guide through there soon."

"What about Alexander?" Myrgen stood, walking past Catriona to set his goblet in the other pigeon hole, next to hers. "That man has walked in some pretty dark places."

She looked away from him. "I don't really know about that. All I know from him is that he wants to marry me, to make me his queen and when I'm around him, when I'm listening to him speak, I can't think of anywhere else I want to be."

He leaned on the desk, next to her, so close he could smell her soap from the Open Lotus filling his senses again. "And when he's not around?"

"I can think clearly. I can't be with him, Myrgen. I have obligations to this ship, this crew. I have a position in Caratia. I have a son who would be devoured by those locusts at court. I can't live in that world." She looked into his eyes. "I want to be here, *right here.*"

He watched her. "*Right* here...?"

The moment hung in the air, begging for release. If she said the word, he would kiss her again and this time there would be no sailors walking up the stairs, no whales catching their attention, no kings threatening his life. She looked down at his lips and he reached up and touched her face. She closed her eyes and he pulled her to him.

Running footsteps in the hallway pulled their attention away, followed almost immediately by a loud knock on Myrgen's door. "Captain, are you in there?"

Myrgen looked at the door, then back at her, questioning the timing. She smiled and stepped away. "Yes, Octavius, I'm here. I was just saying goodnight to Myrgen and checking on his wounds." She opened the door and the First Mate glanced over the former Chancellor, making sure things were still secure.

"You're not healing again, are you?" He looked her over as well.

"No, Octavius." She looked back at Myrgen. "He can take care of himself." She nodded to her Chancellor. "I'll see you tomorrow, then?"

"It's a one hundred fifty foot ship at sea. I doubt I could hide from you."

"You might be surprised. Good night, Myrgen." She smiled and left, closing the door upon his desires.

"Are you sure it's a good idea for you to be alone with that man, Captain?" Octavius was keeping his voice low as he escorted her the few yards to her own bedroom.

"You doubt my ability to handle myself, Octavius?"

"I'm not certain about your ability to keep your guard up. Right now, you're very vulnerable. I don't want him taking advantage of you."

"Vulnerable? How?" She opened her door and they took the conversation into her quarters.

"You just watched your husband die in the streets from an assassin's dart. You let yourself be kissed, *in front of the entire crew* by Alexander. Now you're spending time alone with a man who, from what the ship told me, was a near miss a few minutes before? By the Fae, what is the matter with you?"

"A near miss?" She nodded. "Interesting term. Octavius, are you jealous?"

"Bite your tongue. My wife would kill me and sink this ship if she thought I had feelings for another woman, even you. Don't be daft. I'm talking to you as your friend."

"You're trying to protect me."

"You've saved my life. I'm entitled."

She looked away, out the stained glass window of Galadorn. "I don't know. There's something about him, Octavius. Something… *right*. I can't explain it."

"What about Grymalkin? Isn't that *right*?"

"When I'm standing next to him? Yes. If he had asked me to marry him or lie with him or stay with me and sail to Caratia, I would have done any and all of it when he kissed me. I still don't know how I managed to escape. But when I'm out of his presence, I can think clearly. I know my place in the world, Octavius, and it isn't by his side. I don't know yet what role Myrgen has to play in this, but right now, I don't want him to go."

Octavius watched her eyes. "Catriona, this is dangerous ground. If you're so desperate to be rescued from Alexander's future, then do it yourself. If you use Myrgen, or any other man to do it, all you'll be doing is giving him false hope that there's a life to be had with you, and there won't be. Then, when you figure out what you do want, you'll discard him, *betraying him.*"

He let those words sink in as he backed away to the door and left.

Myrgen heard Octavius leave Catriona's quarters and wondered what they said. It was evident the man did not approve of how close Myrgen and the Captain had gotten. He doubted Octavius would feel better if he knew exactly how they met and all the other events following that fateful meeting. He thought about how best to keep that information from the First Mate, but then he recognized the thought. He shouldn't be trying to cover up this mess. If he was truly going to change his life, he needed to stop the deceptions and misunderstandings instead of perpetuate them.

He got up and pulled on his boots, thinking about what to do next. He knew the approval of her crew was paramount to his continued existence, and the leader of that group was not Catriona. It was Octavius. He stood and tucked in his shirt, then stepped out and went on deck. The First Mate was taking the helm back from one of the other crewmen and the man returned to his previous task. Myrgen took a deep breath and walked up the steps to the man.

"Octavius, may I speak with you a moment?"

Octavius looked him over, a whiff of disapproval around him, and nodded. "What's on your mind, Myrgen?"

"Your Captain, to be honest."

Octavius glanced overboard and nodded. "Yeah, I kind of got that impression. Look, I'll tell you what I told her just now. If she uses you to escape Alexander's proposal, she'll just end up betraying you later, when she's done with you."

Myrgen blinked. "That doesn't strike me as the kind of person she is. I'm related to a woman like that and Catriona doesn't fit that dress."

"No, she doesn't, but like all animals caught in a trap, she's likely to use any means necessary to get out of this and that includes chewing off her own leg."

"And betraying me, that's chewing off her own leg?"

Octavius rolled his eyes, nodding. "Oh yes. She hates betrayal in any form. It's why she does what she does with the whole reading thing. She's been betrayed before, in a most horrible way, and barely came out of that alive."

Myrgen nodded. "You mean Marco Giovanni."

Octavius blinked at Myrgen, the surprise on his face stopping all other expressions. "How did you...?"

"She told me, back in Rouen."

"When?"

"When we went to the Open Lotus for a bath. Uh, *separate* baths." Myrgen waved his hand. "Nothing untoward. Anyway, she told me while we were walking there."

"She did?" Octavius ran his tongue along his cheek. "Hunh. By all the Fae Lords, why would she do that?"

Myrgen furrowed his brow, noting the religious reveal. Apparently, Octavius was a Fae Worshipper. "I don't really know. I guess she needed to talk about it and I was around."

"She doesn't talk about that with anyone."

"Well, you seem to know about it."

"My wife told me."

"So she told your wife?"

Octavius waggled his head. "Well, yeah, but, that's a very special relationship there."

"I see. Look, if it helps, I'm just as baffled by all this as you are. I have no idea why I'm even on this ship right now."

"You're here because she wants you here."

"Yes, but why? I kidnapped her and tried to blackmail her into murdering someone."

"Excuse me?"

Myrgen winced. *Not quite as measured as I had wanted, but it's too late now.* "Er, yes. That's how we actually met."

"You know, if I push you overboard, you might get lucky and *not* survive the fall."

"And I would deserve that."

Octavius blinked, scoping Myrgen out. He squinted. "All right. Talk."

"How far back do you want me to go?"

"Why would you want her to murder someone?"

"I heard she had done it before, and in a very impressive way, an untraceable way. I needed something like that. You might say the person I had in mind to be disposed of was rather high-profile."

"Your source was wrong. The Captain would never murder someone."

Myrgen nodded. "I know that now, but at the time, I had a lot of faith in my source."

Octavius leaned back a bit, analyzing Myrgen. "And you don't anymore?"

Myrgen nodded. "Let's just say I found out they had ulterior motives. I was set up, along with your Captain. I'm certain the conspirators had no intention to do as they promised."

"Well, that's the trouble with conspiracies. No real loyalty."

"I know, but I thought this group was different. I thought I knew them." Myrgen shrugged. "Turns out they knew *me*. I never really knew them."

"What did they do?"

Octavius was acting more interested and Myrgen felt the familiar ground of the right place to start deviating from the truth, but he realized that down that road was the way back to damnation. He needed to focus on the truth. His life depended on it. "They found out a few things about me a while back and used them to get me to try and kill the King."

Octavius' eyebrows made a quick trip to his hairline. "You tried to assassinate the King?"

"I'm wanted for treason, Octavius. What did you think I'd done?"

"Sold state secrets. This is more predatory than I thought you were capable of. But Alexander's brother? You tried to get Catriona to kill Alexander's brother? I take it you didn't know about her and Alex?"

"No. To be fair though, I'd say very few knew about them. They were careful to keep their relationship very quiet. Regardless, when I offered your Captain the job through the underground, she refused to even meet with me. I wanted to go with someone else but my partners refused, insisting on *her* specifically. I told them she wouldn't do it. So they arranged to kidnap her son, then had me capture her and make the offer again, with this as leverage. My

160

partners were convinced she would do as they asked, but I never felt like it was all sewn up."

"Why did they want her specifically? Weren't there others out there willing to be creative in dealing out death?"

"Oh yes. People whose loyalty could be purchased. I was vastly more comfortable with using someone I could pay to be loyal than forcing a woman into service to save her child. I felt like I was being forced to rape her. But it turns out one of my partners had designs on Catriona's husband and was planning on poisoning her to get rid of her. That was why she needed to get her and not just anyone."

"Designs on that chum bucket? What waste of breath would want that man?"

Myrgen took in a breath. "My sister, Tanglwyst de Holloway."

"Embertwist's Beard. That's your sister?"

"I'm sorry to say. I was infatuated with the Queen, Tangl's best friend Elizabeth. It ended up being my downfall. They used that to manipulate me. Luckily, Charles survived the ordeal and came out better from it. It was a huge mess, sloppy and full of unnecessary risks to accomplish a simple task. Had it not been for the Captain, these people would have gotten their way."

"Well, love, even unrequited, is a powerful motivator. Glad to see the villains failed in their task."

"Well, failed to kill him. I think they still got what they wanted: Charles no longer King."

Octavius shook his head. "Were they just trying to put a pretender on the throne, or did they disagree with his foreign policy? I mean, regicide is a pretty big step."

Myrgen walked over to the railing overlooking the Main Deck. "Did you know the man?"

Octavius shook his head. "I know Alexander. Was he anything like his brother?"

"I suspect to an extent. The Captain was loyal to them both during all this. Personally, I don't know Alexander like you folks do, but I know a few things about him. I know he didn't want to be king. I know he is a healer and not a fighter. And I know he was following his mother's lead until the Saint Michael's Day Massacre two years ago, then after that, he didn't trust her to wipe his nose. With him on the throne, Catherine would have no power over Alexander, and that was enough for me."

"It still seems a bit extreme. As a kingdom official, you would know the unrest that could come from a change in power."

Myrgen nodded. "True, but they also told me Charles hit Elizabeth, and she bore a mark from the encounter."

Octavius looked down at the deck, nodding. "Violence against a woman you love. Now I comprehend."

"To tell you the truth, she later displayed some behavior that says she probably did that to herself." Myrgen looked out over the sea, leaning on the railing. "But I was in love with the woman, and that news, coupled with the nightmare I witnessed at the Massacre was all I needed."

Octavius frowned, shaking his head. "I'm sorry, Myrgen, but I'm finding that a bit hard to believe. You strike me as a very sensible, thinking sort of man, not someone ruled by passion."

Myrgen fought against the images of the Massacre in Patras of ten thousand people simply because they believed they could speak directly to Heaven. Such a frivolous difference in religion, yet it destroyed a nation's soul. "Trust me, Octavius. I can be passionate about people I love."

"But to this extreme? Kidnapping a woman's child to get her to murder someone? Why *that* man? Why was *he* the subject of your ire?"

Myrgen snapped, sorrow and anger blending in his voice. "*Because he was weak, Octavius!*" Myrgen fought back the tears, his fists gripped in frustration. "Do you know what the King of Mervolingia possesses that other kings do not?"

Octavius shook his head, straightening up and staying aware.

"The Church grants them the Power of Sovereignty. It is a ritual by which every citizen of Mervolingia who gives their fealty, even if it's just in their minds and hearts, can be controlled by the King. They don't even know it. Charles held the lives and wills of every person who swore their fealty. Every one of them. He held mine. He held my family's. He held those he had murdered that night. The Emilianites were cut down in the streets, some of them fleeing, screaming, begging for mercy, but no! *Every* Augustinian citizen turned against their friends, their neighbors... Their children..." Myrgen's fire dimmed from the pain of reliving that night. "He killed all those people with a single sentence because his mother wanted to get rid of his best friend, because Plantyn had 'too much influence over the King.' Charles held power over every life in Mervolingia, except his own, and someone who had absolutely no repercussions, no responsibility, no *oaths* to any of them was in control of *him*."

Octavius watched Myrgen spit his ire over the side of the ship and look away. "Who did you lose?"

Myrgen returned his attention to the First Mate. "What?"

"No one feels this rage out of empathy. You lost someone that night. Who?"

Myrgen stared at Octavius, surprised the man had forced this story from his lips. "My son." He closed his eyes against the vision of that night. "I lost my son that night. He was cut down while his own mother had to watch, fighting against the King's murder squad. Then, because she renounced her oath of fealty to the King in her attempts to protect him, they tried to kill her too. I didn't let them."

Octavius put a hand on Myrgen's shoulder. "I'm sorry."

Myrgen shook his head. "All this status I had, and I didn't want to ruin it by marrying below my station. All that got me was the memory of seeing my son in two pieces and a woman I had loved once screaming as the killers turned their attention on her. One of them set aside their sword to unbuckle his pants. I guess he was going to rape her. She grabbed his sword and ran him through. His partner knocked her to the ground and as he stood over her, I cut him down. Then I disposed of the bodies while she wept over our son. I catalogued him among the Augustinian dead so he received a burial instead of the mass pyre the Emilianites received. It was the last thing I was able to do for him. She killed herself after the burial."

"Were you working for the King at that time?"

"Yes. I had just started the year before. I had spent a year after I was appointed lingering around the palace just to catch a glimpse of Elizabeth, the queen. But after the massacre, Michael and I left under the pretense that we were going to negotiate some trade agreements for the kingdom. Eventually, Catherine was assigned to be Ambassador to the Papal City and I came back to Patras to stay."

"Was that when they started planning to assassinate Charles?"

"Yes. That's when the first murmurs of it happened. I actually inquired in the Underground about an assassin for hire and got in contact with a rogue named Duncan McVryce. Turns out Duncan knew my sister from before, when she was married to her first husband. He used it as an opportunity to get close to her. I looked into it a few more times, but the final consensus was that I would have to do it myself if it was going to get done right. That's when Tanglwyst talked to me about hiring your Captain."

"But you helped Charles escape, didn't you?"

Myrgen pursed his lips and rubbed his eyes before tapping his fingers on his upper lip. "Yes. Yes, I did."

"If you so despised the man, why did you do that?"

"I don't know, to be honest. When she asked me back in Rouen to take him and his family to their ship, I must say the thought crossed my mind to cut him down, to kill his woman and their child right there and make him drink their blood, choking on it before he died. But when I set foot on the ground from that horse, he turned to me and asked me to hold the baby for a moment while they got their items from the horses. I looked into that infant's eyes and I knew I could never do anything to hurt a child, even the child of my enemy. Charles was powerless before, but now, he no longer had the ability to hurt anyone else. I could see from the way he took care with both his child and his lady that he was a good man." He shook his head. "The truth is I'm not a murderer, Octavius. I've always delegated the bloody work. The only time I've personally taken a life was when that guard went for Fiora." He looked at his companion. "Like I said, I can be quite passionate when dealing with people I love."

"That's not necessarily a bad way to be, Myrgen."

"No, it isn't. And I think that's the sort of person your Captain is, as well. I respect her, more than I think I've ever respected someone before. The fact she could bring herself to save my vile neck after what I allowed to happen astonishes me."

"Have you talked to her about it?"

Myrgen scoffed. "Please. Speak to a woman about my feelings? Don't be foolish. The last time I did that, the woman went crazy after putting me in a cell."

Octavius cocked his head to the side a little. "And when she rescued you from the prison in the palace, was that when you started having feelings for the Captain?"

Myrgen arched an eyebrow at Octavius. "What makes you think I've got feelings for your Captain?"

Octavius arched an eyebrow back, punctuating it with a wry smile. "Don't you?"

Myrgen wondered how Octavius could know what happened below in his cabin, his brush with a fantasized moment. *Best to deny it and figure it out later.* "Well, no, of course not. I'm trying to be professional here, Octavius and if there *were* any inappropriate emotions involved, I'm sure they'll pass once the intense situation calms down."

"Professional, eh?" Octavius nodded towards the rail. "Then what was that over there? Splash over from 'an intense situation'?"

Myrgen looked over at the rail where he and Catriona had almost kissed and understood. Of course, Octavius had either seen or heard about that moment. Myrgen had actually forgotten about it during the conversation, but it had been bound to come up. He turned back to Octavius. "Ah yes. That. Well, no, it was just, it wasn't like it was *planned...* " He felt like he was trying to explain to a father what he was doing with the man's daughter. "Look, there was this whale, see..."

"Oh, a whale, eh? My mistake then, sir. Whales are known to have that effect. I damned near proposed to Thessius over a whale so, I understand completely. Happens all the time." The First Mate waved his hand dismissing the subject and smiled, not fooled at all. He walked back over to the wheel, resting his arms on it.

Myrgen blushed at Octavius' generosity at glossing over the near-kiss and shook it off with a few deep breaths of sea air. He looked at how Octavius was steering the ship and gestured to the "Is that difficult?"

"This part? No. The sea is calm but it is a bit tougher during a squall."

"May I try it?"

"No, I'm afraid not. The ship is extremely touchy about who touches such intimate items. So, if I may ask, what are your heavy thoughts? Something that doesn't involve the romantic purview of whales, I'm guessing?"

"No, not really." Myrgen smiled, feeling refreshed by this banter between them. "I was looking over the life I've led and the new chance I've been given. The last life ended very badly, so I don't want to muck this chance up by walking the same path I've been on."

"How exactly did the last one end?"

"The woman I loved betrayed me and set me up to be killed."

"Oh yes, that's right. Not the Captain, of course, what with you not actually having *unprofessional* feelings for her, of course, outside of the whole whale thing…"

Myrgen smiled and nodded with authority. "Quite right."

"Undoubtedly. You know, for someone who met Catriona under such… *dubious* circumstances, you're being rather forthcoming with all this. Why?"

"Because, Octavius, I've had my fill of lies and deceit. Being hours from death gives a man clarity, they say. They are right."

"So let me make sure I have the story right. You tried to hire the Captain to murder someone who actually turned out to be her friend, but she refused you. So then your *partners* kidnapped Alan in order to force her to do the job. You then, what? Let her go?"

"Yes, pretty much. She couldn't do the deed while we were holding on to her."

"Ok. So, she's released, but you're betting she isn't going to tell anyone about it because you have Alan. While you're waiting for her to do the deed, you got betrayed by the woman you loved?"

"No. Your Captain went to the King and figured out he was being poisoned. That meant someone else was working on him as well."

"Elizabeth."

"Um, well, actually, no. Charles' Mistress, Marie."

"Er, excuse me? The one he took with him?"

"Yes. Catriona and I discovered the Mistress was slipping him a special drug that would make him get ill and appear to die. Then, when he was put in the Royal crypts, she was going to fetch him and they would run away together, free of Catherine and the burden of the Crown, leaving a very capable King Alexander in charge. Unfortunately, Elizabeth was actually trying to poison him and the two drugs interfered with each other. He flew into murderous rages that came out of nowhere. He killed a servant right in front of Alexander."

"Was that when you got thrown in prison?"

"No, I got thrown into prison when Catriona told Charles she had been hired by me to kill him. Charles took that badly. But then Marie realized he was being poisoned by someone else, according to what she told me right before we rescued Charles. She staged the room to look like someone had stabbed him, administered the rest of the drug which would make him appear dead, and watched from the shadows until Alexander was alone with him. She explained what was going on and, in order to save Charles' life from whomever was poisoning him, he 'died' and Alex became king.

"I found out in my cell about the drug being administered to Charles, then Elizabeth showed up with a tray of food that was coated with poison. I figured out that she was going to get rid of all the people who helped her so there would be no witnesses to betray her. I dismissed her from my heart right then. It's one thing to pine away for someone out of your reach, but quite another to finally get your hands on them and they turn out to be insane."

Octavius nodded. "Very few people can actually handle having their wishes granted."

"Very true."

"So, after you were put in prison for trying to assassinate the king, you were almost poisoned and the Captain came and rescued you hours before your execution."

"My *well-deserved* execution."

"Well-deserved, indeed. And she knew this? The well-deserved part?"

"How could she not?"

"So, then…?"

Myrgen shrugged. "I have no idea. I figured I was dead for treason for conspiring against the King, but Catriona saved me."

"Do you know why?"

"I know what I was told. When I was arrested, Catriona's son was still my captive. I told a friend of hers where to find the boy, because I feared he would die before he was found otherwise. She apparently overheard this, somehow, through a solid stone wall a foot thick, and decided I was worth saving."

"Yeah, she does that. So she released you to save her son?"

"No, she already had her son by that point, interestingly enough. I sent Dominic after the boy because Elizabeth made it very clear she had no trouble murdering a child. She actually used the child's life as leverage against *me*. She said she would either personally slit his throat or make sure she watched him starve to death, eating the dog I gave him to survive. The woman was a monster and I cringe at the very thought that I ever had my mouth near such a poisonous person. To be honest, she was as much a reason for my current lifestyle choices as anything. If that's the sort of person I attract, I *really* need to change my ways."

Octavius looked squarely at Myrgen and mulled this over a bit. "Well, that answers a lot of my questions, but it also answers a few I hadn't thought of."

"Like what?" Myrgen was enjoying the conversation with this man, a little surprised to find him so articulate and perceptive. It seemed the more time people spent in Catriona's company, the more clearly they saw the world around them. Myrgen was also getting addicted to the feel of the sea beneath his feet, this intricate piece of wood bearing him forth on liquid destiny to his future.

"Well, it tells me you won't be a permanent member of the *Enigma*."

Myrgen was taken aback by that. "What makes you say that?"

"You don't owe the Cap'n a life debt."

"Interesting, but untrue. I'd be dead right now if she hadn't gotten me out of there."

"No, you said you instigated the release of her son. Your life debt was repaid before it ever was indebted. She rescued you because you rescued her son. You two are square."

"Well, your logic is flawed. She already had her son and she knew it. She didn't need to release me. She chose to save my life, not repay a debt. Just because I didn't know her son was safe doesn't change the fact that he was."

Octavius tilted his head and looked at Myrgen. "Myrgen, there isn't a single person on this ship that she *had* to save, yet she has saved every one of us. She has put her own life in danger, repeatedly. You saw it. She didn't *need* to heal those guards of Alexander's, but she did. Her sense of value is inherent in her, Myrgen. She sees people for what they truly are and she weighs their souls. She's a good judge of character. If she has let you on this ship, *this* ship, then you have some sort of value even you don't understand."

Myrgen looked at Octavius, then let his eyes wander around the ship. The night crew was exactly as plentiful as the day crew, busy men doing their jobs but still managing to keep an eye on him. They were sizing him up and he knew, at some point, there would be a reckoning. "Well, just because she sees it doesn't mean the rest of these fine gentlemen do. What happened earlier this evening wasn't her fault, Octavius. I got too close. That's all. Nothing happened. If any of these men need to talk to me about it, I'm willing to do so. Can you make sure they know that?"

"Oh, I'm quite certain, should they like a word with you, they'll let you know personally."

Myrgen thought about ending the conversation there, but the sheer amount of glares that were bouncing off him from every corner convinced him to stay within sight of the First Mate. At least he was being civil. "So, you mean to tell me there's no one on this ship who doesn't owe Catriona a life debt?"

"At present? No. Several have paid her back, but they tend to be incredibly loyal because she saved them in the first place, and it took them years to return the favor. They get a kind of mentality to them. If a crewman gets to the point where she owes *them* a life debt, it's usually their ticket to their own Captaincy. Every one of her ship captains has repaid their debts to her to the point where she has released them to their own ships, and every one of them started out on the *Enigma*."

"Why does she do that, do you know?"

"Well, like everyone on this ship, I have a theory about that. I think she can't fall in love with someone to whom she doesn't owe a life debt."

"Excuse me?" The contemplations of Catriona's love life were apparently the most theorized and discussed drama available on this ship, and Myrgen had landed himself right in the thick of it. It was like being in a romance novel.

"Well, think about it. If someone saves your life, you feel an obligation to them. If, on the other hand, you save someone's life, you have a power over them, and the ability to abuse that power, rather like your own encounter with a powerful woman. I believe our Captain is too honorable to keep a person around to whom she's indebted because of this crew. Having power over her is having power over us. She'd have to trust someone immensely not to think they would betray us all. That kind of trust generally is a property of an earned love."

"So she sends the people to whom she owes a debt to another ship?"

"Yes. By giving them their own ship, she is giving them a part of her life to govern. That satisfies the debt."

"And this keeps her from falling in love with them?"

"Having a person you have something that intimate with around can cause that trust to blossom into something more than just trust. Not to mention 'intense circumstances', as you know, tend to spark other emotions as well. I've actually done extensive studies on the subject, mainly because it happened to me and I wanted to know why."

Myrgen looked at Octavius with great respect. "Octavius, if I may say so, you are incredibly intelligent and seem to be well-educated. What are you doing aboard this ship?"

"Can you think of a better place to be?"

Myrgen smiled. "No, not really."

"Of course not. Actually, given your own education, I would think it terribly obvious, Master Myrgen. Catriona saved my life once." Octavius smiled and winked.

Myrgen pressed the matter with a look and Octavius continued. "I was a scholar at a private university in upper Latia. She worked a ship for Galadorn, the school. When she was visiting one year for the Midsummer Festival, I was beset by a pack of wolves in the forest around Galadorn. I thought the animals were rabid or something because they charged me without provocation.

She heard my shouts for help and ran to my aid. She managed to determine who the alpha male was and fought this wolf."

Octavius became animated, acting out the encounter with the wolf.

"It was incredible! She let the wolf leap onto her and she shoved her arm into the wolf's mouth crossways, grabbing its head and forcing her arm back against its jaw, like a bit on a horse. It kept trying to get free, and I could see the wolf was hurting because of the hold, so once he broke free, he backed off. Once this wolf was discouraged, he led the pack away. I was afraid she would die in her saving of my life from the bites of the wolf, but she had been wearing a silken shirt and doublet, so the wolf's teeth never broke skin. After that, I left my studies to sail with her, and will until I repay my debt."

"That could be a long time. Don't you worry your studies will suffer severely?"

"There are many ways to study, Myrgen. Books and lectures are only one facet of where one can learn." Octavius winked at Myrgen again, who smiled in understanding.

"Never were truer words spoken, my friend. The thing that amazes me is the amount of speculation that goes on here. Don't these people have better things to do?"

"Hey, not everyone can read, Myrgen. They watch the dramas around them to help them feel alive and involved. That's why gossip is such a popular pastime. And you have landed yourself right in the middle of quite a bit of it. I'd watch my step, if I were you."

"Already got that planned, Octavius. See you in the morning."

Myrgen went down the steps to his cabin. He noticed a light under Catriona's door and thought seriously about knocking to see if she was still awake, then thought better of it. She had told him good night. He decided to leave it at that. He entered his room and closed the door behind him. He undressed for the most part, retaining his breeches in case of a sudden squall or call for emergency. He had noticed the rest of the men did likewise, since it was expected for every hand to pitch in during an emergency, he was sure to prepare himself in a like manner. He poured himself another goblet of wine, draining the bottle, and sat down on the bed, thinking about his conversation with Octavius.

He found the concept of Catriona being the object of infatuations and romantic speculation with most of her crew to be a humorous one, although he could also see its viability. She was a beautiful, competent woman. Many men would be threatened by such a woman, but Myrgen felt the more intelligent of his sex would see the perfection in such a combination. He truly felt Catriona was the sort of woman who would never sell herself short when it came to keeping company with a man.

It pretty much said every man on this ship had proven themselves worthy of her assistance, at one time or another. That's a grand tribute to his gender in and of itself, he thought.

It did bother him a little when he thought about the possibility of his dismissal from her crew because of the lack of a life debt. Although it was possible Octavius was wrong, Myrgen somehow didn't feel this was so. Octavius had known Catriona a lot longer than Myrgen did. That meant he probably knew her more intimately, though not in a sexual, or even a romantic way. He wondered about that when Octavius had mentioned it, but hadn't really pursued that line of questioning. Now it sprang to his mind like a white hart from the forest.

He'd almost kissed her, in front of her crew. It wouldn't take long for that information to go through the ranks. Octavius had handled it well, but if any of the crewmen still harbored romantic feelings for her, it could cause trouble. Of course, nothing had happened on deck, so there was barely anything to witness, but if anyone had seen her come into his room, they might assume more had gone on than just talk. And Saints forbid anyone had heard what she had said about wanting to be *right* here. That almost became what everyone had been thinking. Alone, vulnerable, both of them needing that contact and talking about the previous encounter… He shook his head. *Yes, I'm not thinking right.*

He was glad she had asked him about the kiss in the catacombs. He had needed to sort through that impulse because it certainly seemed to be returning with alarming frequency. When she had said she wanted to be right here, he was ready to throw her onto the bed and claim her. He had never felt such barely-controllable passion. It was as if every experience up to now had been preparing him for this moment. The thought that Nicolai had fantasized about Tanglwyst when he had this incredible woman in his arms was inconceivable.

It was no wonder Alexander wanted her so badly. He could see why the man had spent his summers traveling the coastline. Myrgen had merely kissed her. He could barely imagine what he would be like if they ever became intimate. He hesitated to pursue that particular line of thought right now. He didn't need those kinds of images running through his head. Unfortunately, it seemed he couldn't stop them.

He had spent years studying the arts of lovemaking through books and anecdotes as a young man at university. He possessed a wealth of book learning on the art of love, but only fumbling experience. He pitied Fiora's experience with him in those days, but at least he had honored his responsibility to the boy and she had respected his status. She even allowed him back into her bed on occasion, though, again, he shuddered at the thought of what he had put her through. He must have been so boring.

Then a trip to Yndia changed the practicality of it, and he had brought that knowledge back to Mervolingia when he had gotten the position of Chancellor. The position came with power, and that was an intense aphrodisiac. He had sycophants throwing themselves at him, but he had always turned them down because he had fallen in love with Elizabeth. No other woman was as beautiful, as regal, as majestic as Elizabeth. Her beauty was complimented by her kindness to a scrawny accountant, new to his kingdom position. It was because of her that he took up archery and riding, to be close to her on the hunts. His body had been shaped and hardened by the activities, though he still felt soft around the middle. For him, nothing could have been finer than the days in the woods around the palace, listening to the sound of her laughter.

Then he had kissed her, and his world was suddenly expanded. They had spent a total of four nights in each other's arms and he had never been happier. He finally knew what all those troubadours were going on about. This was love, and love was amazing, although Myrgen realized, looking back on it, that Elizabeth had been quirky, even then. He remembered thinking some of her desires a bit odd, a bit frightening, Now that he knew the nightmare that was rattling around in her skull, he was even more put off by the thought.

He wondered if that was why he was responding to Catriona like this. Getting the taste of that woman out of his mind seemed essential to his next breath when he thought about it. Having Elizabeth under him made him nauseated now, but that wasn't enough reason to transfer those emotions, that *need,* onto Catriona. That wasn't what she deserved.

But is that really what I'm doing? He didn't think of Elizabeth and then quickly think of Catriona. He thought about Catriona. He had explored the incident for her, but now the kiss swelled to his mind again, wanting his personal, private attention. No one was around to walk in now. He leaned his arm and forehead against the wall, letting the memory wash over him.

He had handed Catriona the lantern he held, so as to free his hands to properly kiss her, for he knew in that instant he truly wanted to. He moved before he could talk himself out of the gesture. To him, it all seemed to go in slow motion. He had had accidental brushes of contact with her and saw the effects of those accidents. He knew her, knew her body, her spirit. He reached his already free hand up to her neck, sliding it gently into her hair at the base of her skull, his thumb brushing her jawbone on its way by. He was gratified when he felt the ripple of tingles chase his touch upon her skin. His now free hand had swept along her torso, wrapping around to spread his fingers firmly across the small of her back, gently pressing her to him so she could feel his entire body touch hers.

Her head was tilted up instinctively, responding unbidden to the feel of his fingers in her hair. Her eyes closed as she experienced the thrill of electric sensations which dominated her senses. Her lips were full and parted slightly, her breath captured, and he bent to kiss her. His mouth took in her breath, drinking in the essence of her very soul. He let his lips caress hers in an explosion of sweet passion. She had been so lost in the sensations he gave her that she had dropped the lantern, and he felt her body weep her luscious scent at the ending of the kiss.

He had held her a moment or two longer, reveling in the feeling of her body against his, the taste of her breath, the fire of her pheromones, and the luxury of her silky hair. Her eyes had threatened to capture him, and he had suddenly felt self-conscious of the strength of his impulses and let her go. He marveled now, as he'd marveled then, at how scrumptious was the flavor of a woman, and how addicting such a thing could be. It was grander than the finest food, more seductive than the softest satin, more intoxicating than the sweetest wine. He wanted to taste it again, to feel that moment lingering in his hands for that impossibly long instant when two humans seemed to join internally as well as externally.

He felt a twitch between his legs and he undid his pants, reaching in to stroke his hard member. The silken dream of Catriona returned to the spot behind his eyes and he closed them, begging for the vision to encompass him. He smelled her skin, so close, so rich. He grabbed the image of her on the bed in the Open Lotus and went there with her.

This time, he touched her, taking her soul in exchange for his in a kiss. She responded like it was all she ever wanted. He pulled her to him, hungry lips begging for his flesh. He pushed her back on the bed, throwing himself on top as his hands slipped under that luxurious and tantalizing silk robe. Her breasts were begging for his touch, his lips, and he bowed to their will. His mouth covered her nipples and she arched and moaned. He felt his climax rushing forward. When he got to the point in his mind where he penetrated her, he came hard, calling her name. For a moment, just a moment, he thought her heard her respond in kind.

He breathed heavily. The spot where his arm had been pressed against the wall wore an impression of the wood grain. He stepped back and buttoned his trousers again, finding his decorum. One thing was certain, he would finally be able to sleep. He looked at the towel hanging on the peg by the basin and thought about cleaning up the floor but he found his body too weary at the moment. The tension holding him upright was finally released. He wandered over to the bed and flopped face first into the mattress.

Down the hall, in her room, Catriona lay back on her bed and extracted her hand from beneath her own covers. Her skin was flushed and her own breathing was heavy. She had used her connection to the ship to go to Myrgen in his room and was shocked, at first, when he got up and leaned against the wall, unfettering his breeches. Her curiosity had gotten the better of her and she felt the intensity of the vision he was using as if she had been in the room with him, reading him. His explosive orgasm had brought her very close, but when he had called her name, she joined him.

She had no idea what was going on between them, but if this was the result, she was more than willing to let it happen.

Tanglwyst became aware of the pain in her head just slightly before she became aware of the pains in her wrists. Her hair was matted with drool to her cheek. Her right arm was numb from lying on her side. She rolled onto her stomach and pushed herself onto her knees to look around. She was in a tent of moderate size, alone. It was dark out which worried her. It meant Duncan wasn't around. He never would have left her like this long enough for her arm to go numb or her hair to mat.

Her saddlebags were in the corner of the tent, as were his. She worried for a moment that maybe he *had* come to get her and simply failed. She closed her eyes. That wasn't possible. He had that ability to disappear into thin air. He wouldn't be caught that far off guard unless... Then she remembered making him remove the thread he said tied them together, that made it so he could find her anywhere in the world. She opened her eyes. She was on her own, so far as she knew. That wasn't a bad thing at all. She'd never heard of a band of female bandits so she felt certain there would be at least one man somewhere. If that man got near enough to touch, she would be out of there by sunrise.

A sound outside the tent heralded the person looking in and she was pleased to see it was a man of considerable stature. He had long, dark hair and skin belying a Toledan heritage with dark, dark eyes. He broke into a broad smile at the sight of her. "Ah, you're awake! This is splendid. I was wondering when you would come around. There are men who are interested in your status. I am very much hoping, for your sake, you are someone of importance."

He stepped into the tent and she mentally beckoned him to get close enough to touch. She let a slight smile decorate her face and let her eyes get soft and sexy. She took a breath, letting the air fill her chest, heaving up her bosom. He noticed the activity and smiled, stroking his moustache. He also had one of those tiny beards so popular in Mervolingia and Toledo. On him, it actually was quite attractive. He stepped in and reached down to her bosom. His touch was all she cared about and she sent her love touch throughout him. He shivered and smiled.

"Mmm... the Toque de amor! I *love* those. It very much enhances the lovemaking experience."

Tanglwyst blinked. "What? You... know this...?"

"Of course, woman. I am from Toledo. *Every* woman has this ability there! That must mean you are part Toledan, my dear, unless, of course, you learned this from one of our women. I do not know of a woman in Toledo who would give it to a Mervolingian, and judging from your horrible accent, you must be from Patras itself."

Tanglwyst felt her heart sink. This was not going to be as easy as she thought.

"I am Tulio d'Or, most feared of all bandits in the Disputed Forest."

Tanglwyst arched an eyebrow. "Disputed? This is the King of Mervolingia's forest."

"Ah! See? That is where the dispute comes in. My family was granted this land centuries ago after a great war in York. However, the paperwork was lost in the subsequent skirmishes over the remaining land and I have only recently rediscovered the title given to my family by the King of York. So I am settling here and defending my property from invaders."

"You openly call yourself a bandit."

"Yes. It is far more romantic than 'squatter', don't you think?"

Tanglwyst laughed, despite the circumstances. Tulio's easy and ready smile brightened the tent. "Now, as a lady, you are my guest. You were thrashing around a bit when my Chirurgeon tried to examine your wound, so we had to restrain you. It was a head wound, too, so it was messy." He untied her with such ease that she felt embarrassed she hadn't gotten herself free. "There you are."

Tanglwyst rubbed her arms and wrists, then inspected the back of her head. There was a lump and an abrasion, not unexpected from a knock to the back of the head after falling off a horse. It could have been a lot worse.

"Tulio, there was a man with whom I was traveling. Did you see what happened to him?" She looked around. "I see his saddlebags here. Did he get brought here as well?"

"No, my little iris flower. When we found you, you were alone, although with a very protective horse."

Tanglwyst's eyes narrowed. "Alone?"

"Yes. My men saw two horses and expected to find you escorted when they saw you on the ground, but you were quite alone. It was only proper we take you in," he offered a bow. "For your own protection. The woods can be dangerous for a lone traveler."

"I see that."

Tulio stood, offering a hand to the lady. "Now, if you will be my guest for brunch, I would appreciate the company."

"Brunch? It's dark out."

"Ah, but you did not eat breakfast and so for you, we have held up mealtimes. It is brunch."

Tanglwyst smiled and took the offered hand. She glanced around the tent. Duncan's disappearance worried her. If he was caught by the *gendarme,* he might not be able to leave to fetch her for a while. She knew nothing of the limits of his shadow-leaping power but for her, the further he was away from her, the safer she felt. These people seemed amiable and if she needed to hide from the Mervolingian authorities, the camp of a bunch of Toledan bandits was probably the safest place to be.

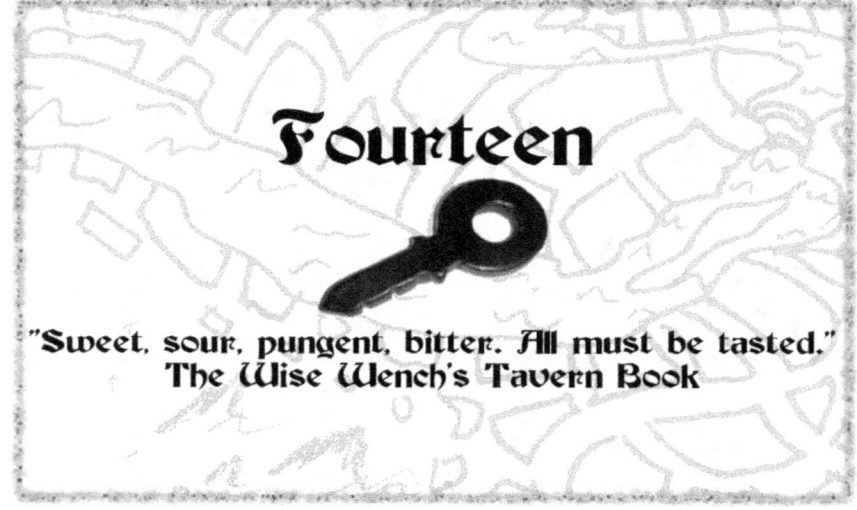

Fourteen

"Sweet, sour, pungent, bitter. All must be tasted."
The Wise Wench's Tavern Book

Morning bustled as the day crew relieved the graveyard crew. The decks were swabbed, and the cook brought the cauldron out onto the main deck to cook the porridge for the crew. The wind was crisp and sharp, the brine from a reef a mile off reaching the Enigma's senses. Myrgen awoke as he heard the wooden buckets hit the fo'c'sle above him. He woke with a furry mouth, a raging erection and a desperate need to urinate. Most of the crew relieved themselves over the side and Catriona always had the decorum to pay it no mind. Granted, she had a chamber pot in her quarters.

This line of thought diminished the erection readily and he slipped into a shirt and boots before he could handle it no longer. He went quickly to the poop deck and hung it over the side. The pressure relieved in his groin, he tucked himself away quickly as another crewman, Drathen Bain he recalled, stepped up. A nod from him belied a lack of knowledge of the near-kiss the night before and Myrgen hoped he actually missed that storm. He breathed deeply at the thought, and got a whiff of rum piss that the sailor produced that nearly gagged him.

Myrgen turned from the rail, covering his mouth and nose with the back of his sleeve. Catriona stepped on deck down below. The wind caught her hair, fluttering it splendidly away from her face and billowing the long coat she wore over her pants. Suddenly, the memories of his dreams the night before overcame him.

He had spent the night wandering in dreams, following her scent, chasing her eyes. She would flutter into shadow and when he pursued her, all he found were remnants and places where her voice echoed in the dark. Finally, he remembered reaching out in the dark and a light had flared right next to him. He had looked and she was there, wearing black Yndian silk with no form to it. With a wind as her tailor, it was pinned to her body. It hid nothing but her skin color, caressing her breasts and thighs, dancing around her neck to play in her hair. Her eyes had beckoned him and she reached out for him.

He had snapped awake with an erection on the verge of exploding. It had taken more than a few minutes to relax and get back to sleep. He had been expecting his pre-bedtime activity to relieve those dreams but it seemed they had merely found a delicious form to catch his attention. Now, here she was and the wind had brought his partial erection back to full alert. What was worse was the knowledge that she could look at him and know everything he had done in the night, and everything he was thinking right now.

He turned quickly away and walked out of sight, willing himself to relax. He was going to have to speak to her soon and he wanted to get his emotions and desires under control. He leaned on the railing and searched the horizon for land markings. They were due into St. Andrew soon and he hoped the distraction of picking out landmarks would ease the pressure against his pants. Drathen came over, a mop in his one hand and a bucket with a rope.

"Mornin' sir," he said with a nod and lowered the bucket over the side. Myrgen nodded back and watched the man draw up sea water for cleaning. Drathen nodded to Myrgen. "Might want to step back a bit."

Myrgen glanced around and did as asked. Drathen upended the bucket over his head with a sputter as Myrgen leapt back another step, still getting splashed.

"What the hell?" He looked up at Drathen, whose longish hair, beard and moustache dripped salt water onto his already soaked shirt and breeches. Drathen shook his head vigorously, casting water like a dog. "Sorry, but that was completely unexpected." Myrgen wiped the water from his shirt and breeches, and inspected the spots on his boots in disgust.

Drathen said, "Sorry sir. Had to be done."

"I thought you were going to clean the deck, not yourself."

"Clean myself? Sir, you ever seen a bucket o' sea water?"

Myrgen stopped wiping and looked at Drathen. "Er, no." He stood up straight. "Why did you douse yourself then?"

Drathen looked at Myrgen. "Because the Captain is a beautiful woman, and I've got things to do." He offered the empty bucket to Myrgen. He noticed a fleck of seaweed caught in Drathen's beard and waved off the gesture in disgust. Drathen shrugged and lowered the bucket to fill it for cleaning the deck. Myrgen turned toward the stairs and walked over to them, shaking his head. Catriona met him at the top of the stairs. The breeze sprang up again, and a lock of her hair fluttered across her face and neck for a moment. She shook it out of her face and smiled.

"Good morning, Myrgen."

Myrgen swallowed, blinked. "Excuse me a moment." He walked back over to Drathen who was just pulling the bucket onto the deck.

"May I?" He grabbed the bucket and dumped it on himself. The chill of the water was colder than he expected and did the trick. He handed the bucket back to Drathen, giving a quick bow of thanks. Myrgen wiped his hair and face with his sleeve as he returned to Catriona.

"Now, my lady," he said, as a drop fell from his chin to his drenched chest, "you were saying?"

"I'd like to get started on the logs today. I think you know the crew and cargo pretty well, as well as the shipping routes. Let's start making headway on interpreting my notes on the manifests. You also seem to think there's a better way to do the books. I'm ready to listen."

Myrgen nodded and went down the stairs. As he turned the corner at the foot of them, he could hear Catriona talking. "Octavius."

"Yes, Captain?"

"You're on deck again."

"Yes, Captain."

"You really don't sleep, do you Octavius?"

"Only at the helm, Captain."

"I see Myrgen has been initiated into the Morning Ritual."

"Bound to happen eventually, Captain. The man has eyes."

Myrgen took a moment and looked around. He noticed four other sailors soaked to the bone, and smiled. For the first time since coming on board, he was actually in on the joke.

He returned to his room and closed the door. He wiped the water from his face and head, finding a small squid, then sat on his bed, leaning his elbows on his knees. He tried to decide what to do. He couldn't avoid her all day, but at the mere sight of her, he felt his groin swelling. She had an unconscious ability to be incredibly sexy without even knowing she was doing it; Bending over the charts, going up and down stairs in front of him, standing in the wind, breathing. Couple that with the need to command all her attention and visions of her wearing only thin cloth and he was going to be a wreck.

How was he supposed to work in conditions like this? He was driven to distraction. If he had to spend the day in her quarters going over the books again, he would make a fool of himself. He needed to be scarce. He smelled his shirt and decided it could be worse. Then he realized it probably couldn't be *much* worse. Between the foul odor in his mouth and the gathering stink of his nocturnal secretions, he guessed he could only smell better in the bilges.

That was it! He would go clean the cargo hold. Last time he went down there to fetch a keg of rum for the cook, it was a bit messy. Apparently the movement of the ship could cause the cargo to shift out of place. He could mop it out as well. That would get rid of some of this tension. He stood up and grabbed a drink of wine from the bottle before heading out. It cut through the paste on his tongue quickly, dissolving the coating like acid eating through metal. He rubbed his teeth with his finger to get the slime off them, and remembered the squid was just in that water. He spat out the mental and actual taste of the water, grimaced and opened the door.

He heard Catriona's voice above him, talking to the helmsman and he waited for her to move off. When she did, he moved quickly to the cargo hold, grabbing an abandoned bucket and mop on his way. He looked around at the disheveled hold and was surprised to see it looked rather tidy for a sailing vessel. Of course, he thought, this ship is populated with men who, as Drathen put it, have things to do. It could be he wasn't the only one who had this idea.

He went about straightening the cargo first. He checked the lashings and tightened several which had come loose overnight. He moved the empty kegs of ale and rum to the back of the section, then realized there was no way to tell an empty keg from a full one that way. He looked around and saw a spare net hanging on a wall. From the looks of it, it didn't get much use and he soon discovered why. There was a large rip down the center of it. Perfect.

Myrgen ripped it the rest of the way, using his dagger on the stubborn knots. He looked around at the hold and found some tools in a crate. He found a keg of nails and set up a net suspended over the collection of full kegs. The idea worked, and he put the empty kegs in the net. This kept them off the hold floor and out of the way, but the net was strong enough to hold several casks more than what were currently empty. He hoped Catriona would like it.

Catriona. There she was again, in his thoughts. Was it even possible for him to be interested in a woman that *wasn't* involved with another man? He didn't seem capable of staying away from women currently involved with kings. He certainly did have expensive taste! Why was he setting himself up for this? As if one narrow brush with death wasn't enough for one lifetime, now he seemed to be daring Fate again. She was the Stâpâna of the only kingdom with an undefeated army and whose ruler was chosen through a trial to the death. Myrgen shook his head, and tightened another rope in a different area.

He couldn't deny his attraction for her, beyond simple appreciation of figure and form. He had the ability to find the beauty in every face and capture that on canvas, but he didn't have to uncover Catriona's beauty. He had it behind his eyes every time he closed them. He was worried that he was tempting Lucifer himself, or being tempted by him. He shook his head again and focused on not focusing on her.

Hours later, he had scrubbed every inch of the cargo hold. He was sweaty and sore, but relaxed. The extra energy was expended, and he just hoped no pirates or storms would attack them tonight because he might have used up some of his reserves as well.

Octavius came down the stairs. "Ah, here you are."

"Hi Octavius. Yes, I'm here. Did you need me?" He tossed a wet rag into the empty bucket at his feet.

"Not really. The Captain wanted to thank you for your efforts. She came by earlier and saw you working hard on some net thing. She wanted me to let you know that dinner was about ready, and she was hoping you would take time out of your busy day to have some." Octavius pointed at Myrgen's chest. "You might want to clean up for it."

Myrgen looked at himself. He had removed his shirt hours ago and was covered in sweat and grime. His pants looked like he had worn them while being dragged through a swamp by a horse and there was a rip in his right boot where the sole met the toe. "Thanks, Octavius." He grabbed his shirt and put it over his shoulder, too tired to put it on just to take it off again when he got to his quarters. The dimming sunlight was noonday strong to him after being in the hold for so long. He shielded his eyes as he emerged from the semi-darkness. The stew Ambrois was making smelled like a Coronation feast compared to the smell of the hold.

Myrgen walked to his quarters, stretching out his legs as he did so. He opened the door and almost stumbled over a half-barrel with two buckets of hot water next to it. Myrgen looked back on deck but no one seemed to own up to the effort, so he went inside and closed the door, dropping his shirt on the floor as he did so. He leaned on the desk to keep his balance and peeled off his all-but-ruined boots. They were wet from scrubbing, torn nigh in half, and he feared they would stink like rotted fish come tomorrow.

He looked around the room. There was a bar of soap on the desk chair and a small stack of towels on his bed. A bottle of white wine was in a pigeon hole in the desk. That made him smile as he remembered Catriona telling him that white wine tasted funny when you were at sea. The white wine, once opened, would absorb the smell of the sea, making it taste like it was made of seaweed instead of grapes, so the transport took extra care and effort. He drank a goblet of the wine quickly to ease his aching muscles, noting the slight briny taste in the last swallow.

He took off his breeches and picked up one of the buckets, testing the water. It was still hot, so he grabbed a pitcher he had on his desk to cool the water down. The cooler water took the edge off enough so it felt good and he reveled in how it refreshed his tired feet. He grabbed the bar of soap on the chair at the desk and got it wet. It wasn't palace quality, but it was good soap and did the trick. He scrubbed his face, arms, body, and hair, scraping the dirt from under his fingernails. He payed extra attention to his groin and backside. Once he was satisfied that he had done all he could, he dumped the other bucket over him. It had cooled down considerably and he felt revitalized when he was finished.

He stepped out of the tub and picked up one of the towels. It had a sweet, spicy scent to it and he held it up to his face. The towel smelled like Catriona and, judging from the intensity of the scent, the towels were sprayed with her perfume before they were stored in her footlocker in her cabin. He realized these must have been from her personal stash, which would mean that it was Catriona, and not the crew members, that set this up for him. He didn't know why, but he appreciated the gesture nonetheless.

He put his face in her towel and drank deep her scent. It was like she was in the room with him and he felt himself responding again. He decided to run with it and buried his face in the towel, letting the feel and smell of her encompass him. His thoughts wandered to the dream from the night before, the one with the silk, and he decided the next chance he got, he would give her that silk. Even if he never saw her like that in reality, he would like to do it for her. She deserved nice things.

He heard a small knock on his door and smelled the food on deck again. He pulled the towel away from his face again and sniffed it before he realized there was a draft in the room suddenly. He opened his eyes and looked in the doorway. Catriona was standing there, holding his shirt in one hand and a bottle of red wine in the other, looking at him. He glanced down and saw that his discarded shirt had stopped the door from closing completely but had failed to notice. He was frightfully aware of the fact that he was naked, dripping wet and sniffing a towel.

They stood across from each other in shocked silence. Catriona recovered first. "Do you have enough towels?"

Myrgen laughed and covered himself with a shake of the towel. "Yes. Sorry. I hoped you were Octavius."

"Would you prefer him? Because I can go get him." She had a smile on her face at Myrgen's blush betraying the truth his brave words denied.

"No," Myrgen said, shaking his head in mock concern. "I wouldn't want to lead him on."

She handed him his filthy shirt from the doorway and smiled warmly. "Are you okay?"

Myrgen glanced at the shirt a moment and took it before returning his gaze to hers. "Yes, I think so.

"I was concerned when you didn't show up to work on the books. Octavius said you were busy in the hold. Thank you for cleaning it. I didn't realize the filth was so pressing."

"It wasn't. I wouldn't want you to think your crew was slacking on the job. It's just that, well, after the last time we worked on the books…"

Catriona took a deep breath, eyes wandering around the ceiling of his chambers. "Would you meet me after you get something to eat?"

Myrgen glanced down at his scantily clad body and nodded quickly. "Of course." Catriona left. He heard her door open and close. He took another drink of wine, then dressed quickly. His boots were still wet, but he had found another pair in his footlocker yesterday and put them on.

There was another knock at the door, and Myrgen tucked in the shirt he had borrowed from Octavius at Catriona's behest as he moved to open it. It was Thessius. "May I 'ave a word with ye, Master Myrgen?"

"Certainly, Thessius. What is it?"

"Woul' ye mind comin' wit' me? I need ta get yar opinion on somethin'."

"Can it wait until morning? I have an appointment with the Captain."

"No, Ah'm afraid it really can't." He moved out the door and down the steps. Myrgen looked over at Catriona's door and sighed, following the crewman to the hold. There were a few lamps in the hold near the furthest bay. Thessius led Myrgen over to this area. They stepped into a ring of boxes and several men stepped in to close the gap they had just walked through.

Myrgen's hackles rose on the back of his neck as he realized he had just walked into a trap. On his guard and wishing for a sword, he turned to Thessius, eyes on the men at his side. "What's the meaning of this, Thessius?"

"Some o' us jus' want ta know what yar intentions are t'wards our Captain. Seems th' two o' ye were a might too cozy las' night. Some o' us want ta make sure ye ain't of questionable charactuh.'"

"Questionable character? What do you mean?"

"Well, someone sai' ye were in prison in Mervolingia for treason, but tha' th' Captain broke ye out. Then someone else said they overheard ye sayin' ye 'ad kidnapped th' Captain's little boy ta get 'er ta kill somebody. That true?"

Myrgen realized what had happened. It was a small ship, and he had engaged in a practice the nobility often fell prey, that of thinking the staff were invisible, dumb, deaf and blind. But these men were none of that, they were quite protective of this lady.

And they had him surrounded.

Fifteen

"The one who first resorts to violence shows that
he has no more arguments."
The Wise Wench's Tavern Book

Catriona got a knock on the door and answered it with a call. Octavius poked his head in the door and asked, "Do you need anything before I go on watch, Captain?" Catriona glanced up at Octavius, expecting Myrgen. She hid her disappointment when it wasn't him. She had been waiting for him for half an hour now, and with him being so close to ready when she had walked in on him, she found it hard to believe he was still primping. She looked at Octavius again, harder, and stood up. There was a light in the far part of the hold behind him. It was flickering. She scanned the ship for trouble.

Octavius saw the look of intensity on her face and turned suddenly along her line of sight. His first thought was that it was a fire, and he moved as if this were the case. Catriona's insight told her to grab her sword. She sprang from the stateroom without a second thought to her own health, sheathed sword in hand.

Octavius' calls of fire caught the attention of the men in the hold as he and several other crewmen accompanied Catriona down there. She paused as she approached, recognizing the situation for what it was: a brawl. She stepped up to the edge of the ring and gazed unbidden upon the spectacle.

Myrgen was bleeding, but he was looking in better shape than his opponent. Thessius was nursing a black eye and a split lip on the sidelines while the bosun's mate tended the bruised ribs of the bosun. Even the Quartermaster was shirtless, awaiting his turn at Myrgen. From the look of things, Myrgen had managed to take on five and was still fighting. Octavius and Ambrois ran to the edge of the ring of crates, shouting for the men to stop immediately.

The combatants turned to face Catriona. She stood straight, a pillar of authority. "Lawrence of Rouen, tell me something."

Lawrence, the bosun, nursing his ribs, turned to his captain and bowed his head before her. "Yes, Captain?"

"What's the wager up to?"

"Five to one odds he'll go down to Johannes the Navigator, Captain."

Catriona folded her arms across her chest, her gaze unwavering on Myrgen's eyes, reading him. His breathing was stabilizing and she could tell he was getting his second, or third, wind. She looked nowhere but at him, and Myrgen glanced about, unsure what to think of it. He was in pain from the other fights, but he was most frightened of her reaction. Myrgen realized when the trap had closed that the time had come to prove his right to be on this ship. Everyone here had something they owed to Catriona. It was only right to have him also earn his way on board. If she stopped the fight, it would be like being rescued from a bully by your mother.

Catriona nodded. "I'll take that bet, Lawrence. Put me in for crow's nest duty on the newcomer."

The crew, who had been silent to this point, erupted in calls and cheers. Myrgen blocked the blow that came in for his head as he turned from his patron, confident that, win or lose, her support of him had enabled him to live through this encounter.

"Put him there gently, please. Octavius, head to your post. Ambrois, please bring me a pan of hot water, some cloths and the poultice pouch from the crew stores." Octavius and Ambrois helped Myrgen to his bed and departed, leaving him alone in his cabin with Catriona. His shirt and skin were bloody, and numerous bruises peppered his body. He ached all over. He opened his good eye and looked at her.

"You owe me crow's nest duty, Myrgen."

"Put it on my roster." His knuckles had fight bites on them and his left cheek was swelling up nicely.

"Actually, I'll just make you sit it with me."

Myrgen smiled and winced from the effort, causing his lip to bleed a tiny bit. "Ugh. I was expecting the final fighter to be the Quartermaster. Who'd have known 'Johannes' would be some little guy from Saint Michael?"

"He's wiry. That's why he wins. People always underestimate him." She took some cool water from his earlier basin bath and started cleaning up his wounds. The wash water ran red as chum very quickly, but by the time the hot water showed up, Myrgen's injuries were at least assessable. She kept him sitting up to check his balance and faculties, saying he could lay down when she was sure he would get up again. She poured some water into a goblet and soaked the poultice to reconstitute it. She watched his eyes carefully to make sure he did not have a concussion. Then she checked for fractured bones. He was fine, aside from the bruises from his initiation. The men knew what they were doing.

She picked the poultice out of the water and opened the fabric surrounding the innards. The water had created a paste which she rubbed in her hand until it was mixed, though not smooth. Using a gentle touch, she placed the poultices precisely on the open wounds on his knuckles.

"These will numb the area during the first six hours, during which it will help the healing process along. Your injuries are mostly superficial, so that will be plenty of time for you to do most of your recovery before the pain is no longer treated by the poultices. When that happens, then you drink the tea I'll bring over."

"When does the numbing happ... oh, now then. Okay. I'm definitely feeling the numbness."

Catriona smiled, in spite of herself. She often found herself smiling around Myrgen. "Sit forward. I want to have a look at your old wound."

Myrgen leaned forward, hissing out his teeth, and Catriona inspected the wound at his beltline. It was almost completely healed, a feat which impressed Catriona quite a bit. He had no old bruises from his interrogation in Patras, just the new ones, and quite a few of those. His entire left side was already one interconnected bruise. "Amazing..."

"Excuse me?"

"Oh," she said, letting him sit upright again. "It's healed. Completely. It's remarkable." She looked at his swollen eye. "How do you do it?"

"It's a matter of concentration, for the most part. I'm not sure how successful I'd be right now."

"Would you try? I'd like to observe the technique."

Myrgen thought about it. "It might actually help me sleep, not being in quite so much pain. Sure." He shifted slowly on the bed to face her and put his hands out in front of him, resting on his lap. The knuckles were swollen and bruised, with a couple cuts from his opponents' teeth. "First, I focus on the place I can afford to take energy away from, and then move that to the injured area. I imagine healing measures being taken, and them working quicker than normal. Watch." He closed his eyes, drawing energy from his legs and feet to feed the healing flow. His sitting position held his legs in place, but they relaxed as he took the energy and brought it up through his thighs to the wounds on his hands.

He tried to call forth the maggots and stitches, but they seemed so weak and not what he needed. He shifted the energy around looking for what he needed and almost gave up when Catriona's hand touched his, inspecting the wounds. He thought about her hands administering the poultices, mixing them with the oils and covering them with bandages. He felt the numbing agents stop the pain and the hearth herbs knit the skin, relieving the swelling with her cool touch. He heard her gasp and opened his eyes, worried.

"What?"

"The wounds, I saw them. They started to pale, the redness started to leave, but then it came back. I thought maybe there was something wrong. Then, when I touched them, I felt it all just repair itself beneath my fingers. It was amazing." She looked at him, the gold flecks dancing in her eyes with excitement, catching the barest of candlelight. "What were you envisioning?"

"You, putting the poultices on." He looked at his hands and they were fully healed, as well as a bruise on his left forearm where he blocked a blow.

"Can you teach me?"

"I'll try. It took me several months to learn it, but I had never had any experience with healing myself or others before either. I take it from your earlier comments that your healing touch is different from this?"

"In Caratia, I am known as the Stâpâna, the Protector. It is my duty to stand before those under my protection and take on their wounds or defend them against attackers. One of the duties I have is to relieve their pain, and that gifts me with healing."

"So it isn't Nubian?"

"No. Why did you think it was Nubian?"

Myrgen gestured to her. "Your skin is dark, like you're half-Nubian. Michael thought you had a Nubian parent."

"Oh. No, I don't think so. I'm not sure though. I don't remember my parents. Drake and Anika adopted me, so they are my family now. But the healing is a gift of the Land."

"But you can't heal yourself?"

"I can a little, but my primary function is to the people. I couldn't have healed you if you hadn't said what you said to Nicolai in the prison. Of course, I couldn't have freed you from that prison cell if you hadn't said it either."

He glanced down at his smooth hands. "I meant every word." He smiled and his lips split more, causing him to wince. "Damn…"

"Here. Let me. I can't practice healing myself without something to practice upon." She closed her eyes and Myrgen felt the bruises flow out of him like they were being pulled through his skin. It hurt, but he gritted his teeth. If the crew were to find out she was healing him after the fight, they might decide to simply pitch him overboard and save her the trouble.

As the swelling in his eye went away, he looked at her. The sight of her face becoming brutalized as he healed nauseated him and he pulled back, severing the link. The cuts and bruises on his arms were gone and he could see fine out of both eyes, but his chest and back still hurt like hell and his right arm felt fractured. He heard her exhale and her breathing became labored from the pain. She started to go limp, and he reached out to catch her, trepidation seizing his heart. "Catriona... can you hear me?"

She groaned and nodded, her body tense and throbbing. "By Calista, they really beat the living hell out of you, didn't they? I think your arm is broken..."

"I thought I heard it snap during one of the fights. In the pause between them as they switched out, I was able to heal it so it was a light wound before getting hit again. That little practice kept me in the fight." He watched her, unsure what to do. He doubted she could return the wounds once they were taken, so he settled his mind and focused on helping her heal herself. "Now, concentrate on the places that *don't* feel like they're on fire. Your legs maybe or your feet."

She furrowed her brow and nodded, closing her good eye.

"Now, do whatever it is you do when you draw energy from around you, only picture it from within instead of from outside."

She winced again, trying to concentrate. He worried that the pain was too much to fight right then. He put his hand on her cheek beneath the swollen eye and watched it for improvement. He felt energy from his healthy body seeping from him and going into her, yet he didn't feel like he was being drained any more than a candle's light diminishes because more than one person is using it to see. He decided to help her heal a bit by offering himself to her. *Perhaps, once we get the injuries on her down to a smaller size, we can see about her doing it on her own.*

He closed his eyes, and let the energy from his arm flow to his hand and into her, helping.

There, it met Catriona's and the two mingled. Her energy was strong and he wasn't sure how to help. So, he did what he usually did on himself and directed it to the wounds he wanted to heal, namely the bruises on her face. Again he imagined the poultices and this time, he mixed them first with her perfumed oil from her cabin. His nostrils filled with the Oriental scent as he smoothed away the swelling with a touch, the poultice coating his fingers and her face. He spread the mixture on her eye, envisioning the swelling melting away like it was excess clay on a sculpture.

His fingers trailed down her shoulder to her injured arm from the guard fight. He could see the injured area as an interruption in the light and again, he smoothed it away, the torn muscles knitting together and flowing with rich, healing blood again. The mixture soaked into her chest, to her heart and began surging through her body, healing every pain and pulled muscle. His energy had never gone so far, done so much on his own body. He felt more alive than he ever knew he could. He could feel the flow of her spirit, like a river, and he followed it. She was a dancing candle flame, scented and vibrant, warm and inviting. He reached out to touch it.

He met an extraordinary thing, colorful but strong and impenetrable. It seemed to be stained glass. He could see his reflection in the glass and his injuries were gone as well, smoothed away as if they never happened. Strange. He looked around and found he was looking at an old cathedral, with stained glass windows at chest level so people could watch the services. He could see someone inside, moving. *What was an Augustinian church doing in the mind of a Land Worshipper?* She had just stated she was the Stâpâna of Caratia, a servant of the Land. This place didn't belong here. The feel of the glass under his fingers was strong, stronger than any glass he'd ever touched. It was more like steel. This place was a fortress. He searched the nearby twilight, trying to figure out what she would need protection from in her own mind.

He felt a presence behind him and turned to see her standing there. She was soft and perfect again, her hair flowing in a wind from nowhere that smelled of incense and candle wax. She took his hand and started to walk away but he stopped her. Instead, he drew her to him, her body clad in silk and moonlight and took her in his arms. He touched her hair and drank in her eyes, their lips so close, he was breathing in her spirit. Light poured out from between them, encompassing them both.

Suddenly, he felt her body go slack and he opened his eyes. He was back in the cabin on the ship and she was falling forward, her eyes closed. He caught her and laid her on the bed beside him, checking for damage. The swelling on her face was gone completely, and he could see no other bruises he had just sustained and she had just acquired. Her hair was splayed out around her and her breathing was normal and soft. She was as beautiful as the dream he had just been in. "Catriona?"

Her eyes opened and she looked around. "What happened?"

"You went slack and started falling." He turned her face and checked her eyes to make sure they were clear. "Is there any pain?"

She sat up and felt her body. "No." She felt her eye, surprised. "I'm fine." Her eyes glittered with excitement as she touched every place that had been suffering. "Myrgen, *I'm fine.* I've never healed like that before!"

She reached over and touched him, pulling aside his shirt to see his skin. "You're healed completely too?"

"Complete...ly..." He swallowed the rest of his statement. Her proximity was overwhelming, and he started having trouble keeping his breathing steady. Between the healing dream and the previous night's occurrence, he felt his will was being tested and he was far too close to deciding to let it break. He tilted his head, kicking himself for what he was about to do. "Catriona..."

She looked at him and stopped, waiting for him to continue. Then she blinked, slowly, and he saw her realize the same thing he had. They were alone, no crew, no king, nothing between them but the distance of a breath. Her eyes fell to her hand on his chest and his heart beat faster beneath her touch. He raised her hand from his chest to his lips and her eyes followed, lingering a moment before she let them meet his again.

"Th...ank you for... healing me, Captain," he swallowed his hesitancy, forcing himself to continue without stuttering, "but seeing as I was just beaten nearly in half by your crew for my lack of decorum while under the effects of a *whale*, I suspect us being unchaperoned right now could get me thrown overboard."

She smiled, a sly, semi-defiant look entering the game. "Are you not a good swimmer?"

He returned the smile. "Not my strongest skill." He could not take his eyes off her, but he also knew he could not do anything more. Part of him wanted to tell her how he felt, but the rest of him couldn't figure out what he would say. He stood and drew her to her feet, regaining his composure a bit. "Are you hurt anywhere?"

She glanced at herself and shook her head. "No, I'm fine."

"Are you sure? I won't receive a lesser punishment if Octavius discovers a bruise on your upper thigh or something."

She tilted her head and arched an eyebrow. "Do you feel the need to check that area?"

He looked at her, eyes narrowing at the challenge. "I might be a little too thorough in my investigations." He released her hand slowly, with great effort.

"I've experienced the results of your investigations first hand, Myrgen. If I recall correctly," she stepped over to the door and looked back at him, "I dropped my lantern. We pull into St. Andrew tomorrow. Try to stay on board until then, if you please." She let her lingering shadow of a smile be the last thing he saw.

Sixteen

"Be grateful when your mother doesn't settle your
fights or your debts."
The Wise Wench's Tavern Book

The next day dawned and Myrgen had barely slept all night.
Thoughts of Catriona overwhelmed him as he thought out and re-
thought out the night before. The dream he fell into was peculiar
and familiar all at once, and he wondered what it meant. The
church still baffled him. He started to wonder if he was the one
who insinuated it into the scene. After all, the presence of an
Augustinian church in the mind of a Land Worshipper was more
foreign than the presence of a mouse in the King's Crown during
his Coronation. He also lingered on her touch on his chest and the
endless visions of unrealized scenarios where they ended up in bed
together or at least in the embrace of a life-altering kiss. As it
stood, her parting comment indicated she had spent some time
thinking about the kiss they had already shared.

In the end, though, he knew he had done the right thing. Catriona had lost her husband and Alexander blundered his chances with her by moving too soon. Myrgen recognized that she might feel very differently about any encounters with him once they were ashore. His relationship with her was too precious, too necessary at this point to jeopardize on something as fleeting as infatuation. Right now, she was his only employment, this ship was his only shelter and these clothes, sadly, were his only clothes.

Myrgen looked at the near rags he had hanging on the pegs on the wall. He had stopped wearing the robe after Xannu washed it and kept it folded in the sea chest at the foot of his bed. He still wore his shirt and pants from that day though. Each sported various blood stains from Alexander's interrogation, rips from the guards dragging him to the holding cells in the dungeon, blue dots from the reagent in the poison he ate, and a few things he couldn't actually identify now. Maybe mildew?

He got out of bed and looked at the assessment he wrote the night before while he had been unable to sleep. He had decided to actually get his wits about him and try to think of his future. He thought seriously about writing a letter to Catriona, or composing a poem, but he knew something like that would invariably fall into the wrong hands. The last thing he needed after all the lessons of yesterday was for a pathetic troubadour endeavor to be read to the crew as dinner entertainment. He also thought about sending a letter to his family requesting money, but he realized that as they were also Tanglwyst's family, they were likely under investigation by the Guard as well. He couldn't even send a letter to Michael because he didn't know where to send it.

So, instead, he had spent the night assessing his situation. The condition of Myrgen's clothes were indicative of the condition of his life: once grand but now in shambles, recognizable only because of the shape of the outline. Catriona was more than generous to offer him employment, even though it would not be on this fine ship he had grown to love.

Myrgen put his boots on and combed his hair. His bath yesterday had been partially eroded from the vigorous fighting afterward. He had washed the blood from his face and hands before he went to bed, and as he looked in the shaving mirror, he realized there were no signs of the brawl in the hold left on his person. Although he definitely *looked* like he hadn't slept all night, he felt fine and was probably going to be able to pass on the bucket bath thanks to the cleaning Catriona had done before she healed him.

He had come to appreciate the Morning Ritual but discovered it added far more in stray creatures than it took away. He thought about starting a collection of the things he had found in his hair and clothes after the bucket was empty, but the beginnings of the list in his mind were enough to stop that impulse. Some things were better left forgotten.

Myrgen decided to ask Octavius when they would be pulling into port. Catriona was right: Octavius was *always* on deck, awake. Myrgen had traveled with the *Enigma* for ten days now and had never gone on deck and not been able to find Octavius. He was as certain as the mast or sails. All he could figure was that the man did nothing but sleep whenever they were in port. Myrgen set the letter back on the desk. He took his shirt from the peg and put it on. It was also irreparably stained from seaweed and sweat. His cuffs were almost black from the deck work he had taken on to help earn his keep and pay off Michael's gambling debts. The time in the hold was still with him as well. He felt tattooed.

Myrgen opened the door, tucking in his shirt. The Captain's door to the chart room was open but he didn't see her inside. She was likewise probably on deck and he felt both excitement and dread at the possibility of seeing her. Anyone who looked at him at this point would know his admiration of her, but he hoped he could pull past that and stay standing. She was admired by her entire crew. Myrgen was truly one of them now.

He stepped on deck and several crewmen cheered him, taking him by surprise. He had apparently made something of an impression with the trials last night. He smiled and acknowledged the cheers with a nod to the men. Octavius was on deck and he turned and greeted Myrgen with nod. "Myrgen."

"Octavius."

"You made quite the impression last night. Only the Quartermaster has ever stood up against Lawrence *and* Johannes in a single night. And that was for actual money in port."

"You actually bet for money?"

"Only when we'll win."

Myrgen smiled and went to take care of pressing morning business, then looked around for Catriona. He saw no sign of her and thought she might still be asleep. Just because he couldn't sleep all night didn't mean she suffered a similar fate. He went back up to Octavius, who was looking him over.

"So, this is the result of that technique you mentioned before, after she healed the guards?"

"You remembered."

"Well, there was some concern that the Captain might try to heal you. I'll tell you now, had she left your cabin sporting the black eye and swollen lip you had when we brought you in there, you would have been suffering through a second round in the hold."

"I will admit she helped heal me, but I usually can take care of my own problems. I learned how to heal my own wounds in Yantap several years ago. Last night, I was pretty beat up though and she was able to supplement my efforts. The effect was a bit more impressive than either of us expected."

"I can see that." Octavius turned his gaze back to the sea. "She has many skills that keep us all intact. Were it not for her leadership, this ship wouldn't sail, I can assure you."

"She is truly an amazing woman."

Myrgen's heart spoke the truth and Octavius blinked at the emotion accidentally displayed within the statement. "Yes, amazing, and worthy of the admiration she has garnered, from all sources. I merely hope she makes the right choice with her future, for all our sakes."

Myrgen pursed his lips and nodded, peering out over the sea towards the land. "She will. The fate of every man on this ship is her primary focus. She thinks of them before she thinks of herself. It is the greatest quality of a leader."

"Yes," Octavius said, watching Myrgen closely, "a good leader is essential to any group. I also appreciate your role in this, Myrgen."

Myrgen looked at Octavius, brow furrowed. "My role?"

"Yes. She has needed someone there for her, someone who would not push himself into the void left by her husband's death. You have been mindful to make sure she did not fall prey to a widow's sorrows."

"You thinking of anyone in particular with that statement? Grymalkin perhaps?"

Octavius winced, his mouth sour with the taste of his judgment. "As much as I like the man, the way he was acting in Rouen was pretty inappropriate. It was like he was celebrating or something."

"I saw that too. I remember at the time it left a very foul taste in my mouth, but I hardly felt close enough to her to say anything. How long have they known each other?"

"Longer than we have. She met him the day her son was born. I understand he saved both their lives."

"Saint's blood. How could someone compete with something like that?"

Octavius looked at Myrgen, a smile commenting on the conversation. "I wouldn't worry about it. You're doing fine, from what I can see."

Myrgen took a deep breath. "It's been that obvious?"

Octavius nodded. "On both sides."

Myrgen cocked his head. "What do you mean, on both sides?"

"Let's just say you don't look as good as she does after not sleeping all night."

He gestured with his chin towards the galley. Catriona was coming out with a steaming mug and a log book in her hand. The book was open and she sipped at the mug but miscalculated the ship's movement and ended up spilling a bit. She swore like a sailor, the first time Myrgen had ever heard her do so. He looked at Octavius. The First Mate clucked his tongue. "Although I must say, your vocabulary is better."

She looked over at the men and nodded. "Myrgen, I have some things to talk about with you. Follow me." She took off for her room and Myrgen nodded to Octavius before following. When they got to her quarters, she set the mug down on the table by her bed and went over to the desk. Myrgen watched this illogical progression with fascination founded in sleep deprivation and waited. She picked up some papers and handed them to him.

"Here are the manifests for the trade we'll be conducting in St. Andrew. I'm going to leave you in charge of getting the wares purchased and catalogued. Theiron will oversee the food and drink supplies." She looked at him. "You look awful."

"And somehow, you don't. I need to discover your secret."

She blushed and looked down at the manifests. "Um, these items here are in high demand at our next stop, so let's make sure we secure as many of them as possible. And although we're low on these, don't get them here. We're going to be at the source in a month. We'll get them there for half the price. Just get enough to get us through 'til then." She looked at him, the blush finally faded. "Any questions?"

"One. Do you ever see a church when you go into your healing trance?"

Seventeen

"If you see in your wine the reflection of a person
not in your range of vision, don't drink it."
The Wise Wench's Tavern Book

Gwen pulled into St. Andrew that morning. She dismounted, grateful to finally be off the animal. She was never really one for horses, having very limited contact with them at home. The horses around the sheep farm had been for pulling wagons or plows and were unfit for travel for one person. The riding horse Michael had graciously provided was beautiful to look at, to be sure, but she would choose a hay wagon over a saddle any day.

She took the animal to the closest inn with a stable, the Black Cat and Anchor, boarded it, and then walked into town. The *Enigma* would be in port for a tenday. If her timing was right, Gwen figured she and the ship would arrive on the same day. The trip to Patras was two days through the woods, four by the main roads. Her inherent Fae sense kept her from ever getting lost or attacked in woodlands unless she was foolish enough to provoke an attack. Otherwise, she was safe in those natural surroundings, far safer than a woman traveling alone on the main roads.

She reached into her riding cloak and made sure the pouch carrying the message from Michael was still closed tightly. It also carried the weak tea she had made from the poultice Alexander had left behind and a special potion she had brought along for her own protection. The latter formula caused a sap to leak from the pores of the skin if the person got excited or scared. Such a strange reaction would often scare off attackers. She had used it before in her travels with Catriona.

She saw the ship pulling into the harbor and smiled. She was right on time. She went into the Harbormaster's office and handed him the message with strict instructions to give them only to Myrgen. She was still too nervous about being seen in the company of a traitor and she couldn't risk Catriona laying eyes on her. The Fae had been sent on task days ago and had undoubtedly worked their charm by now. If Catriona looked at her, she'd know Gwen had been meddling. Best to wait until she got the chance to be with Alexander before coming forward.

She ducked out of the Harbormaster's barely in time to avoid being seen. Luckily, the man had not recognized her and she was dressed like a man traveling, her braided hair bound under a scarf and hat for the journey. He hadn't even looked at her face. She hid in the shadows of the nearby building and watched. Catriona was not the only one with some knowledge of the human animal and she hoped she would be able to tell if the Fae had helped or not.

Catriona and Myrgen came off the ship as the rest of the crew prepped the ship for mooring and shore leave. The first leg of the season was always a little shaky. Crewmen who spent the winter on land needed to regain their sea legs and St. Andrew was the perfect distance from Rouen to accomplish that. By the time the ship pulled into this port, the men were getting the hang of being at sea and were likewise reminded of how nasty hardtack tasted.

Gwen watched her captain and was pleased to see her stride marking a confident and sorrow-free step. Her spell had worked! Now she just needed to get Alexander near Catriona for a while and the situation would be complete.

Catriona looked over her shoulder at Myrgen and handed him a leather pouch of papers. Gwen recognized it as the docking manifests and frowned a little. Was she turning the docking duties over to the *traitor*? That was odd. Michael had said Catriona had taken Myrgen in. She and Dom had the impression that Catriona had decided to rescue the man, but to hand over duties to him like he was going to be permanent? Gwen moved to a slightly better vantage point and watched the two as they approached trying to listen to their conversation. She could hear only snatches of tones, not actual words, but before they parted company, Catriona touched Myrgen's wrist and said something that made him smile and nod. Gwen dodged into the shadows and ran down the alleyway. She came out behind the warehouse she had been near and watched carefully as Catriona walked past the narrow area between the buildings.

Obviously the Fae had worked their charm, but the presence of Myrgen had muddied the waters. She couldn't allow her Mistress to fall in love with a traitor to the very crown she was going to wear. But how to fix it? If she went to Catriona, she'd keelhaul Gwen for her meddling. If she went to Myrgen, she might tip him off that Catriona was attracted to him and make things worse. Men were notoriously stupid when it came to such things. Myrgen might not even know she was having feelings towards him.

The only solution was to go to Alexander, but she needed to make sure Catriona was safe from Myrgen first. The Captain always went to St. Andrew's Net, the local tavern, after arriving in town. Gwen could easily work a little magic and secure Catriona's heart against usurpers there. The place was usually a bit dark, especially after being outside in the daylight, and there were tons of places to hide. She took off down the back street to make sure she got there first.

She slipped into the place from the rear door and snuck into the main room, keeping to the shadows. She had two things she could do to stop things from going badly at this stage. She looked around the tavern with her Fae sight and found a couple brownies, as she had expected. She knew the tavern owner gave them food and drink daily and had always felt the presence of the helpful spirits. A bit of summoning brought one of them to her and she spoke to them quietly in the spirit speech.

Friends, I need you to take this and ready yourself when the lady ship captain enters the hall. She held out the two vials she had in her pouch. *If I give you the request, put this in her drink.*

She felt the protests they gave. Such bad hospitality would hurt the owner of the tavern's business.

I assure you, this is harmless. It will only remind her of the one she loves. Will you not do this, for Love?

The two brownies indicated that no they would not, that she shouldn't meddle in such things.

Will you do it for a biscuit? She reached into her pouch again and brought out the last of the food she had brought from her stores for the trip. The two brownies sniffed the offering and took the biscuits. She watched them trot over to the barkeep's area with their hidden parcels. Should the need arise, she would have them dose the drink Catriona ordered, but only should the need arise. Catriona was smart enough to know not to get herself into a relationship with a surrogate like Myrgen, but just in case...

Gwen crouched down in the back and waited.

Catriona walked away from Myrgen, letting herself relax a bit. She ran her fingers through her hair, wishing St. Andrew had a bath house that wasn't contained in a brothel. She always felt pampered after being at Xannu's and a couple days at sea made her waves frizz while her roots became oily. She paid attention to it and kept it from matting into solid tubes of hair, though many of the sailors with long hair tended to just let theirs mat. Some even used the long locks to decorate them, braiding the hair to help the process. She could see the benefit of it, but had never found the idea of running her fingers through that to be appealing.

She shook off the image of Myrgen's hair as it tried to invade her mind. She had touched it and found it to be very appealing, yet she felt this was an inappropriate road to walk, even within her mind. It was the reason she was leaving him to handle the details on his own. She needed her thoughts clear of him right now. The last few days had confused her.

She had expected them to be like the other times she had left Alexander's presence: Populated with young girl fantasies about joining him in his life, his world, his bed, especially after their time at the cabin on the cliffs. To lie in bed with him as Fae servants tidied the house and repaired their clothing would be worth anything she had. Complete bliss for the price of a bowl of milk per day.

Instead, Alexander had not crossed her mind unless associated with a negative thought, or was mentioned by someone else. Their time in Rouen had even been spoiled, but that was by Alexander more than anything. His advances had driven her away instead of drawing her to them. It disturbed her to have her heart be so fickle.

His touch had been so grateful, so loving in Patras. Seeing him, touching him was a blessing from Heaven and she realized that was what made it so strange. She did not worship Heaven and did not hold a place there. Her fate lay in the soil and stones of the Land. And when she thought of the Land, the man in her mind was not Alexander. The man from her visions was so familiar, and yet, so unknown. She did not understand how he could be both. One dream-memory had her stroking his hair as he died and another had him stroking hers as she passed back to the earth. It was not possible to do both.

Time at sea was supposed to clear her mind and it had, but it cleared it only to put Myrgen in the empty places. Octavius was right. She needed to make sure she wasn't just filling a void and using Myrgen to protect herself from Alexander's future. She knew she couldn't be his queen. She had escaped him and his proposal and she certainly didn't need another man to shield her from Alexander's advances. He had done a good enough job of that on his own.

She had *flirted* with Myrgen, blatantly *flirted*. How she had gotten away with that on this ship was beyond her. Octavius was beyond all knowing on the *Enigma* and she knew why. More than that, she had, well, she dared not confront what she had witnessed through the ship's senses. It was best not to go down that road again. She felt better keeping things in the daylight. In daylight, she was smart. In daylight, Myrgen was proving productive and she felt herself in control, for the most part.

Nighttime was different. Her dreams ignited her in Myrgen's arms. She found it difficult to look at him without wanting to test those dreams' hold in reality. She knew it was undoubtedly driven by the unexpected kiss in the catacombs under the palace. His continued presence on the ship gave her no rest either. Had he not shown restraint after the healing, had he touched her, or moved toward her in any fashion, she would have kissed him, possibly causing his death at the hands of one hundred fifty men. Although that would have been bad, she felt what she did instead was far worse.

She meandered a bit through the market, her arms folded to keep track of her pouch in the crowds. Some of the stalls were closing up shop and she saw a clothing merchant packing the last of his wares away. Myrgen was sadly devoid of clothing right now, not that he needed it. The image of him shirtless, leaning against the bulkhead flashed across her eyes and she blinked it away.

Ale. She needed ale. Something to dull the mind, to make it less nimble, less capable of saying yes, less capable of saying no.

She stepped into her favorite tavern in this town, St. Andrew's Net, and looked around, pleased. The place was half full with a few dark corners with no one around. She would have some quiet and some ale to evaluate her mind. The barkeep recognized her with a nod and she requested her drink and a quiet place to drink it. He poured and gave her a clean table near the back. Despite the intense daylight outside, it was dark and cool inside and she took a draft on her ale, relishing the darkness it relieved in her soul. The place had always had a very homey feel to it, which was why it was her favorite haunt and she had suspected for years that the place had Fae in it. Sometimes, she thought she could sense them nearby, but she had never actually gotten a glimpse of the fantastic creatures.

The first draught of her ale was as welcome as a breeze in the sails. It helped her focus, her attention following the amber drink into her body and soul. This definitely had a Fae's touch, reminding her of Gwen's cooking. She would heartily disapprove of Catriona's behavior during this tenday, no matter which part she inspected. Gwen had spent all winter pining for Alexander on Catriona's behalf. She would be appalled at her mistress's dismissal of her true love.

Gwen couldn't understand. Myrgen had healed Catriona, and not just the bruises and superficial cuts of the brawl. The scar on her leg from an old fight, one which Alexander never saw to treat, was gone. A cramp in her back from the ride from Patras was gone. Even a small burn from the fire in Rouen was gone.

The mending didn't stop at her physical body. Her broken heart from Nicolai was also healed. He no longer was a spot of pain and guilt, but was merely a wonderful man, who endured a terrible loss. Her part in that was unfortunate but it was no longer relevant. She could have held that pain in her heart for decades, but now, she felt released. She forgave Tanglwyst for plotting her death because she was actually in love with Nicolai and did not want him to waste more time unhappy.

Granted, her less savory nature had been fostered by the poisoned wine Elizabeth had given her, but her intentions originally were less murderous. She wanted Nicolai happy. In the end, so did Catriona. With Elizabeth gone, Tanglwyst's head would clear and she would be remorseful, but even if she wasn't, she would be no longer Catriona's problem.

And Alexander. The change there was dramatic. Before, in Rouen, she had been offended by his advances so close to the horrible deed of disposing of Nicolai's body. He had tried to seduce her while her hair still stank of human burnt remains. Even his ability with words could not wipe away that mistake. Had she slept with him that night, before washing, she would have never spoken to him again. Myrgen had helped there as well, even before the healing.

She remembered seeing the church and walking up to it, seeing someone else there. It had been Myrgen, and she had been both surprised and very happy he was there. She had taken his hand and was about to take him to the front, to introduce him to the spirit, Father Benjamin, the priest of Giovanni's who gave his life to help her and her infant son escape. No one had ever been here, although she had told a few people about it: Gwen, Octavius,

Drake, Anika, Alan. No one else, but she was going to take him inside, and make him a part of her soul.

But he had stopped her. Instead he had touched her, brought her close. She had wanted so much to kiss him, to couple with him, unleashing the raging passion she had held in trust for him since Patras. His kiss under the palace had changed her life. Never before had she let someone kiss her in public like she had Alexander on the ship or at the Inn. Even there, with the man she expected to marry eventually, it was not his touch she wanted, but Myrgen's.

When she awakened from the healing, when she touched him, when she realized they could be in an embrace before even Octavius could have gotten to them, it had taken all her will to keep from pulling him to her. She felt the ship around her and knew, without a doubt, if they had done what they clearly wanted, the entire crew would have crashed through the door. Or at least Octavius and the Quartermaster Theiron, probably bristling with weaponry.

It had been quite difficult not to lock that door and tell the ship to keep quiet before leaping on Myrgen, and when she got back to her cabin, she had felt the ship approve of her willpower. She watched him through the ship's senses, saw him pace and drink a bit and put his thoughts on paper. When he got into bed, she did as well, her thoughts being that at last she could sleep.

But sleep was not what he had done, and it was not what she had joined him in doing. Images of him touching her, kissing her, had dominated her dreams and thoughts for long enough and she had used the sensation of him pleasuring himself to drive her own pleasure. When he had called her name, she had joined him in climax.

In the aftermath, she had been unable to sleep, shame at invading such a private moment encompassing her like she were an Augustinian nun. She had never violated her crew's trust, keeping the activities on the ship running in the back of her mind like a water wheel. Only if something foreign invaded or something went wrong would she have probed. But this? This was inexcusable. Worse, she was afraid it would not be the last and only time. She had spent the night busying herself with paperwork and study.

Early in the morning, as the sun was breaking through the hills to port, she had gone for something to eat. She ended up cleaning the entire galley, which was actually kind of dirty after sitting all season when one got on the floor and looked at the baseboards.

It was well after that, while fixing her tea, before she thought of Alexander and only because she overheard, through the ship, Myrgen mention him to Octavius. It startled her and she felt guilty for not thinking of him sooner. Guilt was an emotion that was all too familiar to her, and she was suspicious of it. She knew she couldn't marry Alexander, even before she became a widow. To feel guilty about him when she had just been healed of the emotion irritated her, and she wanted to figure out why. Was she truly so flawed, she clung to guilt like a piece of wreckage in a storm? What would it take for her to set aside this emotion in favor of another?

She closed her eyes and savored the taste of the homemade ale, sensing the presence of something on her periphery.

"If you ever find yourself needing a drink," said a soft, male voice beside her, "you shouldn't have one."

The voice startled Catriona and she almost dropped her ale, catching it before it spilled its contents all over the table. The action did manage to slop some ale onto her lap though.

"By Calista!" She frowned, disgusted at her sudden lack of dexterity. A hand offered her a cloth to clean up and she reached out to take it, glancing up at the man offering it. She did a double take as it registered who he was.

"Alistair?"

"Hello, Catriona." He took her hand and pulled her to her feet, smooth as silk. She smiled into his eyes. "I saw you come in."

"So you followed me?" She arched an eyebrow, her smile taking the edge off her suspicious tone.

Alistair Hapsburg leaned down and hovered near her hand, his eyes still on hers. "I could never resist the view."

He kissed her hand as her smile grew bolder. His honey gold hair shimmered even in this dim light and was so well-behaved, he never felt the need to bind it out of his way. Sea foam green eyes masqueraded as blue in the shadowy atmosphere and his lips were soft as a whisper and strong as an accusation. She had forgotten how much he excited her. It was as if the past several years had never happened.

So much for getting a chance for clear thought. They must smell blood in the water. And I am far too much of a mind to let one of these circling sharks actually feed.

She gestured to the table with a nod. "Would you like to sit?"

"Not really," he said, straightening up to his full height again, but not yet releasing her hand.

"Oh? What would you like to do then?"

He reached up a hand to touch her cheek. "I'd like very much to get you out of those wet things." Then he pulled her to him and kissed her, preventing her from realizing Myrgen had entered the tavern.

Eighteen

"To meet an old friend in a distant country is like
the delight of rain after a long drought."
The Wise Wench's Tavern Book

Myrgen stood transfixed, his heart thumping in his chest. The Harbormaster needed a couple of signatures on the docking papers and Myrgen had brought them to Catriona as instructed. Octavius told him where to find her, but Myrgen had not expected to find her like this. The man kissing Catriona seemed quite comfortable doing so. Myrgen tried to understand what he was seeing. His kiss was too intense to be a relative, but Myrgen had been under the impression that Catriona had no lovers because, until a tenday ago, she had been married.

What was more, the man looked somewhat familiar. Long, golden hair belying a Glarren background was coupled with an almost Yndian flair to his clothing. He wore a coat similar to the ones Catriona favored, but with a large, midnight blue silk sash wrapping his waist instead of a belt. The boots and breeches were

Mervol in design and his gloves were decidedly Mandian. This was the garb of a traveler, but Myrgen had not seen him in the Mervol courts or visiting the palace. Why did he feel he knew this man?

Suddenly, Myrgen realized where he knew him and he moved quickly to interfere. He put his hand on the man's arm, pulling him off her. "That's enough of that, my friend."

Alistair looked at Myrgen's hand on his arm, then to Myrgen. Recognition lit his features as well. "Myrgen the Grey. How unfortunate that we should cross paths again."

"What do you think you're doing here, Alistair?"

"I'm contemplating exactly how little time it would take me to kill you for assuming you can interrupt my conversation."

Myrgen set the paper on the table to free his other hand, eyes not leaving Alistair's. "Is that so? Once again, you've bitten off more than you can chew. This woman isn't some useless creature you can just toss aside. Captain, are you all right?"

Alistair cocked his head, maintaining his eye contact competition with Myrgen. "Captain? So, he's one of yours then, my Dear? That explains the dog-like loyalty."

A few heartbeats passed in silence, then both men realized Catriona had not said anything. They both turned to look at her.

She was watching them, arms folded across her chest. Her smile was gone from her lips, but it was still in her eyes.

"You two finished?"

She picked up the papers Myrgen had brought and strutted them over to the bar, leaving the two men to sort things out between them. Myrgen let go of Alistair's arm and backed up a step to a more gentlemanly distance. Alistair smoothed his sleeve and picked up the tankard of Catriona's ale. He glanced at her as she mounted a stool and began looking at the papers Myrgen had brought.

Alistair took a drink from Catriona's tankard and then looked at Myrgen. "So, you're one of her crew?"

"You could say that. More of an employee of the business than a crew member." Myrgen looked Alistair up and down, lips pursed. "You?"

"Her fiancé, and I haven't seen her in a while. So you can imagine how annoyed I am with you right now."

Myrgen scoffed, folding his arms. "I see. Well, good luck with that." He walked away from the dreamer to Catriona's side. He turned around, leaning backwards on the bar and looking over at Alistair. Alistair leaned on the wall by the table, watching Myrgen talk to his Captain. "That fool just told me he was your fiancé."

Catriona didn't look up from the papers she was inspecting. "He is." She signed something.

Myrgen's neck popped from the speed of his head whipping around to look at her. "What? Ow…" He rubbed his neck.

She moved a paper to the back of the stack and repeated herself. "He is."

Myrgen looked back over at the man and Alistair raised Catriona's tankard in salute. His grin was incredibly smooth and punchable. Myrgen looked back at Catriona. "You're off the ship half an hour and you've gotten engaged? What about all that talk about Alexander and not wanting to marry him because it's too soon?"

Catriona looked at Myrgen. "No, I don't want to marry Alexander because, as Queen, I'll never be able to go to sea. I'll be trapped in Patras. Alistair there is a ship captain as well. That wouldn't be a problem."

Myrgen looked at her, unable to form another question, though he knew he had a couple thousand. For some reason, the words kept on eluding him.

"Is this guy bothering you, Ma'am?" Alistair had come up beside Myrgen so silently, Myrgen would have jumped out of his skin had he not been so stunned by Catriona's comment. He turned to look at Alistair, the numbness in his brain showing in his eyes.

"No, Alistair. He's fine." She nodded to the barkeep. "May we have two more ales, Logan?" The barkeep pulled the tankards full and she put the signed papers back in their leather sheaf and returned them to Myrgen. "Grab your ale and join us Myrgen." She took one of the tankards and returned to the table. Myrgen picked up the other tankard, his hand shifting the papers to a safer position, then walked off the shock on the way to the table.

"All right. Explain." He had to know this story, especially since it didn't fit with everything else he already knew of Catriona. He sat down and leaned forward over the tankard. Alistair put his arm on the table next to Catriona's and leaned forward on it, taking Myrgen into his confidence.

"I met this fine lady about six years ago. She came into a rather seedy port in Yndia, unescorted and fresh off the boat."

Myrgen looked at Alistair. "Yantap port?"

Alistair sat up, then smiled. "Yes. You know it?"

"I was a guest of the Rhamidhal Shalib for two years." He looked at Catriona. "Xannu." Catriona just smiled and nodded.

Alistair rubbed an ugly spot from his tankard. "The Rhamidhal was the owner of the Incense House, wasn't he?"

"Yes. He wished to learn our language. So I taught him and his family in exchange for room, board and a little spending money. He was very generous."

Catriona slapped the table. "The *book*." Myrgen and Alistair looked at her as she pointed to her Chancellor, eyes narrowing. "You said in Rouen you had a book with lots of illustrations. You drew them, didn't you? I thought you meant you had bought one from a publisher."

"Not all the great books have been published, Catriona." Myrgen winked at her and she arched her eyebrow and leaned back, folding her arms.

Alistair eyed Myrgen, smiling despite their earlier exchange. "I remember hearing the Rhamidhal had a silver swan teaching him. I thought he meant something entirely different."

"A silver swan?" Myrgen wasn't sure he needed to be insulted or not.

Catriona leaned in. "It means a noble from the Saintlands. 'Silver' for white, 'Swan' for one of high and noble breeding." She picked up her fresh tankard of ale. "It means he thought very highly of you." She drank as Alistair continued.

"Well, some less than savory characters stumbled upon this lady trying to find a place to stay that would cost no money. As you know, Yantap is warm year 'round and many homeless people sleep in the streets, but they are often molested by ruffians. This time was no different…"

Alistair Hapsburg stepped from the Incense House, a parting kiss to his evening companion, Yishih. He walked towards the docks, going over the itinerary for the next day's travel, when he heard the screams of a woman. He ran to the alleyway from where the screams were ringing and saw five brutes carrying a woman dressed in a torn chemise into a warehouse. Alistair knew this place and slipped around to the front, picking the lock with practiced skill. The screams stopped suddenly as he heard a smack of the back of one of their hands against her face. He slipped inside, the darkness coating him easily and he made his way over to the group.

The woman was on the floor, looking up at her attackers, blood dripping from the corner of her mouth. The thugs were circling her like sharks and she was glaring at each of them, her dark hair barely covering an exposed shoulder. One of them crouched by her and she didn't give him the chance to speak. She lashed out and kicked him in the genitals. The others laughed as their companion fell back, screaming. Alistair leaned against the wall, not certain this woman actually needed his help. Still, he was going to stick around. Just in case.

She spit on one of them, glaring at them, daring them to come too close, but they weren't intimidated by this thin, disheveled thing. The woman looked around for an escape, but the other brutes decided to stop that before it got any ground. One of them stepped on her chemise just as she was going to bolt, and it tore, exposing a thigh. This summoned grunts of pleasure from his fellows and then they were upon her. They pinned her and the one she had kicked said, *"Hold her. She's mine."*

He wrenched the belt open on his pants, then stopped, a knife at his throat. A dark whisper haunted the room from behind him. *"What do you think you're doing to my woman?"* The men holding the woman looked up, the grins fading from their crooked mouths. The man behind their friend was clothed entirely in black, a scarf across his face, hiding his features. He wore a foreign hat, wide *brimmed and spouting straight feathers from one side of the base. The brim hid his eyes in shadow, yet they glinted in the light reflected from the knife that was now sipping a thin line of blood from the throat of their companion.*

The men on the ground released the woman, raising their hands and standing slowly. "We're sorry, Sparrow. We didn't know she was yours."

"Black Sparrow, if you please."

The men nodded, feeble apologies mumbled at the floor. His eyes never wavered from them and once his friends were at the door, Black Sparrow released his quarry and watched the lot of them scurry away. Once they were gone, Black Sparrow took a knee beside the lady. He took off his hat and pulled down his scarf so she could see his face. "Are you hurt?"

The woman reached up to her right cheek, then shook her head, eyes fixed on her rescuer. She peered at him, eyes intense green, discernible even in the gloom of the warehouse. Her eyes narrowed and he worried that her ordeal would make her mute as he had seen happen before. It would be a pity since she is so beautiful, and the way she took on her attackers! Such fire! Would that she would allow him to explore that fire in a more appropriate and gentle setting. He would never dishonor her or any woman by taking her against her will, and he needed to figure out a way to make sure she understood this. He hoped she knew his language. She was foreign and he was hoping to hear her story.

He was thinking of what to say when she reached out her hand to him. He took it and helped her to stand. They found themselves face to face, close enough to kiss. Her hair was tousled, her clothes ripped, and she had dirt and blood on her face, but she still somehow managed to be very beautiful. Sparrow touched her bruised cheek, the swelling still slight but threatening.

"We need to take care of this or it will leave a big bruise. Did they hurt you anywhere else?" He stepped back and looked her over. She glanced down at her rags and covered herself, self-conscious and shivering a bit.

"No, I'm fine. Thank you... for helping me..." Her accent was Latian, with a hint of something else, something indefinable. She

pushed her hair behind her ear. "Are you really interested in my story?"

He blinked, startled by being presented with the thought that had just crossed his mind. "What makes you say that?"

"You were thinking that, just now. You are an honorable man and have no interest in what those men wanted, although you are impressed with my appearance and spirit. You know this port, and it knows you. You also know this way of life. You told those men I was your woman to protect me while I'm here, but you might be willing to take me with you. If I'm worth your time."

He stepped back a bit, looking at her, then stepped in closer. "How do you know that?"

"I saw it. I saw it on your face and your heart. Just now."

"You can do that? Just see things on people's hearts?"

"Yes."

"Have you always been able to do this?"

"No. It just recently started." She shivered again.

Sparrow took off his cloak and put it over her bare arms and ripped chemise. She was so lovely, and fascinating. She clearly had a gift, and he knew she must have recently acquired it. Such witchcraft that could expose the wrongdoings of people in power would have had her executed long ago. She would have learned to hide this gift if she wanted to live, but she seemed too naive to know that right now. That put her in even more danger. "Can you control it?"

"Not always. It comes if I'm scared or hurt."

"Do you have some place to stay?"

She looked around the warehouse. "No, I just got off the ship today. I don't yet know where I want to go. I just needed to escape someone."

He offered his arm to her and said, "I have a place, if you don't mind. I'll expect nothing you aren't willing to give, and you'll be safe. It will be scandalous being seen with me, but if you're willing to do so, I'll be honored to be your host. By the way, I'm Alistair Hapsburg, but you may call me Sparrow."

The lady favored him with a smile at the gentlemanly gesture and nodded, her eyes revealing that she found this man handsome and charming. "I'm Catriona. Pleased to meet you, Alistair." She took his arm and let herself be led from the dark.

Nineteen

"Transgressions should never be forgiven a third time."
The Wise Wench's Tavern Book

"And that's how we met. Before long, the entire town was under the impression that we were engaged because I never went anywhere without her."

Myrgen blinked. "Excuse me, but *you're* Black Sparrow?"

Alistair looked at Catriona. "Well, not so much these days. I turned the name over to my protégé. After a while, I retired. Would have retired married had this lady ever allowed me to." He kissed her hand and she shook her head.

"I was already married, Alistair. I couldn't marry you."

"So you said. Ah, such is the life of a hopeless romantic."

"I thought you found a Glarren woman who would have you?"

"Ah yes, but she was too close. It turned out she was a cousin and I'm not that interested in copying the royalty. Besides, how could she possibly hold a candle to you?"

Myrgen smiled, understanding the game now. Alistair advanced, Catriona parried. He was no more likely to win her than one of her crew members and he knew it as much as she did.

"She can't," Myrgen spoke into his tankard, looking at her over the rim. He swallowed and set the tankard down. "No one can, not even Catriona. Her legend outshines even her."

Catriona smiled at Myrgen, her growing fondness making a rare, but brief, public appearance. "Well, maybe I need to do something about that, my fine gentlemen." She reached out and touched their hands. "Take me upstairs and make me prove my worth."

Alistair grinned, while Myrgen just winked at her. Advance. His turn to parry.

"I don't know you well enough to assess your value, my lady," Myrgen smiled politely, "but as your sworn Chancellor, it would be unseemly to take you up on your offer." He stood up. "Besides, three is a crowd."

He nodded a goodbye and left the tavern.

Catriona watched him as he walked away, then turned her attention to Alistair.

"Well, what about you?"

Alistair searched her eyes for some deception. He found none. "Are you sure about this?"

She took his head and kissed him. "Yes, Alistair. I'm sure."

Moments later, they were in his room upstairs, stripping off their clothes. Alistair pushed Catriona against the wall, pinning her with his kisses. Years of unresolved passion overwhelmed them as they devoured each other, and the fire in their eyes was the only light in the room, save the moonlight cast from a cloudless sky through the open curtains. Alistair pulled her breast free from her clothing, his mouth covering it greedily. Catriona tossed her head back and bumped it against the wall with a thud. Alistair checked her quickly as she rubbed the back of her head.

"I'm fine," she said, anticipating his questions, "No, I don't want to stop." She kissed him again.

"That is still an amazing trick. I thought you couldn't read me." He kissed her neck, ripping a moan of pleasure from her throat.

"Shut up and kiss me." He obliged her while taking off his doublet and shirt as she fought her bodice free. Another bout of kisses and they were out of their clothes. Alistair grabbed Catriona's leg and raised it, giving him access to her privates. She was eager and thrusting her body against his, searching for the same thing he wanted to give. Her head bumped against the wall again, and Alistair picked her up and carried her over to the bed.

"That should put an end to that." He climbed on top of her, kissing her as she back crawled further onto the bed. Alistair put his hand on the pillow next to her head and then suddenly stopped kissing her, staring at the pillow. Catriona looked at her potential lover, then noticed the dark smudge on his chest, black in the moonlight. He knelt back, looking at his hand which was bloody. He looked at his crotch which was not bloody, and neither was hers, but he saw that her arm and chest had a wound that was bleeding freely.

"Calista's Fury, Catriona, you're bleeding."

Catriona looked down at her chest wound from the healing of Alexander's guards and sat up, covering it to stem the flow. Then she realized her arm was also bleeding from the wound from the other guard. She looked up at Alistair who was scrambling off her and grabbing his shirt. He handed her the cloth and wrapped her arm in the sleeve while she tended to the chest wound. She looked at the stomach wound, also bleeding, and her cool demeanor left her.

"Alistair, what's happening?"

He tore his shirt into strips, saying, "I'm not sure, my love. But let's get you back to your ship before you're too weak to walk."

It took only minutes to get dressed but even that small amount of time left her dripping blood in a pool at her feet. Her clothes and bandages were not enough to absorb it all. Alistair refused to leave her alone and run to the ship for supplies. "Then, get me there quickly, Alistair. I need to see Myrgen…"

Myrgen. She could be dying, and the person on her mind was Myrgen. This fact was not lost on Alistair as he rushed to the door. She could see it in his eyes as she slipped out the door at a near run.

Gwen slipped into the stable and walked over to her horse. He was fed, groomed, and rested. Good. From what she had just seen, it was possible she wasn't going to be able to wait. *What a mess.*

First, she had seen her uncle Alistair just before Catriona did. His behavior was, well, more than she could tolerate. Alistair was almost as unacceptable a choice as Myrgen. He had stolen her brother James from the farm and took him on some crazy adventure, insisting he needed a "protégé." Since Alistair was a lazy, brother-stealing, sister-ignoring ne'er-do-well, the last thing she wanted was for Catriona to fall for him. Gwen had nodded to the brownie, who slipped the weak tea into the tankard as Catriona stood and got kissed by Alistair.

Gwen was almost thankful when Myrgen showed up. He interfered just fine with Alistair's machinations. The only trouble was when Alistair started drinking Catriona's ale! Gwen had no idea what would happen if a man took the infusion. She hoped the worst that would happen would be that Alistair would get sick or think highly of Alexander when he met him. She watched him closely to make sure he wasn't poisoned. When it appeared that he wasn't going to choke and die, she turned her attention to Catriona's new tankard.

She watched carefully for a chance to signal the other brownie. When she saw it, she jumped. Catriona handed the papers she had signed back to Myrgen as the barkeep pulled another two ales. Luckily, Catriona grabbed the right one. Gwen felt certain she would have taken it as a sign this wasn't meant to be. Regardless, Gwen now saw that she had to get Alexander to St. Andrew and back on that ship before it set sail. It was too dangerous to leave St. Andrew so she decided to do it through Fae magic.

She patted the horse, then went over and stood in the walkway between the stalls. This spell was one that would bring Grymalkin to her. Her choice to do it in the stables meant he would know to use all haste and to come overland. She closed her eyes and concentrated on the King and the road through the woods. If she told them to, she might be able to give Alexander safe passage through the woods as well. She felt the spell gather strength from her surroundings. Then she opened her eyes and pointed to Patras, Alexander clear in her mind.

She felt the spirit rush along the ether, covering ground like only the wind or thought could. She guided the spirit to the Palace gardens and up to Alexander's window. He was still there and she pushed into the room through the glass to implant the message in his mind. Suddenly, she hit a barrier and then she hit the back wall of the stable. She tried to focus, but only had enough time to realize she had just hit a protection spell of a magnitude she had never encountered before. Then the second wave of the protection spell hit and her world went black.

Noise surrounded her, loud and sharp; the smell of fire and blood overwhelmed her nostrils. She pried open her eyes and saw a smoke-blackened sky choked with ashes above her. She blinked and tried to focus past the throbbing in her head. Her body ached as if one of the horses, or all of them, had stepped on her at various times in the past couple days. She rolled over onto her stomach and was able to raise to her knees before she realized she was kneeling in something wet. She reached down and touched the substance.

It was blood.

She looked around her then. Two great armies were fighting a quarter mile away and on one side, raised above the fighting men and women on a platform of stone to the east was Catriona. She was wearing armor that looked like it was made of dragon scales and wielding a sword of such terrible power, Gwen couldn't look at it. As Catriona swung her sword, spikes of earth and lava erupted beneath the charging foes. She looked to the other end of the battlefield and saw a man standing on a ridge, hailing fire from the sky at his command, ruining Catriona's forces. The smoke from both sources clouded the air so Gwen couldn't see who her opponent was. Then a wind rose from the north and rushed across the war, clearing the air momentarily.

Through the swirling tendrils of smoke and shadow, Gwen saw Catriona's foe was Alexander.

Myrgen leaned on the railing looking out over the bay. The sounds of the port town were cheerful and echoed around the empty ship. He was settling his mind, trying to wrap it around what he had learned in the tavern. *Catriona knew Black Sparrow, the man who had attacked Tanglwyst's ships two years ago. More than that, she was close to him, and if Sparrow was as intelligent as he seemed, he was bedding her at this moment.*

The thought of Alistair doing what he wanted to do, what he could not, infuriated him.

Was it because Catriona had refused Alexander because it was too soon after her husband's death? Of course, that was exacerbated by the fact that Alexander had practically tried to propose while she was still cleaning Nicolai's blood out from under her fingernails. His bad timing and eagerness made it seem like he had planned the whole thing. For all Myrgen knew, that was true. Alexander had been the one to get Marcel, the head of the gendarme in Patras, to go against the Emilianites on Saint Michael's Day. Myrgen wouldn't put it past him to get Nicolai out of the picture.

Or was Myrgen upset for some other reason? Was his problem with the possibility that some other man was doing what he had been dreaming of doing for the last few nights? He was the one who had almost kissed her on the deck in front of her crew. Was Myrgen jealous that there she was, with someone who wasn't afraid to let her know how he felt about her? Alistair had flirted with her and made offers to her just like Alexander had. Was it truly all in the delivery? The timing? Alexander had been callous while Alistair was charming. If Alexander had been more charming, would Catriona be in Rouen with him right now, gripping the headboard while he...

Myrgen shook his head. *What the hell?* He couldn't figure out why he was acting and thinking like this. It was still too soon after Elizabeth and her betrayal for him to be thinking of *any* woman like this, much less this one. Catriona was beyond his reach in so many ways, more than Elizabeth had ever been because Catriona was approachable, while Elizabeth had been on a high shelf. It was an illusion of accessibility that just made her more lofty a goal.

Myrgen took in a breath and rubbed his eyes. They were going to be here for a few more days. Maybe he needed to visit that high end brothel he had heard about, if his mind was walking that path. Rather that than to have her look into his heart and see her own reflection. He heard a man shout good night to someone and saw the Harbormaster waving to a dock hand. He remembered the papers Catriona had signed and reached into his vest pocket.

He walked over to Catriona's room and opened the leather pouch. He had managed to get to the Harbormaster just before he closed for the night to give him the papers he needed and found he had a message that had been left there for him. He opened the sheaf and took out the missive. As he suspected, it was in Michael's handwriting. He set the other papers down on her desk and read the letter:

Your Lordship,

Your sister was placed under house arrest until the King could return and hear her case. Apparently, he left specific instructions that no actions were to be taken dealing with the charges of treason until he had a chance to review the details and oversee the investigation. He has returned as of the writing of this letter.

However, Grande Guard Gomez reports that Tanglwyst was rescued by Duncan McVryce. He suspects dark magic assisted her. No one has seen her or heard anything about her whereabouts since her disappearance two days ago.

I have found a reliable messenger here. Please respond with instructions through this person.

Michael

Myrgen folded the letter again and walked the few paces to his own cabin door. Specific instructions like those probably meant Alexander was expecting to bring Catriona back with him to read Tanglwyst and find out the truth about her involvement in the treason. It was a double-edged sword having her rescued. On the one hand, running made her look guilty. On the other hand, she probably was. Myrgen knew Tanglwyst had set her sights on Nicolai. Now that he knew that man had been married to Catriona, it shed a different light on her actions and intentions. On the off chance she had told him everything, Tanglwyst was still a manipulator. Myrgen didn't necessarily feel safer or better knowing she was loose.

He opened his door and was about to go in when he heard a shout from the dock. He walked down the hall to the deck.

"Myrgen!"

Myrgen stepped up the pace to get to the edge, Catriona's voice ringing through the night. Her arm was wrapped in cloths that were dripping blood, and her coat was open. He could see, even from the ship, the wound that had been on her stomach was leaking blood as well.

"By the Saints… Here! I'm here!" Myrgen ran down the gangplank to meet her and noticed Alistair was with her.

"Myrgen…" She ran up to him, out of breath and holding her side. "Are you alright? …Your wounds? Have your wounds returned?"

He looked her over, his concern trumped by her odd questions. "What? No, no, I'm fine. Let's take care of you." He looked at Alistair. "By the Saints… This much blood?"

"I'm amazed she didn't pass out on the way here," Alistair said to Myrgen as they hurried her to her cabin. "She's been bleeding like that since the Net."

"Probably fear driving her." Myrgen ran ahead of them, opening the door to Catriona's quarters. "Here. Sit down on the bed."

Catriona did as instructed and Myrgen went to her side, looking at her wounds. He turned to Alistair and pointed to the sea chest. "In there are some poultices. Pull them out and drop them in some water, please." Alistair poured water into the bowl on the desk and then opened the chest, looking for the poultices. Myrgen looked up at her. "What happened?"

Catriona looked at Alistair, then back at Myrgen.

Alistair glanced at her. "She suddenly started bleeding, like all her wounds were fresh. How long ago did you get hurt?"

Myrgen reached out a hand. "Wet a cloth for me, will you? I need to see how bad this is."

As Alistair did as he was asked, Catriona answered his question. "Um, about nine or ten days now, back in Rouen. There was a sword fight with my husband."

Myrgen touched the back of her head to look in her eyes for signs the beating damage was returning as well.

She flinched as he felt a bump on the back of her head. Myrgen glanced at her and she tensed under his fingers, "I, uh, ended up with some pretty nasty wounds because of it."

Myrgen studied her, trying to discern why she wasn't telling her alleged fiancé about her healing of the guards, or the healing after the fight with the crewmen. He glanced behind him.

"Thank you."

Myrgen took the wet cloth Alistair held out and returned to his charge. She relaxed and blinked her relief.

He wiped away the blood on her arm and saw that the wound from the guard was still gone, completely healed, just like his own wounds. Not even a mark on her. He then noticed the fluid was an odd color on the cloth. He looked closer, then back at Catriona. Myrgen stood and looked at Alistair. "I'm going to have to remove her shirt to look at her other wounds. Would you mind waiting outside?"

Alistair glanced at Catriona who nodded. "Yeah, I'll be right out there. Call out if you need anything."

After Alistair closed the door, Myrgen looked Catriona. "So, did he try to force himself on you?"

"What? No. Is that why you asked him to leave?"

"To give you the chance to speak freely, if you needed to. What happened to your head?"

"I... bumped it."

Myrgen raised his eyebrows. "*You* bumped it?" He rolled his eyes. "Look, if you're not going to be honest with me…"

"Myrgen, what are you talking about?" She looked at her stained clothes.

He held up the cloth with the efforts of cleaning on it. The color of the fluid was slightly brown, like the blood was already dry. "This is Passion Sap, an herbal potion that has this effect when a person gets touched intimately. My parents used it on Tanglwyst when we were growing up. I saw its effects often. Luckily you have some of that oil Xannu makes for you. It will remove the essence from your skin or you would be foul smelling and sticky for the next tenday." He went over to the basin and rinsed the cloth in the water. "Since it's very unlikely you would be dosed with this and you have an antidote with you at all times through your clever alchemist Xannu, I have to assume you dosed yourself. Would he not accept no for an answer?"

Catriona looked down at her arm and the bloody bandages. "N… no. I wanted…" She looked back at Myrgen. "Excuse me, someone *dosed* me with this?"

He looked back at her. "Are you trying to tell me you didn't know?"

"Trust me, Myrgen, I was *not* interested in having that touching stopped."

He blinked at her, then turned away to walk a few steps, shaking his head. *Had all that intimacy, all those looks and feelings been one sided? The healing, the church, the whale… All nothing.* He looked at her again, hurt in his eyes. "Why?" He looked at the door and stepped closer, lowering his voice. "Why him? Why him and not Alexander?"

She looked at her hands. "Probably because he *wasn't* Alexander, in any way. I can't be physical like that with Alexander without it meaning something more, and I can't let it mean something more."

"So fine. But, with all the options you have," he begged her at that time to see what, see *who* he meant, "why this one?"

She stood up, her anger colored with desperation and a little fear. "Because he wanted me. *He wanted* me, *not your sister.* Do you have any idea how long it's been since I've had a man hold me who *wanted it to be me?*"

He blinked and spoke before he lost his nerve. "Yes." He put the cloth in the basin. "Last night." He left before she could say anything else.

Out in the hallway, Alistair saw him come out and rushed over. "Is she going to be all right?"

"Yes, she's going to be fine. It's just Passion Sap."

"Passion Sap? But those wounds…"

"It's easier for the sap to flow from an area that has had an injury. Trust me, it's more unsettling when it doesn't."

Alistair raised his eyebrows in question.

Myrgen tapped under his eyes.

Alistair shuddered. "Ah, yes. I see your point."

Myrgen opened his door and got a shirt from his sea chest. He handed it to Alistair.

"Thank you." He slipped off his doublet and put his arms in the sleeves of the shirt as Myrgen held the outer garment.

"It's the least I could do after you tore yours to pieces to save her. Thank you, by the way. I don't know what this crew would do without her."

Alistair pulled the shirt on over his head. "But she wasn't in any actual danger."

Myrgen nodded. "That doesn't dismiss the fact that you wanted to save her. This time was not a real threat, but it's nice to know she surrounds herself with people who would act when confronted with something like that, rather than do nothing."

"I've got a lot to make up for with that woman." He stuffed the bottom of the shirt into his breeches. "Speaking of which, how's your sister?"

Twenty

Alistair's conviviality was guarded and Myrgen felt likewise. Last year, Alistair had been a regular merchant to Tanglwyst's house and bed, suddenly disappearing one day from her life without a trace. That same day, she had come up missing as well. She was gone for three tendays and Myrgen, like everyone else in her life, had just decided she had run off with Alistair since Nicolai had left her. When she had returned with Duncan, once again in love, Myrgen, like everyone else in her life, just sighed and went on with their day. Myrgen had approached Duncan with his offer to assassinate Charles, under the impression that the Underground was using this premise as a means to get in contact with Myrgen to fulfill his request. It was after that when Tanglwyst suggested Catriona be approached.

"She might be in a bit of trouble, actually." Myrgen handed the doublet back to Alistair and told him about Tanglwyst's treason, arrest and rescue.

Alistair shrugged when Myrgen finished relating the tale. "Mervolingia doesn't employ women as guards and we both know her power over men. If any guardsman is foolish enough to let her touch him, he'll give his life to save hers." He glanced at Catriona's door and lowered his voice. "Is she in danger with this Duncan fellow?"

"I doubt it," Myrgen gave his own look in the Captain's direction. Tanglwyst was a subject that he felt a strong desire to avoid with her, after all this unpleasantness with Nicolai. "Duncan was her plaything a few months back, after you disappeared. She threw him over for Nicolai as soon as he came sniffing back around."

Alistair tilted his head to the side, watching Myrgen. "Were you there? When they fought?"

"When who fought?"

"Catriona and Nicolai."

"Well, yes, if you could call it a fight. She destroyed him. He never even got a draw on her."

Alistair's face scrunched up in confusion. "Then where did she get those wounds? Those were definitely battle cuts."

Myrgen shifted his feet and folded his arms across his chest, nodding. "She got those afterward, when she healed the guardsmen Nicolai almost killed."

"She took on wounds from someone else's incompetence?" Alistair folded his arms and snorted in anger. "Stupid woman. That stomach wound was fatal."

"That's what Alexander said as well. She couldn't be stopped though."

"Alexander. You mentioned him before, when you spoke of the treason. He's the king that killed your lover. Tanglwyst's friend."

"Probably the best thing, really. She went quite mad at the end."

"And he was on hand to fight Nicolai."

Myrgen took a deep breath, realizing he was about to laud Alistair's only rival for Catriona's affections. "Yes. He protected her. Enabled her to get to her ship and her swords. Once on deck, she had the advantage."

"It's a shame she found out he survived. Last time I spoke with her, she didn't know."

Myrgen watched Alistair's eyes. "Didn't know? That he was alive?"

"No."

"But you did."

"I found out, by accident."

"You didn't tell her?"

Alistair glanced around the hallway and into the night. "It didn't exactly come up." He looked at Myrgen. "She saw me at Tanglwyst's."

Myrgen rolled his eyes. "Oh sweet Saint Anne. I take it from your tone she didn't know you were seeing my sister?"

"Guilty as charged. Except I walked away. When Catriona found out I was responsible for the plot to sabotage Tanglwyst's company, she was... rather judgmental."

"Because you attacked Tangl?"

"Because I sank those ships and put those sailors out of honest work. Even though she tried to take on some of the crews, the damage was already done. I walked away from Tanglwyst that moment and never went back."

Myrgen looked at the man. *So that was what happened. He left because Catriona didn't approve.* He seemed truly remorseful. Myrgen glanced back at Catriona's door. "Then count yourself lucky. If that's the truth, then this woman here might be the only thing that can dispel the hold my sister has over those men she focuses upon."

"I actually count you lucky. When she started bleeding, you were the only one she thought of," Alistair said, stepping away from the wall with an air of egress, "I think you've earned your chance." He nodded good day.

"Wait," Myrgen said, "what do you mean, my chance?"

"Of making her your woman."

Myrgen blinked, stunned as if someone had suddenly hit him in the face with a fish, and run off. Alistair turned to go and Myrgen found his voice. "Why would you think I want her for myself?"

He turned back to look at Myrgen, folding his arms across his chest. "Because every other man does, myself included. You don't?"

"That's not the kind of relationship we have. She's hired me to be her Chancellor. Nothing else."

"You ever kissed her?"

Myrgen blinked, shaken.

Alistair nodded. "Let me let you in on something, Myrgen. Catriona doesn't kiss men in general, part of the practices she learned in the local Incense House from the girls there in Yantap. They told her it is the most intimate thing she can do, the thing that evidences her willingness to be with one man because when she kisses him, she shares a bit of her soul. By the third kiss, she'll be yours, and unlike me, she'll never be able to walk away from you. You have a certain scent about you.

"One more thing: watch this Alexander person. Royalty has access to things commoners like us don't even dare dream." Alistair moved off, leaving Myrgen to his new thought process.

Catriona stepped away from the door, ignoring the pile of oil and sap coated rags she was about to throw away. Myrgen was right. The rags were useless for any other purpose and the only course would be an incinerator. It took the last of her oil to get the sizable amount out of her hair, and that would be a problem within a day. She was about to open the door when she heard the men talking, and decided to listen while she waited for Myrgen to go back to his room.

Now, she was trying desperately to come to grips with everything she had just overheard. Her head was swimming with information. She had bled from wounds that were completely healed, that didn't even have so much as a mark to say they had been there when she had a fresh tiny cut on her head which would have been just as frightening. Could she have possibly, somehow, *forced* the sap to go there? And s*omeone* had dosed her with a potion and she didn't know who, or how. She couldn't read Alistair, but it was unlikely he did it, given that it stopped their intimacy. Myrgen seemed concerned by it and he had been genuine. She could see it wasn't him.

Then how? No one else on the ship seemed to be effected so it wasn't in the food or water. It must have come up when she got here. Alistair didn't start bleeding sap so it wasn't in her tankard. She didn't have time to eat anything either, and that was coming back to haunt her now. She walked over to her chart table and leaned on it, trying to think. Her stomach growled. She stood and went to the bottle of wine in the holder on her desk. The bottle was light. She realized she was going to have to go out there, past quite possibly Alistair and most definitely Myrgen to grab some food from the galley. What was more, the real food would be in town. Perhaps she could ask Octavius to order some from the Net.

This is ridiculous. Leave the ship and go get something to eat. But instead, she sat down on the chair by her desk. Someone had dosed her. That kept sticking in her mind. This was why she couldn't bring herself to marry Alexander. If someone out here, where she was surrounded by her crew and ship, could dose her with a potion, how much more likely was that in the intrigues of court? She had never seen this coming. Perhaps this was just a test to see if it could be done.

She leaned her elbows on her knees and put her face in her hands. At least she had Myrgen here to help her.

She heard his voice in her head.

"Yes. Last night."

She had been callous, and she owed him an apology. He had been the only thing on her mind when she thought she was hurt, her fear that his own wounds would have returned drove her to his side. To turn about and dismiss him like that right on the heels of needing him so much, well, she just didn't know how to make that right. She decided to sleep on it and give it a try on the morrow.

She looked over at her sea chest and remembered she still had some spice cakes from Xannu's kitchen. She often hoarded those and she might have a few stashed in the chest. She got off the chair and went to her sea chest. It had been torn apart to find the poultices, and she knelt beside it to return the contents. As she did so, the flag of Caratia caught her eye, partially unfolded from the rummaging.

She picked it up and held it to her face. The scent of her home enveloped her. It was odd that she could always smell the Land in this fabric. It didn't matter if she flew it or kept it in this chest, when she held it to her face, the scent of home was always there. She thought of the sword she was given by the Land, the stone in the pommel transforming into the marker of the Protector. That had been the Land's choice and it had manifested when the Land had willed it. As a citizen of Caratia, she was always under the jurisdiction of the Land.

Her eye fell upon the area that once had been a scar on her arm from the fight with Nicolai. Her ability to heal was a gift of the Land, as was the key around her neck. This ship was as well, built of timbers from the Caratian forests and sealed with pitch from the Galadorn woods. She was protected here, but yet, this sap had manifested when she had started to couple with Alistair. She could think of no way she could have been dosed with something and it not affect the two men in her company. This was personal. Perhaps it was the Land's way of removing her from Alistair's influence, of saying it did not approve.

But it stopped when she came under Myrgen's care. Myrgen, who had the gift to heal as well. Myrgen, who had taken her soul in the catacombs under the palace in Patras, who had not spared her the truth when she had returned to the ship, nor blocked her path when she went to heal the guards. She had spoken with him, confided in him, even employed him, all without any logical reason to do so, other than it felt right. And now, Alistair had told him to win her heart.

Alistair had obviously believed Myrgen to be a better man for Catriona than even himself, because he told Myrgen he needed to win her. What did he say? By the third kiss, she would be Myrgen's? That was an odd prophecy, but Catriona found herself willing to see if he was right.

His comment about Alexander was likewise odd, and she wondered what he meant by it. The further from Patras they traveled, the less she thought of him. She wasn't certain if it was simply a lack of proximity. She and Alexander had been separated before, for far longer than this. This was different, and she didn't know what to expect next.

She finished putting away the things in the sea chest and was rewarded with finding the pouch with the spice cakes in it. She sat back and ate the cakes, reveling in the Yantap reminiscences they brought her. She had missed Alistair, though she had not realized that until she saw him. But he was right. He did have a lot of making up to do to her. Truth was that he was an ill match for her. She had been about to use him to satisfy her current needs, and nothing more. There was no future there.

She went to her stained glass window and looked out onto the harbor. The moonlight reflected on the still water. She smiled, remembering the last romantic setting she had actually gazed upon, the last time a smile had broken from her hidden cache and displayed itself upon her lips.

Two days. The whale incident. Yes. Perhaps tomorrow, I will look for something with a whale on it, to say thank you. He deserves to be treated like he matters. It's time I stop acting like he doesn't.

Alistair stepped off the *Enigma*, breathing in the scent of the docks. There were drops of the blood-like substance on the gangplank and dock, leading all the way here from the inn. That made Alistair uncomfortable on so many levels. He had never left a trail before. His concern for her had been so overwhelming that he forgot everything. It was amazing what this woman did to him.

He knelt down and inspected the drops of fluid. It had mostly dried, and where it had, it was sticky, like sap. He smelled it, but the scent of the sea overpowered the subtle smell. If this stuff was what Myrgen said it was, he was a lot more concerned for Catriona's safety than if she actually had reopened her wounds. It meant someone had successfully dosed her with a potion. He only hoped that was the only dosing attempted tonight, since he had finished off Catriona's original tankard, but he had not erupted with bloody fluid from his eyes, so he figured it wasn't in the ale she drank at the Net. *Good. I'd hate to have to stop drinking their ale.* He looked around to see if anyone was watching him. If they were, they were better at hiding that he was at spotting them, so he wiped the sticky stuff on his breeches and walked away.

He was actually most concerned about the fact some king was interested in Catriona. He had been straight when he told Myrgen the royalty had access to things the common folk could never imagine. He had seen it before, in Yantap. A nobleman from the mainland had decided he wanted one of the Incense House girls for his own about a year ago. He had shared a tea with her made of a strange herb and then they made love. The next time she tried to perform her duties with a client, she had turned violent, refusing to allow any man to touch her but her nobleman. Horrified, the client called for help and the nobleman arrived to take her away.

He explained to the Incense House that he wanted her for his own and that she was ruined for any other man, for she would react like this at any other man's touch. Unfortunately, he did not realize the fortitude of the laws of the land and he was executed for his impudence. The girl died of a broken heart a few tendays later.

Catriona was no naïve Incense House girl though. Someone approaching her with ill intent would be ferreted out instantly, unless she couldn't read them. To Alistair, *that* idea was frightening. Someone who could deceive *Catriona*? He would have to try and rescue her from that sort of person, and she was considerably less inclined to trust him these days, after the Tanglwyst incident. He would need help, and not just a little bit. Alistair didn't know anything about this drug's other effects, but he knew someone who did: his niece, Gwen. She lived in Patras, a few days' ride from St. Andrew. He could investigate where Tanglwyst might have disappeared to as well.

The thought crossed his mind that perhaps Myrgen had done the dosing. The sap manifested when they had gotten intensely physical, which would fit if Myrgen were in love with her. He was also an inhabitant of the palace up until a tenday ago. The royalty of Patras might have access to the same spell that the nobleman had cast on that tea, and he was, after all, the one she requested when she fell to the drug's effects. But that didn't fit. The girl in the Incense House had gone violent as soon as she was touched by another man. If the potion had taken hold of Catriona like that, she would have fought him as soon as Alistair had kissed her. So if the potion had to have such a high level of sexual desire as what he and Catriona were exhibiting, perhaps it wasn't too late.

Also, it occurred to him, the delivery of such a drug would have been obvious to Catriona when she looked at Myrgen, even if he didn't give it to her directly. Same with the barkeep pulling the ales. She would have read that too. Thus, the dosing must have happened without the barkeep's knowledge either, which would mean the person who dosed her might still be in the tavern. He picked up his step and returned to the Net.

Myrgen signed his name to his reply to Michael and read the message. It told Michael, in code, to go to his parents' house and retrieve a pouch with some money, then meet him in Zara. And not to pursue Tanglwyst. She was more trouble than she was worth at the moment. Myrgen had yet to meet the man alive who could resist or hurt her once she caught his fancy. Myrgen was certain she was safe.

Now he just needed to get it to him. Myrgen didn't know who the messenger was and he felt uncertain about leaving the ship right then. He didn't want to run into Alistair, not after the man's prediction. He wondered if Alistair could know how close he had come to hitting the mark on Myrgen's infatuation. He also didn't want to run the risk of running into Catriona. If she were to read him right now, he would have a difficult time facing her again.

The sound of boots on the deck caught his attention and he grabbed his shirt and put it on before opening the door to see who it was. He was very surprised to find the entire crew returning to the ship. Octavius was speaking to Theiron. Myrgen walked over to them, glancing around. Theiron nodded and left Octavius as

Myrgen arrived. "Octavius. What's the matter? Why is everyone one board?"

"Captain's here. We don't stay off the ship when the Captain's on board."

"Not even in port?"

"Especially not in port. Anyone could walk on if there's no one here to stop them. That was reaffirmed back in Rouen, with Nicolai."

Myrgen recalled how he had knocked Nicolai off the dock into the water and the entire crew left the ship, trying to find him. Catriona had stayed on board and that was where he attacked her. "She came out of that just fine. Nicolai didn't get so much as a drop of harbor water on her."

"Yeah, but it doesn't make it right. She shouldn't have had to do that alone."

"I wasn't alone, Octavius," Catriona said from right behind them. "I was on the *Enigma.*"

"Be that as it may, Captain, the men said they wanted to return to Captain's Watch, just to be sure."

Catriona shook her head and folded her arms. "Fine. Carry on. I'll stay ashore tomorrow. Myrgen, may I see you?" She nodded towards her cabin and Myrgen walked with her. As they reached his door, she turned to him, leaning against the wall. "I wanted to thank you for helping me through that. I'm not certain I would have felt comfortable having Alistair tend my wounds."

"Is that why you asked for me?"

"Yes. I knew you wouldn't take advantage of me. There aren't many men I could say that about."

"I can think of about a hundred, off the top of my head."

Catriona smiled and looked out at the bustling deck. "Maybe so. But if there was no one around to stop them, could they stop themselves?" She looked back at him. "I also wanted to apologize. You were right. You've always made sure I knew you *chose* me, not that I was filler," a small smiled drifted across her lips, "even when we first met. It was inappropriate for me to forget that."

He leaned back against his door, which fell open, almost putting him on his rear. He grabbed the doorjamb just in time. He popped back up, trying to regain his composure, and nodded stiffly. "So, would you like to come in? Have a drink? Get your portrait painted?"

She barely held in her laughter as she stepped past him. "All you had to do was ask."

"I thought the acrobatics might intrigue you, get you off guard for my sneak attack."

"Good thing I saw through your clever ruse." She saw the missive on the desk. "You got a letter?"

"Ah. Yes." He realized the mention of Tanglwyst, who was the cause of both their problems, might be a tender subject for her. He tempered his comment. "I asked Michael to return to Patras to check on my family. Both my parents live in Patras. I needed to know if they had shared Elizabeth's fate, or worse, been arrested in order to draw me back."

"Would you? Go back, I mean."

"Undoubtedly. If my family were threatened, yes."

"Even Tanglwyst?"

Myrgen thought a moment. "Yes."

Catriona looked down at the floor. "Oh. Well that's to be expected. You're her brother, after all." She looked at Myrgen. "Did he tell her about Nicolai?"

"No. She was under house arrest, but she escaped."

"No doubt using some man to get her out of the mess she made."

"No doubt." He stepped over to the desk. "I wrote back that he should let that go. I didn't want him to go looking for her and get himself in trouble with the guard. He's probably as wanted as I am right now."

"Alexander will make sure nothing happens to him."

"Alexander doesn't know everything that goes on in his kingdom. Clearly. Tanglwyst is gone and no one knows where she went."

"Do you?"

He looked in her eyes. "I have a few ideas, but I won't betray her. Especially not to a man who had his sword at my throat a tenday ago. Unfortunately, he said to send it by the same messenger, but he didn't tell me who that was. His letter was left with the Harbormaster, and he's out for the night."

She glanced at the reply missive. "You should go to the Black Cat and Anchor. They have the only stable in town, so messengers regularly use it and you can get your reply to one tonight so they can leave tomorrow. You might get a reply back before we set sail."

"I thought the same thing. I've asked him to pick up a couple things for me and meet me in Zara in two months. That should be plenty of time for him to get there overland without jeopardizing his freedom. He doesn't need to come here."

"What's he getting for you?"

"Money. I'm going to need money if I'm going to live on land. Octavius has explained about your crewman initiation policy and how I don't qualify as someone whose life you've saved."

"It's hardly a policy. It just means I can trust them."

"That's pretty easy for you. Your can read their hearts like they were novels. It's not like anyone could keep a secret from you."

"I've been betrayed before, Myrgen. This keeps me safe."

"But aren't you betraying them by looking? Doesn't that show that you actually *don't* trust them?" Myrgen suddenly found himself feeling a bit betrayed, even though he had nothing to hide, and it irritated him. He looked at the letter he wrote to Michael. "If you'll excuse me, Catriona, I'm going to take your advice and get this letter to the messenger at the Inn. I'll see you in the morning." He grabbed the letter and his vest and started to leave.

"Will you be back on board later? Captain's Watch, and all."

He glanced at her. He became mindful of the things Alistair had said, and figured out the real reason why he was upset. "Do you want me to? Or would I just be a substitute for someone else?"

He almost regretted saying it out loud, but at least that way, he was choosing to let her know what he thought instead of her fishing it and who knew what else out of his skull. She looked at the ground and he stepped into the hallway, shrugging into the vest. She stepped in after him.

"Aren't you afraid we'll set sail without you if you spend the night in town, like the rest of them?"

The look on her face was one of concern and guilt hidden poorly behind bravado. He saw right through it. The annoyance he had felt slipped away as he realized that the Captain's Watch was actually an insult in her eyes, that she didn't value the crew enough to let them board before she left port. When she had given so much to them and risked her life to save theirs, to be shown they didn't have faith in her hurt her. He found it incredible that men who traveled the world with her every year, who had been through so much with her, couldn't see how hurt she was by the very idea of Captain's Watch. How could they be so blind to something so obvious to a stranger?

He pulled his collar and hair out of the vest collar and put the letter in his inner pocket. "Of course not. I know you wouldn't leave without me. You owe me money."

She relaxed and smiled at the floor. He walked back to her, glancing over his shoulder to make sure they weren't being watched. "Look, I don't know what's happening between us. The thing with the whale and the healing yesterday and," he ran his fingers through his hair, "the catacombs…" He leaned his back against the wall across from her. "I just don't know how I'm supposed to act around you. I have no compass, no bearings. I don't know if I should take you in that room right now, throw you on the bed and take you like you were my own, or leave you alone to give you time to process your losses and your future."

He glanced down the hall as several more crewmen came on board, then back to her lovely green eyes. "I'm just choosing the latter option because I can't walk away from the first one. If I go there with you, I'll be too far invested to go back." He pushed off the wall and walked backward down the hallway. "Get some sleep. You were up all night. I'll be back later. You want me to get you anything?"

She smiled at him. "With what?"

"Good point. Very good point." He waved and was gone.

Twenty-One

"When you say one thing, the clever person understands three."
The Wise Wench's Tavern Book

Logan the barkeep took Thessius' tankard and refilled it as he listened to the tale the crewman of the *Enigma* was telling a young local fella named Thomas, fresh from the university. "Every morning? She's *that* beautiful?" He drank alongside the sailor and ordered another ale apiece.

"Yea," nodded Thessius. "Bu'ty got li'le ta dae wath ait, main. Ait's naiturail airges ais mooch ais ennethain. Shay's brave thew, bravuh thain most main. She saved me an' several other crewmen when our Captain wen' mad."

"Mad? Aren't they all a bit off?"

Thessius shook his head. "No' like this. Our Captain, Ramirez, 'ad recently lost 'is wife an' their only child, a daughter, ta sickness. Watched 'em both waste away 'fore 'is eyes. 'E was runnin' one o' the Tanglwyst carracks, and 'ad taken th' winter off ta attend ta 'em. When 'e came back in th' spring, 'e was a different man. 'E was sad all th' time. It was tragic ta see.

"So, we're out off th' Glarren coast when we see this rather frightenin' spectacle. 'T was so 'orrible, I 'esitate to speak of it lest it return to 'aunt us all."

A sturdy, dark-haired man stepped up on the other side of Thessius. "Oi. What are you talking aboot?"

"Ada, Johannes."

Johannes shuddered and shook his head. "'At *was* a noightmare alright."

Thessius said, "Thomas, this be Johannes 'E was one o' th' people on the *Enigma* that day."

Johannes raised his tankard in greeting. "Aye, she was quoite the soight."

Thomas' eyes glittered from the suspense. "What? Was she ugly? Deformed? Big? Tall?"

Johannes shook his head. "Woirse. She was a saimstress."

Thomas lost the thread of the joke. "Huh? A seamstress? You mean like a..."

"Draissmaker, yes," Johannes pointed is tankard at Thomas. "The Captain was in need of proper clothes after she built th' *Enigma*, and it turns out she was in mourning. She 'ad purchased severa' bowts of cloth in black but didn't 'ave time ta stay in port to 'ave the clothes made. So, Ada offered ta make 'er clothes for the cost of materials if Catriona would let 'er sail with 'er. Catriona agreed."

"I've never been afraid of a seamstress before," Thomas' expression was smiling but skeptical.

"You didn't see 'er. She came onto the ship wearing a bright red doublet, blue pants and a large yellow sash."

Thessius turned to Thomas, excited. "Th' sash 'ad little skulls embroidered on the ends. Several of them. Done by 'er in preparation fo' this trip."

"What? Why?"

Johannes leaned over. "Because she wanted to dress the pa't of a proper pirate." The three men laughed heartily, and Johannes continued. "Th' blue was fo' th' sea, th' red for th' blood she would spiw and th' yellow for aw th' gold she was expecting ta foind."

"And the skulls?" Thomas seemed astonished that someone could be so foolish.

Thessius piped up. "Well, pirates *are* dangerous, ya know, Thomas."

"Oh please. How ridiculous."

Johannes said, pointing at Thomas, "An'tha' was just her *boarding* outfit! You should have seen th' othuh stuff she brought out!"

Thomas smiled even bigger, as if imagining different stupid girl definitions of proper attire for piratical crew members. "Did the Captain still allow her to make the clothes, or did she put her off at the next port?"

"Oh no, she fulfilled th' contract. Th' clothes th' Captain wears now are th' ones Ada made. Very capable saimstress. The clothes barely show any wear at aw and they get a lo' of abuse. No, Ada knew what she was doing with th' clothes. She mended aw th' men's clothing while she was on board too. Free o' charge." He unrolled his sleeve. "She mended this shirt where it got snagged on a reef. I though' it was a loss, but she saved it."

Thomas said, "So what does she have to do with this Captain Ramirez?"

"Oh," Johannes said, "wew, th' Captain said Ada could be in charge of th' 'raid' coming up. There was a trader 'at was supposed ta be full of rich cargo and she was going ta commandeer it."

"We like ta refer ta it as pre-emptive salvage," said Thessius.

"Yes," said Johannes, nodding and pointing at Thessius with a wobbling finger. "So she puws up alongside this ship, The *Crimson Veil* and says ta turn over aw th' cargo."

"Captain Ramirez 'ad gone below decks, leaving th' First Mate ta pretend ta be Captain," Thessius injected. "It was standard procedure for raids."

"So Ada starts ordering the First Mate around, cawing him Captain because, believe it or not, he was *dressed bettah* than th' rest of the crew. It didn't occur to her 'at clothes can be swapped in th' course of catching a ship ta raid it."

Thessius got a bit wistful, remembering. "We took th' things from th' 'old that th' Captain 'anded us, figuring 'e was 'olding back th' best fer 'imself. The girl certainly didn't seem competent at picking out wha' were goods and wha' was junk. I noticed we were carrying out casks o' gunpowder, which I found a bit odd, but I didn't question th' Captain. Whatever 'e was doing seemed ta be working because Ada just took it across without thinking twice, standing there in 'er garish red and gold outfit, the wind off th' sea tossing 'er little skulls around 'er legs. I thought they'd surely trip 'er if she tried to run.

"Suddenly, this other woman swung over from th' other ship. She was dressed reasonably and 'er 'air was black as pitch. If it 'adn't flowed behind 'er in a braid, I would 'ave thought she actually put pitch in it ta keep it out o' her eyes. She drew 'er sword and told me to move away from th' hold. Ada got a little irritated at th' interruption, since this was supposed ta be 'er raid and all, and asked what this woman was doing.

"Catriona said she was going after the Captain. Ada revealed then that she thought she had been talking ta th' Captain, and said, 'Look at his outfit!' Catriona tried ta get me ta move but I told her I wasn't going ta let 'er near my Captain. Then she told me my Captain was trying ta kill th' whole crew and sink both ships. I thought she was crazy, but it turned out the gunpowder had been trickling out linking th' two ships as it got put on th' *Enigma*.

"Suddenly, she says, 'Ramirez, put th' lantern down,' and I smelled lamp oil. I turned around and there was my Captain soaked in lamp oil like he'd poured a 'ole barrel on 'im. It was dripping off 'im and all over the stairs. I looked down and saw I was standing on a trail of gunpowder that would cleave the ship in two. I just froze."

Thomas was shocked. This story had obviously gone an entirely different way from where he had seen it going. "What happened? Was he really holding a lantern?"

Johannes said, "Aye. I could see it from the ship. Catriona shouted to th' 'ands to get the othuh crew on board and she started fighting the othuh Captain. She's pretty good with a rapier but she was afraid to just cut him. If he dropped that lantern, both ships would be destroyed before we could ge' awoy. Thessius told us there were still several cas's o' gunpowduh in the 'old."

"Catalogued them m'self," Thessius confirmed. "We 'ad an entire hold full. I thought we were selling it ta someone or something. I would never have brought on so much in one trip. Too dangerous." He turned back to Thomas. "She kept 'im occupied until we 'ad escaped to the ship. I told th' crew about th' gunpowder trail and they removed it from th' ship, rinsing it away with several buckets of water that were everywhere on th' deck."

Johannes smiled and nodded, "Th' Morning Ritual! O' course!"

"Exactly. She shouted ta Octavius ta get th' ship under way, but 'e refused. I'll tell you, I never would 'ave told Ramirez no and I wouldn't tell Catriona no either, but Octavius is a braver man then me."

"An' that's why he's First Mate and you're Galley Master."

"After Ramirez? I'll take Galley Master over me ol' position any day!"

"Wait," said Thomas. *"You* were the First Mate?"

"Didn' I mention 'at?" Thessius turned to Johannes. "Didn' I mention 'at?"

Johannes shook his head and took a drink of his ale. "Not whoile I was sitting 'ere."

"Huh. Yea, 'at was me. Anyway, th' whole crew is brought on board th' *Enigma* and th' Captain is fighting Ramirez and th' worst 'appens. They have been wrestling aroun' as she's tried to get th' lantern from 'im and she gets 'im pinned, and 'e 'its 'er with th' lantern. Th' flame inside spills out onto Ramirez. Now, by this time, she's covered in th' lamp oil too and th' spark of th' flame 'itting Ramirez means she'll go up too if she doesn't get away. There's gunpowder all over 'er from rolling around on the deck. Ramirez runs into the 'old and does she run off th' ship? No. She runs for th' 'elm, dropping th' aft sail on her way by, which, by herself, is about th' most she could do. Th' wind catches and she spins th' ship away from the *Enigma*. She's barely thir'y feet away when th' first cask explodes under th' deck. Fire starts spilling from th' 'old and there are more explosions as she rides th' ship away from th' *Enigma*. It gets abou' a hundred yards away and th' fire must have reached th' gated 'old, where one 'undred casks o' gunpowder are being stored."

Johannes said, "The who'e ship exploded. There were timbers on fire everywhere. If we 'adn't had those buckets o' watuh on deck, the whole ship would 'ave caught. As it stood, only a few things caught fire, an' most of them were folks who dove ovuh. Little fires doused with some watuh. We searched for Catriona an' she popped up near the back of the ship, a littow frazzled, but definitely alive. We 'auled her on deck an' she turned to Thessius 'ere and said, 'You are relieved o' duty.'"

Thessius nodded. "Been on board evuh since."

Thomas whistled. "You've convinced me. I'll serve under a female Captain like that. Sign me up! This ship sounds like quite an adventure magnet."

"We don't need any extra 'ands right now, boy," said Johannes. "Fu' crew."

"You just pulled into port today. Surely some of your crew are staying behind? You'll need to recruit replacements for them." It sounded like Thomas was being thwarted already. He had set his sights on the *Enigma*.

"Not my policy, boy," said Johannes. "I'm not th' one who signs peop'e up, young man. The *Enigma* selects you, you don' select th' *Enigma*."

"The ship chooses? What, does it throw you overboard if it decides you're unworthy or something?"

Just then, a blond man came into the pub. "Thessius, Octavius is 'ere." Johannes nodded to the door and both Thessius and Thomas looked. The blond man stepped over to Thomas' drinking companions. He smelled of fresh air, and Thomas spit out a small chunk of something that had been floating in his ale as he watched the newcomer.

Octavius put his hand on Thessius' shoulder. "The Captain's on board, gentlemen."

Johannes and Thessius immediately downed their ale and stood. A nod to Thomas and then the three men walked away. Alistair heard Thessius tell Octavius that there were about five men at the brothel down the street. As he passed the end of the bar, Johannes reached up and rang a bell that was suspended near a support beam. This dulled the noise for a split second as the patrons turned to see what the ruckus was. Most of them returned readily to their pastimes, but several men abandoned their games of chance and left with Thessius and the others.

Thomas turned to Logan, perplexed. "That was odd. Everyone leaves if the Captain is on board?"

Logan nodded. "Aye. Seen it before."

"But why?"

Alistair, sitting on a stool a few feet down the bar, said, "She's saved every one of them at one point or another. If the Captain of the *Enigma* is on board in port, there's a chance she'll decide to leave, drawn away by danger or instinct. They return to the ship so they aren't left behind. They call it Captain's Watch."

"An' who are you that you know so much about what goes on on that ship?" Thomas folded his arms. "Were you left behind?"

"Yes, young man. I was. But that was my own damned fault."

Logan turned to him and leaned on the bar. "I saw you leave with her a bit ago. Is she all right, Alistair?"

Alistair nodded. "I left her in good hands, Logan. Hey, you got a moment?"

Logan moved down the bar and leaned in.

"It looks like she might have been dosed with something. Did anybody have access to the ale or tankards except you?"

"Course not! I'm the only one who pulls here."

"See anyone acting shifty or odd?"

Logan thought for a moment. "There was one fella, earlier. Right before Catriona came in. Victoria said she saw someone duck in the back door and duck out a bit later. She came and asked me if anyone had skipped out on their bill. He wasn't one of the *Enigma's* crew and no other ships pulled in today. He was probably here overland."

Alistair nodded. There was only one inn with a stable in St. Andrew and that was the Black Cat and Anchor. He paid Logan and left. The streets were a bit busy with traffic heading towards the docks. Alistair didn't know for sure but a hundred men returning to the *Enigma* might take a bit of time. The movement might hide the stranger who did the dosing and he didn't know all the crew members she employed. Luckily, her crew did, so no one would be getting on that ship who didn't belong there. Her crew was definitely her greatest asset, He knew from experience the kind of man she inspired men to become.

Myrgen appeared to already be that type of man. It was odd, but Alistair found he rather liked Myrgen. The man definitely didn't back down from a challenge but he had decorum, class, dignity, respect. Fine qualities. Yep, if Alistair couldn't have her, he approved of Myrgen, provided Myrgen wasn't the one dosing her. If he *was* the one doing this to her, he was a dead man because she was capable of going to those dark places where even Alistair couldn't go, and he was a regular resident. She could more than take care of herself. Still, he wished he had gotten the chance to see her fight, especially against Nicolai. Conquering him meant regaining her life.

That Myrgen was sharp. He picked up immediately on the fact that Alistair had known Nicolai was alive before Catriona did. He had hoped to talk to her about that in the morning, or right before they fell asleep in each other's arms, but that didn't seem meant to be. He had learned last summer that Nicolai lived, but he had not found her in time to tell her before the winter months had set in. Alistair wondered how different things would be now if he had been able to do so. He reached up and pulled a locket the length of his thumb from where he wore it, next to his heart.

In Yantap, Catriona had a locket with a miniature portrait of Nicolai in it, the twin of this one he held in his hand. She told Alistair that they were wedding gifts and that Nicolai had one just like it with her portrait in it, and they each had a secret engraving behind the pictures. She never let Alistair see what that said, but he had seen the picture of Nicolai often enough.

When Catriona went to break things off with her husband, Alistair actually went with her to Latia, for moral support. He had hung around in town, waiting. He hadn't known what would happen, but he had seen enough of these situations to know it would be difficult and she would be emotionally sore for a bit afterward, but he felt she was more than strong enough to weather anything. Maybe they were going to be lucky and Nicolai had found someone else as well.

Catriona had returned to the ship, heart-broken and struck. There was a couple living in her old house who told her that the previous tenant, Nicolai, had fallen ill, gone blind and wandered off into the woods. Some hunters had found a body in the woods a few tendays later and determined it was probably him. His wife had left him, they had explained, and he grew ill shortly after. Many people said he died of a broken heart. Catriona blamed herself. She told Alistair she needed some time alone to come to grips with this information. He told her he would be there when she was ready, that his offer would always be there for her. She thanked him and they had parted company.

Then, one night in Cheryb, while on his way to his room at a local inn after offering condolences to the widow of one of his own sailors, he saw a man in the company of woman Alistair knew, a man he recognized from a certain portrait that was all too familiar. Alistair followed them and watched as Tanglwyst hit on this man, and watched the man turn her offer down. He instead reminded her that his heart already belonged to someone else. Tanglwyst had respectfully left him for the night. Alistair followed him, trying to be certain it really was Nicolai and not just someone who could pass for him. The man walked around town for a while and seemed to be sussing something out.

He went to a cliff near the town, where a lighthouse illuminated the ship-crushing crags of a coral reef. From there, he took off and cast a necklace from the precipice. Alistair was in the shadows below him, and saw it land on some rocks near the sea's edge. The man left, and Alistair had realized he *had* to see what was on that necklace. He risked his life on the jagged, slimy boulders to get that piece of jewelry, only to find his worst fears realized. The locket on the necklace had a picture of Catriona in it.

This locket, the one in his hand. Usually he wore it in case he ran into her, removing it only to bathe. When she made her offer in the tavern, he was so focused on what she had just said that he forgot all about the locket. In all the commotion afterward, he was only just remembering. Hopefully they were going to be in port for a few days so he could give it to her. Worst case, if she wasn't better by morning, he would entrust it to Myrgen.

The thought of the locket and the potion burned in Alistair's blood. When Catriona gave herself to someone, they had something very valuable. Those few who had experienced it first hand found it nearly impossible to live without it. Maybe that was what had happened. Maybe this king Myrgen mentioned had been testing her, trying to see if she could be dosed, using that harmless deterrent this time. Who knew what they might use next? Perhaps that drug the nobleman had used, the one that would seal her to one man. Her commitment was not something to be coerced or taken lightly. Alistair knew this better than anyone and he would make sure they didn't get away with this.

Alistair got to the Black Cat and stepped inside. The common room was separated from the stairs heading to the rooms by a foyer before opening into a room of full tankards, heaping plates and conversation. The absence of the *Enigma's* crew made the place a bit quieter than would be expected. From the looks of things, several of them had left partially full plates. The innkeeper, a lovely widow named Ce'Nedra, was placing several roasted chickens into a large laundry basket, along with loaves of bread and some turnips. He realized he had seen a few of these baskets leaving the area as he had walked here. True to its name, a sleek black cat watched over things from its perch in an old anchor on a shelf near the hearth. A tabby cat sat on the other side acting like the second book end.

The sailors nodded thanks and left as she saw them off with a wave. She wiped her hands and began looking around the room. She saw Alistair and put her hands on her hips. "Alistair Hapsburg, as I live and breathe. You usually stay at the Net. What brings you out my way?"

"I'm looking for a man who might have arrived overland, a messenger. I need to speak with him."

Ce'Nedra walked over to one of the empty tables and started clearing it off. She glanced at one of the few remaining customers in the room and nodded Alistair over. "The tone in your voice makes it sound like you have intentions of a rough nature for this fellow. I can't have people thinking I let ruffians control my place."

Alistair glanced around and leaned on the table next to her. "Ce'Nedra, the *Enigma* is on Captain's Watch. That's why your patrons cleared out so fast. Someone did something to the Captain and I think that messenger might have seen who." Ce'Nedra still looked skeptical and Alistair went for his pouch. "Look, I'll pay you for the information…"

Ce'Nedra put her hand on his, drawing his attention back to her. "Trust me, it's not your money I've had my eye on for the past three tendays." She glanced at his lips and he took the hint and kissed her. A call from the back of the room broke the moment and they both turned to see a young man carrying another over his shoulder.

"Lady, I found him knocked out in the stable."

She went over to the body and lifted the head. She turned to Alistair. "It's him. It's the messenger." She looked at the stable hand. "Saiban, take him to his room, third one on the right. Alistair, help him, would you?"

Alistair preceded Saiban up the stairs and got the door open before turning to offer assistance with the load. Saiban waved him off, definitely much stronger than he looked under that loose shirt, and put the body on the bed. Alistair took the young messenger's hat off him and stared at the face beneath it. He looked at Saiban. "I've got this, sir. Here." He tossed him a gold. "Tell your mistress I'll be down in a bit. I know this messenger."

The stable hand nodded to the messenger. "He must be from a pretty rich house."

Alistair looked at the man, a little nervous. *Could Gwen have confided in this young man her heritage as a Glarren royal?* "What makes you say that?"

"That horse he came in on is an exceptional animal. High quality, very well trained and very expensive. Nothin' like the beast that other fella came in on."

"Other fellow?"

"The messenger from St. Giles. He went straight to the brothel, but he was riding a common trade-off horse, probably from Rouen from the looks of it. Damn near spent too. Musta had one helluva powerful need for a lady."

As Saiban left the room, Alistair frowned. Tanglwyst had a vineyard in St. Giles. He wondered if the two were connected. He looked at Gwen and patted his niece's hand. Gwen started to stir and he said her name.

She opened her eyes and saw Alistair. "Oh no…"

"Oh yes, young lady. So you were the one that dosed her."

"Just with Passion Sap. Scary but completely harmless. She's probably already up and ordering people about. It's designed to help with an escape, not make the person more vulnerable. She's fine." Gwen sat up, then put her hand to her head. "Ow…"

"What happened in the stable?"

Gwen looked at him. "I slipped trying to climb onto the horse from the stall fence."

Alistair leaned back, pursing his lips. "Serves you right for meddling." He pointed at her. "That's Karma, balancing things."

"Don't start spewing that odd religion you favor. I'm not interested. The study of the Fae and the spiritual magics are the only thing I'll stake my soul upon."

"That's how you did it, didn't you? You got a Fae to dose her, knowing she couldn't see the ruddy things." When Gwen looked away, he got up and stormed around the room. "Why would you do that?"

"Because she deserves better than you, Alistair."

Alistair stopped and closed his eyes. *That hurt.* "I know that, Gwen. Better than you do, in fact. That doesn't make it right. Besides, it didn't work anyway."

"What are you talking about? You're here, aren't you? She's not?" Gwen folded her arms. "That's a considerable improvement over what I saw in the tavern."

Alistair rolled his eyes. "Gwen, she was never going to be with me, at least not permanently. Not yet. I have already seen to that, and it had nothing to do with you or your meddling. It was Karma and I haven't set anything right enough yet to balance what I did wrong, though I'm pretty sure you've helped *that* cause, thank you."

"You're welcome."

"Why did you come here? Surely not to dose her with Passion Sap."

"I had a message for Myrgen, about Tanglwyst."

"And you saw me and Catriona kissing and decided to interfere. Well, she's safe now. She's with Myrgen on the ship."

"*What?!*" She started to get up and got very shaky on her feet, dropping back onto the bed.

"Gwen, you've had a bit of a fall. Just get back into bed. It's none of your business who she's with and frankly, Myrgen's a decent fellow. You should be happy if they get together."

"Myrgen is a traitor and a betrayer."

"If that's so," he knelt down before her and looked into her eyes, "then don't you think she can see that better than you?" Gwen looked for a moment like she was going to say something, but then thought better of it. Alistair sat back on his heel and looked down at her feet. "Come on. Let's get these boots off you and get you into bed. I have a date."

Twenty-Two

"Where a chest lies open, a righteous man may sin."
The Wise Wench's Tavern Book

Myrgen entered the Black Cat and looked around, spying Ce'Nedra. "My Lady, may I trouble you? I'm looking for the Innkeeper."

"That's me."

Myrgen was only slightly surprised the inn's owner was a woman. *Probably a widow.* That was how most Mervol women became land owners outside of Royal appointment or ecumenical interference, as in the case of his sister. Tanglwyst actually had all three dispensations. "I am looking for a messenger who rode in today? From Patras? I have a return message for him."

Ce'Nedra glanced at the rooms upstairs. "Well, there were two messengers that came in today. I'm not certain where the one was from. He has retired for the night. The other made all due haste to the brothel."

"When was that, the brothel fellow?"

"Oh, hours ago. Arrived just after lunchtime. It was strange. He looked at the food like he couldn't bring himself to eat again. I guess he must have seen something on the way from St. Giles that really put him off."

Myrgen blinked, startled. "St. Giles? How do you know he was from St. Giles?"

"He's a regular. He's the messenger Lady Elina sends with word between her two houses. He knows several shortcuts through the woods so he avoids bandits and being slowed by caravans. He can get from Giles to Andrew in four days if he must, but it's terribly expensive."

"Thank you, my lady." He left, heading off to the brothel. Tanglwyst's vineyard was outside of St. Giles, and a perfect first stop for her. The time frame was right too. It was about four days travel from Patras to St. Giles. Duncan would hardly be afraid of running into bandits on the way. Even if her rescuer fell, it would only be a matter of hours before she was the controller of any bandits fool enough to lay a hand on her. The news from St. Giles might be about her. Myrgen needed to find out. She was probably safe, but something wasn't sitting right and he felt nervous. He quickened his step and reached the brothel.

The lady inside was pacing when he entered and looked up at him with a hint of fear as he came in. Her gown was emerald silk with black velvet trim, Mandian in style. Her long, dark hair matched her dark eyes. The elaborate braids and pearls within it would have rivaled any courtesan in Patras. Her shoes carried the theme. At first, he at felt this was not a brothel a sailor could afford. He bowed.

"Can I help you?" Her voice was curt and sharp.

Myrgen realized she must not work here and was decidedly uncomfortable being in a brothel, locating a spouse or relative. "Forgive me, my Lady. I was looking for the Madam."

She looked at him. Her doeskin gloves were on a table nearby and the fingers wore deep scars from twisting them in her hands. Her hair, upon closer inspection, revealed it had been unattended and her make up showed signs of wear. "I am the Madam. I am

Lucia Ilaria Malatesta, Proprietress of the Red Sky at Night. What business have you with me, sir?"

Something is wrong. This probably didn't have anything to do with Tanglwyst at all, but it concerned him that this lady, of obvious fine quality, good breeding and money, was looking so spent. With the crew of the *Enigma* back on board, she would have had plenty of time to get herself ready again, in case they returned, yet she had not. He glanced at the room, noting none of the girls were down here, waiting.

The Madam put on her managerial face and smiled. "Can I get you a companion for the evening?"

Myrgen realized at that moment he still had absolutely no money, and could not offer this woman a proper bribe for her information. "I heard a messenger from St. Giles arrived today. My sister has gone missing and I have reason to believe she might be in St. Giles. I was hoping to possibly ask if he had seen her."

The Madam glanced at the rooms upstairs and dropped her façade for a moment. "I went missing six years ago in St. Giles." She spat out the bitter words, a glare in her eyes. "Trust me. No one has seen her. If you're lucky, she'll prove her worth and you will see her here in three years, after her training is complete."

Myrgen sized the woman up. She would not be in this trusted position days away from the owner if she were not suited to it. This house was one of high caliber, not full of street-walkers, but of women of quality, like the Incense House. They could choose their clientele and would not have a bitter, spiteful person running it. Bad for business.

"Something is wrong, something dire. Isn't it?" He looked around the room. "You don't get to be the proprietor of an elegant house of companions by being surly to the customers, and if you were training for three years, then you've been here at least that long to have this position. You could have escaped at any time, but you haven't." He put his hand on her shoulder, gently, to help reassure her. "Please. I might be able to help."

The woman closed her eyes and relaxed a little, exhaling deeply. "I apologize. It's just this thing… You're right, but we need to be careful. We can't run the risk of it damaging business." She looked at Myrgen. "Come with me."

She took him to the back room, her private chambers. There was a long message on her desk and she gestured towards it, folding her arms across her chest as if protecting herself from its contents. Myrgen went over and picked up the letter. It was from the Elina the Innkeeper had mentioned and the handwriting was shaky and difficult to read at first. She obviously turned the writing over to someone else because the writing became smoother and more legible. The fact that she didn't have the person begin with a fresh sheet implied a strong sense of urgency.

"Lucia,

Forgive the brusque nature of this missive. I am distraught beyond measure and can barely bring myself to think about this, much less write it down. Putting the words on paper makes them somehow more real.

Celeste is dead. She was murdered by a..."

(Here, the handwriting changed.)

"...monster disguised as a man. A client came in to the Red Sky. He had a black scar on his face, as if a fiery stone was drug across his cheek. I thought nothing of it. Many disfigured men seek our companions, thinking wrongly no whole woman would want them. I set him up with Celeste because she never has problems with the way men look, being blind. She has a very loyal clientele because she is so enthusiastic in her work.

I heard an unusual amount of ruckus in the room and thought at first they were just being energetic. Then I heard her scream in pain and I knocked on the door. It was locked and when I pushed against it, there seemed to be something blocking it. I brought the key to open the room and two guards to break down the door. Her screams will torment me for the rest of my life, they never stopped the entire time. Eventually, we got the door open. The bed had been shoved against it with such force, it broke the frame. A rancid smell filled my nostrils, like burnt flesh.

Celeste lay on the bed under a sheet, still screaming. The man was no where to be seen, and the room had only the one exit. When we pulled back the covers, Celeste's body was so empty, as if her entire body had been drained of all moisture and life, her eyes were gone, black holes crying blood in their place. Her mouth was open and she was somehow still alive. Her chest had carvings through the skin and into the bones. I could see her ribs through the flesh. He had managed to take every bit of blood from her body, but kept her mind trapped there, awake throughout the ordeal.

I ran from the room and the guards managed to end the screaming. The guards said they found dark stains on her skin, like someone had spilled ink on her. They looked around for a trail of ink but no one saw any so it remains unexplained.

Lucia, don't let this man near you, or any of the girls. If he arrives, put him in a room alone and get the guards. Under no circumstances, be alone with him yourself. Take care.

Elina"

"Land's blood…" Myrgen looked at Lucia. "Has there been any sign of this person in Andrew?"

Lucia shook her head. "Not that I've seen or heard. I need to take this to the gendarme but I'm afraid to leave the house. If he were to come in while I was gone…"

"Is there no one here you trust with this?"

Lucia shook her head. "Not yet. It's early in the season now. We're still getting mostly noblemen who wintered nearby. There is a resort within a day's ride of here and we get a lot of clientele during winter from them because the road is so well maintained. Our summer guards won't be in town until next week, sent early by Elina. I have the girls in their rooms for the night."

Myrgen looked down at the missive. "I'll do it."

She looked at him, hope returning to her eyes. "You will?"

"Yes," he folded the missive and put it in his doublet. *And may the Saints preserve me from my Captain's wrath.*

She smiled a desperate smile, filled with relief. "Thank you, sir."

He offered a slight bow and left the brothel only *slightly* concerned he would be arrested on sight.

Gwen opened her eyes and listened. She couldn't hear anyone else in the room and she let her breath out. She needed to get to

Alexander and get him back to St. Andrew before Catriona left. Alistair's support of Myrgen and Catriona getting together bothered her, enough to wake her in the night with an urgent need to go right away to fetch the man. She was still a little uncomfortable with the idea that she could simply walk in and have an audience with the King of Mervolingia, but she knew she would not be stopped.

She was still dressed in her traveling clothes, her boots by the bedside. She slipped them on and checked her disguise in the moonlit mirror. It might need checking in the light of day, but for now, it would do. She gathered the rest of her things and made her way downstairs. There was a fire in the fireplace and someone writing something at a table near it, but other than that, the place was deserted. She looked over at the person near the fireplace to make sure it wasn't Alistair.

The man looked up and saw Gwen and perked up. "Excuse me, are you the messenger from Patras?"

Gwen dropped her voice to be more like her brother's. "Um, yes."

"Good." The man stood and gathered together the papers he had been writing on. He folded them together and tied the packet closed. He walked over, holding it out to her. It wasn't until he was practically next to her that she realized it was Myrgen. She dropped her head, respectfully as he continued. "I have the reply. I was hoping to catch you in the morning, but Fate has intervened, it seems. Could you return this to the one who sent it?"

"Yes, of course."

Myrgen looked at her a moment longer and Gwen felt certain he had recognized her. "Wait," he said, reaching into his doublet and retrieving another missive, "I have another letter, one that needs to be taken to the local authorities. I, uh, have other duties to attend to at present. Could you go by the local gendarme and give them this as well. I recommend not reading it."

Gwen looked at the letter, which had already been opened. "Not a problem, sir. I can't read."

Myrgen sighed. "You have no idea what a blessing that is at this moment. Thank you for your help."

"Of course, Sir." She took the packet and bowed.

Myrgen clapped her on the back. "Good man. Be careful. There are very bad men out there on the road these days." The concern in his voice was genuine and Gwen swallowed her instinct to reassure him. Instead, she nodded and turned to be on her way. Myrgen left via the front door at the same time.

Myrgen looked around at the night life of St. Andrew. It was late and he was feeling the hour. With the crew on board, the streets were far less populated than expected. He figured the townsfolk were feeling the financial losses. Port towns like this one survived because of the added irregular population increases. Catriona's presence on the ship was damaging to the economy. According to the trade logs, there were supplies and goods to take on here. The *Enigma* was scheduled to be in port for a tenday and at this moment, that made Myrgen very nervous.

He made his way back to the ship and looked around for Octavius. Catriona's comment seemed to be true: obviously, the man never slept. He nodded to Myrgen as he stepped onto the deck and the Chancellor waited for him to finish examining the manifest in his hand. "Myrgen. What's on your mind?"

Myrgen stepped in close to make sure he was not overheard by the rest of the crew. "I've come into some information that's very disturbing, and might jeopardize the Captain's safety, as well as the safety of every man on this crew. As First Mate, I thought you should know." He told Octavius about the missive from St. Giles.

Octavius glanced around and rubbed the back of his neck. "That's horrible. How did you get hold of a missive like that?"

"My sister has a vineyard up there. I was wondering if the information had to do with her. She escaped Patras, apparently."

"You think she might have run afoul of this scarred man?"

Myrgen shrugged. "I hope not. I was more worried that the scarred guy might be the one who rescued her: Duncan McVryce."

"That disreputable pirate?" Octavius swore and put his hand on Myrgen's shoulder. "I'm sorry, mate."

Myrgen realized what Octavius was thinking and smiled. "Don't write my sister off just yet, Octavius. She has an odd power. Maybe it's a scent she gives off, maybe it's something in her breath or kiss, but it is a very rare man indeed who can raise a hand against her and Duncan is not one of them. He's one of those who are addicted to her. Most men don't get over her. In fact, I think I've only met one." He folded his arms and shook his head. "No, this is something different. I've seen men get angry and lash out because she has jilted them, but I've never heard of anyone killing someone like this. I don't think it's Duncan."

"Men haven't killed for her before?"

"Oh yes. Her first husband was one of those rare men who could raise a hand to her. Consequently, he met with a messy end from a man who couldn't. Most men, if they end up killing someone, it's in her defense. Bandits or street thugs, that sort of thing. No, this is different. She's extremely Augustinian. She would never stay in the company of someone so steeped in the black arts, not to mention her vineyards are the easiest place to look for her."

"Where would she go?"

"Probably the Papal City. Our Grandfather lives there and it's a holy place. Someone using the black arts would find themselves bereft of any contact with the unholy there if it turns out she's caught that kind of attention, and provided she knows. I have no way of getting a message to her to warn her though."

Octavius nodded. "That's a smart move. I'm sure she has the means to get there unscathed."

"Well, if she's with Duncan, she's got a good shot."

Octavius frowned. "So, do you know anything about Duncan?"

Myrgen glanced around the ship out of habit. Discussing this part of his life, the part he was trying to leave behind as he tried to walk in the light, was risky. But he needed to be able to trust someone and Catriona trusted Octavius with her life. More importantly, she trusted him with this ship, and that told Myrgen all he needed to know. He covered his mouth casually with his hand as he leaned against the main mast, his less savory habits coming to his aid as he sussed out potential listeners and directed his voice away from them. "A few months back, when my sister was seeing him, I sent word to the Patrasian Underground that I was looking for an assassin to get rid of someone. Duncan responded to the call, but he turned down the job. Apparently, he's a true citizen of Mervolingia because he refused to raise a hand against the King."

Octavius nodded, recalling their first real conversation. "Ah yes, the predatory side you mentioned before. You know, your actions since I've known you make it almost hard to believe you could be as bad as you claim."

"Trust me, when it comes to protecting someone I love," he returned his attention to his partner, "I don't draw the bow lightly. They get my full force."

"Good to know. So, you don't think the monster at the brothel was Duncan. Any idea who it was?"

Myrgen shook his head. "The message said he had a deep scar. I haven't seen anyone like that in my travels. I just hope, since Duncan rescued Tangl, that he knows enough to get her somewhere safe. I don't like the idea of her being near a place with a killer on the loose."

Octavius folded his arms, his eyebrow and edge of his mouth curled, pinching his cheek. "It's not like Duncan is a saint, you know."

"No, but he lost her once. This was a grand gesture to get back in her good graces."

"What happened the first time?"

"Nicolai returned to her."

Octavius' eyebrows made their familiar trip to his hairline. He glanced at the hallway to the Captain's Quarters. "Catriona's Nicolai?"

"Yes. When Catriona and Nicolai found each other again, they left Tangl without a lover. Duncan showed up and she was with him until Nicolai came back. I walked in on her and Nicolai together and asked what she had done with Duncan. She said she'd left him."

"But you said men don't just get on after Tanglwyst has been with them."

"No, they don't. I was expecting some sort of grand gesture. Duncan is nothing if not an opportunist. But even if she was in St. Giles before that, I'm pretty sure he'd have her out of there now. One thing you learn when you walk the shady side of the street, a killer like this doesn't see what he did as a crime. He sees it as practice." Myrgen glanced around the ship, causing Octavius to do likewise. "Octavius, you said before nothing could be on this ship without you knowing, right?"

"Correct."

"Because the ship speaks to you."

Octavius nodded.

"Is there anything on the ship now that shouldn't be here? Or in the water near the ship?"

Octavius glanced at the helm of the ship and seemed as though he were searching for a memory. He blinked back to the present and shook his head. "Nope. Nothing and no one here."

Myrgen glanced at the helm, curious, but took a deep breath and nodded. There was so much about this place he didn't know. "I'm going to check on the Captain."

Myrgen barely knocked on Catriona's door. He thought he heard movement, and he knocked again, slightly heavier. No more movement, so he opened the door quietly. His concern regarding the Scarred Man outweighed his sense of respect for the lady's privacy. If Duncan had fallen into a shadow, as Michael had conveyed, then who was to say he couldn't emerge from one? Catriona could be in danger before even Octavius could be alerted.

He stepped over to her bedside where she was sleeping. She had cleaned away the Passion Sap and changed clothes, as was expected. She seemed to be resting heavily, something Myrgen figured she didn't do regularly. The truth was she felt safe on this ship, and he would do all in his rather miniscule power to protect that safety. His main weapon was foreknowledge of the threat.

He touched her temple, smoothing a hair from her face. She stirred at the touch, but didn't seem to waken. *By the third kiss,*

Alistair had said. But he had kissed her only once, in reality. In his dreams and fantasies, which were recurring with alarming frequency, they coupled nightly, but when he had had the opportunity to kiss her two nights ago on deck, he stayed his hand, or rather, his lips. The possibility that they would be seen stopped him then, but even he acknowledged it was just barely.

But now, he thought, *there is no one to see. We are alone and she would never even know.* Her hair decorated the pillow in sensual swirls. The smell of her skin was back, that spice and musk scent that reminded him of Yantap. Her lips were full and available and he leaned over her, hovering over her lips. Her breathing quickened and he imagined her waking to find him all but kissing her. Would she take the initiative and close the distance, or would she throw him off her ship for daring to violate her while she was vulnerable?

Myrgen closed his eyes and pulled back, letting out an unconsciously held breath. He would never do that to her. If she wanted him, then she would kiss him. He would not impose himself upon her. He stood quietly and moved to the door. The desire to look back once more was almost overpowering. He instead opened the door quietly and left.

Twenty-Three

"Sliced turnips or green Mandian squash, cooked
with cinnamon and sugar, are indistinguishable
from apples."
The Wise Wench's Tavern Book

The next morning, Myrgen opened the door and entered the tavern, looking around for Alistair. The place was busy and louder than he expected at this hour of the day, full of wet wood and dust. Most of the inhabitants were from ships by the look of them. Some were coming in, some were going out. He saw Alistair at the back of the tavern, at the table he had shared with Myrgen and Catriona the night before. He saw a few of the sailors from the *Enigma*, now on solid ground because Catriona had left the ship. He had forgotten to address Captain's Watch with Octavius like he planned and hoped he would remember during their next conversation.

He made his way to the bar and waited for acknowledgment before ordering tea from the barkeep. The Yorkish fluid was passed his way and he carried it carefully over to the man in the shadows. "Sparrow," he said as he approached the table, aware to use proper address in so busy a room.

Alistair looked up and nodded. "Chancellor! Sit." Myrgen did so. "How is your Lady?"

"My *Captain* is fine, thank you. She's up and about. Taking care of the purchase of supplies today. Couldn't keep her on the ship, in fact. She insisted on going ashore."

"How long have you been at sea?" Alistair took a sip of his own beverage, a frothy black liquid in a very small cup.

"About a tenday. We escorted one of her ships to an island, then made our way here. This is the first time we've been in a port city overnight."

"And the crew returned to the ship last night? Stayed on board?"

"Right. Captain's Watch. She hates that practice, you know."

"I know. Doesn't stop the men from doing it though."

Myrgen leaned in, curious. "Is a sudden departure common?"

"No, it's decidedly *uncommon*. It means something's wrong. If the threat ends up meaning danger for either the ship or crew, Octavius doesn't want to have to try and track them down. It's usually temporary though. She picks good men. But they'll stay on that ship the entire tenday she's scheduled in port if she doesn't leave it."

"So she left to give them shore leave. That's undoubtedly a good thing for the economy. These people depend upon the traffic of the ships. Most likely she'll stay in town tonight, then."

Alistair noticed a frown impose itself upon Myrgen's face, like the thought of her in town bothered him. He guessed the Chancellor might think the more intimate surroundings of the ship had a greater chance for romance. He hid a smile in his cup. "Isn't that what she tried to do last night?"

Myrgen didn't produce a jealous scowl as Alistair had expected. Instead he said, "Yes, about that. Could you two try again tonight?"

Alistair blinked. "I doubt it. You might say I have a prior engagement. Ce'Nedra, the lovely Innkeeper has invited me to dinner."

"Oh."

Alistair leaned in, confused. "Myrgen, you seem somehow vexed by my lack of interest in Catriona."

"I just… I didn't want her to be alone."

"Then see after her yourself." He reached into his doublet and pulled a key from his pouch. "Here." He set the iron key on the table. "Use my room here at the Net. It's paid up through the tenday."

Myrgen looked at the key, then at Alistair. "Aren't you going to need it?"

"No. As I said, Ce'Nedra has invited me to dinner."

Myrgen arched an eyebrow. "You're certainly sure of yourself." He picked up the key.

"Merely following instructions. She was quite clear in her ambitions."

Myrgen smiled. "I see. And you're not in the habit of telling these fine women no?"

"It would be unseemly." Alistair watched him as he seemed to mull over the concept of taking care of Catriona's needs. From her zeal last night, Alistair felt quite certain she was ready for such an engagement and by Karma's Hand, Myrgen certainly looked like he needed the same thing. Alistair decided to nudge him a bit. He turned the tankard in his hands and saw a crack in the side near the top, wording his next question carefully. He wanted to confirm that Myrgen did indeed have strong feelings for Catriona. His presence by her side all night as she recovered would be that final impulse he needed to be sure. "So, were you there with her when she woke up this morning?"

"No. We have a young man on board named Jack. I had him sit in there with her. He's about fifteen years old and an orphan that Catriona saved from drowning."

"You let a teenaged boy watch her in her bedroom?"

"Yes. Octavius figured he'd be the only one who would stay awake with such a duty. He's still in the throes of wanting to impress her with his chivalry."

Alistair smiled at that. "Octavius is a very smart man."

Myrgen agreed.

Alistair sipped the ale. "Did you know Octavius turned down captaining a ship in order to stay First Mate on the *Enigma*?"

Myrgen sat back, folding his arms. "No, he never mentioned that."

Alistair nodded confirmation. "It's true. He also gets himself into nearly fatally dangerous situations periodically in order to stay in debt to her. So he can stay on the ship." Alistair leaned back, noting idly the shininess of the ale that had dripped from the small crack in the tankard. Pity it wasn't an ugly spot. "Did she, uh, happen to ask for me this morning?"

Myrgen shook his head. "No. She really didn't ask for anyone, according to Jack."

Alistair nodded. "She did last night." He looked up at Myrgen. "She asked for you."

Myrgen blinked, and studied his companion, remembering the night he healed Catriona on the ship. "Did she say why?"

"Thought maybe you could tell me. Here she was, seeping large quantities of fluid that looked a lot like blood pouring from some rather serious and potentially fatal wounds, and she wanted to make sure I got her to you." He crossed his arms. "You have an idea?"

"I... might." He leaned on the table again, trying to figure out how to explain what would easily be construed as magic by most folks. He decided to go with what the Captain had told him. "I tried teaching her the Fusion of Flesh Technique on the way here. I learned it from the Rhamidhal Shalib. Her ability to heal others is something she got from the Land but it seems to allow her to heal herself from the brink of death as well, but only just. I thought it might couple with the Technique well so she wouldn't need... outside help anymore."

"She has a surgeon on board now?"

"No. Remember that King I mentioned? He spent a lot of his time these past few years traveling under an assumed name and being her healer when they met up in various ports."

"So, he's had access to her for years? Tending wounds? How does she feel about him?" The concern Alistair displayed was more than casual, like he suspected something.

"He has been a bit inappropriate around her of late and she is put off by him, at present." When Alistair relaxed, Myrgen leaned forward. "What's on your mind, Alistair?"

"Remember what I said about her being dosed? Well, I understand now what happened and it was... an accident. Wrong cup. Just make sure she knows who is giving her what, would you?"

"I'll let her know." Myrgen took a drink of his lukewarm tea.

Alistair watched him and scowled a little. "How can you drink that swill? Boiled leaves that cool off so quickly."

Myrgen glanced at the cup. "It's convenient. It tastes roughly the same whether it's warm or cold. It doesn't distract me with trivialities of temperature. When you live in a castle, and your schedule is based upon the whim of a spineless, abusive wretch, you adapt."

"My! You must have hated the King."

"I was actually thinking of Elizabeth." He set his cup down. "It amazes me how much can change in the space of a few days. Three tendays ago, I would have given my life for that woman. Now, all I can remember is her insanity and the danger she put everyone in. I also have a much higher respect for the man she married. Anyone who can call themselves Catriona's friend means they have a lot more character than perhaps they've deigned to show someone of lesser quality like myself." He raised his cup in a slight toast. "Present company included." He drank.

"Yes, about that... Myrgen, remember when I told you last night to beware a royal suitor because they have access to things us commoners have not? I need to warn you about an herb I encountered when I was at the Incense House in Yantap..."

Myrgen pushed his empty mug away as Alistair finished telling about the girl and the nobleman. "So, do you remember anything about this herb?"

Alistair shook his head. "No."

"Was the man questioned as to where he got the herb?"

"I don't know. I actually wasn't in on the trial."

Myrgen thought about it. "Did they record what was said?"

Alistair looked at his tankard and shrugged with his face. "Probably. The Rhamidhal are very meticulous about writing things down, as you may remember. He might have the records of the trial."

"How long before you're due to return there?"

"Well, at present, I don't really have plans to go for a few months. There's this Innkeeper, see…"

Myrgen nodded, holding up his hands in surrender. "Maybe I can convince her to make a trip there."

"Why are you concerned about this? It's not like she would be caught off guard like that Incense House girl, not with her ability."

"She was last night."

His gaze wandered down to his sleeve, still carrying a hint of dark brown staining on the cuffs. "Also a concern but at least it wasn't malicious. It does denote a hole in her defenses. One I'm sure you can cover." He scratched his temple. "That's why I decided to go see Ce'Nedra. I knew she has a fancy for me and frankly, you have a hole to cover."

Myrgen looked at the leaves floating in the last of the water, his brow furrowing. Her dismissal of his affection in favor of Alistair's still stung but he understood it now. Alistair was temporary, something to fill a void, something she knew would never stay, or at least that she would never keep. "The thing that killed Nicolai was so virulent, the spasms it caused broke his back. Afterwards, to prevent the poison from accidentally getting in the water or food, Catriona had to *burn* his body." He looked at Alistair. "She doesn't need someone to bed her. She needs time to heal on her own."

Alistair raised his eyebrows.

"Uh, no."

He leaned forward as Myrgen fought with such a statement. "What she needs, more than anything right now is to be bedded and hard. She needs confirmation that she's alive and desirable. That man she married was one of Tanglwyst's pets and from what I know of your sister's abilities, Catriona was cast aside in favor of that woman by the man whose death she mourned, needlessly, for seven years. Now she *knows* he's actually dead. She needs to know she's actually alive." He picked up his tankard. "I'd do it, but I'm secured for the rest of this tenday. That's where you come in."

"I can't do that to her. For one thing, she's my Captain. She'd throw me off the ship and I'm wanted for treason in this country still."

"What'd ya do?"

Myrgen kept his steam, despite the effort to divert it. "Attempted regicide."

Alistair blinked. "I woulda pegged you as a state secret sort of man."

"Yeah, I'm full of surprises. My point is I'm opposed to her jumping into bed to ease her suffering."

"Even if she's jumping in with you?"

"Yes." He looked at his empty mug again. "Yes. She's way too good for the likes of me." He looked at Alistair who started to get a comment on his face. He pointed a finger at the man. "She's too good for the likes of you too. So is that lady Innkeeper."

Alistair smiled. "*That* is probably too true." He ran his thumb across the rim of the tankard. "You know yet where you will be heading after she's done here in St. Andrew?"

"We're going to Caratia, I guess. That's where her business has its home base. Since she wants me to be her Chancellor, and since I'm not actually a part of her crew what with the whole life debt thing, I imagine I'll be staying behind in Zara."

Alistair glanced down at the table, then back at Myrgen. "You're not a part of the crew? I'm quite surprised. I felt certain you had a life debt to her. Although I can't say as I blame her. Knowing these men are good and true and feel beholden to her for their lives means they will keep her safe."

"Well," said Myrgen pointing at the two of them, "clearly, she doesn't have to save us to have us want to protect her."

"Speak for yourself. She's already saved my life." He stood and put a coin down on the table for the barmaid. "She got me away from your sister. Here, let me have that room key. My things are still in the room. I'll clear it out and return the key to you in a few minutes. I was planning on staying longer so I unpacked everything."

"You don't need to do this, you know."

"You turning down a free room, Mr. Accountant?"

Myrgen tightened his lips, shaking as if from great effort. Suddenly, he relaxed, as if exhausted from the failed attempt. "No."

"I thought not." Alistair smiled and left the grinning Chancellor with a swirl of impeccably tailored clothing.

A tap on Myrgen's shoulder a few minutes later surprised him when it *wasn't* Alistair. Octavius sat down across from the Chancellor. "How are you this morning, Myrgen?"

"Good. Had a cup of tea, which was actually quite good for a pub *not* in York. What more could I want from my day?"

"Good. I was coming to find you to see if you needed any money for a room for the night? In an attempt to make sure she stays off the ship and in town tonight, the Captain has ordered all the mattresses and bedding pulled onto the deck, washed, and left to dry. It occurred to her afterwards that you had said something about not having any money, so she sent me to find you."

Myrgen smiled. "No, thank you. I have a room for the entire tenday, as a matter of fact. I also found a small pouch of silver this morning on my desk for my tenday's work on the books." He raised his empty mug. "Hence, the tea."

"So you found it. Very good. Well, I have been authorized to front you up to fifteen gold ducats, should you need it."

"*Fifteen? Gold?* That's three months wages at the palace. Why so much?"

"She said it will encourage you to stick around."

Myrgen smiled and examined his mug. He set it down again, shaking his head. "Again, thank you, but I decline. Maybe if we were further along in the voyage, but right now she needs that money to buy supplies for her real crewmen. The silver she…?" He looked at Octavius, who shook his head, "You…? You gave me will take care of me while we're in town. Please, tell her thank you, though."

Octavius smiled, nodded and left the tavern.

Catriona saw Octavius leave the Net and nodded him over as she turned her attention to the fruits at the stall. He bowed quickly and handed her the pouch with the fifteen gold ducats in it. "He said thank you, but no. Pay up."

She reached into her doublet and handed him a piece of paper. It was a voucher to finish cleaning the mattresses on the deck. "I can't believe you made me write this down. What kind of trust is that?"

"The trust of a man who wants bragging rights." He held it up and smiled. "I'm surprised you bet against him after that incident in the hold."

"Well, this will teach me, won't it?"

Octavius nodded and put the voucher in his pouch as he went on his way. Catriona looked at the fruit again, not really seeing it. A soft, sexy male voice next to her said, "I'm surprised you bet against him as well."

She looked at Alistair who stepped half into the light from the shadow of the stall. "He is not accustomed to being without resources and he was probably paid twice that at the palace. I was actually more concerned he would find it an insult."

"I highly doubt you could say anything to insult him."

She dropped her gaze, that horrible feeling of guilt invading her again. "You'd be wrong." She met his eyes again. "I managed to do it last night. Twice."

Alistair sighed and reached into his pocket. He pulled out a room key. "Here. This is the key to my room here at the Net. I have promised to do some things for some folks, but come there tonight. If I'm not there, I won't be long."

She smiled as she took the key. "I might be pretty smelly. I'm scheduled to clean mattresses all day."

"I'll endeavor to have water for a bath and some good wine waiting for you then. Maybe dinner as well."

"You're quite the romantic, Alistair."

"Oh, more than you know, my dear. 'Til tonight then?"

She nodded and put the key away in her pouch. When she looked up again, he had disappeared into the crowd.

Twenty-Four

"Do not rush to serve a lain-in mead."
The Wise Wench's Tavern Book

An iron key was set on Myrgen's table and he looked up. Again, he was surprised by the lack of an Alistair. "Ma'am?"

"Alistair's cutting some wood for me. His room key fell out of his pouch and he asked me to bring it in to ye."

Myrgen picked up the key. "What's he doing chopping wood?"

The barkeep's wife nodded her pretty red head. "Logan's got his hands full with all the ships and crew due in today. Alistair offered to do it for me."

Myrgen looked at the key. "Well, that's just not equitable. Where did you say he was, my Lady?"

She smiled a sly smile. "He's out back."

Myrgen got up and Victoria retrieved the key from the table before following him. Alistair was splitting a log. Myrgen saw about twenty logs behind him, leaning up against a small storage shed behind the tavern. "Hey, Alistair!"

The man looked up, his golden hair already showing signs of dishevelment. He stood from where he had just set a log to split. "Myrgen. Victoria, I told you to give him the key, not ask him to come out here."

"He insisted, Alistair. Said something about it not being equitable?" She leaned her shoulder against the wall and folded her arms.

Myrgen nodded. "It's not right that you, who have already paid for your room here, should be splitting wood while I freeload. I can't stand by and do it. Besides, I wouldn't want you to pull something for your date tonight. As I have no such engagements, please, allow me to earn the right to stay here."

Victoria piped up. "If you split all that wood for me, I'll feed you for the tenday, sir."

Myrgen said, "We have a contract then, my lady. I accept your offer and I'll chop any other deliveries the woodcutter brings while I'm in town."

"Oh, I doubt I'll have to worry about that. That wood hasn't been split in a month."

Myrgen looked at the shed and noticed the logs were not setting near the wall of the shed. They were spilling out from beside it. He walked around to the side. There, easily a forest of uncut logs was piled haphazardly as if dumped from a wagon on several occasions. He swallowed and looked at Alistair.

The man put his hand on Myrgen's shoulder. "That seem more equitable?"

Myrgen blinked and nodded through a deep breath. "I'm going to need some wine at the end of this."

"I'll be certain there's wine, a bath and dinner awaiting you in the room when you are finished here. Maybe even a lady for the evening."

"You're insane if you think I'll be in any shape whatsoever to do anything with a lady after this."

"Good point. Ah well. Great way to work off that frustration though. Hard labor always clears the head. Well, my friend, as it would be inequitable for me to aide you in this since you have a contract with Victoria, I will leave you to your task. Good day."

Catriona brushed the hair out of her face for about the hundredth time and stepped back to survey her work. It had taken quite a bit of scrubbing but the mattresses were finally all cleaned. She had set them on their edges, leaning against the railings to dry. Most of the stains had come out. She had several bales delivered and re-stuffed the mattresses back to their original firmness. She was actually quite proud of herself for accomplishing such a feat unaided and the weariness of manual labor felt good.

She walked over to the latest bucket of water she had used and dumped it over the side of the ship. She had pretty much used all the extra water they had on board to do this, but she knew she had water ordered for the next leg of the voyage. The bad news was that there was no water left to clean herself a bit before seeing Alistair. Had her own mattress not also been leaning against a railing, she would have been inclined to send word to her suitor and beg off. Regardless, she was going to be useless tonight.

She went to her quarters and got a few things for the next couple days at the Net. In the end, a change of clothes and a kit bag were all she could carry. She walked in a tired haze to the tavern. A wave to Logan at the bar and she was up the stairs, pulling the key from her pouch. The door opened easily and she was quite pleased to find the room blissfully empty. The bed called to her. He had apparently not gotten around to the bath or the dinner yet, but she was fine with that. She would nap for a while and then indulge afterward.

She pulled off her boots with great effort and put them under the bed. The room was dim. She had removed her filthy clothes and just barely got under the covers before she was unconscious.

Myrgen set the split logs he carried in next to the stove and waved at Victoria. "Here you are. Do you need anything else?"

"No, Myrgen. I'm fine. Did you actually get that entire pile done today?"

"Saints, no, my lady," he leaned against the stove and instantly recoiled from the burn. He swore as Victoria rushed him over and put his hand in a bucket of water. "What is *wrong* with me? I have never been so clumsy in all my life?"

Victoria grinned. "I take it this has happened a lot recently?"

"Like it was intentional. I have tripped, fallen backwards, or any number of things in the past few tendays that would have given anybody watching me the impression I am inept and apparently endowed with multiple left feet, some of them actually attached to my wrists."

Victoria laughed into the back of her hand until tears streamed down her face. "I'm, I'm sorry, Myrgen…Would you like something to drink?"

"Yes, please. Is there some water I can use to clean up?"

"Well, that water your hand's in is available."

He looked at the damage to his hand and realized he could heal that pretty quick, but his level of exhaustion was impairing concentration right then. *I'll just have to do it in the morning.* "Is there a bath house in St. Andrew?"

"Yes, at the Red Sky at Night."

Myrgen remembered Lucia and hoped there were a few city guards inside the doors by now. Definitely not a smart choice for a wanted traitor. "I see. Do you have anything here? That place is a little out of my price range."

"There's a tub down here, if you want to use it. A lot easier to haul water to it than up the stairs repeatedly to your own room."

"Actually, I think I may do this a quicker way, if you don't mind." He grabbed a sea sponge and some soap and took the bucket outside. He set it on the stump he had been using to split logs, then took off his boots and socks so they wouldn't get wet. He used the sponge to soak up a load of water and squeezed it over his head. Although the water was cool, it felt good on his sore muscles.

He soaped up quickly as the encroaching night air chilled the dampness on his skin, then he soaked the sponge again to pour some water over his face and body. Finally, with the last of the water in the bucket, he upended it over his head, rinsing away most of the last of the soap. He couldn't feel anymore soap in his hair or on his face or chest, but he was sure his pants and feet were still less than clean. He really didn't care right then. He took the bucket and accessories back inside and set them by the sink.

"Feel better?"

"Much."

"I poured you some stew. Sit and eat before you head on up to bed."

It took some effort but he managed to eat the stew without falling asleep in the bowl and by the time he was finished, he was dead on his feet. Victoria gave him the key and took him up to his room. The main room had been loud, but he barely heard any of it. He dropped his boots, shirt and pants inside the door and fell into the bed.

The movement woke Catriona and she rolled over. Her companion was wet and nude, but he was also already snoring, asleep on his stomach which gave her some mixed messages. Perhaps he had gotten to drinking or dicing with the other sailors in town and forgotten her. Maybe he listened to her when she had said she wasn't going to be worth anything tonight. No matter the cause, she wasn't about to tempt fate by disturbing him.

She turned her back to him and fell asleep.

The sound of a door being quietly opened woke her again. She realized that she had been asleep longer than she thought. She was resting on his chest and he had crawled under the covers and was cradling her in his arms.

She raised her head to see who was entering the room, unconcerned about such an entry for some reason. What could barely be called pre-morning light was seeping into the room and she figured it must be well after midnight. She looked at the intruder to see what they wanted. Her adrenaline spiked when she realized she couldn't read him. She sat up, pressing her hand against Alistair's chest, which woke him as well. He rolled off the bed and threw open the curtains to gain some light. She was extremely surprised to see the person who had snuck into the room was *Alistair!*

She looked at the man who had been in bed with her and saw that it was Myrgen. She quickly turned her eye on the intruder. "Alistair! What is the meaning of this?"

"I was just checking to see how you kids were getting on." He smiled. "Looks like you're getting on very well."

Myrgen looked at the bed and saw Catriona, but she kept her eyes on Alistair. Catriona scowled. "Please toss him his pants."

"Aye, Captain. That I can do."

"And explain this."

Alistair tossed Myrgen his pants. Myrgen's anger flared as he put them on. "Oh please Catriona, do you really need this spelled out for you? He set us up." He fastened his buttons and a twitch indicated his hand was injured. "You gave her a key and told her to use the room, then you did the same thing to me."

"I was just trying to give things a little nudge."

"I don't need your help getting a woman!" He pointed at Catriona. "Especially not that one." He grabbed his boots and socks by the door and shoved past Alistair to leave the two of them in the room.

Alistair looked around the room, pursing his lips. Catriona glared at him. He finally spoke up. "Well, that didn't exactly go as I expected."

"Is he right? Is that what you did?"

"Look, Catriona, I'm not the right one for you…"

"On that we agree."

"But I didn't want to leave you alone again. I saw how you two were together, how much you two obviously care for each other." He pointed at her. "But you're a stubborn woman, Catriona Morsdatora. You won't allow yourself to experience real happiness because you don't think you deserve it."

"What in the Land and sea were you thinking, Alistair? That you could put us in the same bed together and we would fall in love?"

He nodded, eyes wide. "Pretty much, yes."

"Then what are you doing here?"

He glanced at the floor, then pulled his hand from behind his back. "I came to leave this."

He opened his hand and let the locket Nicolai had worn dangle before her eyes. She got out of bed, holding the covers to her chest. She looked at him, her eyes confused and hurt.

"I acquired it a year ago, about this time. He cast it off a cliff outside of Cheryb, the night he decided he wanted her instead of you."

"You knew? You knew all this time and you didn't tell me?"

"I couldn't find you, not before it was too late."

"You could have left a message at *any* port."

"What makes you think I *didn't?*" He stepped away from her, pacing. "I left messages in St. Giles, St. Augustine and St. Marguerite for you to contact me, but you never did."

Catriona cast her eyes at the ground. She *had* received those messages, but she had not gotten the missives until after she had seen him at Tanglwyst's. She had thought they were just attempts to get back in her good graces and had torn them up without reading them. She leaned against the wall, her head back and her eyes filling with tears. "I'm so sorry, Alistair."

He looked at her, She could see he was surprised at her apology. He went over to her and took her in his arms. She started crying and all the years of grieving her lost love invaded her vulnerable walls. She dropped to her knees and Alistair went to the floor with her, not letting her go. She cried for almost half an hour before she was able to stop. Her exhaustion was so overwhelming she could barely stand to get back into the bed. He sat next to her and tucked her in.

"Do you want me to get him? Myrgen?"

She shook her head. "No. He's very angry right now, but he's exhausted too. Leave him be. Go back to your lady friend."

He sat back a bit. "How did you know...?"

She sniffed and rubbed her red nose with the back of her hand. "When I took the locket from you, I noticed a perfume. You don't wear perfume."

He nodded and got up.

"Tell me something," she said, her voice still thick with mucus. "Are *all* Glarrens such incredible meddlers?"

He smiled at her. "Only the royal ones." He kissed her forehead. "Get some sleep."

Twenty-Five

Myrgen folded his arms across his bare chest in the pre-dawn chill and cursed Alistair for getting him so angry that he forgot to get dressed completely. A light sea spray coated everything in heavy fog. It didn't take long for him to be soaked through to the skin. He decided to return to the ship and get his long coat he had been wearing the day of his imprisonment. It was made of a heavy wool and silk brocade and would go a long way towards keeping him warm. He had given Alistair his only other shirt, one borrowed from Octavius' stores. He now needed to make sure he replaced it. He damned sure wasn't going to speak to Alistair again, even to ask for it back. About then, it occurred to him that he could sleep on the ship. *I must be exhausted to have not thought of that in the first place. Where, I wonder, was I planning on going once I got my coat?*

The fog covered most of the streets and got heavier as he approached the docks. He could see very little and was glad he actually knew the way well since a mere passing acquaintance with the route to the *Enigma* would have resulted in a miscalculation of the length of one of these piers and the subsequent dousing in the harbor. Myrgen entertained the thought of Alistair doing that, his impeccable hair and smile covered in the grimy oils and flotsam that marked the water around the ships.

Myrgen stepped onto the ship and looked around. There were strange shapes on the deck, lining the railings. He walked up to them and found them to be the mattresses from the berthing quarters. He touched them and, sure enough, they were soaking wet from the fog. He shook his head. There went the idea to stay on board for the rest of the night. He looked around and noticed a mast rising out of the shadows across the dock from him. The fog at ground level had hidden the other ship from him, but on deck the fog was thinner and he could see the hulking shadows of about six other ships. If each one was the size of the *Enigma*, that would mean every available room in town, including the ones at the brothel, would be full up. Alistair had really outdone himself in setting them up.

He went to his cabin and took off his pants, hanging them over the back of the desk chair to dry. He changed clothes into the set he had been imprisoned in, minus the shirt, and was quite pleased to rediscover that Xannu had cleaned and repaired his clothing the night he had spent at the Open Lotus. He could still smell the fragrant soaps used to clean them. The smell reminded him of Catriona and he closed his eyes and sat down on his bed frame.

What am I going to do? I can't see her, not after this. I thank the Saints I didn't molest her, thinking she was the prostitute Alistair mentioned. Although at least that way, she would have killed me and I wouldn't be sitting on an empty ship in the middle of the night, kicking myself for trusting that man.

He felt the wood of the frame digging in to his legs and felt the soreness from chopping the wood. It was actually a lot worse than he thought it would be. The light work he had done around the ship did not qualify as exercise in any way. He was actually grateful the food served on the ship was sustaining but not fattening or he would have been unable to actually wear his only (almost) full set of clothes any longer. The soreness in his muscles was a good soreness, a good tired, but right then, it felt like it was Alistair's own personal torture. On the other hand, that extreme bone-tiredness had been the reason nothing untoward happened between him and the Captain.

He got up and went to her cabin. The door was surprisingly unlocked. They must have forgotten to lock it when they removed her mattress for airing out. He stepped in and breathed in the scent of her. It was everywhere, marking her territory. He looked in on her bed, but her mattress was gone as well. No chance there of reprieve, though he was unsure her finding him in her bed on the ship would be any less horrifying than finding him in her bed at the Net had been.

A sound behind him called his attention and he found himself looking into the eyes of a very suspicious-looking Octavius. "Myrgen, what are you doing here?"

"Looking for a place to sleep. What are you doing here?"

"I was in bed, like a sane person."

"So you actually do sleep?"

"I didn't say that. I said I was in bed."

"What happened here?"

"All the mattresses are being cleaned. Captain's orders, remember? I told you this morning. There's no beds made except mine."

"Why is yours made?"

"Because I made it? No offense, but why are you sleeping on the ship? Why aren't you sleeping in town like the rest of the crew?"

"I ca, can't..." A serious yawn interrupted Myrgen's commentary, which, surprisingly did not illicit one from Octavius. "Sorry. I can't. No room. Is that why you're here too?"

"Not exactly. I can't spend a night off the *Enigma* until we reach Zara."

"Is that also Captains' orders?"

"No. It's the ship's." He scratched his chest and rubbed his face. "I promised her I would never leave her alone. It's why I'm First Mate. The ship likes me."

"So she holds you prisoner?"

"No, it's not like that, Myrgen. More like I wouldn't leave my wife's side at night. Why would I leave the *Enigma*?"

"Because it's not a person? It's a ship?"

"You have so much to learn. What are you doing here?"

"I told you, looking for a place to sleep."

"No, I mean what are you doing *here*, in the Captain's Quarters? And you'd better not tell me you were looking to sleep here. I'll throw you off this ship so fast they'll never find your body before the tide takes it."

Myrgen looked around the room. "I guess I was apologizing." He sat with Octavius and told him of the trick Alistair had pulled on both of them. "I told him I didn't need his help getting a woman, especially *that* one and left. I came here right afterward."

"Callista's Fury, Myrgen, that was incredibly arrogant. I can see why you would want to apologize."

"Huh? Arrogant?"

"Yes. Saying you didn't need help getting the Captain? Like you pretty much have that handled?"

Myrgen slapped his hand to his forehead and then ran it back through his entangled hair. "By the bleeding Saints and Martyrs! *What is wrong with me?*" He got up with a shove of the chair from the table and stormed around the room, shaking his head.

"I'm not this *inept*. I can usually see plots coming at me. I don't step into them like they're a new pair of shoes left out by elves, but apparently not today. I can't seem to stand without a solid, rigid surface on at least three sides, or walk through a door without it hitting me in the face. And I may not be Alexander when it comes to speaking, but I'm hardly a bumbling *cow herd*. I'm an educated man, Octavius! I know a few things about the world. I know how to talk and hold and kiss a woman. Even Catriona herself can attest to *that*, but I'm acting like I've never been around upright humans before, much less the feminine kind. Hell, my *sister* is *Tanglwyst de Holloway,* the most notorious mantrap on the continent! I've been around beautiful women before! So why am I acting like this around *her?*"

He turned to Octavius as if asking him for the answer. The First Mate's eyebrows were on full alert. "You kissed her?"

"By the Saints..." He raised his head and closed his eyes. He doubted highly that their intimate moments were something she wanted the men on her ship to know. "Should I just go ahead and jump over the side of the ship now, or would you like to tie some weights on my feet first? Before you do, though, you should probably know I gave away the shirt you loaned me so you'll probably want the one in Catriona's room at the Net in its stead."

Octavius smiled and got up. He clapped his friend on the shoulder. "Mate, just accept it. You are infatuated with the Captain. The sooner you admit that, the sooner you'll be able to go on with your life. The reason you're having so much trouble isn't because you are attracted to her. It's because you're trying to *deny* that you're attracted to her. Accept your infatuation, acknowledge it and you will find you can function again, think like an adult and perform your duties like you know how."

He raised his hand as Myrgen started to question. "Trust me. I've been dealing with this for a decade now. I know from whence I speak. Do as I say." He turned and walked backwards a few steps, keeping his eye on Myrgen. "I need you in top form, Myrgen. Duncan is still out there and like you said, Tangl may want a grand gesture." He opened the door and stepped out of the way.

Myrgen blinked. "Callista's Fury. I left her alone." He ran out the open door without a thought to the fact Octavius had known he would.

Catriona woke as the door to her room opened again. The light in the room was a bit brighter, a soft grey covering all color but the most garish. She saw Myrgen come in quietly and lock the door behind him. He was obviously planning to stay in the room. She could see he was worried and that he had been back to the ship because he was wearing his long coat from the palace. His hair was damp from the morning fog. She suddenly remembered the mattresses and realized they would be all but soaked through by now. She would need to get them indoors before dusk tonight to prevent that from happening again. Hopefully, it was going to be a warm day and not a rainy spring morning.

He walked over to the hearth and pulled the chair about an inch before the noise stopped him, swearing quietly. He looked over at her and saw her eyes open.

"Sorry, Captain. I was trying not to wake you."

"Try lifting the chair next time."

He straightened, groaning as aches exploded through his body and across his face. She sat up, holding the covers to her chest. "What's wrong?" Her voice was sharp and alert. *Had he and Alistair fought after they left?* Catriona wouldn't have put it past them. He confirmed her fears with his reply.

"Alistair. He played me very well. He put me to splitting wood for the proprietress of this tavern and there's probably about three days worth of work out back. I'm stiff and sore and tired and…" He sighed. "And my mattress on the ship is soaking wet and outdoors."

"Why didn't you try to get another room?"

He leaned on the arms of the chair and took a breath. "Two reasons. One," he picked up the chair and walked it over to in front of the door, "there are about six ships in dock right now. I couldn't tell through the fog, but if they are merely the size of the *Enigma*, that's an extra nine hundred men in town looking for berth. It will take some looking to find another room, and in the twilight of sunrise is not the best time to be doing that.

"Two," he thunked the chair in place by the door and turned to face her, "I think you might be targeted for assassination."

Catriona blinked, worried. "You mean like Nicolai was in Rouen?"

Myrgen looked away in thought as the idea walked into his mind and had a seat. "Saint's blood. That would make sense. Tanglwyst jilted Duncan for Nicolai. It would not be a far stretch of the imagination to believe the man would take him out before rushing off to rescue her."

"Who is Duncan?"

Myrgen looked at her and glanced at the ground. He took a deep breath and spread his arms. "Maybe you should read me on this one. There's a lot to convey."

Catriona nodded and blinked her gift into being. She looked at his hair and saw it had been washed recently, despite the work he had been doing the day before. There were a few blisters on the heels and fingers of his hands from the unaccustomed grip of an axe and his muscles twitched from the effort of holding his arms out to the sides, even for such a small amount of time. The palm of one of his hands was red and had blisters starting to form on the soft parts of it, the ones not already attacked by the axe handle. It looked painful, but treatable with immediate care. He obviously thought he could heal it himself and chose not to bandage it, but his exhaustion from the physical labor had not yet enabled that.

He was wearing the coat he wore when she rescued him, when they kissed under the palace in the burnt out church. His shirt was missing, still on the floor where he had dropped his clothes and the coat was open, not being designed to close. The scent of the soap from the Open Lotus still lingered on the coat. He had kept it folded and safe since that encounter, and the smell reminded him of that time. His pants had a line of soap and salt just under the waistband, indicating he had cleaned up after his work wearing them. She could see the bulge of the key in his pocket against his thigh and his boots had wet wood dust clotting the seams.

She blinked back up to his eyes and pushed into his soul. She opened his spirit and it was easy because he let her in. She wasn't sneaking in like she often did, or ripping her way in as she had done to others in the past. She stepped in, like an honored guest, and the visions lined up politely for her to view. She saw his actions at the palace, his objection to using Catriona when she had refused the job to kill King Charles, and his intense anger at being manipulated by his sister and the Queen. She pushed those aside. *The past is the past, Myrgen. That is not this time.*

The next vision was of the fight in Rouen. She saw that he had heard the exchange between her and Nicolai, borne somehow to only him through the ground. *The Land told him? Why?* She did not know, but she thought that was quite important. Something in the exchange between them was significant to the Land. That Myrgen was the recipient when Alexander was right there being tended by him indicated a choice. She nodded, recognizing the wishes of her deity.

She saw the whale incident, colored in moonlight and attraction. Her own feelings on this subject were too passionate and she likewise moved that vision aside for a better day. That was not what she was here for. She would not violate his trust by delving beyond her purpose. Likewise, she saw his feelings for her after they put into port, when she and Alistair returned to the ship because of the Passion Sap. She saw how cast aside he had felt when she had complained that she was in need of being touched by someone who wanted her because he wanted nothing else.

Yet, despite this, she saw him decide not to take advantage of her and kiss her as she slept. His integrity was powerful. She knew beyond all else that she was safe with him.

She glanced around, trying to figure out what it was he specifically wanted her to know and two memories stepped forward. One was a letter from a friend, one from a stranger. She went to the friend first. Michael's tale of Tangl's rescue caught her attention, especially the description of Duncan McVryce's disappearance into shadow with his beloved. Tangl had caught another poor bastard and Myrgen was worried he might step out of a shadow and slay Catriona to prove his love to Tangl. Catriona nodded acknowledgment of the threat.

Then she saw the letter from Elina in St. Giles. The nightmare of stealing the prostitute's blood and life, but leaving her alive to suffer snapped her out of the visions and out of Myrgen's soul. Her face turned away as if slapped, the picture of what he imagined described in that letter frightening her as much as it frightened him. She leaned on the bed, weak and nauseous, trying to shake off the image of that girl. Myrgen put his arms down and sat on the chair. "My sentiments exactly."

"That poor girl." Catriona shuddered. "I cannot imagine such a thing, but you seemed capable. I cannot say I prefer yours to mine. What do you make of the ink?"

"The ink?"

"It was the thing that was odd. The other details were horrific, but the ink stains are the clue. She was blind. She would have no need for writing implements so it clearly wasn't hers."

"Well, we're not about to go hunting murderers of blind illiterate girls, Catriona. Did you see the news about Duncan, and Tangl?"

Catriona nodded.

He took a stabilizing breath before going on. "I think you need to be back on the ship. So you can see him coming."

"He deals in subterfuge and distance weapons, Myrgen. It's why you sought him out for your task originally. It's decidedly difficult to block an attack I can't see coming, even on the *Enigma*. If I registered the attack the moment it crossed the deck rail, it wouldn't stop me from dying of the poison if I'm right by the edge. Besides, if he's the one who killed Nicolai, like you suspect, that poison worked fast."

"Then we'll keep you away from the edge, keep people all around you at all times so you'd have fair warning."

"You mean put a human shield around me so if he attacks, they die instead of me?"

"Yes." He stood. "Again, I can think of a hundred men who would step up to protect you."

She softened her gaze with reason. "Myrgen, I can think of no person's life that is less valuable than mine. Every man on my crew I would trust with my life and I would not allow any of them to put themselves in such peril, even if they volunteered. I have a responsibility to them and their families to keep them safe."

He turned away, running his fingers through his hair, his other hand on his hip. She saw his jaw set as he came to a conclusion. "Fine." He turned back to her. "I resign as your Chancellor. Scoot over."

"*What?*"

"I'm not a member of your crew, and now, I'm no longer your employee. It is because of my sister that you are, quite possibly, in this predicament, or did you not see that when you read me? Scoot over." He walked over to the bed and sat down on it, removing his boots again as she scrambled back a bit to make room. "Since this assassin is coming after you because of one of my family, it is well within my legal duties to protect you until I can void the contract between them. You're *my* charge now and are under *my* protection." He lay down and closed his eyes.

She looked at him, amazement that he would think she would allow this practically dripping from her eyelashes. "Myrgen, I'm not going..."

"You don't have a choice." He turned on his side to face her. "Whether you choose to believe it or not, I owe you my life. I'm not about to let some insane adolescent infatuation deny me the chance to repay that debt. It would be inequitable." He rolled onto his back again and closed his eyes. "Now, please. Lay down. I'm still very sore and very tired and it's still very early."

She lay on her side, watching him. She could not push aside her own feelings on this matter. She had been fighting her attraction to him from the first stumble, when she released him from his cell in Patras. His determination on this appeared unshakable. She could not help but be flattered. She smiled and glanced down at her hand. The locket Alistair had given her was still in it and the emotion of that item coupled with the visions she had just gotten from Myrgen threatened to break her again. She managed to sniff them back, but not before he heard her. His eyes fluttered open and he looked at her.

"Are you crying?"

"It's nothing. Go to sleep, Myrgen." She closed her eyes. The silence was long and she almost thought she would drift off again when she was pulled back to consciousness.

"Catriona, I didn't mean to insult you earlier."

She opened her eyes. He was laying there, blatantly *not* sleeping, staring at the ceiling. "Which time? When you told me on the ship that I was treating my men like I didn't trust them, or just now when you told me I was your ward and I didn't have the right to dispute it?"

"When I said I didn't need Alistair's help to get you. I just meant it was inappropriate for him to be trying to fix me up with you in particular, given our working relationship."

"Well, like you said, we no longer have a working relationship, meaning neither one of us is employed by the other. Or were you going to apologize for that as well?"

"No. I meant that."

"And the other two? The no choice and the issues of distrust?"

"No, I meant those too." He smiled at her.

"If you don't stop talking so I can get back to sleep, I will gag you."

Myrgen blinked at her. "*You* will gag *me?*"

She put her fingers on his mouth and raised up to look him in the eyes. She pressed her fingers on his lips, her eyes sparkling in the pre-dawn twilight. "Shhhh." *Remember, you asked for this, Myrgen...*

He looked into those eyes and smiled under her fingers, then turned his gaze back to the ceiling and closed his eyes. Before long, they both were sleeping sound.

Duncan sat in the room, looking at the light rune. The amulet felt thick and heavy. He was worried because he had lost his charge the Pope had given him. He had not found Tanglwyst in the guard house, nor the prison. She had disappeared and he was concerned because he could not fulfill the primary order he had been given. All he felt he could do now was wait. He felt impotent and returned to the last place he had held her in his arms. She had made him remove her thread. He couldn't feel her, he couldn't jump to her, and he couldn't summon her to him. He was powerless.

He caught darkness swirling at the edge of his vision, but he didn't care now. The darkness spoke to him in whispers and he closed his eyes to hear it better. He got vague impressions instead of direct instructions, but in the black, he heard them.

Go to your king.

Have him summon your woman.

Impregnate her.

Then she'll never leave you again.

Duncan nodded, never feeling the drool spill onto his hands in his lap, never seeing the black stain it left there.

Twenty-Six

"You're better off buying your produce locally
than risk the farmer's price when your
shipment is late."
The Wise Wench's Tavern Book

Alexander left his bedroom and walked down the hall to the Royal Chambers, glancing over a report regarding the latest figures on trade with York. He had to admit, Dominic was very thorough. Alexander thanked the Saints he didn't have to do this himself. He opened the door and saw Gomez there, signing a report. "Ah, Your Majesty." The Grande Guard stood and bowed.

"Gomez. What can I do for you?"

"I have the latest report on the Tanglwyst investigation."

"Ah." He took the report from his Guard.

"Turns out she had a lover outside of Duncan. Nicolai Moriarity. He was a guard here. We suspect he was involved in the plot. I understand he's the man who attacked you and the guards when you were pursuing Myrgen de Sablonnieres in Rouen."

"Yes." Alexander set the report down on his desk. "But the man is dead. He's no longer a threat."

"Yes, Sire. She may have told him where she was going. It's possible they had planned to meet in Rouen and Duncan murdered him to have her to himself. I'm also not ruling out the possibility that Tanglwyst had him killed to limit the amount of people who were in on the plot. We plan to take the investigation to his house, to see if there might be evidence of the conspiracy naming anyone else."

"His... house..." It caught Alexander off guard to think about that. His house. *Her house.*

"Yes. Did you want to come with us?"

He looked at the report. "Uh... yes. I think I would. In case there's anything else we don't know about this situation. When are you leaving?"

"Soon. Shall I come and get you or simply wait for you?"

"Please, wait for me. I'll be down shortly."

Gomez bowed and left and Alexander sat down at the desk. Her house. He had wanted to go there before, to see her, but she had asked him not to seek her out. The thought of going to the place where she had lived felt very bittersweet. Would she return there at the end of the season? Would she ever be that close again? He wanted to have something of hers, something common that she would have touched every day, like a goblet or a fork. Anything to feel close to her.

But *he* was going to be there too. Nicolai. For every goblet she touched, he had as well. He might not be able to discern between the two and touching something of his felt foul in Alexander's mouth. The man had hurt her every day, betrayed her and scarred her heart. That it took Alexander so long to decide to remove the vermin haunted him. If he had just chosen to have Nicolai killed at the beginning of the year, Catriona might be preparing to be Queen right now.

The door opened and Marie Elizabeth came in with her governess. "She was looking for you again, Your Majesty."

"Hello, Dear One." He held out his arms and she ran to him. He scooped her up and hugged her. "What do you need, Emmy?"

"Where's Awan?"

Alexander felt his heart seize. Alan used to play at the castle with her, but now that the season had started, he was gone. "Alan has gone to his grandparents' house, Emmy."

"When will he be back?"

"You want him to come back?"

She nodded. "I'm gonna mawwy him."

He turned her to face him. "You're going to marry him? When?"

"Next time I see him. Then he won't go away."

"But I thought you were going to marry me."

She looked at him and smiled, then laid her head against his chest. "Are you gonna get mawwied, Unca Awex?"

"I'm trying to, Emmy. And if I do, maybe you'll see Alan again. Would that be nice?"

"Yes. Gamma says Awan's a commonew and that I can't marry him."

"Gamma's wrong. You can do whatever you want to do. You're the Princess." He stroked her hair. "You tell Gamma I said so."

He held her a while longer until he realized he needed to go downstairs. Gomez was waiting.

"Hey, I've got to go help Gomez. I'll see you later."

"Ok." She got up and left and he followed her.

The group of horses pulled up outside Nicolai and Catriona's house and Alexander was full of butterflies. He could not understand why he was so nervous about going here. Gomez opened the door and looked around before admitting the King. He leaned in close to Gomez to keep it confidential. "Keep it to just the two of us initially. No sense tromping the entire unit through here."

Gomez nodded and told the men to guard the perimeter. Alexander walked inside the place. It was a moderate sized house with two levels. The main floor had the common room and the kitchen and a set of stairs on the north wall took them up to the bedrooms. There was a desk and several shelves of books and logs along the south wall with firewood piled beneath the wall mounted shelves. For it being so close on the heels of winter, there was very little wood in the house.

Gomez went over to the desk and Alexander went to the stairs. "I'm going to check out the bedrooms."

Gomez nodded and Alexander went upstairs. There was a narrow hallway and two doors. He opened the first door and found it to be the master bedroom. The bed was a full sized one with a pair of pillows and some nice bedding. He walked over to the bed and looked at the pillows.

One of them had a long, almost black hair in it that fell in waves and he picked up the pillow and sniffed it. Instantly, the smell of spice and musk filled his sensual memory and he realized he had found her pillow. The thought of coming here to sleep in this bed and smell her like she had just gotten up to check on Alan was overwhelming. He almost did it then. He wanted to take the pillow back with him, but he couldn't figure out a way to do it without appearing to be part of the conspiracy for which Gomez was looking. If he managed to win Catriona as his Queen, he didn't want Gomez investigating her all the time and making her uncomfortable. Reluctantly, he put the pillow back.

There was little else in the room besides two wardrobes and a trunk. All three were empty. He left and went to the next room. This was obviously where Alan had been. The walls had colorful drawings on them that were somewhat disturbing. Pictures of tall mountains and a large, rather frightening-looking man in armor with a sword. On the other side of the room was a picture of a dark woman with long black hair in waves, also bearing a sword. In the background was a black ship. Alexander touched the drawing and smiled.

"I wish the princess had some playmates."

Alexander looked up from his reports as he walked past the nursery. Marie-Elizabeth's nurse was standing in the doorway, leaning against the jam, watching her. "Excuse me, Fallon."

She looked at His Highness, startled. "I'm sorry?"

"You just said something about playmates?"

"Oh. I didn't realize I spoke." She looked back into the room and Alexander poked his head in to look at his niece. She was playing with some dolls dressed in Mandian fashions, a common way for tailors to exchange styles each season. "I was just saying, I wish the princess had some playmates or siblings. It's not good for a child to grow up so isolated from other children."

"Well, several servants here have children. In fact, I know Gomez has a daughter, though, honestly, she may be too old for Emmy by now."

"Well, I thought of that before, Sire, but the Queen-mother said that was the way royal children got kidnapped."

Alexander snorted. "Well, the Queen-mother is…" he managed to restrain himself with some effort, "…not here. She is also a poor judge of such things. Please, tell some of the other staff they are welcome to bring their children by on occasion, so long as you do not get overwhelmed, Fallon. Maybe one or two until you find a group she fits with."

About a week later, he walked by again, and stopped at the sound of children laughing. He stepped in to see what was so funny and Marie-Elizabeth had run over to him.

"Alex!" She hugged his legs and he picked her up.

"Good morning, Emmy! Why are you so happy?"

"Come, Alex." She wriggled to be put down and he followed her to a structure of pillows and table cloths. She knelt down. "Come out an' meet Alex."

A dark-haired boy crawled out of the structure and stood before the Prince. He bowed, then raised his mother's eyes to meet Alexander's.

"Alex, this is Alan."

Alexander froze, barely daring to breathe. "Alan? Who are your parents, son?"

"Nicolai and Catriona Moriarity, Sire."

Alexander put his hand on the boy's shoulder. "Welcome, Alan. Welcome. Did you come here with your father or your mother?"

"My father, Sire. He works as a guard here. My mother says she is not of sufficient status to come to the palace," Alan leaned in to whisper in Alexander's ear, "but that's not true."

Alexander looked the boy, smiling a conspirator's smile. "I know. But you must listen to your mother and we'll keep that our secret."

Alan seemed satisfied with that answer and went back to playing. Alexander had sat in the room with them, not really reading the reports in his lap, for the next few hours. When Alan finally left, he told Fallon, "Please let me know whenever Alan or his mother comes to the palace. I wish to meet the woman of such a fine boy."

"Of course, Your Highness."

Of course, she had never come and he was very careful to never push. He had sent a few gifts home during the Feast Days, things that would mean something to her. She never returned them, so he assumed she approved. They were always expendables, like cakes and flowers, never anything permanent. He knew she would not accept anything with a lasting presence, and that would have been cruel on his part. He had promoted Nicolai shortly after meeting Alan, to encourage him coming to the palace more often, even to making sure the child had a tutor. One of his most treasured items was a drawing Alan did during one of the playtimes, showing Alexander, Catriona and Alan together at the palace. Alan had whispered when he gave Alexander the drawing, that he wished the Prince was his father.

He truly loved this house now. Nicolai could be purged from it easily. Apparently Alan had not liked him because there were no pictures Alexander recognized as his former guardsman. He looked around at some of the smaller pictures on the walls and noticed something when he went by the window.

The curtains were drawn, but he could see out the crack between the folds of fabric. He opened the curtains and saw the palace. From this window, he could see his room and he remembered sitting at that window, night after night, wishing he knew which light was hers. Now he could see he had been looking in her eyes every minute. There was a chair next to the window and he sat down and looked around. There was a place on the window sill where the paint was marred with drink rings and he moved the curtain aside.

On the sill was an empty ceramic cup with a ship carved into the side. The glaze was yellow with the ship glazed black and he knew instantly that it was hers. What's more, he had drank from this cup himself at the cabin the first night they made love. That she had brought it with her and kept it made his heart ache. Now he regretted even more that he had never come when she was here. A thousand scenarios crossed his mind every night and to discover that she had been this close, that had he ever gotten out his spyglass, he would have seen her, was maddening. He stood and put the cup in his doublet.

He saw a drawing of Alan and Emmy on the wall, held up with a small bit of pitch and he carefully took it from the wall. He rolled it and put it in his doublet on the other side as Gomez entered the room. "Ah, his son's room. Abraham?"

"Alan." He looked up at Gomez. "He used to play with Emmy all the time. Nicolai would bring him to the palace with him and the boy played with my niece. She was telling me this morning that she misses him."

Gomez looked at him a few moments. Alexander looked around the room, then moved over to the door. "Your Majesty?"

Alexander stopped in the doorway. "Yes?"

"Your grandfather was named Alan, wasn't he? Alan Youngforest?"

"Yes. He was actually my grandmother's father. He was a very good man."

"He died when you were quite young, didn't he?"

"When I was this boy's age, yes. He was quite advanced in age, but he was amazingly spry and cheerful. He died when he fell from a horse. It was because of him I first looked into healing. I tried to fix him when he fell, but I was too late." Alexander looked at the picture of Catriona on the wall, remembering their first meeting and how he had finally healed someone, and realized he was having a difficult time breathing. "I miss him."

"And this boy, did you ever meet his mother?"

Alexander's eyes wandered to the window, looking out on the palace, to the sill where she sat and watched his window. He shook his head and looked at Gomez. "No. I'm afraid I never met her. But judging from her son, she must have been beautiful." He stepped out into the hallway and got himself under control as he went down the stairs.

Gomez stopped him partway down. "Your Majesty, should we look for the woman?"

"What? Why?"

"To make certain she has not suffered a similar fate as her husband. To make sure the boy is safe as well." He glanced down at the ceramic cup peeking out from the king's doublet. "To make sure *your* son is safe…"

Alexander looked at what Gomez was referencing and realized his conclusion. His first instinct was to straighten him out, stop the confusion before it got any farther. Then he thought about Charles and the joy he had leading a simple, normal life with Marie Touchet. Alexander had always wanted to claim Alan as his own and he had been more of a father to the boy than Nicolai ever had. What better way to establish him as his heir than to legitimize the boy through rumor now? He had already established Alan as his heir when he took the Power of Sovereignty, Alan or his own child, once conceived. All it would take is four words to change the world. Four words…

He looked at Gomez and swallowed. "Is it that obvious?"

Gomez nodded, relieved that the King had not told him to mind his investigation. He had worked with Alexander closely for the entire winter and had always felt a kinship with the man, ever since he saved his family from Giovanni a decade ago. Still, he was the monarch and Gomez was the servant. Alexander would have been well within his rights to dismiss Gomez for being so bold. He had figured something like this was the case. The King's desire to get personally involved in this investigation had been concerning him. He was praying that Tanglwyst woman had not gotten her claws into him as well, having seen entire groups fall before her powers. It was good to discover his interest was in the woman left behind, crushed beneath the onslaught of Tanglwyst's desires.

The drawing on the wall revealed absolutely nothing about the lady, but Gomez had to admit the child had striking features and that he looked nothing like Nicolai. He had always suspected another rooster in the henhouse, but never had he dreamed it was the Prince. It explained a lot though. All those times where the man disappeared for tendays or months. Not dissimilar to his brother's jaunts into town, though he was certain Charles never knew. Gomez had been far too worried about where his king was to concern himself with the excursions of the Prince as well, but now his focus was upon this man on the stairs.

"Yes, Your Majesty. It is. If I may ask, how did you meet the lady?"

"I came upon her after Giovanni left her for dead outside a burning church about a decade ago…"

"Wait. This is *that* lady? The one who took Giovanni's eye?"

Alexander nodded. "Yes."

"So the two of you had a child after you rescued us. I remember her own child was killed during that attack." Gomez smiled. "I'm glad you two found each other."

"Thank you, Gomez."

"And Nicolai? How did he factor into this?"

"Nicolai was the baby's father, the one the priest was holding. She was married to him when she was taken. However, Giovanni told her he was dead so she would believe no one would come to save her. When Charles and I came upon her, she was so bloody and broken…" He turned away from the memory in genuine disgust.

Gomez remembered the horror from countless nightmares he had after the incident. He had been barely a man, having married and just recently become a father at eighteen. The time at the Giovanni estate was a stain on his soul he feared could never be cleansed. "Did she know, about your change in status, before she left here?"

He nodded.

"Is that why she left? To set you free to marry for the good of the Kingdom?"

Alexander took a deep breath. "Undoubtedly. She would never put herself before the welfare of others. She's a very giving woman."

Gomez looked at the drawing of the woman on the wall. She had long wavy hair like he remembered, and a sword, and wore black. The wall drawing was in charcoal, no color, so he had no idea beyond those factors what to think. "She uses a sword now?"

Alexander looked at Gomez, then at the drawing. "Yes. Quite adept at it too."

"I could tell it was random chance that took Giovanni's eye. Glad to know she picked up the skill. You teach her?"

"No. She decided not to be victimized again. I did patch her up on more than one occasion though."

"So she came back from her ordeal. That's good. Too often, I have seen the opposite effect in those who have been captured. I have no doubt your influence had a lot to do with that."

"You assume far too much, Gomez. The woman is magnificent all on her own. She can inspire the stars to spin."

Gomez smiled. He felt the same way about his own lady, Mauda. It was different when one was a commoner. Marrying the one you love was far easier. He looked at his sovereign and suddenly found himself a bit irritated. "Majesty, may I ask a question?"

Alexander narrowed his eyes. "Yeeees?"

"Her husband is dead, undoubtedly murdered on a lover's rivalry. The boy needs a father…"

"Gomez. Are you advising your King to chase a woman he loves over a marriage that would benefit the kingdom?"

"If my king is happy, *that* benefits the kingdom far better than a loveless marriage like the kingdom has just endured. Now I'm not certain who the most eligible ladies are for a king and what they bring to the bargaining table, but I will say that marrying a commoner will bring your people under you in a way that marrying a noble never could."

Alexander smiled, then got rather serious. "Well, you need not worry about that. She's actually rather prominent in the royal house of Caratia. She's the daughter of the Dûce."

Gomez blinked. "Nicolai has been married all this time to a Caratian princess?"

Alexander smiled. "Apparently."

"Why would she be in Patras then?"

"She stayed here all winter because she discovered her husband was alive. She was trying to make things work between them."

Gomez leaned back against the wall. "But she couldn't, because she was in love with someone else."

Alexander shrugged.

Gomez narrowed his eyes in thought. "Giovanni was foolish enough to kidnap a noblewoman from Caratia? How can it be the place stood for as long as it did? I understand those people can be vicious."

"The Dûce did not adopt her as his own daughter until after her escape from Giovanni."

"Oh. So she isn't of noble birth. That explains why she thinks she is unworthy and left you to marry for the good of the State."

Alexander looked askance at Gomez. "Of course, I disagree with her, Gomez but I'm worried about traveling so soon after Charles death. I'm not sure how to pursue her without risking being kidnapped and held ransom or simply put to death by Emilianite scum or worse, Mandians. I need a distraction."

"Do you know how she plans on returning to Caratia?"

"Yes, she has a ship."

Gomez nodded, impressed that she had really left the torture of Giovanni behind and become accomplished. "Then go overland. With a good horse, it's only six tendays. If you travel with only a couple companions, you could be there before she arrived and speak to the Dûce and Dûcesa. Get their blessing."

"Six tendays though, Gomez. That's a lot of time for some noble to decide to take the throne when I have yet to be crowned."

"We'll send word you are visiting nobles in search of a wife before your Coronation, looking to pick from the finest Mervolingian families instead of looking outside the kingdom for a change. We can even send people out in groups to 'prepare' for your arrival. The nobles will be scrambling so fast to make the best impression, they won't have time to fight or consider thinking about a coup."

Alexander raised his eyebrows, then nodded. "You are a rather insidious plotter, my man. Do you have designs upon the throne yourself?"

"Saint's no, Sire. It's just, well... my own wife, Mauda, is the light of my life. I could never love someone more than her and I saw your brother, every day. I saw you every day. Believe it or not, you look happier now, just *thinking* about this, than I have seen you in months. Please, Sire, go get her and bring her back."

Alexander broke into a very wide grin and clapped Gomez on the shoulder. "Thank you. I'll not forget this." He went down the stairs with a skip in his step and they left the house.

Twenty-Seven

"If you dream a new recipe, don't wake and make
the same old roast."
The Wise Wench's Tavern Book

Alexander entered his room grinning and started packing his travel bags. It was good to be taking to the road again. He had been worried he would no longer be able to leave Patras without a massive contingency of retinue, but the idea Gomez came up with was brilliant. Sending out groups to the eligible nobility would most definitely tie up their plots. It also meant he could follow Catriona's actual route and take the time with her he needed without worrying that he would be assaulted if he didn't encumber himself with fifty guards and a hundred servants. Since no one else heard their comments, he felt quite safe.

He stopped a moment. Or had they? They were in the empty house, no one around them, and they had kept their voices relatively low. However, he had put that Writ of Destruction against Nicolai on the desk with the other business, yet Alexander didn't recall ever hearing about it through any of the royal channels. Duncan must have used that trick that allowed him to materialize from nowhere. He vaguely recalled a scent of something, but it was gone before he could identify it.

Being able to travel like that would mean he could be a good scout. I could send him ahead to stall Catriona, make sure she's safe and alive. Traveling with Myrgen, she might be betrayed at any moment. He decided to summon the man to him again.

"Did you need something, Your Majesty?"

Alexander leapt at least twenty feet in the air and spun to face his attacker. A brilliant light burst around him, creating a globe of force which pinned Duncan McVryce to the wall beside the king. Duncan struggled and it looked like he was having trouble breathing. Alexander relaxed and stepped away from him. Duncan fell from the wall, gasping. The strength of the Power of Sovereignty again surprised him and he stumbled, trying to rein it in.

"Are you...?" Alexander tried to form the words of his chosen profession as healer, but the meanings escaped him. "Pregnant?"

Duncan arched an eyebrow. "Uh, no."

Alexander blinked and gave his head a little shake. "I'm sorry. I mean hurt, are you hurt?"

Duncan coughed through a smile. "Nothing lasting."

"Forgive me. You... you startled me."

Duncan rubbed his chest. "Yeah, I got that. I apologize, Your Majesty."

"I'm still getting used to that. I thought you'd appear in front of me."

"It's a kind of magic, ancient, from a holy war a long time ago. From what I understand, it was to help the Inquisition. I don't think they wanted to be seen coming. However, it could be I'm not using it right. I'm not a mage."

Alexander nodded. "Thank the Saints for that. You'd be put to death for trucking with demons. Speaking of which, do you smell that?"

Duncan sniffed, a frown and a scowl at Alexander. "How does the smell of lemons make you think demons, unless you are going by the spelling?"

"That's not lemons. It's sulfur."

Duncan blinked, clearly confused. It occurred to Alexander that, on board Catriona's ship, the smell of sulfur was not uncommon, since boiled eggs were a regular part of a seafarer's diet. It was possible the summons had caused Duncan to pass gas upon arrival. Alexander decided to be polite to his servant and change the subject. "How is Tanglwyst?"

"I cannot answer because I do not know. I lost her a few days ago, after your last summoning, and I have not found her again."

Alexander heard a note of bitterness, despite Duncan's disciplined attempt to hide it. "Do you know where to look?"

"I'm afraid not, Your Majesty. She's gone."

Alexander frowned. "What are your plans for her now?"

Duncan maintained his composure, impressing his King. "I suspect she will make her way to safety, bartering on the kindness of those she meets along the way. Regardless, her plans are no longer known to me, Sire."

That meant, since he hadn't seen her after the last summoning, Alexander's secrets were still his own. Tanglwyst would not know about Alexander's order on Nicolai's life. He doubted she would share that information with Catriona, but having that come out to the Pope after the whole mess with that massacre a few years back could cause his family to be excommunicated. That would mean Duncan's fealty, along with his entire kingdom's, would be nullified and he would no longer be protected by Duncan's hierarchy. Instead, he might be hunted by the man, and with that ability to show up instantly, Alexander feared he would never even feel the dart that slew him.

"In fact, I come to you with a request, Your Majesty. I cannot find her, but you can. You can summon her to you, through your Power of Sovereignty."

"If that were true, I would have done so already. She has taken back her fealty, Duncan. I cannot reach her. She was no longer part of Mervolingia the moment she decided to murder the king." He put his hand on Duncan's shoulder. "I'm sorry."

"Then I shall trust in the Saints to see her to safety."

Alexander nodded. "If you are willing, I have another assignment for you. The woman I love is currently on her way to

Caratia on board the *Enigma*. She travels in the company of a man named Myrgen the Grey. This man is a traitor. I cannot act against him personally, but you can. Go there and watch him. If you see anything suspicious, report back to me immediately. However, if he betrays her or hurts her in any way, I want you to kill him. Can you take this assignment?"

"Yes, My King."

"Then Saint Gabriel's speed to you. Be on your way."

Duncan stepped into the shadows and was gone.

Duncan stepped out of the shadows of an alley in St. Andrew, a port he frequented often. He had discovered, shortly after being given the traveling amulet he wore, that he could only visit places he had been. It had been decidedly difficult to get to the King's bedchamber, but the Archbishop had arranged that when Duncan started working for the King at the Church's request. Now, his shadow webs alerted him to any Writs of Destruction that crossed that desk.

He was actually quite confused by the encounter with the King. Never before had he had any trouble being that close to his Sovereign, or anybody, for that matter. However, when the King turned and saw him, he had felt a white hot force knock him away from the man. The incident worried him. As a representative of the Church, he should have access to the king the Church put on the throne. The protection circle was so powerful, he had not been able to fight it. He wasn't sure why the Power of Sovereignty would repel a servant of Heaven, unless it was not from Heaven as well.

Perhaps it was the amulet that was the problem. It was made during a time when magic was being destroyed. It was likely the king's protection was Heaven's rejection of those old magicks. It would explain why only a sinner could serve the Church through its use. He had found the amulet on his pallet at the Archbishop's See in Patras after finishing up his first assignment. Surely something given to him by the Church would not damage his soul.

He had a thin memory of the night or so spent in the secret room after failing to find Tanglwyst. His right hand still bore a stain from whatever he spilled on it, though he could remember no ink open in the room. It had been tucked away in the desk drawer, yet he must have not only spilled ink on himself, but held the quill in his mouth for his lips had been stained as well. That was at least gone, but the webbing between his thumb and forefinger still had black in the creases and grey everywhere else. He shook his head. He had not been paying much attention to his surroundings. Maybe he wrote her a letter?

He looked around the streets. The evening fog was starting to settle in and he was glad for the cover. Tanglwyst had commented on his eyes and their swirling changes, an after-effect of shadow travel, but that usually faded after a few minutes. His eyes had been swirling for days now. He was trying very hard not to scream.

Several ships were in port and he had heard of the *Enigma* before. Allegedly a woman commanded the ship and that sort of thing was rare and distinctive. Since St. Andrew was the first major port after Rouen heading south, with St. Giles to the north, and one cannot travel by ship directly to Caratia from Patras, he decided to start his search here. The Harbormaster would know if the *Enigma* had been through here or not. He felt hungry and the discomfort he had suffered at the King's presence still rippled through his body. He wanted to rest and eat.

He went to the Net and looked around. The place was thronging. Sailors from every country seemed to be in here. Duncan missed being at sea. When Tanglwyst had first broken with Nicolai, she had put the word out that she was in the market for a new captain. Duncan had been planning on taking that position, the possibility of being with the woman he had loved from afar for years too enticing to pass up. His time working for Maitre Guillaume and the Underground was easy to leave behind.

When he went to apply for the position, he discovered another man there before him, a rogue named Alistair who he knew had a tendency to get women to fall in love with him and then he would leave them. He didn't want to be pushed aside again, so Duncan had kidnapped Tangl under the pretense that the man was an assassin sent to murder her. They had spent three tendays at sea, with no interruptions and by the time they had set foot on solid ground again, he was in.

Their time together had been cut short by the return of Nicolai. Tanglwyst had sent Duncan to prepare the ship for the two of them to sail away for the winter and when he had returned a few days later, he found Nicolai, begging for her to take him back. She had relented, but Duncan knew it was only a matter of time before that man would return to his wife and Tanglwyst would be heart-broken again. Then the Writ of Destruction on him had come through and Duncan had leapt at the chance to kill the man as he lay with his beloved.

He had followed Nicolai from the palace and was surprised to find he was making all due haste to the city of Rouen. It would not be as satisfying to kill him out of Tanglwyst's sight, but he followed the man nonetheless. The fight in the street between Nicolai and Alexander and his men had shown Duncan the man's fighting style and he had realized immediately that Nicolai, drunk or not, was far more of a sword master than he. That's when he decided to use the poisoned dart.

It occurred to him that the woman on the ship, the one who beat Nicolai readily was probably the woman the King meant. She had a foreign beauty to her, like that of the slaves, but she could not hold a candle to his Tanglwyst. He remembered now that the King had called her name a few times in the street. He knew the name, but for some reason, it was swirling in the darkness now, another side effect of the shadow travel... *Caitlyn...Catherine...Katrina... something like that.* It would come to him once his head cleared.

And he knew Myrgen.

Myrgen had tried to hire Duncan to kill the King of his beloved Mervolingia. Duncan had refused and the only thing that had stopped him from reporting this to Gomez himself was Tanglwyst's revelation that Myrgen was her brother. But the King had sanctioned the man's destruction now. If Duncan felt he was betraying the King's lover, then Duncan could kill him. That suited him just fine.

He sat down at the counter and looked around. The barkeep was quite busy and gave Duncan a nod. "Be right with you, sir."

Duncan nodded and continued to scan the room. He didn't recognize any of Tanglwyst's sailors here and the smell of the food was nauseating instead of attractive. That surprised him. He felt hungry, but none of this was sounding good. Even the ale, which was some of the best on the coast, sickened him to think of it. Logan came over to him, cleaning a tankard with a cloth.

"What can I get for ya, sailor?"

Duncan looked around, feeling his stomach churn. "I'm looking for the captain or passengers from the *Enigma*. Is she in port?"

"Yeah, came in day before yesterday. The Captain's staying here at the Net, in fact." He glanced around the room and spied his daughter, waiting tables. "Don't see her though. Bianca! Do you see Catriona?"

Catriona! That was her name! Duncan suddenly realized who the King wanted him to protect. He felt the nausea advance in his stomach, the taste of bile heavy in his mouth. The shadows within him balked at the idea of protecting someone, calling out for human contact for an entirely different purpose. He could smell the bodies around him and for some reason, the fact they were alive called out to him like the scent of the roast beef called to the other patrons. He felt horror at the thought of consuming them and suddenly he realized simply bumping into one of them could result in something dreadful. He shook his head to clear the impending madness before it took hold as the barkeep watched him.

"Sir, you look pale. Can I get you anything?"

Duncan shook his head, said thank you to Logan and carefully made his way outside. The Net was dusty and a bit dark, and the blast of afternoon sun gave him a headache. He had been in his safe room underground before going to the palace, trying to rest and stop his eyes from swirling like ink in water. The effort had made him dizzy. This was the first time since he had lost Tanglwyst that he had seen the sun, and it scorched now like a fire. He ducked into the shadows of an alleyway and caught his breath. He tried to focus upon what was happening. He closed his eyes and tried to dispel the shadows. Instead they seemed to gain voices and spoke in cacophony, unintelligible. He felt very much that they were doing it on purpose.

"Catriona! Myrgen!"

The shout from the street called him from his introspection and he looked out for the speaker. Myrgen and the woman from the fight on the ship came into view as a lovely golden haired woman escorted by the rogue, Alistair Hapsburg, greeted them.

Myrgen bowed to the lady. "Ce'Nedra, wasn't it?"

The companion nodded. "I'm impressed, sir. I did not catch your name the other night."

Alistair put a hand on her lower back and nodded, gesturing towards the other couple. "Ce'Nedra, may I present Captain Catriona Moriarity and Myrgen de Sablonnieres. "

Myrgen bowed and kissed her hand. "Truly a pleasure, my lady."

Catriona offered a pleasant nod. "Actually, it's Catriona Morsdatora these days."

Alistair raised his eyebrows. "Good for you, Captain."

Ce'Nedra curtsied. "Congratulations?" She glanced at Catriona's gloved hands, which revealed nothing.

She shrugged. "It was time." She acknowledged Myrgen's questioning look. "Morsdatora was the name I received when I became Stapana. There is a special ritual where the Land tells you your true name. It usually happens in a person's tenth year. It also happens when someone from outside is accepted publicly in a role for the Land."

Ce'Nedra furrowed her brow while smiling. "It sounds foreign. What does it mean?"

"It's an ancient tongue. It means Death Bringer."

Alistair took a deep breath. "Not unfitting for the Protector of the Land's People."

"I agree."

Myrgen shifted, looking into her eyes. "Alan is ten."

She nodded. "Yes. It's part of why I am returning to Caratia."

"And you want me there?"

She glanced at Alistair, shifting a little on her feet. Alistair suppressed his smile. "Yes, I do."

Duncan saw his opportunity as Catriona put her back to the alley. *If the shadows wish to feed, then let them feast on her!* He moved in behind her, soundless as a thought and breathed in slowly, preparing himself. He could taste the purity in her soul and a strange sweetness, just from proximity. Her soul was hard and black, like onyx, but lit from within by a thousand sparkles of gold. She lit up like the night sky to him and he reached out to drain her.

A searing pain burst through his head causing him to scream. Alexander's voice pierced his mind. *You are here to protect my beloved. She is mine.* Duncan fell to his knees, grabbing his head.

"No! She's the one I was told to destroy." He gritted his teeth against the pain, hissing his protest. "She's the danger to the kingdom... to the Chur..."

The sound of his inner fight brought the people at the front of the alley to him and Alistair knelt beside him. "Sir, can we help you?"

Duncan looked at him and Alistair snatched his hand away from his shoulder like it was made of snakes. "Callista's Fury. He's a Shadowalker. Ce'Nedra! Get back to the Inn. Go to my room and stay with my niece!" He got to his feet and backed away, drawing his sword.

Myrgen's eyes grew wide as he also recognized Duncan. He, too, backed away, reaching behind him. "Catriona, it's him. It's Duncan."

"By the Land..." She drew her sword as well.

Duncan slowly got to his feet and Myrgen said, "Catriona, get to the ship."

"No."

"Don't argue."

"I'm not going to *leave* you."

"Catriona, your crew can't lose you. They'll do just fine without me."

The shadows swirling within Duncan grew gleeful. They spoke in a hundred voices, but they all seemed to say the same thing. *I may not be able to kill her, but treason is punishable by death...*

"Well then," Duncan hissed, the blackness within him becoming a cyclone, "I accept."

He reached out his hand, leaping for Myrgen's chest. Catriona gasped and pushed Myrgen just enough to cause Duncan to miss and hit his shoulder instead of his heart. Myrgen cried out as contact caused blackness to spread across his face and neck. The shadows drank and Duncan heard the cacophony harmonize, losing himself in the darkness. Suddenly, Duncan's hand parted company with his wrist and he looked up. Alistair had cut his hand off. Catriona grabbed Myrgen's collar and dragged him as Alistair held Duncan at bay. Duncan hissed at the rogue and stepped into the shadows, disappearing.

Twenty-Eight

"Everyone should carefully observe which way his heart draws him, and then choose that way with all his strength."
The Wise Wench's Tavern Book

Alistair sheathed his sword and helped Myrgen to his feet. "Get him to your ship, Catriona. Get him inside."

"What about you?" She shouldered Myrgen who breathed through his teeth, the agony plain. She was going to return with him and heal him once on board. She was almost afraid to look at him. She could see black veins where Duncan had touched his shoulder.

"I need to check on Gwen."

Catriona blinked. "Gwen? Why would you think of Gwen right now? She's in Patras."

"Yeah, about that. I'll have to explain that later. Right now, she's a priority."

"Why?"

"She's part Fae and she uses magic. That amulet will tell him she's here. I've seen them before."

"Go. Make sure she's safe. Then tell her I'm probably going to kill her when I see her."

Alistair furrowed his brow. "Excuse me?"

"Your family's eternal meddling. She's the one who delivered the Passion Sap, isn't she?"

"Oh." Alistair glanced down the street. "Yes, well, better get him onto the ship." He left quickly and Catriona couldn't help but smile, despite the circumstances.

"Catriona, stop."

She looked at Myrgen, whose pale skin was worrying her. His cheeks were hollow and he looked dehydrated. She could see dark circles under his eyes like he hadn't slept in days. "What is it?"

"You need to let go of me." His eyes were closed and his breathing was thin and thready.

She loosened her hold on him, worried she was causing his shoulder wound to hurt. She needed to get him someplace safe and she cast about for a place away from the afternoon shadows. She could see nowhere that wasn't at least partially in darkness. "Am I hurting you?"

"No. Well, yes, but that's… to be expected…. I mean, you need to get… away from me."

Her eyes scrunched in confusion. "What? Why would I do that?"

"Because I'm not sure I can control this…"

He opened his eyes and she saw they were swirling with blackness, like ink in water.

Myrgen watched her reaction, scared. He could feel the presence of every foul thing he had ever done, and was disgusted to find it was actually quite a lot. Images of people he'd made disapper when they got in his way, others he had cheated or deceived out of money flowed behind his eyes like eddies in a river, reminding him over and over that he had no right to be with this woman, in any capacity. *How can you possibly think you won't do the same to her?*

"By the stones…"

She recoiled from the sight of his eyes and he realized his greatest fear had come true. The darkness from his life had returned to haunt him, and he was no different from Duncan, except that the bastard was more honest about it. Duncan wasn't trying to pretend he wasn't evil. He accepted it and owned it. Myrgen had been trying for days to pretend he was better than a common thug, that he had changed. All he had done was try and seduce another man's woman. Again.

He looked away from her and pushed her away. He was hurting, that was true, but he was alive and he didn't want her near him in this state. What if the shadows were to fasten onto her like they had from Duncan? He felt the poison of his infernal touch coursing through his neck and head, threatening to destroy his mind and will. There was a desire to destroy that was hard to isolate, and harder to resist. The thought of some tendril of blackness injecting this into her repelled him. He was here to protect her, even if that meant protecting her from himself.

She caught his wrist and he looked at her again. Her eyes had softened and her touch was gentle but firm. "Myrgen, let me help you."

She closed her eyes and he realized what she was about to do. He pulled his wrist from her grasp, wresting control of his thoughts from the black invading him and gave her a stern look.

"Catriona, if you think… for a moment I will let you take on these wounds… you are dead wrong. This is more than… an injury… This is a *sin*. This is my… penance for all the horrible things I've… done in my life. I can't… jeopardize… you with this. Not after all… you've done for me."

"I've got to do something."

"Then take me to our room… Get me away from people… I can see them… they glow…"

"I can't. It's dark in there."

He pushed away from her and spat. Ink swirled on the street and he almost swore he saw wisps of smoke. "Then get the hell away from me."

"Myrgen, *no. I won't leave you.*"

He grabbed her shoulder. "*You have to.*" He looked into her eyes. "I can see what this is doing to me. I… I won't allow you to end up like that blind girl…" He reached up to touch her face and saw drops like ink on the skin where his saliva had sprayed. "Land's blood…"

Suddenly he realized how close she was, how he could feel her essence and how precious and sweet she smelled. Spice, musk, rich, rich fluid. Every part of her ached to be touched, to be *violated.* His breath became ragged and his eyes traced her lips.

"Catriona… I need something from you… desperately…" He looked into her eyes, dark green with gold flecks at the edges. "Please… *read me…*"

She blinked and her eyes flared. She gasped, stepped back and the last thing he saw before the darkness took him was the bottom of her boot.

Octavius saw the altercation with Myrgen and ran over to her. "Captain! What's wrong?"

"Octavius, help me get him in the Net. He's hurt."

"Of course he's hurt. You just kicked him in the face."

"I mean he was hurt in a fight in town. I need to get him to our room to heal him."

"Why did you kick him in the first place?" He lifted Myrgen under the arms as she took his feet.

"He was attacked by a shadowsomethingorother. It caused his eyes to have swirls of blackness in them. I knocked him out so I could get him to safety without being attacked."

Octavius stopped, dropping him. "A Shadowalker?"

"Yes. You've heard of them?"

"Yes. Fae Slayers. Of course I've heard of them."

"That's what Alistair said but he said Fae have no souls so they prefer half Fae."

"The Church saw such unions as the ultimate soul betrayal. Fae and magic could exist in a creature with a soul, which the

Church claimed was the purview of Heaven alone. That doesn't stop them from killing others, though. They just prefer half-breeds. They contain a disease mixed with death and corruption. It destroys what it touches, if it doesn't follow the Church's beliefs, and poisons the souls of those contaminated by it. Catriona, you need to leave him."

"Why?"

"Because if you get infected with that stuff, I'll kill you rather than let you *touch* the *Enigma*. It's him or us and frankly, he won't be allowed back on board either."

"Octavius?" Catriona blinked, her First Mate's defiance shocking her too much to be angry. Yet.

"I mean it. Don't make me choose."

She looked around at the emptying streets. It was starting to get dark and soon, the wrong kind of company would be entering the streets. She looked at Myrgen.

"I'm sorry."

Myrgen opened his eyes and looked around. He was in a place of thick ink and it felt oppressive, like he was under water. He could feel tendrils holding him, like snakes, and he fought against them. They seemed to stretch easily and his shoulder burned from their touch. He shouted out in the darkness but no sound escaped.

You want out? You are hurt…

Myrgen stopped. "You're the ones who hurt me."

We can help. We can heal your wound, if you'll let us. Make you whole.

He looked around for a source of the sound, and realized they seemed to be coming from within him. "Get away from me, you monsters! I've heard what you do to people."

We can make her yours… Make her love you…

"The hell you can. You have no power here. Your fight is with me, not her."

Just get us on the ship. We can change everything.

"No. You'll not have the ship either. If you could do all that, you would have already. You are nothing. Wisps of my own evil. If I don't let you win, you can't do anything!"

Oh...?

The creatures made the veins in his neck and shoulder grow, stretching and rippling. Myrgen breathed through his teeth, hissing in pain. He shook his head and snarled at the shadows, which consumed the sound, leaving not a scrap. Still, they heard him. *Fine. So be it...* They began to enter his head, pushing through his blood like lumps of glass.

Myrgen screamed again and closed his eyes. He searched for something to help him and felt Catriona's presence. He recognized the candle glow of her essence, even through pressed eyelids, and he felt the shadows focus upon it.

Ah! What's that? Something precious to you? Perhaps she will succumb, if you will not.

"Captain?"

"I won't leave him, Octavius. I can't, no more than you could leave Estelle."

Octavius straightened. "That was a poignant statement."

She looked at him. "If you tell him I said it, I'll deny it."

Octavius nodded. "Duly noted. Do you want to bring him to the docks?"

She shook her head. "I need contact with the Land. These stones will be better than hovering over water. At least I can feel its presence here, unlike Patras."

"What do you need?"

She looked back at Myrgen. "Light."

Myrgen's eyes snapped open as they began to release him and he grabbed at the tendrils, keeping them from her. He struggled with the creatures, fighting this thing that seemed to be like a bush with many branches, and found the central core. He slammed it into the ground beneath him, his predominant objective to keep this thing away from her, away from the ship. He reached out and touched the ground, grabbing for something to destroy this thing with. A large rock was instantly available beneath his fingers and he picked it up and crushed the shadow beneath it.

The shadow creature screamed and attacked. Myrgen felt the poison burn from him as he used the weapon against all the shadows. Every movement was met with impact from the weapon. Within minutes, they stopped. He stood in the darkness, the air around him empty and quiet. He looked over at the candle glow of Catriona's presence and steadied his breathing. He was going to be okay. He walked towards the candle.

Duncan fell onto the ground, grasping his wrist. Blood sped over his fingers to the floor despite his grip. He tried to steady his breathing and think. He looked around to assess his surroundings. He had gone to the secret room underground, the one where he had taken Tanglwyst when they fled Patras. This was good. There were bandages and things here to help. He scooted over to the dresser and pulled the drawer open with his remaining pinky. The drawer caught on its track, shifted by the inconsistent pull and he swore before letting go of his injured wrist long enough to correct it and pull it open. He found the bandages and next to them, a bottle of brandy and some matches.

He felt the shadows in his head whisper to use the fire, to burn himself, but the shock of the battle in the alley had shaken him free of their grasp. He reached down and took off the amulet, throwing it across the room. More blood decorated the floor and his pants and he started to feel weak. *By the Saints, my only choice may be to burn it. It's not like I'll ever use that hand again.*

He took the brandy out of the drawer and took a drink of it to steady himself. He was unaccustomed to such fine drink, having had only ship ales and meads from harbor taverns with regularity.

He remembered hearing that brandy burned. Time to test it. He took the bandages out of the drawer and quickly wrapped his wrist to stop the bleeding. It would also give him time to set himself on fire, something that was causing his heart to threaten his ribs with violence. He poured the brandy on the bloody bandages, took out a match, struck it, and set the bandages on fire.

The flame burned blue and Duncan figured he was probably going to die because he felt no pain, no burning. The fire danced across the top of the material but he felt no heat. After a moment, the fire burned out but he could see the bleeding was not lessened and the bandages showed very little sign of scorching. He lit another match and tried again.

This time, the bandage burned, yellow flame leaping down his wrist. The wet of the blood stopped the flame from advancing to the wound, but he put out the flame as it burnt the flesh under it. Beating the fire caused his nerves to wake up and between the pain from the burn and the pain from the severing, he passed out.

Myrgen opened his eyes and saw lanterns around him. He could feel the cobblestones of the street beneath him and the sea air felt wonderful in his lungs after the heaviness of the shadows.

"Hello." Catriona was sitting next to him, stroking his hair.

He blinked at her and sat up. "What happened? Why are all these lanterns here?"

"To keep the shadows away."

He looked around. She had pulled him into the alley behind the tavern, then ringed the place with lanterns. A couple of her crewmen were at the end, looking back at them now that she was speaking. It was well into night. The moon was a quarter of its way through the sky and was barely a sliver. "How long was I out?"

"A while. How do you feel?"

He reached up and felt his jaw. It was a little sore, but not bad. His shoulder and neck still held a residual ache, but he could neither see nor feel the veins thick with poison. He looked at her.

"Did you heal me?" He was ready to yell if she had.

"No. You did that yourself. I couldn't heal you. I tried."

"I told you not to try."

"Well, you're not *my* Captain. And I wasn't going to just sit by and let you die. At least, that wasn't my original intent. It turned out, all I *could* do was sit by and watch."

He touched her hand. "Thank you for staying with me."

She smiled and glanced down at their hands. "Blame Octavius. He wouldn't let me take you on the ship."

"Bless him. If I had hurt one of your men…"

"Yes, well, *he* seems to like you so, since I trust his opinion, I'll let you live. In fact, you have quite a few supporters. Johannes and Thessius insisted on standing watch." She let the smile infect her whole body and she touched his face. "Now, let me look at your eyes." She examined them and was satisfied with their condition so he guessed the blackness there was also gone. "Good. Let's get you up then. Can you stand?"

"I'm sure I can. Steady as a rock." He blinked, remembering his fight. *Where had the rock come from?* He glanced around and there was a hole in the ground where a cobblestone had once been set. He looked around for a moment but didn't find it. Catriona stood and reached out her hand for him.

He took her hand when she offered it and stood. His legs were a little wobbly, but he felt fine. Thirsty. He swallowed and his throat was very dry. He gestured to the docks. "Shall we? Or did you want to stay at the Net?"

They started walking to the docks.

"No, I think tonight, I need to have you on the ship." She gathered a couple of the lanterns as they passed them and Johannes and Thessius grabbed the rest.

"Ah well. It was good while it lasted." He picked up the last lantern and took one of the ones from her.

"Oh, that part might not be over. I want to stay by you and make sure you're not going to have a relapse."

He stopped and looked at her. "Do you think that's a possibility?"

"I don't know."

"Then I think I should stay away until we *are* sure. I can't… I don't want to risk…"

Octavius came down the gangplank. "Captain. The ship says to bring him on board. He's clean."

Myrgen looked at the First Mate. "The... ship? She can tell?"

Catriona and Octavius smiled and nodded. Myrgen exhaled. "Then there *is* a way to detect them. Thank the Stones and Soil."

Octavius and Catriona exchanged a look and Octavius turned around and returned to the deck. Myrgen looked at her as she gestured him up the plank. "What about the crew? If you're on board..."

She nodded to the deck. Myrgen looked as he got to the top of the plank. Every sailor seemed to be on board. Supplies were lining the main deck and all hands were standing by their places, ready to go.

"I don't think that will be a problem." She stepped on after he did.

"Captain on deck!"

"Men," Catriona nodded to Octavius, "weigh anchor! Get us out of here. Set course for Caratia."

"Aye Captain!"

Myrgen looked around, astonished. "You're sailing at night?"

Catriona smiled and Octavius patted Myrgen on the back. Octavius said, "Son, you've got a lot to learn about this ship and this Captain."

The ship was pushed from the dock as if the crew had been waiting for this moment, and the ship was under way as if they were trying to impress Myrgen specifically. It worked. He looked at Catriona. "What about shore leave, and getting the trade goods?"

"Goods are already loaded, as are the supplies for the next month. They did it this afternoon, while you were out. As for the crew, well," she looked at them as the men bustled at their posts, "let's just say I didn't order them back to the ship. They found out what happened and returned on their own." She looked at him. "Apparently, they like you."

Ambrois came up and took the lanterns from Catriona and she stepped over to the stairs that took her to the helm. Myrgen watched her ascend them and then took his own lanterns to their respective holders. As he walked, the crew nodded greeting or patted his shoulder or back. He knew he had found a home.

Octavius spoke to the Captain and Myrgen decided to take the remaining lantern to his room. When he entered, he saw an item sitting on his desk. It was about eight inches long and wrapped in black silk. He opened it and found a Damascus steel dagger with a handle shaped like a whale tail.

Had she given it to him in public, like on the streets of the market, he would have taken it as a light reminder to watch his step when dealing with odd sea creatures. But she had not. She had given him this in private, where they had almost ended up. This was a different message. Like the layers of steel in the blade, this went deeper.

He stepped outside and went down the hall. She glanced down at him and he smiled, offering a small bow of thanks. She nodded in return. He knew without fail he would do anything in his power to be by her side, no matter the need.

Duncan awoke in the dark, the smell of cooked flesh surrounding him. His right hand hurt, and he flexed his fingers, trying to work out the ache before remembering he had no right hand. He reached out for the lantern that he knew existed nearby and fumbled around, not locating it. He did find the sulfur sticks he used to cauterize the wound and grabbed one with his left hand. It argued against the task, snapping the sulfur stick without striking a spark. He swore and grabbed another one.

Instinctively, he reached out with his right hand, forgetting about his handicap. He felt the matches beneath his fingers and picked one up. He held the match in his thumb and forefinger, then struck it on the floor. It sparked and glowed and he saw his missing hand attached to his wrist. It appeared to be stitched on with black thread to his wrist and he moved the fingers, testing. They worked, though he felt numb. He blinked, wondering what this meant. *Has Heaven healed me?*

He looked at the amulet and then touched it with his right hand. The stitches were the same color and consistency as the threads he used to keep track of the King and Tanglwyst and panic flashed through. He reached out to feel for the threads and found the one he was reserving for Tanglwyst was now gone. To make him complete, the amulet had sacrificed his beloved.

Now, more than before, he had no intention of letting those who had wronged him escape his revenge.

The black cat leapt from the mantle displaying the anchor and slipped between the sailors as they returned. Ce'Nedra greeted them and they commented on the bright lights just as the door quieted their discussion. He walked along the streets, common as an alley cat in a fish market, and he stopped to sniff at some water near one of the stalls which had closed for the night. He looked up the street, deciding instead to move to the other tavern. The door was propped open and he stepped in, looking around.

Alistair sat in a booth, sipping a tankard. The cat leapt onto the seat across from Alistair and cleared his throat. Alistair looked at the man across from him and sighed. He turned around in the booth, raised his hand to Victoria and pointed, ordering another mug of ale for his companion. He turned back to his friend.

"Hi Raven."

The man nodded, his hood hiding most of his hair, but a single green lock slipped its confines and dropped in front of his right eye. Alistair glanced at it and took a sip of his ale. "You should do something about that before Victoria gets here."

Raven glanced at the dangling hair and moved his hood back, smoothing it back into place. His hair went from green to a similar shade of chestnut, which matched his eyes. Victoria brought the ale to the table and Raven gave her a ducat in return. She smiled and left the two.

Alistair looked at the bar owner. "That's not going to turn into dust come sunrise, is it?"

Raven shrugged. "I don't think so." He picked up his tankard and sipped the ale. "Hmm. Brownies. I thought so." He squinted at the bar and saw one wiping down the large keg from behind it.

Alistair set his tankard on the table. "What are you doing out of the Anchor?"

"I saw sailors returning talking about some woman sitting in an alley with a man, ringed in lanterns. Sounded like the attack Ce'Nedra fled. She's worried about you. I figured I'd see what was keeping you."

"Thinking. Things I didn't want to explain, nor be distracted from."

"Have you told him yet?"

Alistair tipped his tankard toward him, renewing his interest. "No…"

Raven's brow furrowed. "Why not?" He glanced at the door, then leaned in. "Heaven has until Genevary to choose a Champion or lose the Well of Souls to the Land. I think the Land needs to have its own Champion ready for the ensuing discussions. Right now, she's adrift, at sea."

Alistair took a drink. "That's right where she needs to be."

"She needs to be anchored."

"That will happen soon enough."

Raven sat back. He had been afraid of this. "Alistair. Don't make me do it. You have a rapport with this man. It will be better coming from you."

"There's no way to make this better. You know what this will do to her."

"Alistair."

Alistair waved a hand, irritation darkening his features. "Don't 'Alistair' me. Your people did this in the first place. You put her to sea, with that pitch for the ship and what Corrigan did to his daughter. If the Land gets the Well of Souls, that's a victory for you. The hold the Church has on the people will be broken and magic will be allowed to return. For someone like you," Alistair pointed to Raven, "both Fae *and* a Land Worshipper, that's perfect."

"The war is coming. Heaven has fought for souls for three hundred years now, and the First Dûcesa was lost in the Soulless War, as was her Stapan. I am only partially inclined to say this Catriona is her current incarnation."

"It's her. The Land even named her Morsdatora."

"Death Bringer."

"I almost shuddered when I heard that."

Raven inhaled, leaning on the table. "That does suit her. Once her eyes turn to jade..." Raven shook his head. Her power had caused the cliffs surrounding Caratia to rise, sealing it from the world. To that day, no Mandian could even get near Caratia, even though they shared a border. Even ships were turned away. The ravages and destruction perpetrated by the Church created a scar that was visible to any traveler heading to the Papal City. It wasn't the only one either.

Raven watched Alistair. Time had been kind to his old friend, almost as kind as it had been to Raven, and for almost the same reason. "How is Gloriana?"

Alistair looked away. "Last time I saw her, I was barely able to get out of the pass before Tooele closed it with a storm. I think I only got out because I was ahead of the scream of her anger and he didn't know to seal me in a snow bank."

Raven smiled. "I'm sure Embertwist would have enjoyed being the one who rescued you. You don't owe him a debt anymore."

"Yes, but I didn't want my baby girl to start life owing a debt to a Master Thief."

Raven grinned, surprised. "You stole a child from the Midwinter Queen?"

Alistair got an incredulous look. "She was half mine! And, as it happened, half hers..."

Raven folded his arms across his chest. "Amazing. And what did you do with this child?"

"I took her to be raised by a relative, a human one. After all, she needed to know about the other half of her heritage."

"All that and you weren't going to raise her yourself?"

Alistair gestured with his mug. "Well, you and Wilge weren't available."

Raven's smile drained away at the mention of his wife. He glanced down at his own mug.

Alistair's own smile faded as well. "How long has it been?"

Raven blinked. "About a hundred fifty years. She decided not to take the longevity potion again. I wandered in the Caratian

Mountains for a few decades until I was fit to be around people again."

"And your children?"

Raven smiled. "I run into our great-greats periodically. How about you? Have you been back to York since the War?"

"Not really. My brother's queen turned the place into a matriarchy, at my request. I told her the mother was the only sure parent. She agreed. I understand the woman on the throne now is quite impressive."

Raven nodded. "Do you ever see any of the others?"

Alistair shook his head. "I hear Embertwist and the Glove are somewhere in the forests in Mervolingia these days. Corrigan still resides in the south. Gloriana in Glarren, of course, and Calpurnia is still asleep in the tower at Sovereignlumen."

"There are rumors she is stirring. She may awaken soon."

Alistair set his cup on the table, his hand trembling the ale inside. "If she awakens, what will that do to the spell holding the Soulless?"

"She's not the lock, Alistair, merely a key. Merrick watches over her still though even he is getting old."

"Three hundred years is a long time for any human to draw breath. I know."

"But unlike you, he still ages. A mage can only take the potions for so long before they still die. You are alive solely because Gloriana has not released you to age. I can't tell if she loves you or hates you."

"If that's the measure, then I don't know either. But there's still the two of us wandering the world." Alistair lifted his mug again, this time in toast.

Raven took a deep breath. "I am going to take an apprentice."

Alistair's brow furrowed. "Is it time?"

"Oh yes. It might even be past time. I'm sure to join Wilgefortis in Summerland soon and with this year approaching, I fear there may be too much to learn. I hope I have a quick study to teach the magics. There's so little left in the world now."

"Who's your choice?"

Raven shrugged. "Haven't met them yet. I really need to get on with it."

Alistair sat back in the seat, folding his arms. "You mean you feel the approach of your own death and you're just *now* thinking an apprentice might be a good idea? Raven, you're the last mage left walking the world right now. You survived the Soulless Wars that changed the face of human history. You've sired Fae-blooded folks across the continent. You've been to Nubia and Yokotama, which is no small feat, my friend. You are probably the only person alive now who knows how to find an Ancient Dragon. This knowledge... You have written it down somewhere at least, right?"

Raven narrowed his eyes. Writing it down probably would have been a good idea. "I've kind of been a cat for a while, you see. We cats don't really *record* things, per se."

Alistair closed his eyes and steadied his breathing.

Raven stroked his chin. "I suppose I could take my apprentice to Kūki Doragon. The Air Walkers could record this at the same time I teach it. I hope they won't be afraid of heights."

Alistair opened his eyes. "I think I have the perfect candidate. Not afraid of heights, part Fae and definitely magically inclined. And my own progeny. You truly could not ask for a finer apprentice."

He drained his tankard and stood. "Let me talk to them first though. This could take some explaining."

Raven nodded. "I'll be around."

Book Two

"Life is partly what we make it, and partly what it is made by the friends we choose."
The Wise Wench's Tavern Book

Twenty-Nine

"Men fated to be happy need not make haste."
The Wise Wench's Tavern Book

Alexander sat in the King's Chambers and looked out the window. The chair his brother had been found in a tenday ago had been removed and destroyed, replaced by another ostentatious furnishing. He hoped Catriona wouldn't prefer this room, but if she were the one in it, he would be willing to tolerate the place. She would probably decorate it with ships and sailing themes to remind herself of her beloved sea.

He blinked away from the window, the thought catching him in a thin web of guilt. She loved the sea, as did he. To trap her here could be seen by many to be heartless and unbecoming a man expressing such love for someone. He stood, and leaned on the window sill. The morning sun had burned off the frost from the glass and caused the foliage below in the royal gardens to glimmer. He found it all too pretentious. He wanted to be sharing it with her, or with no one, and sharing it with no one was boring. He'd done that all winter.

He left the room, taking the mug from the cabin with him. It had become his almost constant companion since he had rescued it from her house a few days ago. The palace bustled with excitement and activity, as different from the other side of those doors as a wet cat from a dry dog. He had decided to come to the King's Chamber for silence sake. He wanted very much to be on the road by now, on his way to find his bride. But his ruse was precise and important. He needed to be seen leaving town. The preparations were taking far too much time and he was antsy. Another day, and he would not be able to catch her in St. Andrew. Perhaps Gwen had managed to convince her to wait for him. He wanted to hear from her, to have Gwen tell him Catriona loved him and wanted to be there when he arrived.

"Your Majesty!" Alexander saw Dominic coming down the hallway towards him and he took a deep breath to be able to deal with the Mandian right then. Every time he saw Dominic, he though of Gwen, and the cyclic imagery made him dizzy.

"Yes, Dominic, what can I do for you?"

"I'm told Gwen is downstairs. She has asked for an audience with you."

Alexander smiled and he sharpened his step, making Dominic sprint to catch up. "Where?"

"Um, the antechamber, Sire. With the velvet tapestry."

"Ah, very good. See to it we are not disturbed." Alexander ran down the stairs two at a time in his excitement. It took a moment to remember where the anteroom was. Usually, if he left his room, he left through the catacombs, avoiding the downstairs and all the politicians and courtiers. As he entered the first floor, he was reminded as to exactly why he did this. Within seconds, he was all but mobbed by sycophants and servants, bureaucrats and bystanders. Papers were shoved at him and at least six lockets with miniature portraits painted in them of young women were thrust into his hand. He moved them aside and entered the anteroom.

Gwen turned as he entered and curtsied. "Grymalkin."

"Ah, you remembered! Thank you, Gwen. Did you want anything? Food, drink?"

She waved him off. "No thank you."

He sat down, smiling. "What news have you?"

She joined him, choosing a hearth chair upholstered in shepherdesses and lambs. "She's well. She was in St. Andrew three days ago, and tends to be in that port for a tenday. I'm not sure if we can make it, but if we leave right now, we might be able to make it back before she leaves."

"Right now?" He leaned back. "I can't. I'm not ready."

"Well, how long would it take to pack a saddlebag and throw it on a horse?"

"It's not that. I'm packed for *that* trip. I've managed to set up a trip to several nobles' estates in search of a wife, to throw the dogs off the scent. The visits should keep the nobility focused inward so they won't be thinking about how to bring me down. It will enable me to go to Caratia, if necessary, and bring her back."

"That's brilliant. What can I do to help?"

"You, my pixie, are going to accompany me on my trip to get her. With you on my side, how can she refuse me?"

Gwen smiled. "Quite right. When do we leave?"

"Well, it looks like preparations are still two days out. I was thinking of sneaking away for a night or two."

Gwen blinked and sat back. "With who?"

He smiled at her suspicions. "No one. I went to her house a few days ago and I've been dying to return. To lie there, well… Let's just say I've thought of little else than to be close to her."

"You miss her, don't you?"

"More than life." He stood and paced a bit, rubbing the mug from the cabin. "I've been anticipating your return, hoping she would be waiting in St. Andrew. Did she send a message?"

"Um, well, no… I didn't actually *speak* to her, you see…"

"What?" He stopped and stared at her. "Why not?"

"Um, well, you see…" She wrung her hands and he furrowed his brow at her. She cleared her throat. "Alexander, I have a confession to make…"

Alexander stared at her as she finished her tale.

"So, between the Passion Sap to scare off Alistair and Myrgen being a traitor, I'm *certain* she's safe." Gwen offered a smile, but it was turned down.

Alexander blinked and leaned forward. "Gwen, you sent a Fae to slip her some Passion Sap, which she miraculously drank? And you are certain this Alistair character did not have his way with her?"

Gwen straightened and nodded. "I'm sure of it. I was told by that same Fae he carried her to her ship. Octavius would never allow such tawdriness on the *Enigma*. None of the sailors sully the ship by bringing lovers on board."

"Hmm. That explains why she never wanted me to spend the night with her on the ship."

Gwen nodded. "And why I was sent to prepare the Cabin on the Cliffs. She suspected she might be tempted by you. That place remained very special to her."

Alexander nodded and produced the mug from his doublet. "I know."

Gwen leaned forward, recognizing it. "Where did you get that?" Her voice reflected her excited smile.

"Gomez and I went to her home and I found this in Alan's window. It looked onto the palace, to my window. It looked like she used it every day."

Gwen looked at it and seemed to get an idea. "You know what you should do? You should let me have this. I'll send it to her via a Fae messenger. It means so much to her and you, and is a great reminder of your love."

He looked down at the cup. It had come to symbolize the time they had been together, had been happy and in love. He could barely bring himself to put it down during the day for fear it might be broken. "I don't know. This means a lot to me. More than it probably should, in fact. It's from the Cabin on the Cliffs. I used it when we sat up all night talking, the night she first kissed me."

Gwen knelt down and put her hand on his. "I know. And so does she. I'm certain she regrets leaving it behind."

He looked at it a few more moments, then nodded and handed it to her. "Please. Do this then. I need her not to forget me."

Gwen jumped up. "That could never happen. I'll get right on it, Grymalkin. She'll have it within the tenday." She tucked the mug into her doublet as she left and ran off down the hall.

Alexander saw something flutter from her doublet, a message. He picked it up and started to shout out for her when the throng of courtiers saw him and started to come his way. He ducked quickly back inside the anteroom and locked the door against them.

He looked at the letter. It had no writing on the outside and was sealed on the back. He looked at the seal. It was an "M". Alexander looked at the sizable missive. Whatever was inside this, it must be from Myrgen. But why would Gwen have a message from *Myrgen?* She couldn't read. It's possible she didn't even know it was from him. And Gwen would never have exposed herself with Catriona around in person. Her plot with the Passion Sap would have been instantly discovered.

He set his jaw and opened the letter. The first page was covered in gibberish, obviously some kind of code. There was normal writing from at least two different people on the rest of the pages, but none of them were in Catriona's handwriting or Myrgen's, so he went back to the first page.

He looked at the gibberish letter, but he couldn't decipher it. If it threatened him or Catriona or was a grocery list, Alexander couldn't tell and he wasn't certain who could. He could show it to Dominic. Maybe he was familiar with Myrgen's codes, but he doubted it. Dominic was more of a rival than a confidant. This was probably meant for someone else, though Alexander wasn't sure who. Michael was on the *Enigma* with Myrgen and he obviously had spoken to Gwen in order to give her this letter. It might be for Tanglwyst.

Alexander tapped his hand with the missive. *Maybe Myrgen knows where Tanglwyst is hiding. It wasn't out of the question. He protected her when he was interrogated. Unfortunately, I don't know her at all. All I'm certain of is that she and Catriona are enemies now.*

It occurred to him that this was obvious to him because of his insight into this situation. He knew Catriona and Nicolai weren't working out, but he only knew that now because Catriona had told him, but no details. Tanglwyst probably knew the details, if only through pillow talk. Not that it really mattered. The details of a relationship that was no longer around wouldn't be the subject of a missive like this, unless Myrgen were informing Tanglwyst that her lover was killed. Since Duncan was the one who had rescued her, Alexander felt secure that she was aware of that fact by now.

But where was she now? She had evaded Duncan. Had he found her again? He wasn't really certain if he cared. She was Elizabeth's friend and the only reason he had wanted her kept under house arrest until he could investigate this was because Catriona was involved. If the woman he loved was in danger of being scandalized, Alexander was quite willing to put Tanglwyst's head on a pike next to Elizabeth's. From what Gomez had indicated, the woman was a menace and her association with a treacherous Queen was reason enough to put her to death for treason.

However, if she was still alive, and Myrgen knew where she was, Alexander might be able to draw him back to Patras to stand trial. His closeness to Catriona was unsettling. If what Gwen had confessed was true, the longer he stayed in her presence, the greater the chance for Myrgen to win her away from Alexander, and he couldn't bear the thought of that. He wasn't certain if Tanglwyst's ties to Myrgen were enough to get him back to protect her, but it was definitely worth it to have her around for leverage. Now he just had to get her here.

He thought about questioning Duncan, but that had not worked before. Maybe Gomez knew. He had talked to Dominic about her holdings. He would ask for an update on the search. He reached down to the small table for the mug he had been using and it took a moment to register that he had given it to Gwen. He sighed and shook his head. He had no idea what he would do if Catriona refused him.

"Gomez. The King wants to see you."

Gomez looked up from the letter he had just received from St. Giles. The report from the town's Constable, Philippe, was unsettling. The information given in the report was frightening and Gomez wasn't at all sure this scarred man was even human. It told of a lingering sulfur smell in the room and the details made Philippe think dark magic was afoot, though he didn't elaborate, and that was more than a match for most soldiers. That dark power had put the killer on a level well above what Gomez could counter, and he had no idea what to do. Saints forbid the man came after the King. He stood, folding the report. This was something he wanted to tell the King about anyway. Now was as good a time as any.

"Thank you, Colin. Where is he?"

"In the anteroom, on the main floor."

"What? He never comes down to the main floor."

Colin shrugged. "He's here now, sir. Had a female visitor a bit ago. That's where they met." Colin smiled at the implication that Alexander might have had a woman for gratification purposes. "Maybe he didn't want to go all the way back upstairs with her."

Gomez scoffed. His experience with Alexander had shown him it was very unlikely the man would be serviced by a strumpet, or even a mistress. The fact that he had kept a secret lover all these years, and had an heir by her, had colored the lieutenant's image of his sovereign. *A man as devoted to a woman as the King is to her is exactly what this kingdom needs and deserves. It must be killing him not to be pursuing her as we speak.*

Suddenly, an idea occurred to him. "Colin, did you get a look at the woman?"

"Yes."

"Did she have long black hair?"

"No. Blonde."

Gomez felt his face fall. "Oh." He was surprised at how much he really wanted to see Catriona again. Gomez had a lot of respect for Alexander. He wanted to see him happy. He checked his uniform in the mirror and went to meet his sovereign. He went downstairs, noting the sickening amount of sycophants and courtiers buzzing about the main floor. The servants had been taught to keep these people fed, watered and amused during Henry and Catherine's reign and the Queen Mother liked to keep them around to boost her ego. Gomez had no time or interest for any of them.

He knocked on the door to the anteroom and heard the door unlock from the inside. He slipped in and closed the door behind him. Alexander nodded to it. "Lock it, would you? Those locusts in the foyer can smell an open door."

Alexander was pacing and looking at a sheet of paper with a lot of writing on it. A few more pages were discarded on a small end table. Gomez waited as the King got to a stopping place, then bowed. "You sent for me, Sire?"

"Yes. I had a question for you. How goes the investigation into Tanglwyst's escape?"

"Nothing new. I got a report from St. Giles that I thought may be about her. She has a vineyard up there."

"But it didn't, I take it?"

Gomez shrugged. "I'm not sure yet, to be honest. A woman was murdered in a brothel. The description of her killer, who escaped by the way, didn't match Duncan, but it's obvious to me and others that dark magic was used. The way she died was gruesome. Duncan used dark magic to rescue Tanglwyst. Either the two are connected, or there's a new cult in the kingdom and I don't know if I can protect you from it."

Alexander frowned. "Well, I'll be safe soon enough. What about the woman that was murdered. Could that have been Tanglwyst?"

Gomez shook his head. "Doubtful. I've yet to meet the man that could raise a hand to Tanglwyst de Holloway, though to be honest, I don't know what her abilities are against dark magic."

"You seemed to indicate such a thing before, when we were at her manor. Tell me about her."

Gomez raised his eyebrows. "Where to start? When I was stationed in St. Marguerite several years back, I was told to go investigate some flotsam that had washed ashore a half mile down the coast. I took three men and went there. The flotsam we were investigating was a masthead from a ship called the Bishop of Canterbury, registered to the Tanglwyst Trading Company. It had gone missing several tendays before and was overdue from a routine trip from the Glarren lowlands. The reason it was noteworthy was because it was recorded that the Lady Tanglwyst herself was on board.

"We followed the debris from what we determined to be a shipwreck up the coast to an elaborate estate overlooking a treacherous reef. It was a league away from town, there were no docks or landing sites near it and the estate itself was high on a cliff. It was the home of Urien Atriedes, Tanglwyst's chief rival. We began to suspect foul play. The debris indicated an explosion and although there had been a terrible thunderstorm about the time the Bishop went missing, these scorch marks could have been the work of a saboteur."

Alexander arched an eyebrow and Gomez shrugged. "I was young and saw conspiracies in everything at the time.

"Anyway, we went to the manor and knocked. We were greeted by a head man and escorted into the foyer. I knew Urien and Tanglwyst had been fighting over a Mandian glass work factory in Veniche for six years. Every year, it seemed to switch ownership. It was like a local sport to hear the rumors and stories about who had the glass works this season. I believed Urien might have done the Lady in to end the rivalry.

"The head man goes to fetch Urien and he comes down with none other than the Lady Tanglwyst herself. She is wearing a diamond the size of which I have seen only upon your mother's fingers, and never with a matching necklace and earrings like she had on. They bow and Urien introduces her. I told her that she was listed to us as missing and her ship overdue. She explained that the ship had exploded and it had killed nearly every person on board. She had survived, along with three other crewmen. Two of the three were lost in the subsequent days, but they had seen the Atriedes estate not far off and, according to the last survivor, whom I personally interviewed, the others gave their lives to get the lady to shore floating on a chunk of the hull only big enough for one.

"Urien, of course, was ready to have her be lost at sea as well, but the crewman said she stepped over and touched his arm and asked him to please spare them. The sailor swore he saw the light of Heaven itself spread from her fingers across Urien's skin. After that, he couldn't have been more accommodating. He engaged and married the woman, and as far as I know, they remain married even now. I refused to believe such nonsense and wanted to take her to the Magister. I suspected she was being held captive against her will.

"Urien offered to let her go and explain things to the Magister. One of my men, a rough surly bastard named Shannon, blasted a few ill-mannered remarks at the lady. I watched her walk over to him and put her hand on his arm. Sure as I'm standing here, Sire, a pale pinkish-orange glow spread across him and he apologized immediately. He was still a surly, loud-mouth bastard, but when it came to her, he was well-mannered and kind. I have never seen the like.

"I've heard tales of this over and over. She doesn't need to touch them. If she talks with a man for four hours in a row, he falls in love with her. If there were a way to harness her ability, we could quell the army of Caratia."

Alexander blinked, rolling his eyes. "That might be the only way to take them. Luckily, we don't have to worry about that. So, you find it unlikely Duncan would have hurt Tanglwyst?"

"From what I saw in that alley, I find it impossible to believe he would hurt her."

"I see."

"Why do you ask, Sire?"

Alexander handed him the encoded letter from Myrgen. "I have no idea what it says. I've been studying it for about half an hour. I keep feeling like I'm on the verge of getting it, but I have yet to actually hit upon something. It's from Myrgen."

Gomez looked up from the letter. "*Myrgen?*" He looked back at the letter again.

"Yes. I suspect it might be going to Tanglwyst. It's unlikely he would know she had been taken. It occurred to me he might know where to find her. I just wish I had the means to summon her here."

"Are you sure you don't?"

Alexander looked at his guard. "Excuse me?"

"She was never charged. Maybe her Oath is intact. Remember, an enemy is never a villain to themselves. She might have thought she was being a patriot. It's worth a try, at least. Honestly, what have you got to lose?"

Alexander shrugged. "Alright." He closed his eyes and felt around for the people. He felt decidedly foolish for groping around in the dark for a thread but he didn't know what to do. He just wanted to know if Tanglwyst's Oath of Fealty was intact.

And there it was. A small, distant dot of gold light, but he knew instantly it was her.

"By the Saints... She's still here. I figured treason could only be committed by someone with no Oath." He opened his eyes. "I guess you were right. She must consider herself a patriot. But how can I summon her? Again, to break the Oath, she just has to believe herself free."

"Your Majesty, think about it. She plotted the King's destruction, yet her fealty is intact. Either she still holds it, in which case, she comes to the summons, or she never violated it, which amounts to the same. Of all the people in this kingdom, you have the ability to find out."

Alexander exhaled. "Alright, I'm going to need your help."

"What do you need of me, Sire?"

"Believe it or not, I only need one witness whose Oath is intact." He smiled at Gomez, who bowed.

"I would be honored. And I will take the necessary precautions not to let her touch you."

"Thank you." He picked up a quill and ink that was nested on a blotter on a console against a wall. There were small scraps of paper on the console, nothing of official size. He glanced around the room. "Do you have a piece of paper?"

Gomez looked around and then turned the message from Myrgen over. "The back of this is blank."

Alexander nodded, smiling at the irony. "I like it." He wrote a paragraph on the paper and then nicked a knuckle with the pen knife on the console. He put his blood to the paper. "So It Is Written..."

Gomez felt a small compulsion to finish the Ritual. "So Shall It Be Done." He blinked, and looked at his King. "What will happen now?"

"Well, did you feel a compulsion just now?"

"Yes. Faint, not like I would die or anything if didn't speak the final words, but yes."

"Good. Then it worked. Wherever Tanglwyst is at this moment, she will feel compelled to bring herself before me. The longer she delays, the more of her health she loses. Between the compulsion and the damage to her physically, she will crawl across Mervolingia if she must to get to me."

"What if she takes too much damage before she can get to you and dies?"

"I don't know. As far as I know, that's never happened." He handed the Summons to his Grande Guard. "Keep that in a safe place."

"Of course, Your Majesty." Gomez took the Summons and folded it. "What do you plan to do when she arrives?"

"Put her in a cell with solid walls and surround her with female guards. You'd better have some by then." He walked over to the discarded pages were and picked them up.

"I'll make sure it is done." Gomez put the Summons in a pocket in his doublet as the King glanced over the other pages

"I have every faith… in… you… By the Saints." He read quickly over the pages and grew paler with each word. When he finished it, he looked at Gomez. "Is this the murder you spoke of?"

Gomez looked at the pages the king handed him. The account was graphic and far more vivid that his report. He could see why.

Alexander said, "Your report. Did it mention sulfur?"

"Sulfur?"

"Yes!"

Gomez nodded. "Yes, it did. Why?"

"Didn't you say Duncan disappeared in a stink of sulfur?"

Gomez straightened, eyes wide. "You think it might be him? That he has been scarred by the experience with black magic and has become the monster who did this?"

"By the blood of the Saints, I hope not. Excuse me, Gomez, I need to go to my room. I have preparations to make." Alexander left the anteroom with Gomez clearing the way.

Alexander entered his room and closed the door. Gomez had said as he moved up the stairs that a threat like this scarred man was too great to ignore. He proposed putting off leaving the palace

until he could ensure Alexander's safety. Alexander knew well enough that such a thing was not possible. The way Duncan moved through shadow, and the things the Scarred Man did, made Alexander hope he did not just send a monster to protect his most valuable treasure. If Duncan slew Myrgen, Alexander wouldn't care. But if he missed and caught Catriona? That would be the death of them both and she could be quite unpredictable. He wouldn't deny the possibility that she would throw herself between Duncan's dart and Myrgen. Besides, he saw Duncan yesterday. He wasn't wearing a scar like the one described.

Alexander stopped where he was and willed his blood to slow. Duncan was a citizen, with very specific ties. He had said so. The only one outranking Alexander right now was the Church. He focused upon Duncan, trying to sense his fealty oath, but it was murky, like he was looking through a swamp for Duncan. He tried contacting him, but again, the murky feeling intervened. Perhaps he was on a mission for the Church. But why would that prevent Alexander from summoning Duncan unless...

He had to go. Now.

Alexander pulled on the travel cloak he had set out and shouldered his pack. He locked his bedroom door and opened the door to the catacombs in his prayer nave. He moved through the familiar corridors and out into the gardens by the kitchen. He slipped past the hedge and moved with purpose through the forest to Gwen's house. He saw smoke rising from the chimney and he hoped she had enough horses so they could get moving. He *had* to get to Catriona.

He knocked on the door and she opened it. "Hi. Before you start choking, listen. We have to go. Now."

Gwen chewed her bread thoroughly and swallowed. "That was fast. I haven't done the Fae calling."

"I'll adjust. Do you have a couple horses?"

"Only the one I rode here."

"We'll ride double until the first Inn on the way to St. Andrew then. It will make it easier to talk to you anyway. Get your cloak." He glanced out the door to make sure he wasn't being followed. When he looked back, Gwen had fastened her cloak and grabbed a loaf of bread, which she was stuffing into a satchel. He saw the mug on the table and fetched it up, putting it in his own pack.

"Why the sudden urgency, Grymalkin?"

"I think the Church may be trying to assassinate Catriona."

"What? Why?"

"Well, because my own assassin, who serves the church above me, is unreachable."

Gwen stopped moving. "*Your* assassin?"

He looked at Gwen. "I'm King, Gwen. As an office, it comes with a Royal Assassin."

"Why would you know about an assassin? Were you trying to have someone killed?"

Alexander swallowed. "Yes." He looked directly into her eyes. "A scarred man murdered a woman in St. Giles, in a horrible way. I'll have nightmares just from of the description in a letter that was in that message you dropped. The one from Myrgen."

Gwen stepped back and Alexander read guilt on her features.

"So," he continued, "you *did* know whom it was from?"

"He was looking for a messenger to go to Patras. The innkeeper told him I was that person. He gave me a letter to bring back here. I had thought I might give it to you, just in case it was state secrets. He seems like the type."

"Well, I read it. I don't know who the letter was meant for, but inside was a report of this murder. I tried to reach out and summon my assassin, to have him look into this. I couldn't reach him."

"Wait. Myrgen was telling someone about the murder?" Gwen reached into her travel doublet, finding it empty. "Oh no... He asked me to drop a message off with the city guard there in St. Andrew. He told me not to read it and he looked queasy when he mentioned it. I completely forgot it in my haste to tell you about Catriona."

"Well, the message got to Gomez anyway, which is truly where it belongs. Nonetheless, I need to get to St. Andrew right away, as fast as we can. You said before you could get Fae to help you. Can they make a horse run faster?"

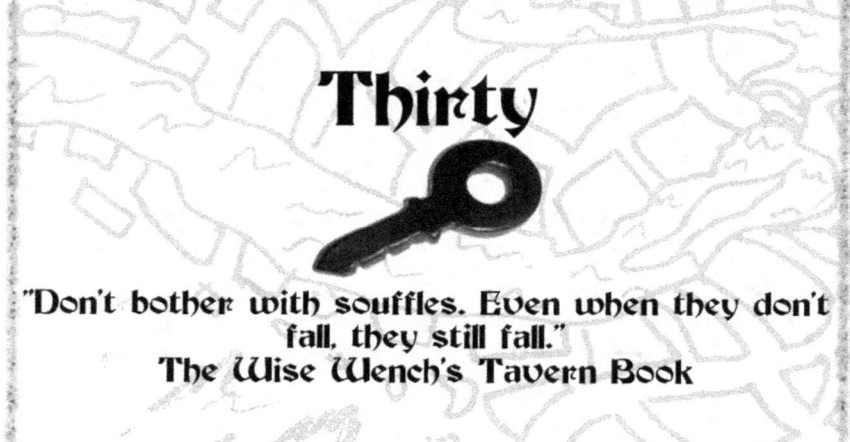

Thirty

"Don't bother with souffles. Even when they don't
fall, they still fall."
The Wise Wench's Tavern Book

James Douglas stepped off the *Raven's Watch* and scratched his shoulder. The clothes he had been wearing for the past three tendays as he traveled from Yantap were extremely well made, durable and beautiful, but they still stunk after not being properly washed. So did he. He was literally itching for a bath. He ran his fingers through his short blond hair and sniffed the air. Usually, he could find the local bath house/ brothel within minutes of setting foot on shore by the smell of heavy perfumes on the wind, but all he could smell was fish and fog. Not very promising.

He saw a few figures coming toward him and figured out that one of them was the assistant harbormaster by the sheer amount of secondary authority he exuded. James knew this feeling well because of the man the assistant was walking alongside. James waited as they approached and nodded greeting. "Assistant Harbormaster. Uncle."

Alistair caught James in a hug and James returned the gesture. He put his hands upon James' shoulders and looked him over. "You have any problems getting here?"

"Of course not. The new ship handles, well, like a new ship." James rubbed the back of his neck. "I'll be happy to tell you all about her over a bath. Care to direct me? I've never spent time in St. Andrew. Just load and unload, then off."

"Gladly. I have much to tell you." Alistair nodded to the assistant.

James recognized a sense of urgency about Alistair and it made him a little nervous. He turned to the assistant. "Please find the Quartermaster. He'll take care of the manifests." The assistant nodded and Alistair took James by the shoulder and walked him away from the docks. When they were pretty much away from the ship, but not near any heavily populated areas, he stopped Alistair. "Now, what's going on?"

Alistair shot a furtive glance at the alleyways around them and lowered his voice. "What makes you think there's something wrong?"

"The furtive glances you keep shooting into the alleyways around us?"

Alistair stood straight and blinked. "Good word use. You sound like a romance novel though."

"I get that a lot. What's wrong?"

Alistair smiled and waved his hand. "You promised we'd talk about that over a bath. Let's save it for there."

Alistair nudged them along and the two men started walking down the streets of St. Andrew, making their way to the brothel. The market opened before them, raising the ambient noise level. The air was thick with the scream of gulls and the smell of fish. It was a good smell after a tenday at sea because it was mixed with earth and James was grateful for the opportunity to talk with his uncle. "So, how long have you been in St. Andrew?"

"For about three tendays. How was Yantap?"

"It was everything you ever told me it was. Of course," said James, "you've never allowed me to come to Yantap before, and now it was only after you had left to be here at the beginning of the season. Why is that, Uncle?"

Alistair favored James with a sly smile. "Because two incredibly handsome men in a town that size would ruin the economy."

"That's you. Always so civic minded." They walked past some fishermen lugging a net full of fish from the docks, and managed to side step a slew of roughy when one of the young men dropped the net. "I thought maybe it was to meet a girl. She lands here first every season, right?"

Alistair pursed his lips. "I'm going to have to remove the tattooed skin of the Quartermaster, I see. For being such a large, frightening man, he's certainly a gossip."

"What can I say? I was speaking that fancy talk to him the entire trip." James stopped at a fruit stand and picked up an apple. "So, did you meet with her?"

Alistair leaned against the stall post. "What do you think?"

James paid for the apple, pocketing it for later, and looked closer at his uncle. He looked well and healthy, with a glow of refreshed relaxation about him, tinged with a healthy dose of shattered delusions and a bit of something else... *fear?* "I'm not at all certain. I have no idea what's going on."

"Good!" Alistair pushed off the post. "Then I did it right. Let's get you bathed."

"You can't possibly think that will stop me from prying."

Alistair shook his head. "Of course not. I taught you better than that." He glanced into the shadows of an alley and James frowned slightly. He started rubbing his hand with his thumb, a nervous habit he had from childhood when he had to regularly remove splinters. His uncle was being frustratingly vague, more so than usual. His concern was even more unsettling. In the several years he had been in his uncle's service, James had never seen the man nervous.

They arrived at the Red Sky at Night and Alistair nodded to James. "You go ahead and get cleaned up and I'll go check on some things. I'll meet you at the Net after you're done." He turned to leave, glancing into the shadows again.

James grabbed his arm. "Uncle, what's going on? Does it have to do with the woman the Quartermaster told me about?"

"Yes, James, but it also has to do with you and your sister."

"Gwen?"

"Yes. Look, go get cleaned up. I want to go check on Ce'Nedra."

"*Ce'Nedra? Who's Ce'Nedra?*"

"A lady I'm friends with. Excuse me." He left.

James blinked after him. His uncle had left Yantap early in order to meet with a woman, according to the Quartermaster. Could this be the lady? Would James finally meet the woman who outranked all others in his uncle's heart? He smiled and strode through the bright red doors of the brothel.

Alistair moved through the streets towards the Inn. He had a strange feeling of unease and he felt the need to check on Ce'Nedra. He opened the front doors and found Saiban puttering in the dining area, serving a few folks. Ce'Nedra was cleaning glasses behind the bar and the room was better lit than usual. There was nary a shadow in the place. Alistair went over to her and leaned on the bar, touching her hand as she brought it up to his arm. "Any trouble, my lady?"

Ce'Nedra shook her head. "No. No sign of him."

"Good. Just keep things well lit. You should be fine. My nephew has arrived in town. He's getting a bath right now. He's been at sea for three tendays so I expect he'll take full use of the Red Sky's facilities before he's done. We have a while."

"Would you like something to eat?"

He looked into her golden eyes and smiled. "Of your excellent cooking? Of course." He sat down on a stool by the bar and kept watch while Ce'Nedra went in back to make him a serving of the night's fare. Saiban had finished cleaning up a wine stain from the night before, and was returning to the back with his bucket and rags. He nodded to Alistair as he went past. The room's extra lights brought out the small, dismissible sins of a poorly lit tavern floor and Saiban had been obviously put to work to clean those marks.

Alistair spotted several clean spots on the floor, which served to draw attention to the normal wear of the rest of the floor. Chances were Ce'Nedra would either paint the floor or decide this fear of the dark was too expensive. Frankly, she wasn't Duncan's target anyway but she too had been unsettled by the attack in the alley. When Alistair had told her to stay out of the shadows, she had apparently taken him literally. He wasn't sure if this was going to work out for her business or not. People rather liked their taverns a bit dark.

A couple sailors from the *Raven's Watch* came in and Alistair recognized them. He nodded to them and glanced towards the back of the room in the direction of the kitchen. Ce'Nedra was taking longer than he expected and Saiban hadn't returned yet either. Just then, the young man returned, the bucket full again and a handful of clean rags were tucked into his belt. He saw the two men sitting down at one of the tables and set down his bucket. He walked over and talked to the sailors. A couple more men came in the front door and Alistair looked them over. He didn't recognize them, but the other two men seemed to and called them to share the table.

Saiban came over to the bar and poured a few mugs of ale. Alistair glanced at the back again, certain the sound of customers would draw the innkeeper back out, but he saw not even a flicker of movement. He leaned to Saiban. "What's taking her so long?"

Saiban glanced at the kitchen area and shrugged. "Oi dunno, suh. Ait's nevuh toiken 'er this long ta git woine b'fore."

"To… get *wine!*" Alistair jumped up and flew into the kitchen, looking around. The door to the wine cellar was open and he could see a light hinting at its existence in the dark. His heart turned cold as he saw the light was not moving at all. He drew his sword and stepped onto the stairs leading down. He wanted to call out to her, but if he wanted to maintain the chance for surprise, he needed to be silent. Just in case. He saw some movement near the foot of the stairs and Ce'Nedra stepped into view carrying several bottles of wine. She almost dropped them when she saw Alistair.

He smiled and sheathed as she gave a sigh. "You scared me! Here," she came up the stairs, trying to hand him the wine. He took a couple bottles from her and let her go past him. They brought the bottles to the bar and she turned to go back.

Alistair stopped her. "I'll get them. How many more do you need?"

"This should be enough wine, but I'll need at least two kegs of ale and two of mead, please."

He nodded and returned to the cellar. He watched the shadows carefully, sword out, and grabbed a keg of mead. It would take four trips, he decided, but he would keep his sword out, just in case. He brought out the two mead kegs and met Saiban at the top of the stairs, who took them from him and brought them out to Ce'Nedra. Alistair saw the ale kegs were bigger, too big, in fact, to carry one handed. He glanced around and sheathed his sword, picking up the ale keg and getting it up the stairs before his mind had time to fill his head with images of what lingered in the dark.

Saiban nodded and took the keg and Alistair managed to return with the second one unscathed as well. He started to close the cellar door when the young man stopped him. He nodded to the opening. "Th' lantoirn. Wuh coin't laive it down thair, not with all thet woine." He started to go down the stairs but Alistair took his shoulder.

"I'll get it. You go help Ce'Nedra."

Saiban nodded and Alistair went back down the stairs. He walked over to the lantern and retrieved it, heading up the stairs. He blew it out and hung it on the hook by the cellar. A noise out the back of the inn drew his attention and he felt a sting on his neck right before he hit the floor.

Duncan watched Alistair crumple and smiled. He had decided to be kind and give him a heart-stopping poison, killing him quick instead of the thrashing poison Alexander had chosen. Duncan had debated for a while about whether to kill him, or to simply give the poison that made Alistair *appear* dead. Then he could wake up in a box underground and try to claw his way out. In the end, it was the urgings of the shadow whispers that made him turn from the crueler method. He didn't like the sound of their voices.

He heard the people in the inn talking and thought again about their discovery of Alistair. The shadows delighted in the idea of such pain and he felt guilt. He stepped into the kitchen as he heard the woman replying to someone in the other room. Any moment, she would turn that corner and find his body. He swallowed and ran into the room. He put his hand on the body as a sweep of golden curls turned in the doorway back to the dining room and in a flash of light and lemons, he was in the secret room where he had fled before.

He stood and looked at the lifeless body of Alistair Hapsburg and thought about it rotting in this place. He would never return here again because it would stink of death, at least for the next several months, though he might be wrong. With no natural environment, it may not. No insects, no external air. Just this glowing symbol to treat the body. It may remain like this for the rest of time. He had nowhere else to take it right then so he left it on the floor and returned to the alley behind the inn.

Duncan walked around to the front of the building, the darkness settling in feeling comfortable. He breathed in the air. He may have lost his current quarry, but he had just got a great second prize. He flexed his hand in the lantern light, then put on his glove. The stitches were still too obvious, but he was pleased to find his hand worked just fine. The glove caught for a second and he almost didn't hear the person step out of the alley behind him in time.

Thirty-One

"Don't stand by the water and long for fish. Go
home and weave a net."
The Wise Wench's Tavern Book

James stepped into the Inn and looked around. He expected to have to let his eyes adjust to a common gloom, but this room was extremely well lit. The glare caused him to shield his eyes a bit. He looked around for Alistair, but he wasn't in the room. However, there was a pretty blonde woman behind the bar, loading an ale keg by herself. James suspected Alistair was somewhere else because he would never allow a woman to strain herself if he was interested in her. It would take away from his dashing demeanor.

Well, his loss! James strode quickly over to the lady and came in from the opposite side of the keg. "Here, allow me."

The lady jumped, nearly dropping the keg. James had his hands on it before it could fall and moved it into the slot where she had been trying to place it. He looked at her and smiled. "I'm sorry. I didn't mean to startle you."

Her eyes remained wide and she glanced around, looking for someone.

His smile had somehow failed to put her at ease, and he knew he was clean, so she couldn't be responding to some foul smell or a bit of something in his teeth. Her hands were shaking. He reached out to touch her shoulder. "Hey, it's fine. No one is here to hurt you. Are you Ce'Nedra?"

She arched an eyebrow at him and pulled back a little. "Yes. Who are you?"

"I'm looking for Alistair. I'm his nephew, James. He said he was coming here to see you and to meet him here."

"Oh. He's downstairs, helping Saiban get supplies for tonight." She finally relaxed, but her twitchiness put him on edge. *What was going on?*

"Thank you." James glanced back into the kitchen and went back there, looking for his Uncle. The door to the wine cellar was closed, but James heard a noise out the back door. He opened the door and looked out. He saw a form step around the corner of a building and wondered if Alistair was going somewhere for the innkeeper. He followed the form around the corner and looked around, but his uncle was nowhere to be seen.

He turned and looked the other direction.

"James? James Douglas?"

James looked at the man standing in front of the Black Cat and Anchor. The tall man was beaming friendship and James recognized him. He had been one of the men James had sailed with after Catriona defeated him in the Firth of Glarren several years ago, though James' pride had not let him tell that tale at the time. He smiled and caught the man's gloved hand in a worker's grip of companionship.

"Duncan McVryce! What in the scope of the Saints brings you to St. Andrew?"

Gwen and Alexander crested a hill and saw the sea village of St. Andrew glistening on the shoreline. He stopped for a moment, various memories of days and evenings spent in this small port city welling to the surface of his mind. Their focus upon getting here had precluded the usual chatter of traveling companions and the hours spent not on the horses had been filled with sleeping off the rigors of travel. He and Gwen had barely spoken outside necessary exchanges after he had told her about the letter from the brothel owner in St. Giles.

Now that their target was before them, he felt hopeful again. He knew his Sovereignty protected him against being touched by Duncan and if he could get to Catriona in time, he would make sure he stayed close enough to protect her. He had left her side for the last time. He spurred the horse and caught up to Gwen. She turned to him.

"When we get into town, we should probably split up. We stand a better chance of finding her that way." Gwen flicked a stray wisp of blonde from her eyes.

Alexander smiled. "You just don't want her to know you've been meddling."

Gwen blushed and kicked her horse into a run. Alexander joined her and they rode into town like they were being chased. They reined in at an inn on the north end of town. She nodded towards it as they dismounted. "I'm going to check on Alistair. He can update me as to what's going on with her."

Alexander pulled his satchel from the saddlebags on his horse. "I'll head to the docks, looking in at the Net on the way. Be careful. Stay out of the shadows."

Gwen stopped and looked at him. "Why?"

He realized he might have just shown his hand. He glanced into the alleyway where a couple men were talking in the cover the darkness provided. "Because of thieves. Besides, we don't know if that killer is around. I just want to make sure you're safe."

She smiled. "Thanks, Grymalkin."

He moved off towards the docks as she took the horses to the stable. He ducked his head into the Net on his way through town. Lots of people were in there, but only a few women. Catriona tended to be a solitary drinker, and he could see no single parties at any of the back tables where she was wont to frequent. He stepped back onto the streets again and moved through the noonday crowds in the marketplace. He kept his hand on his pouch and sword to keep track of them, scanning the throngs for her familiar ebony hair and flashing, rare eyes. He got to the docks and stopped, looking around for the *Enigma.*

His heart seized as he recognized none of the ships. The *Enigma* was gone.

Gwen walked both horses over to the stable and looked around for Saiban. There was no sound of him out back either. She walked over near the back of the Inn and saw two unsavory types plotting in the shadows. Alexander's warning came quickly to mind and she walked away from the alley toward the front doors.

Suddenly, an arm was around her neck from behind and a husky voice growled in her ear.

"Move one inch and I'll break your neck."

Her cloak clasp dug into her windpipe. The voice was muffled through her hood, but the threat was very clear. *Think, Gwen! Think! You can't fall here. Alexander needs you to help him win Catriona's heart!* She focused through the pain and realized she could sense there was a chink in his hold of her.

She held her breath and slammed her elbow into her attacker's kidneys. He flinched, clearly not expecting her to fight back. His hold fell away and she slipped out, turning on him with a vicious kick to the knee.

The man collapsed and glared up at her as her hood fell away. His eyes, the only thing she could see above the cloth covering the rest of his face, grew wide. His brow furrowed. "Ow! You brat!"

"James?"

"You kicked me. I can't believe you kicked me."

"You said you were going to break my neck!"

"Yes, but I wouldn't have really done it. Ouch!"

Gwen knelt down and felt his knee. It was starting to swell. "We are gonna have to get that looked at by a healer. Can you stand?"

"Maybe. You are in trouble. I'm gonna tell Mom."

Gwen folded her arms. "Yeah? And I'll tell Alistair you're being a girl."

"You would *not!*"

"Try me."

James shook his head and she helped him to his feet. "Saints, Gwen, when did you get so tough?" He turned to look down the alley. "Hey, Duncan, meet my sis...ter." He looked around, but his friend was gone. "Hunh. Must not have wanted to intrude upon our reunion." He waved a hand at the empty end of the alley. "Eh, he'll turn up later." He turned his attention back to Gwen. "My friend Duncan."

She nodded. "Oh. I thought you two were thieves plotting mischief."

James smiled. "Maybe we were and you just saved some innocent from our pranks! Come on. I'll buy you a drink." He dusted his rear clean and limped into the Inn with his sister.

Duncan watched the exchange between the siblings from the shadow of a wall. He could feel something about the girl, and something about his former shipmate as well. He had never noticed it when they had sailed together, but now it was painfully obvious, a nectar-sweetness that surpassed all else. It was far more prominent in her and he wondered if it was because he preferred women to men. Then again, he'd never been with a man. For all he knew, it might be interesting.

He glanced down the street and saw a man dodging through the marketplace, looking for someone. The man turned and Duncan saw that it was Alexander. He closed his eyes and felt his thread, confirming his identity, then slipped through a few shadowy areas to get closer. He stepped out in the alleyway the man was walking past, striding with purpose. The King stopped as he reached the dock area, looking around. His search grew frantic as he did not find what he sought and Duncan stepped in behind him, head bowed.

"She's gone, Your Majesty."

Alexander turned and his Sovereign's protection flared, subtle in the noonday light. He toned it down, but not out, and glanced around once he saw Duncan.

"You let her go?" The king at once seemed relieved and annoyed.

Duncan motioned them back into the alley where they could talk undisturbed. "No. I couldn't get on the ship. One of her companions attacked me and I was injured." He peeled off the glove and showed Alexander the sewn hand. Then he put the glove back on.

Alexander looked around, then back at Duncan. "Which companion? Myrgen?"

"No. The Black Sparrow himself, Alistair Hapsburg. He will, however, no longer be a problem." He smiled, but he felt the smile carry no mirth. "Though I will tell you I managed to injure Myrgen quite heavily."

"He fought you?"

"Not really. Merely got in the way."

"Was she hurt?"

Duncan shook his head. "No, Your Majesty. I couldn't have raised a hand against her had I wanted to."

Alexander focused upon Duncan for a moment, then blinked. "No, you still have your Oath intact. For the time being."

"I don't expect it will falter, Your Majesty."

"I see. It was murky before. I couldn't reach you. I feared the worst."

"Which would be what?"

Alexander glanced at the amulet on Duncan's neck. "That the Church had ordered her execution and sent you to do it."

Duncan nodded. "That would be the worst in your opinion. But no, Your Majesty. She left three nights ago, after the incident."

"*Three days?*" Alexander looked at Duncan. "Why didn't you come to me immediately?"

Duncan held up his hand. "I was incapacitated."

Alexander exhaled and his irritation left with the bad air. "Of course. You were probably unconscious when I tried to summon you. That's why it didn't work." He looked at the sea. "Three days... so she's not far. They'll dock in St. Marguerite next. Go there, and follow them until they reach Caratia. If you get the chance, slow them down. We'll take another ship and follow. Go, and stay hidden. Don't let her capture you and don't let her read you."

Yes, Your Majesty." He stepped into the shadows and stepped out in St. Marguerite.

Alexander stepped out of the alleyway and looked around. He saw no one he knew back towards the marketplace and the Inn was too far away with too many people between him and where Gwen was going. He didn't need to talk to Gwen about this anyway. Her knowledge of a royal assassin was bad enough. She didn't need to meet the man. Moreover, he still wasn't certain he trusted Duncan as much as he did before. Alexander had fantasized about having Catriona to himself, and even abusing his royal status to get it, but the St. Michael's Day massacre had ended his taste for that. Or so he had thought. When the idea to kill Nicolai had come to him along with the Power of Sovereignty, he wasn't certain if it was just a side effect of his new position. In the end, he believed it was the corrupting influence of power.

Duncan must fight that as well, and his ability to disappear from one place and arrive in another instantly was accompanied by the stink of sulfur and darkness within his eyes, and those were the external costs. Such ease of movement could not possibly come without a greater price.

Alexander had wanted to go with Duncan through the shadows. To be there ahead of Catriona and greet her as she pulled into port would be amazing and undoubtedly irresistible. He had felt the truth in Duncan's words when he said he could not have hurt her, and, nearly as important, he had hurt Myrgen. Alexander found himself pleased by this news.

He walked toward the Harbormaster's office. He needed to find a ship going south and soon. Duncan could probably slow them down, provided they pulled into a port. Worst case, he could get on board and rip up the sails, forcing a port stop. Of course, if he could get on board, he would have. Alexander stopped and thought about that for a moment.

Duncan couldn't get on board the *Enigma* for some reason. Probably because Catriona knows her ship so well, it was almost like it was part of her, an extension of her, like her rapier or her clothes. Her crew was vigilant and she never took on new crew members she didn't personally introduce. Passengers? Yes, but even those were hand chosen by her. There was also something about a life debt, but since he didn't have one to her, they had never discussed it. She had always been mysterious to him, and rarely revealed anything without it being her idea. He had always felt that she was full of secrets and that was something that excited him.

He supposed it was wrong, but he had often looked forward to her being hurt, because it was then that she needed him. He learned things about her through mending her body, like what she had been through and what she could handle. He had learned her most intimate pleasure places, testing them occasionally when she was knocked out from the herbs he gave her to help her sleep. It had begun as an accident, dealing with a set of broken ribs. He had brushed against her breast with his sleeve as he had been checking her bandages. She had moaned in response.

He had almost taken her that night. Had she been less wounded, he might have. Instead, he had realized to do that would have soiled their relationship. When she gave herself to him, he wanted it to be with complete abandon, of her own free will. Moreover, he wanted her to be conscious, an active part of the play. He wanted to see his reflection in her eyes.

He still needed a ship, and entered the Harbormaster's Office. The Harbormaster was a grizzled looking thing, with strong shoulders like a blacksmiths and deep canyons of experience on his face. His hair was white as sea foam and he wore a red shirt and blue doublet and breeches. His hands were the size of a child's head and he was knitting a green sock with metal needles the size of horseshoe nails when Alexander came in.

"Sorry to disturb you."

The Harbormaster looked up and smiled. "No bother at'all, young man. I was just taking care of a long overdue task. There's only so long yeh can wear a pair of stockings before yeh need a new set."

"And you make them yourself?"

"Yep. Learned to do it on muh first ship. Found it rather soothin' and been doing it ever since. Seemed appropriate, considerin'." He tapped his head. "Helps me organize. Ended up being muh claim to fame, as it happens. When Kirkwood passed on this winter, the Mayor came tuh me. Name's Esau Stocking. What cen uh do fer yeh, young man?"

Alexander smiled. *That really is appropriate, a knitter named Stocking.* "I'm looking for a ship that's for hire. I need to head to St. Marguerite, and possibly on to Caratia after that. Are there any ships available?"

"Well, lessee…" Esau thought for a moment, his hands knitting the entire time. "The *Raven's Watch* just pulled in t'day. It hasn't filed orders for where it's off tuh next. Captain's a fella named James Douglas, but the person you might want tuh talk tuh about gettin' a charter is Alistair Hapsburg. He's the registered owner."

Alexander's eyes narrowed. "Alistair… does he, by chance, know the captain of the *Enigma*?"

"Catriona? Yep. Saw them t'gether t'other day, when that Myrgen fella was injured." He checked his stitches on his knitting. "He an' her musta had some sort a altercation or something. First, she hit that fella and knocked him clean out. I think Octavius musta disapproved because he refused to help her move him afterwards and she sat in the street with him 'til 'e came to. Took a while too. It was well past dark, but she didn't leave 'is side once. Methinks she might be smitten."

He waved his hand at Alexander. "But that's just sailor gossip. Can't really put no faith in talk and appearances. Folks get it wrong all the time."

"Excuse me, but she knocked out *Alistair*, then sat by him in the streets?"

"Neh. Sorry. Musta been confusin' the way I told it. She knocked out that *Myrgen* fella."

"The man who was already injured?"

"Yep. They strted arguin' when she tried to take him somewhere, I think t' the ship. Once Octavius refused t' help her, she just sat there in an alley, surrounded by lanterns, just glowin' like it was midday. Whatever the altercation between her and Octavius di'n't stop him from sending crew t' guard the two of 'em while she tended him. Nice fella, that Myrgen."

Alexander got a sinking feeling, like his stomach had decided to move to his left ankle all of a sudden, marked by the tiny ticking of the small metal knitting needles. He didn't want to ask any more questions. He didn't want to find out anything more. For some reason, he just couldn't stop himself. "Were you around when Myrgen woke up? Did you see what happened then?"

"As a matter o' fact, I was. I was closin' up for the night and was gonna see if they needed anything. I saw Myrgen sit up and she and he gathered up th' lanterns and went on board. Set sail within the hour."

"Was he still injured?"

Esau stopped knitting and cocked his head in thought. "Come tuh think of it, no. He helped her gather them lanterns just fine. He had a nasty-lookin' bite or somethin' on him when he was injured, too, all black and vein-y. Saw it m'self."

Alexander closed his eyes. *She healed him. She HEALED him!* The wound Duncan gave that traitor had not gone on to destroy Myrgen. It *had* wounded the woman Alexander loved. *Damn them!*

"Hey. You well over there?"

Alexander shook his head. "No... not, not really... Thank you for your help." He turned to open the door, then he stopped. "How long does it take to travel to St. Marguerite?"

"By sea? 'Bout three days. Longer overland on account o' th' mountains."

"Thank you." Alexander left the man to his knitting, closing the door behind him.

Thirty-Two

"Four things come not back: The past life, the sped arrow, the spoken word and the neglected opportunity."
The Wise Wench's Tavern Book

Gwen and James entered the inn and she led him to a table to sit and rest his wounded leg and wounded pride. "Did you want some food or something? I stayed here before. Ce'Nedra's a good cook."

"Ce'Nedra? That's the woman Alistair was coming to see."

Gwen frowned at James. "He's already telling you about his latest conquest? How long have you been here?"

"Almost two hours!"

Gwen rolled her eyes and galumphed over to the innkeeper. Ce'Nedra looked back in the kitchen again, then at Gwen. "I understand you know my uncle, Alistair. He has blond hair and ice blue eyes?"

"Yes. Not half an hour ago. He went downstairs to help Saiban with bringing up some ales and wine. The lantern's on the hook by the cellar, so he obviously came up, but he's disappeared suddenly. He's been so protective since the incident in the alley, I'm a little surprised he let himself get distracted. You must be Gwen. He was very worried when he couldn't find you the other day."

"Why?"

A sharp sound from the dining room caused the innkeeper to jump half out of her skin and both women looked to see James had scooted away from the table to have a closer look at his bruised shin, scraping the chair across the floor. Gwen noticed how bright everything was in the room. The black cat that usually sat on the mantelpiece near the striped one was nowhere to be seen. She put her hand on Ce'Nedra's. "What's wrong?"

Ce'Nedra steadied herself with a deep breath and a long drought from a glass of wine. "Alistair and I were attacked in town a few days ago, along with a couple of his friends. His friends left on board the *Enigma,* but he stayed here to make sure the man didn't return. Alistair cut off his hand and even with such an injury, he wasn't certain the man wouldn't return." She took another swig of wine. "He was right by my side for most of the last two days. He left late this morning to see if a ship of his had arrived and came back in time to help me out with bringing up spirits for the day. But I haven't seen him in a while and he would have told me he was going somewhere."

Gwen took her over to James, who stood as the ladies approached. "James, this is Ce'Nedra."

"My lady! I have heard your name spoken on the fairest of winds."

Ce'Nedra drew a small smile. "You *are* related to him, though I certainly would have pegged you for a son, not a nephew."

James kissed her hand. "That is a frequent assumption. But enough about me. You look troubled, my lady."

Gwen nodded. Ce'Nedra repeated her concerns and James shook his head. "No, we were just outside *and* in the alleyway, and from the smell of her, Gwen was just at the stables." James ducked Gwen's punch without stopping. "We've not seen him."

"I see. You're the James that brought in the *Raven's Watch,* right?"

"The same."

"I'll wait up for him, but I have something for the two of you. He gave it to me in case something happened before you got here." Ce'Nedra produced the key to his room. "He said you would know how to get into his sea chest."

James frowned at that and looked at the key. "He left his sea chest up there?"

Ce'Nedra nodded towards the stairs. "Third door on the left."

James took a breath and nodded to Gwen. "We'll be right back, my lady. I should be ready for lunch by then and with any luck, our uncle will join us."

James led his sister upstairs.

James opened the door and then closed and locked it behind Gwen. He ignored her puzzled look and scanned the room for the chest. It wasn't immediately visible, but he didn't expect it to be.

"Look around. You want a small rectangular box about this big." He held his fingers and thumb in a rectangle about eight inches across.

"I thought she said it was a sea chest."

"It is. You'll understand once you see it." He went through the drawers in the room and looked under the dresser. Gwen looked under the bed and under the pillows and chair cushion. They had practically torn the room apart when James noticed a slight bulge in the mattress. He lifted it and found the box. He pulled it from the straw-filled canvas.

"Wow," Gwen said as she came around to his side of the bed. "I see what you mean." Her fingers traced the ripples on the box, sea green and curling foam like in a small breeze. Her touch caused the waves to roll and move and James smelled the salt and sea spray fill the room. Gwen's eyes widened. "It's *Fae!*"

James nodded. "After I lost the war with Catriona against Tanglwyst's shipping company, Alistair showed me this to cheer me up. He said it contained his most precious items and that if anything ever happened to him, it would take both you and I to open it. He said our mother was the only other one who could."

James put his hands on the back and front of the box. "Put your hands on the top and bottom. It's the only way I can figure it would take both of us to open it."

Gwen did as directed and the box grew a wavy seam around it, tracking the flow of the waves. He lifted the lid and looked in. It held a thick book, a snow white glove with a "G" embroidered upon the cuff and two small lockets. James picked up the book while Gwen took a look at the lockets. The book was old, but it was in his uncle's handwriting.

"Here is an accounting of the actions of the Covenant of Persephone and the saving of the World in the year of Heaven twelve hundred seventy-six, as told by Prince Alistair Hapsburg, Heir to the Crown of York."

"What the hell...?" James glanced through a few pages. There were several drawings and a portrait of a stunning woman wearing white and fur. She was reaching out a gloved hand with a "G" embroidered upon it. He looked at Gwen. "Let me see that glove."

Gwen brought over the glove and looked at the portrait drawn in the book. James compared the two. It was a match to the ones in the portrait. "This glove belongs to this woman."

Gwen touched the portrait. "James, this is Gloriana, the Winter Queen of the Fae. Mother told me about her from tales uncle brought for us. I saw her in a book once."

"This is a first hand account of something that happened three hundred years ago. And it's Alistair's handwriting." He nodded to the lockets. "What's in there?"

Gwen opened the locket and her face went bright with glee. "Look!" She turned the small portrait inside to him and he saw his sister, exactly as she was right that second, including the flush of excitement in her cheeks. He took the other locket and looked into his own features. He noticed a small bit of white soap on his left ear and rubbed it away. The portrait reflected the change. He looked at the other side of the hinged door at the inscription.

"For my Beloved, so you will always know the faces of our children."

The siblings looked at one another. Gwen spoke what James was thinking. "What is going on?"

Gwen and James came downstairs and Gwen raised her head, looking for Alexander. "Grymalkin, you're back."

Alexander lifted his eyes to her and her brother. He did not look to Gwen like he had found what he wanted. "Grymalkin, this is my brother, James."

Alexander nodded and clasped the forearm offered him. "Grymalkin." He looked at Gwen. "She's gone, we missed her."

Gwen blinked, lost. "Her?"

Alexander arched his eyebrows. "Catriona? The reason we're here?"

"Oh! Yes, of course." She shook her head. "How long ago?"

"Three days."

"Three days? That's not very far. She's probably going to stop in the next port of call. If we sail quickly, we can catch her."

"We need a ship for that."

"I have a ship." Gwen and Alexander looked at James. "Brand new. Been on the seas three tendays from its home port. The *Raven's Watch*."

Alexander smiled. "That was considerably easier than I thought it would be. The Harbormaster, Stocking, suggested you. I came here in hopes of meeting up with Gwen and then looking for you. How soon can we get under weigh? As you heard, I'm actually trying to catch up to someone."

"Well, I need to restock supplies right now, but I know from experience we can do that in two hours. We can be eating dinner on the open sea."

"Are you sure? You said her maiden voyage had taken three tendays. Won't your men be ready for shore leave by now?"

"I can always take on new crewmen and get going. That's how I did it for years."

"*Years?*" Alexander arched an eyebrow.

"Yes. Started about eight years ago, sailing with my uncle." James looked at Gwen and she patted his shoulder.

He'll turn up. Don't worry.

Alexander put a hand on Gwen's. "Are you sure you're up to this? If you need time for your family, I can find another way, another ship."

"I don't want to abandon you, Grymalkin. Not during your time of need here." She looked at James, then back at Alexander.

"Gwen, you're not abandoning me. I'll find my own way. Look," Alexander leaned a little closer to Gwen, glancing at the nearby tables first, "in your," he waved his fingers in front of his chest, "*meddling* with these Fae powers, can they speed a ship along?"

Gwen thought about it. "Not really. Just horses, like I said before. You mean for this trip?"

Alexander winced. "We're three days behind, but I don't remember her spending three days in any port outside of this one."

James leaned in as well, joining the conspiracy. "Well, our ship isn't laden. Maybe we can make it there faster. Possibly two and a half."

Alexander looked around, running his hand through his hair. He looked like he wanted to ask her something and was having trouble wording it. He also glanced at James a couple times and she determined he was worried about looking weak and lovesick in front of a stranger. Gwen put her hand on his arm.

"Hey, don't worry. We'll catch her. At the very least, we know where she's going. With minimal stops, we will get there about a day behind her. She'll be in Caratia for a while."

Alexander stood, frustration showing on his face and body. "With *him* courting her the entire time. And now with her husband dead, there's nothing stopping her from giving in to him."

He walked away a few steps, hands in his hair, then saw the sitting room with the fireplace and entered it. The weather was such the fire had not been tended during the day and the room was empty and out of earshot of much of the dining room, secluded by a partial wall. Gwen and James followed him. "She healed him, Gwen. Don't you understand?"

"Alexander, why are you doubting her love for you? She's remained faithful despite her circumstances all winter. Now, a few tendays will turn her eye?"

He looked at her again. "She *healed* him. She took on his wounds so he wouldn't suffer. With all she's been through, that's becoming increasingly difficult for her. If she ever suffers a major injury directly, her body will *not* be able to handle it, and I'll lose her. Myrgen is a manipulating slime and he's clearly working his will upon her. What's more, she's walking right into it. I can't do it. I can't wait a month to see her again, not with him doing this."

Gwen drew a breath and closed her eyes. She knew this was her fault and she could tell he was only barely holding back his outrage that this had happened. She didn't want James to get the wrong impression of Alexander either. In his current state of mind, he'd tear Alexander apart.

James put a hand on her shoulder. "I think your tone is out of place here, sir. My sister is hardly at fault because you can't keep your woman."

Gwen touched his hand. "James, please…"

Alexander seemed not to even notice James' aggressive tone. "What's more I don't know why she healed him, or why she isn't seeing through his ruses. She's better than this. She *must* know his intentions. It's like she's…"

"Like she's under a spell." Gwen opened her eyes and looked at Alexander.

Alexander returned her look, though his was slowly becoming a simmer, with the potential to not only boil, but explode.

James' eyes widened a touch. "Oh no. Please…"

"I cast a spell to heal her heart, Alexander. I'm sorry. She's acting like this because of me."

Alexander tilted his head the barest of inches, eyes betraying his moving anger. "Heal her heart? What do you mean?"

"I sent a sea spirit to her. It heals broken hearts. Since her heart was in mourning over the loss of Nicolai, I thought it would help her realize her love for you and have her return to you. It opens up hearts for love again."

"So, you sent a spirit to her to heal her heart when I couldn't be there to fill the void?"

Gwen blinked. "Well, no. It won't make her fall in love. Even if you *were* there, she'd have to have feelings for you," Gwen hesitated a moment as Alexander stepped back from her, "*which she does*. Alexander, she loves you. She does. I've seen it all winter. She never once wanted to be with Nicolai."

"Then why didn't she *come to me?*" He balled his fist and thumped the arm of a chair, his anger mounting. "Why did she *never* come to the palace to see me? If her love for me was so great and so strong, why was she not in my arms instead of in a filthy alleyway healing a *traitor?*" He turned back to Gwen. "That man murdered my brother and set the woman I want for my *queen* up to harbor him from justice! Is that *also* the work of your interference, or did your spell just take away the only thing keeping her *sane?*"

James stepped up to Alexander and put a strong hand upon his shoulder. "Lower your voice when you speak of spells and my sister or so help me, I'll put you in the ground next to your brother. I'll not have her burned as a witch because of your indiscretion."

Gwen grabbed her brother's hands. "James, don't! Please. He's the King of Mervolingia. He can have you put to death for touching him."

A gasp from behind them and the sound of crashing ceramics drew all their attention. Ce'Nedra looked at the trio. "The King of Mervolingia? In *my* inn?" She glanced at the coins in her hand, then back at Alexander. "Your Majesty!" She dropped to her knee.

Behind her, every head in the tavern stopped speaking, turned to look and then rose and bowed before him. A young man by the door stood aghast, then bolted out the door, shouting as he ran that the King was in the Black Cat and Anchor. Within minutes, people were flowing in the door like a tidal wave to see the King and Ce'Nedra staved off Gwen's almost certain execution by bustling Alexander into the main hall and up the stairs to a private room before he could get mobbed.

Thirty-Three

"Sooner or later, a Mandian always shows his scales."
The Wise Wench's Tavern Book

Alexander closed the door to the room Ce'Nedra had given him and leaned his head against it. She had refused payment, but he was going to leave a hefty tip when he left. The trouble with traveling as the King was that nothing was ever quick and nothing was ever easy. Gwen's slip of the tongue had just pinned them here for at least another day. And all the time, Catriona was getting farther away and Myrgen was getting farther with her. He was going to lose her if he didn't act fast.

His mind brought up something that he had been avoiding thinking about all day, but now he let the idea gel completely in his mind. He took a deep breath and closed his eyes.

"Duncan, come here." He had no idea if this would work, but it was worth a try. If he had suffered another blow or was asleep, he might not hear the call. He needn't have worried.

"I am here, Your Majesty."

Alexander turned and saw the tall, bald man on a knee, head bowed in respect on the other side of the room, respecting the Royal Presence of ten feet. "I didn't know if that was going to work, after last time."

"I'm not injured this time."

Alexander looked at Duncan's gloved hand. "Would it work if you were asleep?"

"I would be alerted to your need for me, but I would be able to get dressed. But that was not necessary this time."

"No, it wasn't. But it brings up a question I have. You rescued Tanglwyst and took her with you and you've just come from St. Marguerite." Alexander took a deep breath. "Take me to her. Take me to Catriona."

Duncan nodded and took Alexander by the shoulders and the world went black. Alexander felt his stomach reel from the overwhelming stench of sulfur and the disorienting darkness. He felt tendrils clawing at him and he felt his Sovereign protection ignite, then he was pulled from the pit of this nightmare. He emerged into the light of day into an alley with a few shadows still around. Duncan released him and he dropped to a knee, coughing the stench from his lungs.

A door opened in the alley and Catriona stepped out of the back of the shop.

"I'll be by in an hour then. Thank you."

She closed the door and turned to see the two men standing in the shadowy corridor. Recognition displayed on her face as she looked at Alexander. The surprised light of seeing him was extinguished immediately upon laying eyes upon the Shadowalker. Her gaze grew bright in the late afternoon light, and Alexander hissed, "Leave. *Now*."

Duncan stepped into a shadow, exuding the stink of infernal magic into the alleyway. He had seen her eyes flash, but he knew from watching her before that she hadn't had time to do her deep reading of the man, what she called "flaying the soul." Regardless, even with only the brief time she had laid eyes upon him, he feared she may still have discovered Alexander's worst secret, that he had contracted Nicolai's murder.

Catriona looked at Alexander, puzzled and wary. "Alex?"

"Catriona," he began but he saw her look over the alley, her nostrils flaring from the sharp scent. It suddenly occurred to him that Duncan's eyes were black with shadows from the trip and reached up to his own eyes, as if he could feel the shadows dancing there. They felt normal, but the guilty gesture was not lost upon her.

"That man. I know him."

He dropped his hand. "I can explain." He moved towards her but she stepped back.

"That man attacked us a few days ago, in St. Andrew. He was hiding something just now. Did you send him?"

Alexander closed his eyes. His greatest nightmare had just come true.

Duncan stepped out from the shadows into the secret room out of habit. Even if unconscious, the amulet would take him here and he had not had time to think of a place to go before he was moving. This was as good as any, until he remembered he had left Alistair's body in this room. It had been less than two hours so he was not concerned. There would be no more smell now really than when he dropped the body into this place.

Well, he's still here, I see. The body lay where dropped, but he noticed what looked like dust or ash upon the man's skin. Duncan bent near it and studied it. He touched a bit and inspected his finger. The dust was sparkling, even in the faint glow of the symbol, and he looked around for what could have deposited it. He heard a shuffle and smelled what seemed like cedar and sandalwood and when he looked at Alistair's body again, he caught the last glimpse of it disintegrating into ancient dust which rode the small eddies of fresh air the room has always somehow supplied. Within seconds, all trace of him disappeared.

Thirty-Four

"If you wish to know the mind of a man, listen to
his words."
The Wise Wench's Tavern Book

"Catriona, wait, it's not…"

"No. Don't." She waved him off and turned, making her way down the alley, her original intention of crossing to the tavern kitchens across from the shop's back entrance forgotten. She moved quickly as Alexander moved after her, his footfalls on the cobblestones echoing off the building walls.

"Catriona, please."

She stepped into the street without looking where she was going and ran into Myrgen. "Whoa! Here you are. I thought I saw… you…"

Catriona looked at Myrgen, then at Alexander emerging from the alley. Myrgen looked as well. "Your Majesty?"

Catriona brushed by and headed towards the docks. She would get on the ship and get away. Maybe duck into a shop and escape out the back, or blend into the crowd here. Anything. She just couldn't deal with what she had just seen. Tears were welling up in her eyes, threatening to crest. She heard Alexander's voice calling to her, but she didn't dare look back. She didn't want to hear his point of view right now.

She slipped through a heavily populated area and got to the docks. Her ship was in the middle pier and she felt desperate to get to it. She ran up the gangplank and saw Octavius.

"Don't let Grymalkin on board. He's had contact with the Shadowalker that attacked us in St. Andrew. I think he sent it after Myrgen."

Octavius looked at her, then to the street. He called over Lioncourt and they stood at the top of the gangplank as she entered her quarters. She was trying to wrap her head around what she had just witnessed. The Shadowalker was not injured, yet she had seen Alistair remove his hand. He had left before she could read him, but she saw he had a few very important secrets. Had he just been there, Catriona might have believed Duncan had been after Alexander.

But then Alexander had *commanded* him to go, and she knew why: because of her gift. Alexander knew she would be able to read the Shadowalker and there was something between them he didn't want her to find out, something more than the guilt the creature was wearing on its skin in plain sight. Alexander's eyes were clear, but she was too unfamiliar with its disease to know if that was significant. Alexander may have fought off the shadows like Myrgen, but a single touch from Duncan had turned Myrgen's eyes into orbs of swirling filth. Had he wanted Alexander dead, the King would have a dagger through his heart right now. When Alexander commanded him, it took him out of the realm of victim and into the realm of accomplice.

She walked over to her chart table and leaned on it. *What? What had Alexander done that he didn't want her to know? He had been Sovereign barely two tendays. Was he ashamed of something before that time, or since?* She had run from him because she knew he could talk, could charm her into believing anything he said, and right then, she didn't feel comfortable with that. She didn't want to let him smooth this over and suddenly, she wasn't sure she could trust him anymore. Then she realized she had left Myrgen with him, vulnerable, and her heart seized. She moved to her desk chair and grabbed her sword, which Myrgen had convinced her to leave behind when they had gone out that day.

A knock at her door made her jump and she spun to see she had failed to actually close her door. Myrgen looked in from the doorway. "Are you alright?"

She smiled, relief filling her voice. "I just realized I had abandoned you."

He looked at her sword. "Expecting trouble?"

She looked down, then put the sword back on the chair back. "Maybe a little. Where is he?"

Myrgen came in and closed the door. "Some nice people are taking him to an inn. He'll wake up soon."

"Wake up?"

"Well, he was kind of insisting on following you so I punched him." He shrugged. "Hey, I'm already wanted for treason. What are they going to do? Hang me twice?"

She walked over to him. "Are you hurt?" She found she almost wanted him to be, so she could simultaneously fuel her righteous anger at Alexander and fulfill the inexplicable need to touch Myrgen.

"Oh no," he said, stepping back from her. "None of that. I don't know if that black stuff is still in me. You keep your healing off me." She smiled and nodded, then cast her eyes down at the floor. Myrgen put a hand on her shoulder and she raised her eyes. "You want to tell me what happened?"

"I was going out the back of the supply store. They have a door across from the kitchens of the Seafarer's Way tavern. I was going to drop in on a friend of mine and say hello. That's when I saw Alexander and that Duncan monster in the alley together."

"I didn't see anyone else in the alley. Are you sure it was him?"

"Yes. The reason he was gone when you looked was because Alexander commanded him to go. He knew I could read Duncan and got rid of him before that could happen."

"Are you sure that's what it was?"

"Pretty sure, though I could be wrong."

"Are your visions fallible?"

Catriona turned and walked over to her desk, picking up the bottle of wine in the wine holder. "Well, usually, no. The visions work in two ways, actually. I can take a cursory look, only what the person has recently done," she nodded to him, "like with the letter you read. If they actually want me to read something, if they open up to it like you have, I can get everything they want to convey very quickly." She poured the wine into one of the goblets in the wine holder set.

"However, if they don't want me to see what they've done, it's harder. In that case, a brief glance over the surface will produce only that they are guilty of something and I use the surroundings to put together what they are hiding. If I don't get results from that, I can look harder, scan them for their transgression. It's akin to pulling hair out by the roots. A few details are easy and just itch a little. More details are more difficult and hurt more."

She handed Myrgen the goblet she poured. "Wait," he said. "So this can hurt physically?"

"Oh yes. If I choose to do a deep reading, I've been told it is like being flayed alive, like their soul has been cut open and folded back, bared before me. I can see everything then, every horrible thing they've ever done, said, seen or felt."

"You've been *told* this? By whom?"

She glanced down at the floor. "Giovanni."

The memory hit her like a punch in the gut.

"You little bitch! How dare you attack me!" Marco Giovanni slapped her, the ichor from his popped eye flinging with the effort. She hit the ground hard, and the adrenaline rush suddenly abandoned her. She was still weak from giving birth a few hours before and the fight had drained the last of her strength.

He dropped down on top of her, pushing his knee between her legs as he pushed her onto her back. His forearm was across her throat and he growled at her. "You will pay for this, my pet. But it's nice to see you've regained your fight. I thought you'd lost that. I like that in a victim." He leaned down and some blood and fluid dripped onto her cheek. He smiled. "See, I like causing pain, because I don't have the ability to feel it. I never have. You, though, you will feel pain."

He pressed down upon her throat and she struggled to breathe. The world around her started to pop with spots of white light and she felt the blood in her face and head pushing against her skin, trying to get out en masse. She barely felt him spread her legs and undo his breeches, his semi-hard crotch brushing against her inner thighs. She felt like she was going to pass out and he let up on her pressure.

"Oh no. You don't get to go anywhere, darling. Nowhere but here." He thrust into her, kicking into her bloody vagina, still ripped from the birth. Her womb was still open, and there was swelling and bruising from the birth. She could barely feel him inside her, but she could feel the tears from the birth getting bigger. She tried to scream and he let her, but it was soft and raspy, barely a whisper from the crushed windpipe. He smiled and thrust into her, repeatedly, picking up speed and roughness.

She glanced over to the body of Father Benjamin. He had been holding her son when he had been beheaded by a sword blow. His sizable girth fell forward and she felt certain her hours-old son was crushed beneath the man. She strained, trying to hear the slightest muffled cry, anything to indicate that her son still lived, that he might be able to escape this, forgotten by Giovanni. She begged whatever force guided the earth to please, save her son.

And the Land had answered.

She had felt a surge of power enter her body from the ground beneath her and a flood of insight swell behind her eyes. She saw a rock, sizable but amazing in its placement, shielding her son from suffocation beneath the priest. He was in a small pocket of air, and she could see his small body wiggling there, like the priest was translucent. She looked at the guard standing nearby, who looked into Catriona's eyes, an apology sitting there, obvious to her and realized Giovanni had his wife and daughter hostage on the Giovanni estate. Only by working for the vile man was his family not being subjected to the tortures she had been put through. She also saw a small glimmer of hope in his eyes. With her injuring Giovanni, it would take him time to heal, even if he couldn't feel pain, and the guard had been waiting for just such an opportunity to flee with his family. Catriona had just saved them, but he felt helpless to save her.

She turned this insight onto her attacker and suddenly, her pain, fear, anger and hatred had forced themselves out. She looked at Giovanni and it was as if she had stepped into his mind and encountered large walls made of heavy paper. She punched her fingers through the walls and ripped them open, hoping to find something inside the wall that would help her son. His entire life fell before her like a tapestry.

He never felt pain, even as a child, but he studied it in animals, pets, servant children and governesses, even his mother. Those he killed, he kept in the cellars beneath his family's manor, going back and looking at their rotting bodies to study the decomposition process.

Then, he had learned about how to cause intense pain without killing the victim and he had blossomed as a nightmare. People who randomly wandered into his web were caught and tortured to death. He got very good at it. Then, he had kidnapped the daughter of a nobleman who was there to talk marriage, and his parents had rescued the girl before he could actually hurt her. The D'Medici girl never knew how close she had come to seeing her own death. She had, instead, taken it as he had presented it, as an opportunity for him to be alone with her because he had fallen instantly in love upon sight of her. He had deceived her into lying with him and he had taken her virtue before she had been rescued.

The father had demanded the marriage between them and had only left once the contract had been signed. His parents had sent him away to Nubia in the hopes the girl would be spared his sadism by his bloody death in the jungles and plains of the continent. He had not died, but had instead inflicted horrors upon the villages there whenever he encountered them, citing the Wrath of Heaven upon the heathens. He had found a village's holy woman there and stolen her from her family. Giovanni, with the flames of her village as the backdrop, had raped her in front of her father as he burnt to death.

Over and over, torture after torture, death after death, rape after rape, she saw many fall before him and finally, she broke. Catriona, in that instant, had screamed inside his head. Blood had burst from his nose and mouth and he leapt back, gripping his head and crying out with something he had never known before.

Pain.

His eyes grew wide, the one she had stabbed actually falling from the socket at that moment. He backed away, looking like one of his own experiments, until he hit the legs of the guard whose family he held. Giovanni gripped the man's sword belt and looked up at him. "She's a demon! She stepped into my soul and flayed it! Kill her! <u>Kill her!</u>*"*

Catriona saw the guard look at her and beg her with his eyes to play dead, and she had done so, passing out from the pain and exhaustion. That was when she had first lain eyes upon the church in her mind, the living replica of the one burning behind Giovanni, and Father Benjamin beckoning to her to seek shelter in the sanctuary of the doors. She had done so and when she had opened her eyes, Alexander had been kneeling over her, healing her wounds as the local midwife retrieved Catriona's son from under Father Benjamin's body with the help of Charles.

"Giovanni. The man who assaulted you."

She blinked and turned to the bottle of wine. "Yes. Giovanni did not exactly mean it as a dissertation on what happens when I do that, but it looked quite painful."

"Why didn't it hurt when you did it to me?"

She looked at him. "Because you let me. If you want me to see, it's painless."

"And that's how you choose your crew, isn't it? If they are innocent of wrongdoing, they want you to see that and they're willing to let you look, aren't they?"

"Sometimes they are interested in having me see, even if they are guilty as charged."

He caught her meaning easily and glanced down at his goblet, then set it on the desk. "Then you know I'm not exactly innocent of wrongdoing."

She looked away. "I haven't actually looked that deeply into you, Myrgen."

"Maybe you should." He caught her eyes again. "I may be as bad as Duncan, dangerous to have around your ship and crew. Despite what you think, Catriona, I'm not a good person. I'm an evil, money-lending bastard, who has ordered the deaths of more than a few men. You really should know what you're sailing with, what you're protecting." He continued as she stepped over and put her goblet down next to his. "After my assault on the King of Mervolingia today, your harboring of me could cause your ships to be banished from her shores." He turned her face to meet his.

"Look at me, Catriona. *See me.*"

He opened his soul to her and the visions came without her bidding them. He revealed to her the plots and schemes in which he had played a part. Some were minor roles, some major and yet, the one crime he was being charged with was one he had not orchestrated nor even truly wanted a part in, yet he had bounced as his strings were pulled, something which disgusted him now. His forbidden love affair with Elizabeth had been ill-conceived and he had walked blindly into that trap. He felt betrayed, but even through all that had happened he did not regret any of it because it had brought him to this moment.

This moment here where he realized he was falling in love with her.

She blinked slowly, severing the visions and she felt the warmth of his hand still on her chin. Their eyes held each other and he bent in and kissed her, gently but with confirmation. It wasn't like the kiss in the catacombs. This was an offer, an opportunity to explore a depth of feeling she had wanted as long as she could remember. It was an offer she wanted to take.

A knock at the door interrupted them and he rested his head upon her forehead. "Captain? Grymalkin is here. He says he needs to speak with you immediately."

Catriona looked into Myrgen's eyes and pulled away with great effort. She opened the door. "Octavius, I told you I didn't want him on board. He's been dealing with the Shadowalker."

"The ship says he isn't corrupted. In fact, she says he can't be touched by the darkness. He's protected. Surely he knew this going in?"

Catriona shook her head. "I don't care. He trucked with a killer who hurt someone under my protection. If he was doing it at Alexander's command…" She looked back at Myrgen. He looked away, picking up his goblet of wine.

Behind them, Alexander looked into the room, fighting against Lioncourt's strong restraint. "Catriona, please! I have to speak with you! It's important."

"I don't want to hear any of his lies. I have better things to do." She looked at Myrgen, who returned her gaze.

Myrgen smirked. "He may try to command you as king."

"He has no power over me. He's never been my king." She looked at him again, for what she hoped would be the last time. He spoke to Octavius and her First Mate looked to Catriona. He nodded and came over to her.

"Captain, you might want to hear what he has to say. He says you're under a spell." He looked at Myrgen. "Both of you."

She folded her arms. "You can't possibly trust him."

Octavius shook his head. "I don't. But I trust the ship. She says he's right."

Myrgen frowned, setting down his goblet. "We're under a spell?"

Octavius nodded.

Catriona's jaw set. "Hülyeseg." She stormed out to the gangplank where Lioncourt had Alexander on his knees with his arm behind him, face almost touching the deck. Myrgen followed. She put her boot under his chin and nudged his face with her toe. Alexander looked up.

"Speak."

Alexander swallowed. "Gwen cast a spell upon you, sending some Fae or something to remove the sorrow in your heart and open it to love. She intended to speed your healing in order for us to finally be together." Alexander wriggled under Lioncourt's grasp, but Catriona did not order his release. "I must say her heart was in the right place, but her spell was indiscriminant." He looked at Myrgen. "I'm sorry, Myrgen."

"What makes you so sure?" Myrgen seemed very suspicious and Catriona did not disagree.

"Because I know you, Catriona. You wouldn't let another man touch you for years after you were told Nicolai had died. Don't you find it inappropriate, with Nicolai's actual death so recent, to want Myrgen to court you? And you, Myrgen," he said, looking at his rival. "You were involved with Elizabeth enough to cause you to cover for her in a charge of treason. Didn't you think it odd that you two, who were enemies two tendays ago, would suddenly be exchanging meaningful glances and charming gestures?"

Myrgen shook his head and ran his hand through his hair, taking a few steps away from them.

Alexander followed him with his eyes. "It started with a seemingly innocuous incident, but all of a sudden, you couldn't think of anything but each other. You both stopped caring about your broken hearts and considerable losses and family in danger?"

Catriona looked at Alexander again. "So, you mean none of this has been real?"

"No. I'm afraid not. That's why I contacted that man. He's the one who rescued Tanglwyst. Gomez told me he traveled instantly through the shadows." He lowered his head to a less-strained position. "When I heard about how you responded to Myrgen's injury in St. Andrew, I knew I needed to get here, to warn you before you did something you would regret."

Catriona nodded to Lioncourt to release Alexander and took a few steps away from him. "What do you think I might regret?"

Alexander glanced at the other man. "Myrgen, would you excuse us momentarily?"

Myrgen rolled his eyes and leaned on the railing, looking over the water. Alexander stood, stretching his shoulder and moved towards her quarters. He paused by the door, waiting. Myrgen turned to her. "What are you going to do?"

She touched Myrgen's arm. "I don't know yet. I should talk to Gwen though, not just take his word for it." She looked at Alexander, who looked away from their exchange.

Myrgen put his hand on hers. "What do you think? Could what he said be true?"

"Well, Gwen *is* a meddlesome creature, to be sure. It's not out of the realm of possibility. And he described what's been happening with us as if he had been standing there the whole time. I'll see what he has to say." She stole into Myrgen's guarded eyes. "But yes, it's possible it's true."

Myrgen closed his eyes, shutting her out. She squeezed his arm and went to speak with Alexander. She was glad to leave Myrgen on deck with Octavius. Real or not, she still cared about his feelings. She entered her cabin.

"I'm sorry. I didn't mean to upset you. I just wanted you to know the truth."

She wasn't entirely certain she believed him, but she stayed open minded. "If it's the truth, you were right to tell us. Traveling through darkness with a killer was foolish."

He came over to her and touched her cheek. "I'd do it again in an instant if it meant I could be by your side."

She pushed his hand from her face. "It's not that simple anymore, Alex. You're King now. You can't be putting yourself at risk like this. There's no heir to the Mervol throne. If you die, the realm will be split with chaos. Thousands will die in the struggle for power. Look at what happened with Elizabeth."

"Elizabeth is dead. She'll be no trouble now."

"I know. I saw you stab her."

Alexander blinked. "You did? How?"

"I was helping Myrgen escape. We were in the corridor of the Royal Crypts."

He pursed his lips. "I see. Your compassion for the man is going to be your undoing, Kikotu."

"And your obsession with me will be yours. Alex, it's not safe for you to be unescorted. What if Duncan had hurt you or left you in the darkness?"

"My Power of Sovereignty protected me the entire time I was with him. And as for my obsession with you," he reached down and took her hand, drawing her to him. "The only way to keep me safe is for you to be my wife."

He kissed her with great ardor and she felt that dread of being trapped again. She didn't understand why her soul resisted his advances when she had loved him not four months before. She pushed him away. "Alexander, stop."

"Stop? What do you mean stop?"

"I can't do this."

"What do you mean?" He frowned as she stepped away from him. "Catriona, I love you. I'll accept no other woman in my bed."

"Then you'll sleep alone, Alexander. I don't love you." She walked away from him towards the door, intent on talking to Myrgen. She didn't know if Alexander was right or not about Gwen's meddling, but being with Alexander felt wrong, and being with Myrgen, well...

"I saw Alan's bedroom in Patras."

She stopped, her hand on the door.

Thirty-Five

"All things change and we change with them."
The Wise Wench's Tavern Book

Myrgen stood looking at Catriona's door, ready in case she needed him. Octavius leaned on the railing next to him so as not to block the view. "Private talk, eh?"

"Yeah…" Myrgen looked out over the city docks. "Apparently Gwen cast some sort of Fae spell upon Catriona and I got caught in the spillover."

"The whale?"

Myrgen looked at Octavius and raised his eyebrows. "Yeah, that probably was it, now that you mention it. So it's all been something neither of us had any control over."

"Well, I don't know about your experiences with love, but I've never known it to be polite enough to ask what I've wanted. That's the thing about love. You never had control over it in the first place."

Myrgen smiled. "That's very true, but it's not the same. This has been false, from the very beginning. I thought I was… that maybe she would…" He shook his head. "Of course, that was stupid on my part. I'm a wanted man, a traitor to king and country. She's a ship's captain, and easily the finest woman I've ever met."

"Better even than that Queen?"

Myrgen looked at Octavius, who arched an eyebrow. Myrgen nodded and looked back over the railing. "Yes, better by far than Elizabeth. For one thing, she isn't insane."

"There are those that would disagree, of course."

"And I wouldn't trust a one of them."

"Neither would I, my friend. Neither would I." Octavius looked over the city as well. "So, what are you going to do now?"

"Keep my distance until the spell wears off, I guess. That's the thing about this. I can't pursue her now. No matter what, I would always question whether it was the real thing or just the spell." Myrgen shook his head. "That's no way to be in love, having it forced upon you."

Catriona stopped and Alexander knew he had gotten through to her. She spoke without looking at him. "What were you doing in Alan's room?"

"Gomez wanted to see if there was any connection between Nicolai's death and Tanglwyst's disappearance. I couldn't help myself." He stepped over and put a hand on her shoulder. "You were so close. I had no idea how near you were to me."

"It means nothing, Alexander."

"Nothing?" He reached into his doublet and pulled out the mug from the cabin. "Then why was this on the windowsill?"

She turned and saw the mug and closed her eyes. A thin line of water divided her lashes and she opened them, the tears threatening her composure.

"Tell me again you don't love me."

"Alex…"

He shook the mug. "*This is real, Catriona.* That infatuation with Myrgen is a spell, a passing fancy that wasn't even your idea in the first place. It was Gwen's, and she didn't mean for it to bring you and him together." He put the mug in her hand. "It was meant for us, because of this night. You watched my bedroom window from your son's room. You came to me at the castle, through the catacombs, seeking *me* out in this whole mess. Catriona, you were meant for me. We were brought together by Heaven itself. Outside the church, remember?"

He touched her face and stroked her hair. "My beloved, it was only for you that I have ever healed through my will alone. It was for you alone that I have given up my crown, my kingdom, my life for the chance to be by your side. When I was in darkness, you were the beacon that guided me to safety. Kikotu, I do not wish to go back in the dark. Tell me you love me and save my life."

He looked into her eyes, almost pressing his will into hers, and she closed hers and nodded. "Yes..."

Myrgen felt a ripple rush across his skin and he shivered. His eyes grew wide and his stomach turned. He leaned on the railing. Octavius put a hand on his shoulder. "Myrgen?"

"Something's wrong..."

Octavius glanced toward the Captain's quarters and seemed to focus somewhere between himself and her door. "Damn."

Myrgen looked at Octavius. "He's done it, hasn't he? He's won her heart again."

Octavius nodded, then looked at his friend. "I'm sorry."

Myrgen shook his head and ran to the other side of the ship to vomit over the rail.

Catriona felt her stomach turn and sweat popped out on her brow. She opened her eyes, confused.

"Catriona?"

Before she could stop it, she vomited, coating Alexander before he could leap out of the way. He spread his hands, looking down at his clothes as she ran to the chamber pot in the corner. She could hear him fighting his own war with previous meals which only aided her in completing the process of losing the wine she and Myrgen had shared. She closed her eyes. *It could have been worse. I could have had to taste that hard tack again.*

A towel came into her vision and she glanced up. Alexander had grabbed a towel from her sea chest and handed it to her. She used it to wipe her mouth, then glanced at him. His traveling clothes, which had seen better days, were now stained with dark red wine.

"I'm so sorry, Alexander." She handed the towel back to him and he used it to wipe off the worst of it.

"Perhaps I pressed a bit too hard."

She had no idea what to say to that, so she decided to say nothing. The fact was he was right. He *had* pressed too hard, and something within her had fought against it the only way it could.

"I have clothes in my saddlebags. I think I need to go change into them." He dropped the towel on the floor near the chamber pot. "In case you still feel sick while I'm gone."

She nodded. "Thank you."

He knelt next to her and touched her shoulder. She felt the convulsions threaten again, but this time she was ready for them and used her healing ability to fight the urge. "I'll be back after I've changed. Will you be alright for a little while?"

She nodded and he stood. He looked back once more before leaving. She looked over at the area near her desk where they had been standing and saw that the mug he had handed her had fallen to the floor and broken on impact. She closed her eyes against the image and cried.

Thirty-Six

"Better to have two good brownies than to
accept a gift from a troll."
The Wise Wench's Tavern Book

Alexander stepped into the corridor and closed her door behind him. Her response was probably stress-induced and his healer nature advised him to leave her be for a while, to give her time to adjust to the things she was experiencing. It was probably her will fighting the spell, purging it from her system. From the looks of things, the spell had caused more trouble than he had originally thought. Luckily, he had gotten her to admit she loved him and that seemed to have broken the spell.

He got on deck and noticed Octavius and Myrgen talking at the railing on the other side of the ship. He was going to tell Octavius that Catriona needed some attention when he realized what was going on. Myrgen was retching as well. *Good. It looks like they will both be free of the spell's effects soon. Catriona won't allow Myrgen to get close to her anymore, not now, and*

Myrgen will feel the loss of a love. Serves him right for moving in on my woman.

He walked past Octavius and Myrgen unnoticed, which pleased him. It made it less likely that Myrgen would talk to Catriona without Alexander around. He slipped to the inn where he had awoken and went inside. The innkeeper came over to him immediately. "Your room is ready, Your Majesty."

Great. Another innkeeper who knows who I am. Myrgen has done a fantastic job of making it harder for me to get around undetected. "Thank you, master innkeeper."

"Would you like some food sent up, sire?"

Alexander swallowed the bile that rose in his throat at the thought of food. "Not at present. I do need a bath, though. And laundry service."

The innkeeper noticed his clothing. "Of course, Sire. At once."

"That won't be necessary, Martin."

The deep voice came from behind them, from a nearby table. Alexander turned to see who had spoken. A short man with long light brown hair and a full beard with streaks of grey dripping from his mouth bowed before the King. "I am Vicar Morgan Wolf, Sire. I would like to invite you to stay at my home. My lady has already got a room prepared and a bath ready. No waiting."

Alexander wanted to refuse the man, but word had spread that he was here now and it was expected that he stay in more secure surroundings than the local inn. He would have an armed escort by the time he walked out of this building. He took a deep breath, caught a whiff of vomit, and sighed. "Thank you, Vicar. I have had a run-in with a street person who was ill, however, and I don't want to meet your good lady smelling of sick."

"I understand completely, Sire. I'll wait down here for you and let you have your privacy, unless you need a dresser?"

"No, thank you. I can manage this attire myself." He followed the innkeeper to his room where two men were rolling a large wooden half-barrel, obviously for his bath. He shook his head as he got undressed. He had wanted to return to the ship as soon as he was changed, but his discretion had been compromised in his situation. Now he had been identified as the King and etiquette dictated he now had to spend time with the local official.

I should go get Catriona as soon as I'm changed. Since I'm going to make her my Queen, why not start here, introducing her to the mayor? Show her what her life will be like once she's Queen. She deserves to be treated like she matters.

He looked over the things in his room and realized this was not his room at the Black Cat and Anchor, where his saddlebags were currently. He had nothing here. He looked in the mirror to see if maybe the clothes he had were salvageable. The wine was definitely going to stain and the smell was gagging him now that he was back in an enclosed area. He doubted he could take off the clothing without vomiting.

It turned out that was true. When he pulled the shirt and doublet off at once, some of the vomit scraped off inside his nose and he lost it. He threw up while the shirt and doublet were still covering his face and all that fine food Ce'Nedra had fed him became his new attire. The proximity of both vomits caused even more to come up and by the time he had actually gotten the clothes off, he looked as though he had been painted in the stuff. Chunks of partially digested food caked his hair and beard and stuck to everything. He hung his head, on all fours, and tried not to faint.

The room spun, threatening to dislodge even more stomach fluid, and he closed his eyes against the urge. It took a moment, but he managed to finally get the room to stop spinning and he crawled away from the bile-soaked clothes and sat on one of the chairs to catch his breath. His mind crumpled beneath the weight of exhaustion and he tumbled into sleep.

He was back in St. Andrew, at the Black Cat and Anchor, standing before a door. He knew this door, knew this room. He looked around and saw the populace below, milling and flirting, completely unaware of him. He was dressed in his finest, or rather, in someone's finest because he did not recognize the clothes. Rich royal blue embroidered with fleurs of singular beauty and amazing detail when taken alone. In the abundant present, they were as gifts from Heaven. The doublet fit him with expert tailoring, breeches of blue embroidered strips with gold silk flowing between them. His stockings were gold, and the blue knee high boots were likewise tooled with gold fleurs-de-lys. Golden garters stood out above the knee and a gold silk shirt, also heavily embroidered with the same fleur pattern peeked with whimsy from the front of his doublet. Blue leather that matched the boots gloved his hands, also accented by gold silk and fleurs with slashes at the knuckles to show off the Royal Seal upon his right hand.

He was dressed for his Coronation.

He thought, this is wrong. If I'm ready for my Coronation, why am I here? I should be before Catriona's door. He looked around again and saw a room across the hall a few steps away. The door was closed, but he could see light from a seaward facing window under the door. He went to it and found it locked. He knocked and after a moment, a yawning man opened the door. It was Duncan McVryce.

"Sire?"

"I need to come in. I need to use your window." Alexander pushed past Duncan to the window and saw what he needed to see. The Enigma was in port.

Alexander turned to leave, but Duncan caught his arm. "Sire, don't do this. She is not the one for you."

"That's my decision. No one will arrange a marriage for me but me."

"She is not the one for you. She is an enemy, poison to our people. Look."

Duncan pointed to the window. Alexander went over to it again and looked out. Lining the streets were people sick or injured, some badly maimed. Several children were there as well, hollow eyes and sunken cheeks marking great trauma and sadness. He felt their pain, felt every tear, every sorrow. It overwhelmed him, hitting him like waves of heat in the desert.

"What's wrong with them?"

Duncan sighed. "They are hurt. But you are a healer. You can save them, but you must do so personally. Without you, they will continue to suffer. Go to the other room. Start with the one there who needs to be healed."

Alexander turned from the window and went down the hall to the door he stood before when he came here. He opened it, and found Gwen sitting on a chair beside the bed. Upon the bed lay a golden silk pall covering a distinctly feminine shape. The pall was embroidered all over with the same fleur design as on his shirt, but the pall was almost sheer. The woman beneath it breathed a heavy slumber, her auburn hair cascading across the pillow beneath her head. She was likewise dressed in blue silk embroidered with gold fleurs and her gown flowed like water across the bed upon which she lay.

He stepped to the bedside and pulled the pall from her face. It made a shushing sound as it slipped from her face and body and he felt almost as if the silk were telling him to be quiet for the lady was sleeping. The scent of vanilla rose from her skin, reminding him of cookies and cakes Lawrence had made them as children. He knelt beside her, enraptured by her beauty. He touched her hand and felt it warm beneath his touch. Her lips beckoned him, as they had done before.

"I am not worthy of such a lady."

Duncan stepped up beside him. "There is none more worthy of her than you, Sire. Heaven has set her aside for you."

Alexander looked at Duncan. "But you love her. How can you give her away?"

"It is because I love her that I will step aside for you."

Alexander looked at Tanglwyst again, then stood. "No. I'll not take your woman. I have one of my own."

Gwen looked up from her chair. "Grymalkin?"

"You know my heart, Gwen. I must remain true to it."

Gwen stood, then clasped her chest. Blood formed upon her apron dress, staining the front and her hand. "Alex?"

Alexander's eyes grew wide with terror and he backed away from Gwen. He turned, but Duncan was there, a knife protruding from his chest. "Sire, please..." He fell to his knees before his King, sprawling upon the floor. Alexander moved aside, then ran out the door and down the stairs. All the people in the tavern knelt and he saw every one of them wounded, sick and maimed. Parents held children in the arms, offering them up to him, men knelt beside their wives as wasting sickness and disease wracked their bodies and everywhere was the smell of urine and vomit. They grabbed at his fine clothing as he passed, begging him to help them, tearing the clothes into rags.

He got outside and looked up. He could see the mast of the Enigma *and he ran towards the docks as it shifted in the waves.*

400

Then he realized it was not shifting, it was moving, setting sail. He ran faster, but the people in the streets continued to grab him and slow his progress. Finally, he shouted an Order Which Must Be Obeyed to let him pass, and they fell back, dead. He ran unhindered to the docks, Catriona's ship still barely within reach.

He called her name, called for her to stop the ship, to drop anchor and let him come aboard. Myrgen stepped into view on deck and lifted a great bow to his shoulder. He nocked an arrow of considerable weight and drew back the bowstring. Alexander turned to run, dodging the missile about to fly at him and felt the stone arrow pierce his chest from behind. Alexander screamed as he looked down and saw a bloody hole in his body which had sprouted a granite barb as he fell forwards onto the dock.

Thirty-Seven

"A single rat will clear the whole pantry."
The Wise Wench's Tavern Book

The sound of a scream woke Alistair and he sat up, his breathing heavy. Flickering candles and soft perfumes met his senses, silken sheets beneath his fingers. The pale orange glow revealed a series of translucent curtains moving in a slight breeze from somewhere. He reached up and grabbed his neck where the dart had hit, but felt no weapon and his body showed no signs of poison. He looked around, trying to figure out where he was. Movement on the other side of the curtains caught his attention.

"Who's there?"

Although she was clearly on the other side of the fabric, a woman's voice answered from the other side of the world, impossibly distant. "Ah. You're awake."

She moved up to the curtains and he saw she was covered by a thin swathe of opaque gold silk, her figure occasionally revealed in the breeze, but all other features hidden. The sunset colors of the curtain sheers blended with the gold of her caul. Her voice sounded almost familiar, but he could not place it.

"Yes," he replied. "I seem to be healed. Did you do that?"

"Once you died, that body was no longer of use. It was destroyed in the passage to your destiny."

Alistair's brow furrowed. "Wait, died? So I'm dead? But I have obligations I haven't fulfilled. I can't be dead." He looked at his hands and body, trying to assess. *Gloriana...*

She started to walk around the circular bed upon which he lay, fingers running along the curtains. "You're incredibly unique, Alistair. Did you know that? At the moment of your death, you had spent as much time on land as you have at sea, to the moment. You have been part of the Fae Nation as well as heir to a country's throne. You have been exactly as selfish as you have been generous, exactly as fearless as you have been timid, exactly as lustful as you have been chaste. You have saved and harmed the exact same amount of people, and to the same degree. You have learned the languages of the Air Walkers of Yokotama, the Jungle Dwellers of Nubia and the Scented Gardens of Yndia. Your accomplishments have met in number and magnitude the failures. You have loved deeply, loved protectively, loved dishonorably and loved dismissively, spanning all ranges of emotion, and have despised to the exact same degree. You have been just as wise as you have been foolish and all in a little more than three hundred years. In all my years walking this world's soil, I have never encountered such a being in balance. And I can assure you, that has been my focus. To find you was as much as to be called to you. It seems Fate has a plan for you."

Alistair narrowed his eyes. "You are so familiar to me. We have met before, you and I."

"Yes we have, in a moment intensely memorable that was instantly forgotten."

He snorted. "I apologize. I feel I have done something wrong, but I am having a hard time feeling guilty."

She laughed. "That is as much as I would expect from you."

He looked around. "So, where am I?"

"You are in Karma's Hand. Such a creature as yourself could hardly go elsewhere."

"Karma's Hand?"

"Yes. You see, something important is happening and it is Karma's role in this to maintain the balance. You have come to us in a very interesting time."

The Woman in Gold stepped away from the curtains, fading from view. Alistair threw the covers off his legs and stood, trying to find her. He was wearing blue breeches with gold embroidery upon the cuffs and no shirt. He saw no sign of his other clothes.

"Us? Who else is here?"

He pushed open the curtains and was met by a huge blue woman with many arms and many heads, bare breasted and wearing a necklace of men's heads. Beneath her feet was a pale man being stepped upon wearing a crescent upon his head. In her many hands were different objects, a sword, a head, a goblet, a bowl. She was gleeful in her dance upon the man, her forked tongue lashing and her eyes glittering.

"Kali Ma," said Alistair, identifying the portrait. "The Destroyer."

"And the Mother. Her dance with Shiva is the ultimate in male-female relationships."

He looked around the room and saw candles on low tables and hundreds of colorful cushions decorating every surface. The tables had gold inlay in them, reflecting the firelight that managed to heat the room without overheating it. Goblets and decanters set on the tables, and bowls of fruit set alongside plates hosting meats, cheeses and small flat breads. Bowls of soups, dips and creams were interspersed in an almost organized chaos with the food and drink. He realized he was hungry, almost forgetting why he had gotten out of bed in the first place.

The opposite wall had a mosaic of Shiva, the white man from the other portrait. Here he was smiling, benevolent, kind, supportive. The two gods in Yndian mythology were best friends as well as the keepers of balance. Some of the tomes he had perused in Yantap, Yndia's capital city, had even used these characters to illustrate lovemaking positions. Tomes of this appearance set in a stack on a nearby table. He looked, but could not see his hostess.

"Where did you go?"

Her voice, again distant, melted into his ears like warm butter. "I'm still here. Rest, eat, drink. Relax. The tomes will guide you in the past and present. What happens in the future will be your responsibility."

He picked up one of the tomes and opened it. It was an account of the places where Karma had stepped into people's lives, changing their course. One fellow had two mages walk into his workplace, a gambling room hidden in a bath house in upper Mervolingia, and they slaughtered several creatures of infernal nature. Another spoke of the intervention of a man in the life of a woman that enabled her to become a saint and through this act, save the world. He closed the book, looking around. "This has accounts of the Soulless War. I just saw Raven referenced in it."

"Yes. Karma felt it necessary to intervene. It was unprecedented for all aspects of the mystical world to convene and cause such a virulent anomaly. The only way for the world to survive was by setting an equal number of the same factors together to stop that anomaly. It is because of your familiarity with the Soulless War that makes you so perfect for your current role."

Alistair shuddered. When he was younger, he had been with a group of people who fought in a battle so destructive, it had changed the world. Magic and the Fae nation and even Heaven, the Land and Hell itself had all touched a group of children and the effects of this convergence of powers had caused a disease of such virulence, the only way to end it had been through the direct intervention of a Saint. One of them hid and survived, and with the help of a mage, had swept through all of his home kingdom of York, destroying nearly everyone and everything, including his brother, Antoine, the original heir to the throne. Alistair and his allies defeated the threat only by banishing the Last Child and everything it had touched into a void, a pocket aside from reality where nothing could enter, and nothing could leave. Alistair had lost a brother, the Land had lost a protector, and one of the mages had had the infant within her womb turned by the Last Child. The damage was significant to all.

"Are the Soulless returning?"

"That is undetermined. When the Fae Lords and the arcane casters trapped the Soulless in the Void, it seemed the plague was contained. However, because of the nature of the spell that trapped them, we cannot trace their movements. They are hidden from us all. Certain things have happened for which we cannot account. It is my duty to investigate these occurrences, to see where to attribute credit or blame. Also, the Fae Lord Calpurnia stirs from her slumber. Whispers say her sleep is what has held the monsters at bay, but we do not know if this is true. And ancient artifacts from that war have been used of late. We are not certain what happens to the user, but they disappear from creation, then reappear somewhere else. It is the disappearance that worries us."

"What artifacts are these?"

One of the tomes shifted on the stack and fell off. It opened to a drawing of an amulet. The Woman in Gold fluttered behind him. "There used to be twelve of these, back when they were created. A circle of mages sworn to Heaven made these artifacts to enable their Inquisition to go instantly to places where the Soulless appeared. You see, Alistair, despite your coterie's best efforts, a few creatures escaped the trap before it closed."

"That's not possible. That plague infected any living creature, sentient or not. It destroyed their souls, leaving them hungering monsters neither dead nor alive. A single touch destroyed my brother in seconds, before my eyes. If any creature had escaped, the world would be consumed."

"There were many ways to destroy the monsters, and each encounter had a unique solution. The Church decided to create amulets that moved the holder anywhere a Church to Heaven resided. They merely needed the name of the church's patron saint and its location. But the mages who made it were deceived. They used an essence they believed they controlled, but that essence came from an Infernal. To have an infernal essence serving the church turned the holders of the amulets slowly into creatures that served Hell. Their souls were forfeit and have not been seen since.

"As time has gone on, Karma has placed them in the path of Champions, and they have been destroyed. But in so doing, many of the Champions have fallen as well. However, their nature, as teleporters, takes them momentarily from our sight. We do not know where they go, but there are only three left in the world below at this time. The only way to track them is by the destruction left in their wake."

Alistair took a deep breath of the warring but complimenting scents. "So, what can I do from here?"

"Guide. You need to guide people towards these amulets and you must hurry. There is a war coming and we must not have these creatures available to be called upon."

"A war?"

"Yes, Alistair. There is a War coming between Heaven and Earth, and they have been seeking their Champions for generations. The Battle for the Well of Souls is very important. The Hour of Observation is approaching and both sides are running out of time."

Alistair looked at the book again, then set it aside. "The Champions, have they been chosen?"

"Often for some, but once for the other."

"You actually can't give a straight answer, can you?"

He heard her giggle and the sound was exhilarating and slightly annoying.

"The Champion of Heaven has been chosen several times. Each Saint has chosen someone and when the current one dies or becomes corrupted, they are considered a failure and the next saint steps up to bring in their choice. In one case, the saint has yet to be able to offer their choice, but their choice has been made for centuries. In such cases, it has been their task to keep their choice preserved. As for the Land, its choice has always been the same."

Alistair sighed. "You mean the Dûcesa?"

"Yes. Though she dies, it is her destiny to always be reborn. The Land always knows her, and always returns her. The problem is that she is currently incomplete."

"Incomplete?"

"Her Protector is trapped."

Alistair's heart broke a little. "Slade."

"Yes. As such, she is incapable of remembering her true role in this battle, for she has always known her destiny. But to realize her place, she must regain her memories of her past. The Keeper of her Memories has always been Slade, just as she has always been the Dûcesa. Once the Last Child stole him from the world, she has not had a companion capable of staying by her side. You know this. You have a friend who was once her Stapan."

Alistair nodded, thinking of Raven. He had spent two years serving as her Stapan after he inadvertently caused her death right after her renewal on the heels of the Soulless War. But Raven wasn't known for sticking around and turned the Stone Sword, the symbol of the Stapan, back to her keeping to be with his family. As far as Alistair had ever heard, the First Dûcesa had not been seen in this world since.

"The Role of the Land's Servant is quite significant. Not only does she gather the dead and return them to the Land, she stands as Champion, protecting its people. She has been missing for centuries."

"Why didn't the Land just make a new one?"

"Once the Land made her, it never thought to make another."

"That is strangely balanced."

The Woman in Gold whispered in his ear. "That is our place in this."

"And the Well of Souls you mentioned. What is that?"

The woman rustled beside him. He turned to look at her and she gestured to the pillows and food. He picked up a piece of cheese, his attention upon her.

"The Well of Souls is where all souls are kept until they are put into a human body. At present, Heaven is the caretaker of the Well, but the incident with the Soulless Ones caused a question of whether or not this is the best course. Currently, balance is in place with Heaven maintaining souls and the Land maintaining the bodies. The land grows food, provides water and takes in the bodies of those walking upon her. Heaven holds the souls before they are inserted into a body, and collects them after the body ceases.

"But some concerns have arisen regarding Heaven's management of the souls. Its current practice is to have the souls in the Well. When a human is named on Earth, the soul is inserted. When the body dies, the soul is gathered. It is then judged and if it does not meet the criteria for Heaven, it is cast out and becomes the purview of Lucifer, the harvester of punishment. If the soul can be purged of its impurity in the fires of Hell, it is returned, fresh and untainted, to the Well of Souls. But Lucifer has never returned a soul, claiming no soul has ever been clean enough for Heaven.

"The Land has a different way of dealing with those that worship it. When a believer dies, the Land takes the body into the ground, allowing the soil to filter the sin from the soul. The soul retires to Summerland, a place where it lives out the rest of its allotted days. If it was the person's time to die, their soul goes to Well as it was when they died. If they were taken before their time, they live in Summerland, resting until they die a second time, filtering their soul of its sins. It then takes the remaining parts of the filtered soul and returns it to Heaven to be added to the Well.

"This method is less wasteful, but it does not return whole souls and the end result is that it takes several pieces to meld together to form a complete soul. Since these souls are fragments sewn together, the personalities are often not compatible and chaotic people are the result. These are often artists or bards, but they can sometimes be violent or insane. The Land maintains that if the Well were under its purview, the souls would have more time to melt together, making them cohesive, but because Heaven limits the souls in the Well, not allowing them to mingle, the fragments don't have time to bond."

Alistair picked up a piece of meat. "Which method is better?"

"It is unknown. The coherency of the souls under the purview of the Land might be more consistent, but likewise, it would be less individual. It is unknown if the life experiences alone would be enough to make each person different. Some other factor might need to assert itself in order to grant that individuality, such as star positions or the tides, but the Land believes the souls would be more receptive to those factors if they were a cohesive soup awaiting the human to develop that potential. It would give them no definition, allowing them to define themselves. However, since this is not the method currently in use, it is untested."

Alistair swallowed his mouthful. He could see the importance of being impartial in this, but it sounded like a nasty fight was coming and he didn't like the idea of his family, his friends, being in the world when it did. "What do I do then? Decide? I don't want a war to shatter the lives of everyone I know."

"You know people from each culture that would prosper from this, and you are more aware of that impact than anyone in the world at present. You have lived in every culture and been accepted among them. There is no way to have a war that would not affect someone you know."

"Why does it have to be a war?" Alistair dropped the date back onto the plate of tidbits where he got it. "Why can't the Champions meet and fight it out? Why do whole populations need to be destroyed?"

"Do you think you could get the Champions to battle without involving everything at their disposal for something so very important?"

Alistair exhaled, scowling in defeat. "This world has suffered enough. To be put through this again is unreasonable." He looked at the Woman. "Why now? The Soulless conflict happened centuries ago."

"When the argument first happened, during The Purge, it was set for a certain point in time. A light passes across the sky and can be seen from every place in creation. It is a portent of great things. According to the Angels, it is the time when God looks in upon his grand experiment. The conflict must be resolved on that day."

"When is it?"

"On the equinox of winter, in two years."

Alistair stood. "*Two years?*" He looked around. "What do I do?"

"Watch. Intervene when you must, but watch. In the end, you must be impartial."

"And if I can't be?"

The Woman bowed. "That is why *I* am here."

"And exactly how do I do this? Are you going to send me back?"

She bowed her head. "You have no body any longer. You can never again set foot upon the world, at least, not until this is resolved."

"What happens then?"

"You'll declare a winner." She gestured to the bed. "You may watch overall upon the curtains when they are drawn, or you can choose a single individual. You can also access dreams from here."

"So, not a play place nor a sleeping area."

"You are beyond the need for sleep, just as you are beyond the need for food or drink." She waved her hand and all the room's trappings disappeared. He was alone, nude, in a white void with a disc floating nearby. He walked over to the disc and saw swirling fog. An image began to form in the disc's surface and her voice whispered behind him. He turned and the room was decadent again. "But that would be boring."

He reached out to touch her and she was gone, a lingering scent of sandalwood and cedar fluttering on the breeze.

Thirty-Eight

"You can never have too much chocolate or garlic, but never at the same time."
The Wise Wench's Tavern Book

Myrgen walked over to his room on his own, despite Octavius' concerns. He got to his door just as Catriona opened hers. Her skin was pale and shiny and she looked a bit worn out. They had only been alone a few minutes. Had Alexander hurt her in that time? Or had they already made love? "Catriona, are you all right?"

"Myrgen? What happened to you?" She came over to him and he was surprised to find he felt better almost immediately. He saw the color return to her cheeks as well and she straightened up, noticing the change.

"I was... on deck." He nudged his chin towards her door. "What happened in there?"

"I... By the Land, Myrgen, I don't know." She leaned back against the wall. "I told him I wasn't in love with him, but then, suddenly, I was crying in his arms and he was telling me I did. And then I threw up."

Myrgen blinked a couple times. "You… threw up?"

"Yes. All over Alex."

Myrgen started laughing and even though Catriona tried to stop him, it didn't work. His laughter caused her to laugh and within a minute, they were sitting on the floor in tears when Octavius came over to find out what was going on.

Finally, they got their wits about them and Catriona got to her feet and offered a hand up to Myrgen. He accepted and stood up next to her. They looked at each other, and Myrgen realized he was thinking about the moment right before Alexander had interrupted them. *What would have happened if he had not?* Myrgen blinked and released her hand, clearing his throat. *Down that path lies madness.*

Catriona watched his eyes a moment, then cast her eyes at the floor. Octavius looked at Myrgen and nodded to the pair before leaving. Catriona nodded her head towards her cabin. "You want to talk?"

He shrugged. "I'm not sure what there is to say. The truth is he's right. I was in love with Elizabeth for two years. I finally got my greatest wish, only to be betrayed by her and then watch her cut down in front of me. Yet, an hour ago, I couldn't stop myself from…"

She nodded. "I know what you mean. It didn't sound odd until he brought it up to us. Suddenly, I realized he was right. That *was* out of character for me, and that I have been noticing. I just didn't care."

"You think the spell made you not care?"

"Do you think the spell made you kiss me?"

Myrgen glanced at his feet. "I guess that's the point, isn't it?" He looked back up at her. "I can't say for sure that I would have done something like that on my own."

She swallowed, like she was weighing something, not certain if she should say what was on her mind. "So, under the castle, in the catacombs…"

He reached out and touched her face. "No, that was… something else. That was real."

"Then how do we know the rest isn't real as well?"

Myrgen brushed her cheek with his thumb. He didn't want this to be imagined. He wanted it to be real, and that desire for it to be real was what worried him. "I want this to be real. I truly do. But I'm not going to take you away from a life you deserve over something that could be a fleeting emotion."

"A life I deserve?"

A noise behind them caught his attention as some of the crew came on board with supplies. He didn't want to abandon this discussion though. He opened his door. "Here, let's take this out of the public eye." He glanced over his shoulder, "Unless that's something you need to oversee."

Catriona looked over at the crates being brought on board and shook her head. "Octavius is there. If they need me, he'll let me know." She stepped into the room and Myrgen followed her. The moment the door closed, he wanted to grab her and kiss her, letting the passion he felt for her be known. He didn't know what would happen next, but he thought of what Alistair had said about the third kiss. If he was right, she could be his, spell or no spell.

She turned to him and he worried his desires would be blatantly evident, but she politely kept her gaze from his. "So, this life you think I deserve...?"

"Yes. Well, Alexander clearly loves you and he's going against Mervol tradition in pursuing you instead of going with a political marriage. According to what you told me before, he's been there for you for years and his affection for you has been unshakable. He's forsaken his duties as Prince to be by your side and puts his life and soul in jeopardy to woo you now.

"Catriona, there's a lot of effort being put forth on your behalf. I just want to make sure this spell isn't interfering with something that's right. The only person who can answer that is you. Now, you've told me before how you feel about Alexander's advances and how you don't want to leave your ship, your crew and your home to be his Queen. I understand that. What I don't understand is how he can continue to think you love him as well."

Catriona exhaled and folded her hands in front of her. "Here, come with me." She opened his door and went to her own room, Myrgen following. Inside, she closed the door and walked him over to a small sack resting on her desk. "Alexander went to my home in Patras a few days ago. He said Gomez wanted to see if Nicolai's death and your sister's disappearance were connected. So he went to the house, to my son's bedroom, where he found this." She picked up the sack which chinked when it moved. Myrgen opened the sack and saw shards of a broken ceramic mug.

"What is it?' He picked up the handle, surprised to see it so simple and unimportant-looking for something that seemed to be life-changing.

"It's the mug Alexander used at the Cabin on the Cliffs, the night we…" She looked away. "He found it on the window sill of Alan's room, where I used to sit nights and stare at his bedroom window in the palace. Nicolai chose this house because he could see Tanglwyst's manor roof from our bedroom, and I chose it because I could see Alexander from Alan's. I used to sit at the window and drink tea from that mug. It made me feel closer to him, to share something he had held. I pretended I could still feel the warmth of his hand."

Myrgen noticed how her voice had softened talking about the connection between her and the King. "Did you ever go see him over the winter?"

"Once. Nicolai and I had been talking and getting to know each other again. I had put Alan to bed and went back downstairs to have some tea. Nicolai poured us some wine that he had received as a congratulatory gesture when he got the promotion to head of a unit. It was good wine and I must admit I allowed myself to get a little drunk. Nicolai made advances and I let him. He pushed me down on the table in our kitchen and we began to… well…"

She shrugged. "That was when he asked me to use that technique Tanglwyst used with him. I was so disgusted, I couldn't see straight. I got dressed, gathered up Alan and went to Gwen's.

"After I put Alan to bed there, I sat up with Gwen for a while, and then I went for a walk." She wrapped her arms around herself, remembering. "It was very cold and I walked through the woods behind Gwen's house. I was standing behind the palace, near the kitchen, before I knew where I was. And then I heard his voice." She looked at the mug handle in Myrgen's hand. "He was visiting the baker in the kitchen and he stood in the open doorway to get some air. It took all my will to keep from running to him in that moment. I was so lonely, so hurt. I needed him, Myrgen, more than I needed my next breath, but somehow, I didn't go to him, or call out to him, because I was married."

She looked at Myrgen. "Eventually, he went back inside and I returned to Gwen's, but I have always wondered what would have happened had I gone to him."

Myrgen watched her a few moments, then put the handle back into the small bag. "Well, thank you for answering my question."

"So, you understand now?"

"Yes. Completely." He handed her the bag. "I understand that Alexander is right. You *are* in love with him, and it would be wrong for me to interfere with that."

"But with him, it doesn't feel *right*. When I'm alone, when I can think clearly, I know he isn't right for me. But when I'm near him, I lose all sense of perspective. I don't like being that out of control. After Giovanni…" She shook her head and turned away.

Myrgen put a hand on her shoulder. "Hey, that's what love is. I know. I did things very similar to what you're describing, with Elizabeth. Watching her, arranging to be near her, painting life-sized portraits of her so I could imagine being with her. Granted," he raised his eyebrows and bobbed his head for emphasis, "that didn't exactly end well so it might not be the best example, but it's the only one I have."

Catriona laughed and he smiled. "Alexander cares about you. He loves you. I think you need to give him a chance to be with you."

She looked at him and he felt her scan. "You really do feel that way, Myrgen. How can you feel that way when, an hour ago… Hell, minutes ago, you wanted me for yourself?"

He dropped his hand from her shoulder and pursed his lips. "I'm not going to try and deny what I'm feeling for you. I agree, this feels right. When I touch you, it's like the earth hums beneath my feet. I don't mind you looking into me for truth. In fact, I *want* you to, to make sure I'm staying honest with you. But part of being honest with you is being honest with myself. And frankly, I haven't been tested like you and Alexander have been. I don't know if what I feel for you right now would hold up. Knowing it comes from a spell throws the entire thing into shadow, and we know what a nightmare that is.

"And I think your fears are just that: fears. You are a fearless woman, Catriona, and it is foolish for you to let those fears take away from Mervolingia the finest queen her people could ever know." He took her hand. "You are destined to be more than what you are right now. Don't be afraid of your destiny." He kissed her hand and bowed.

A knock at the door called their attention and Myrgen walked over to open it. Alexander stood in the hallway. He was wearing a fresh doublet, jerkin and breeches, of good quality and dark blue in color. His hair was clean and he smelled scrubbed and perfumed. "Myrgen. It seems I'm always interrupting something here."

Myrgen smiled a genuine smile, which seemed to take Alexander a bit off guard. "True, Your Majesty, but no longer. Take good care of this fine lady, Sire. She deserves all you can give her."

Myrgen clapped Alexander on the shoulder and left the room.

Thirty-Nine

"Honey in his mouth, but knives in his heart."
The Wise Wench's Tavern Book

"What was that?" Alexander looked at the closed door, then back at Catriona.

"That was Myrgen, imparting wisdom. He told me you were right, and that I am in love with you." She walked over and handed him the bag of shards. "I'm sorry I broke this. It was so precious to me for so long."

He took her hand. "What need have you for a memory when you have in your hands the very thing you were remembering?"

"That's a very good point." She stepped in and reached her gloved hand up to his face. His eyes searched hers like they had the first night she had kissed him, when that mug had been intact and filled with mulled wine. She smiled and leaned in to kiss him. He responded rather similar to the way he had originally, with a bit of surprise when she first touched him, but then with passion he had been holding back.

When they finally broke apart, he looked at her, a questioning smile dancing on his lips. "Does this mean I might be able to convince you to accompany me somewhere this evening? Perhaps give you a taste of things to come?"

"What did you have in mind?"

"The Mayor here has asked me to join him for dinner. I would love it if you would accompany me."

She glanced at his clothes and smiled. "I'm afraid I don't have the proper attire for such an endeavor."

"Well, it turns out, I have thought of that as well. I had something sent to a salon here in St. Marguerite. They have promised to take good care of you. Please?"

She touched his face, her leather gloves smooth on his skin. "Of course I will, Especially since it seems you have already availed yourself of their services. You look quite refreshed and invigorated."

"They are rumored to be miracle-workers." He stepped back and took her hand, escorting her out of the cabin and out on deck. Myrgen was leaning on the railing looking over the city and she smiled at him as they approached. He stood and bowed. "Now that's what I like to see. Your Majesty, she looks radiant."

Alexander looked at her, his own smile reflecting in his eyes. "She does, doesn't she?"

Catriona put a hand on Myrgen's arm. "We're going out to dinner. Keep an eye on things here?"

Myrgen winked at her. "Will do."

Myrgen watched them walk down the docks together and didn't look away until they moved down the street out of sight behind a neighboring ship. Octavius came over to him and leaned on the railing as well.

"You alright?"

Myrgen nodded. "Yeah. I feel it, trust me, but it's the right thing to do. I need a few more right things in my life."

"How do you know it's the right thing?"

"To be honest, it's because I want her, but I'm not the best thing for her. He was here first. She spent all winter pining for him. Then some spell causes her to change her mind and I just can't let that set. She's worthy of being queen, worthy of being in love and very worthy of being loved. It's very possible I'm not in love with her, not really, and I'll end up breaking her heart. Better to move her where she belongs than end up being the source of her sorrow."

Octavius looked at him, his brow not furrowed despite the fact he seemed to be thinking. Myrgen was astounded. Eventually, he nodded. "What will you do now?"

"Work. I have a lot of logs to read and manifests to enter into the books. No reason to put it off." He pushed away from the railing and nodded to Octavius and was very impressed with himself when he managed to get to his room and close the door before the tears actually fell.

Alexander and Catriona walked through town looking at the local color and a few booths. Before long, they left the main road and went into a nice part of town. Catriona had to admit she had never been in this section of town and was a little nervous. With each nicer house, she felt more and more under dressed. As her clothes got shabbier and shabbier in her mind, they arrived at a beautiful manor at the end of a street of beautiful manors. It was set back from the others and she was patently aware of how dusty her boots had gotten in the trip.

A servant greeted them at the end of the walk. "Your Majesty. The Mayor is expecting you."

Catriona pulled on Alexander's arm. "I thought you were taking me someplace to cleanup first?"

"Yes. The finest salon in the city. The Mayor's lady specifically requested the opportunity to dress you. It's quite an honor for her, being as you may be the next Queen."

Catriona scowled at him. This was not the sort of surprise she appreciated. The servant glanced at her and she decided not to bring up her irritation in front of the man. They followed the servant to the front door and followed him in. A portly man in his forties came forward to greet them. He was well dressed and had shoulder-length hair that had once been brown, but was now fine and grey, despite there being a lot of it. He had rich blue eyes and he smiled, extending his hand to her. "My dear lady. I am Morgan Wolf. Welcome to my home."

"Vicar Morgan, this is the Stâpâna Catriona of Caratia. I have brought her to you, as requested."

"Indeed, indeed. Please, come this way, Lady. I have someone who is dying to meet you." He looked over his shoulder and called out. "Ysabel! The Lady is here!"

A lovely young woman with ample hips and thick, long hair came from the back. She curtsied before Catriona and the King. "My lady, it is a pleasure to meet you. Please, come with me."

Catriona looked at Alexander, who kissed her hand. "Take your time and let them pamper you. We have a while before dinner, isn't that right, Vicar?"

"Indeed. His Majesty alerted us when the dress was delivered that you were interested in experiencing the finest salon treatment in the Kingdom."

She looked at Alexander and cocked her head. "Dress? You *are* expecting a lot."

"I promised you a taste of things to come." He smiled and moved her off down the hallway after Ysabel. She heard the Vicar invite Alexander into the study for a brandy and a pipe and Alexander agreed, but she did not turn around to watch him go. The irritation with him was fading a bit as she followed the girl down the corridor.

"The gown His Majesty picked out is amazing, My Lady. I'm sure it will look stunning on you."

"Thank you Ysabel. And please, call me Catriona."

"Yes, My... I mean Catriona." She opened a door in the back of the manor and they entered a vast chamber. The entire thing was tiled in cobalt blue and gold with several fleurs-de-lis in mosaics on every surface. A square tub to the left of the room held steaming water and several cakes of soaps and bottles of hair oils, lotions and perfumes. And a pile of the largest towels Catriona had ever seen. Ysabel turned and stood before her. "Do you wish to wash alone, or would you like a bather?"

"I'll wash alone. Is there someplace for my things until I leave?"

"I was told to return them to your ship for you. Is that alright?"

Catriona looked at the door they had come through. "Yes, I suppose that will be fine. May I see this gown you mentioned first?"

"Of course." She led Catriona over to a large enclosed changing room with velvet seats and three huge mirrors. The cost of this changing room alone would have funded one of her ships for a year. Hanging on one of the mirrors was a gown like no other she had ever seen. It was made of the same shimmering silk Alexander's was, but it was gold instead of blue. It was woven with black threads in the warp, so it shimmered and danced, looking almost alive. He had supplied stockings, shoes and gloves as well, all made of the same material.

"Well, Ysabel. You were right. I can't even be in the same room with this gown."

The girl chuckled. "We'll work on it, then, ma'am. It won't take long before you'll measure up to that dress."

Catriona walked over to the tub, got undressed and got in. Ysabel came over and gathered up her clothing. She sat on a settee and folded the garments while Catriona bathed. She didn't like the soaps scent as much as she liked the one Xannu had made, but she had not come prepared for such a thing either.

Ysabel inspected the seams of Catriona's clothing. "These clothes are extremely well made. Who is your seamstress?"

"Oh, a young woman named Ada. She made all my clothes for me in exchange for a summer of traveling the seas about three years ago."

"These are three years old? I'm even more impressed! They show no wear at all!"

Catriona dipped her head back, wetting her hair. "Well, don't look at the elbows too closely. They get a lot of use."

"Usually, the armscye is the place that tells the tale. A bad tailor or seamstress will skimp there and the salt from the sweat destroys the threads."

"The armscye. That's the armpit, right?"

"Actually, where the entire sleeve attaches. She put a gusset there though, so the threads don't come in contact with the sweat. This is especially important if you live in a sea air environment."

"You certainly seem to know your clothes."

Ysabel shrugged verbally. "I sew clothes for the Vicar and a local Duchess who lives inland."

"You must be pretty good. Did you make the dress there?"

"Oh no. I've never worked with fabric that fine. A man brought a large velvet bag by with it and all the accessories in it. It was huge. I don't know who he was though. He must have been traveling with the King."

Catriona sat up in the tub. *Alexander had come to town through the shadows, with Duncan. Is that where this came from?* "What did he look like?"

"Who? The delivery man? I don't know. I didn't see him. Lysette brought it from the foyer."

"Oh." Catriona settled back into the water, nervous. *Alexander couldn't have brought something like that with him and Ysabel here would have known if it had been made locally.* She looked over at the closed room. It was very well lit, so the person in the room could inspect every aspect. As long as she stayed in the light, she was certain the dress couldn't attack her.

Ysabel noticed Catriona's unease and cleared her throat. "I can get Lysette, if you like."

"Would you please? I would like to know."

Ysabel stood, putting the garment she was folding on the settee. "Of course. There are special soaps in those bottles, specifically for thick hair. The blue ones. Use that and I'll be back in a few moments."

Catriona went over to the basket as Ysabel left, and examined the bottles. They smelled nice and she opened the one to which she had been directed. She had used similar treatments ever since Yantap, where the people's hair was usually thick and straight. Hers had a wave to it which, when she first began traveling on the sea, had been a massive problem. She had braided it constantly to keep the salt air and water from causing it to poof and frizz. The braiding helped immensely, but made it grow longer because it didn't suffer individual breakage as much. Once she had met up with Xannu and her specialty, Catriona had not dealt with such matters outside of regular cleaning.

Ysabel returned as she was rinsing her hair and Lysette, a tall woman with light brown hair and sweet features bowed respectfully to Catriona. "I understand you wanted to see me?"

"Yes. The man who delivered the gown today. What did he look like?"

"Look like? Oh, he was a local messenger. Daniel is his name."

"Oh. Was it made by a local tailor then?"

Lysette shook her head. "I suspect it was a gift from the Duchess. They are preparing to attend the Coronation and she had the clothes His Majesty is wearing brought. This came just after his arrived."

"How did she find out we were here?"

Ysabel answered. "The Vicar. He sent a message as soon as he heard His Majesty was here. They were preparing for His Majesty's visit in search of a wife. This dress was a gift for his wedding. All their children are already married off and none of their grandchildren are of age yet."

"I see. Thank you Lysette."

Ysabel instructed her companion to return later to help with dressing and Lysette bowed and left the room. Catriona sat back into the bath. Ysabel's comment about "His Majesty's visit in search of a wife" unsettled her. Alexander had advertised he was searching for a wife? Enough that people were preparing for it with gifts. Of course, it could have been set aside for something already. She doubted a dress with that much detail work could have been done since Charles' death, and it bothered her that it might have been a gown set aside for one of their children or grandchildren. Such an heirloom should remain in their family.

She looked at the gown again and ducked under the water to wash away the image.

Forty

"He who carves the oak leaves for the mantle
never worships the Fae."
The Wise Wench's Tavern Book

Alexander lifted his glass to his lips. "And Mother never tried to arrange a marriage for me again."

Morgan Wolf was laughing so hard, tears were running down his face. He pulled his shirt sleeve cuff out of his doublet a bit and wiped the tears away, then reached for his brandy. "By the Saints! I'm surprised we still have dealings with York at all!"

Alexander swallowed the brandy and set the glass on the low table before him. "Well, Charles and Mother went in afterward and did damage control, but I wasn't about to have her make such a decision for me. She was Charles' regent, not mine. That's why I'm making this tour of my kingdom, to find my bride. This is a decision for the good of the entire kingdom, and I'm not going to take it lightly."

Morgan nodded. "And this lady, the, what was her title?"

"The Stâpâna."

"Yes, the Stâpâna of Caratia. She is not without her own political ties, it seems."

"I didn't say I would marry a commoner. I merely said I wouldn't exclude them. However, this lady does mean an alliance with the largest, undefeated army in the world. That does have a certain charm all its own." He glanced down the hall as a noise caught his attention. "Could that be her now?"

Morgan leaned forward and saw Ysabel come into the room. "May I present Catriona Morsdatora, Stâpâna of Caratia."

The men stood as she stepped into view and Alexander felt his heart seize in his chest. The gown was glistening gold against her dark skin, enriching the color on both. Her eyes and lips were decorated with cinnamon color, highlighted with a subtle sparkle of gold and the black weft of the dress was more prominent on her than it had been when he approved it from the messenger.

The skirt was full and lavish, with small golden slippers peeking out as she walked. The embroidered bodice was secured over a corset which only served to emphasize her beautiful breasts and clavicle. A necklace of gold and topaz mirrored the ones dancing in her hair and ears and when she curtsied before them, Morgan supported himself on the back of his chair as he bowed in response.

"Your Majesty," he whispered to Alexander, "might I suggest you quit your search."

"I quite agree," he whispered back and then stepped forward to take Catriona's hand. "My dear, you are a vision stepped from my dreams." He raised her fingers to his lips and her gaze followed.

She turned to face their host. "Vicar Morgan, I must say the rumors about your salon here are absolutely true."

"They had a fabulous start, my good Lady. Your beauty is beyond anything we could create. All we did here was remove some of the dust." He turned to the King. "Shall we go dinner then? It should be about ready."

Alexander was pleased to see her moving so smoothly in this setting. He had to admit he worried she would be a sailor on the land as well and putting a nice dress on her would change but the outside. *Perhaps the role she plays in Caratia isn't some honorary title after all.*

A servant pulled out her chair and poured some wine as Alexander was seated opposite her near the Vicar. Alexander was a little surprised to see many others at the table with them and when Catriona nodded and smiled to a couple of the ladies present, he guessed they were the ones who had helped her get dressed. He rather appreciated his host's generosity with his staff. The more people who saw Catriona with him, the more they would not be surprised when he married her. Rumor would spread by word of mouth, preparing his people for this woman to be their ruler.

Conversation was relegated to food selection and simple instruction for a while, with comments regarding the quality. Catriona and the young woman next to her seemed to be engaging in a bit of congenial conversation for most of the meal, leaving Alexander and Morgan to continue their conversation. Toward the end, Catriona looked over at Morgan with a discerning eye.

"Vicar, your name, Morgan Wolf, it is an odd surname."

"Well, yes, but it is not my paternal surname, obviously. I earned it fighting a wolf to save a couple children in the woods nearby. My paternal surname is de Sablonnieres."

"*De Sablonnieres?* So you are related to Myrgen the Grey?"

Morgan snorted. "I prefer not to be associated with that traitor."

"Traitor? So, the news has already reached here from Patras. How unfortunate."

"Unfortunate? He assassinated the King, did he not?"

"I am certain his innocence will be determined as the investigation progresses."

Morgan frowned at Catriona and Alexander saw a perfect opportunity. "The Stâpâna has reason to believe the plan was solely the product of the former Queen and that Myrgen was a puppet being manipulated by her. He is actually currently a guest on her ship, under her protection. Her ship is registered to Caratia and is considered Caratian soil. As long as he is on that ship, he does not fall under our jurisdiction." He sipped the wine Morgan served with dinner.

"Is that so?" Morgan's eyebrows raised in shock.

Catriona remained calm and polite. "I must follow my heart, Vicar."

"The Laws of Caratia must be very different from the Laws of Mervolingia."

Alexander nodded. "There are differences, yes, but I value the lady's integrity enough to allow her the fugitive's company while the investigation is carried out, to keep him safe. It is possible your brother may be innocent, but what is thought and what can be proven are two different things."

Catriona smiled at Alexander and he could tell she was grateful for his defense of Myrgen.

Morgan leaned on his elbows. "As king, Your Majesty, you could simply issue a pardon for him, could you not?"

"I fear that would jeopardize the Oaths of Fealty the people, such as yourself and your staff here, have sworn to the Crown. It would make it look like I approved of the murder of my brother. Thus, until the investigation concludes, his status must remain the same."

Catriona bowed her head graciously to Morgan. "You are welcome to visit your brother on my ship, if you like. He is there now."

"He is? Is this known?" Morgan looked a little panicked.

Catriona shook her head gently. "No. He has been traveling incognito at all the ports. Those who have met him have not known him as anything other than my Chancellor. Not to mention that the word is not out that he has escaped. For all the populace knows, he is rotting in a cell in Patras as we speak."

"And you would not mind if I went to visit him?"

"Of course not, Vicar. I understand completely. I'm sure he would like to explain his side of the story to his brother."

The Vicar bowed to her and stood. "Your Majesty, if you would not mind, I would like very much to do just that."

"Understood, my good man. I do not know how much longer the *Enigma* will be in your fine port city and so long as you allow me and the Stâpâna to utilize the beauty of your gardens, you are more than welcome to take your leave."

"Thank you, Sire. Thank you very much. My lady, I am in your debt." He stepped over and lifted her hand to kiss it.

"It is the least I can do after you have opened your home and salon to me."

"It was my pleasure. Now, please, enjoy the rest of the meal and dessert. My lady, I have extended my home and hospitality to His Majesty during his stay here in St. Marguerite. I would extend the same courtesy to you. We have several extra rooms here for visiting dignitaries. It would be my great honor if you would stay the night with us."

Catriona looked over at Alexander, who let a sly smile decorate his lips. She got his message and nodded to her host. "I have not brought appropriate attire to stay the night, unless..." she turned to the young woman beside her. "Ysabel, have the clothes I wore here been returned to my ship yet?"

Ysabel nodded. "I'm afraid so, my Lady. As soon as they were folded."

Catriona looked at Morgan. "Then I will simply have to request that you ask my First Mate, Octavius, to send some clothes here once you get to my ship, as payment for setting foot on Caratian soil, Vicar."

Morgan smiled and bowed. "Consider it done, Stâpâna." He bowed once more to the King and then left the room.

Once dinner was done, dessert and tea were offered in the parlor and Catriona waved off the additional food. The corset she was trussed into was already pressing against her ribs and stomach and she didn't dare try to force more into it. Alexander stood and came over to her.

"My lady, you are incredibly beautiful tonight. If I may tear you away from your companion, I would like the opportunity to walk in the moonlight with you."

"I am always at Your Majesty's service." She turned to the woman next to her. "Ysabel, have you met His Majesty formally?"

Ysabel curtsied and nodded. "Yes, my lady, he was so polite as to introduce himself to me earlier."

"I take it, Ysabel, that you assisted my lady in preparing for dinner?"

Ysabel nodded.

Alexander took her hand and kissed it. "My compliments. Should this lady find herself as my queen, your experience assisting her will not be overlooked."

The idea of having someone familiar at the palace was comforting to Catriona, especially if this was going to be her attire for the rest of her life. Perhaps, once Myrgen was cleared of the charges, he would be able to be an ambassador to Mervolingia from Caratia. Then she could feel safe with him at her back, protecting her. She blinked, stopping herself from walking that path of thought. She was here with Alexander. She had said she loved him and Myrgen had stepped away, acknowledging this. It would be difficult, and possibly cruel, to call him to her and have him nearby. She didn't need him close anymore than she had needed to spend time with Alexander this winter.

He looked at Catriona and offered his arm. "Shall we, my lady?"

Catriona took his arm and smiled as they left the room.

Alexander seemed to know where he was going, having apparently been given the grand tour when he had arrived before. He took her out towards the salon, but diverted down a separate hallway at the last minute. At the end of a few turns, he opened a door to a beautiful garden bordering the entire salon. She drew in a breath. "Alex, it's beautiful. I didn't realize this was on the other side of those curtains they had drawn in the salon."

"Well, they were probably interested in keeping you a secret until the final moment. Otherwise, I might have been tempted to peek."

"Well, you would have seen me washing the sea salt out of my hair, if you had. Not the best sight, I'm sure."

He stepped in front of her and looked into her eyes. "I'll be the judge of that." He leaned in and kissed her. The setting was as romantic as possible and she was definitely feeling the effects of the efforts. His hands upon her waist pulled her into him and she surrendered to her fate. For too long, she had fought what he offered under the false dream that she would die if she were away

430

from the sea. Listening to him again had shown she would die away from his side. And she made certain to convey that surrender in her kiss.

Alexander pulled back, breathless. "By the Saints, I want you, Catriona."

She seized his eyes in hers. "Then take me, Alex."

He blinked searching for jest. Finding none, he pulled her to him and kissed her with authority. Passion flowed between them and she liked the feel of his embrace, more than she remembered. She felt his hand slide down her corset, but the impairing masses of fabric between them interfered with the feel of his hands anywhere else. Then she felt his hand on her leg through the skirt and felt a draft as he began hitching it up. She looked at him, then cast her gaze around the garden, watching for voyeurs. She got distracted almost immediately by the feel of his lips on her neck, kissing his way down to the cleavage the corset afforded.

He moved her over to the wall of the salon and pressed her up against it. The gown and corset kept her from feeling the stone bricks behind her and the heat of Alexander's desire kept her from feeling the late night air anywhere else. She felt as well as heard his codpiece unbuckle and wasn't surprised to discover the bulk pressing against her crotch failed completely to diminish with the freeing of him. He grabbed her leg and lifted it, feeling around with the head of his penis for the right place on her.

He found it and thrust into her. The feel of him entering her, claiming her was exquisite and she cried out at his penetration. She arched her back, trying to feel more of him, but the gown interfered and he popped out. He shuddered immediately, his own desire to feel her overwhelming him and she felt him pulse onto her, his orgasm spreading his semen all over her thighs. He rested his forehead on hers and exhaled. "By the Saints and Martyrs... I can't believe it..."

She started to snicker and stroked his hair. "A little too much excitement?"

"Apparently. I'm so sorry, Catriona." He laughed a little too, his smile easy and apologetic. "So, was it good for you?"

She laughed. "Not exactly how I remember it..."

"Must be the clothes."

She touched his face. "Then maybe we should see about getting rid of them."

His eyes glittered and he nuzzled her neck. "Maybe we should."

Forty-One

"All people are your relatives; therefore expect
only trouble from them."
The Wise Wench's Tavern Book

Myrgen heard a knock on his door and looked up from the log books he was working upon. "Enter."

Octavius poked his head in. "Myrgen, there's a man here to see you."

"A man?" He closed the books and got up, following the First Mate out onto the deck. The man on the deck turned and smiled at Myrgen.

"So it's true, you *are* here. My sources are better than I thought."

"*Morgan?* What are you doing here?"

"I live here. Have for a few years now."

"And I'm just learning this now?"

Morgan shrugged. "I wasn't aware you were in a position to care very much."

Myrgen rolled his eyes at the cliché his brother seemed intent on reliving every time he and Myrgen met. Morgan was a half-brother, the product of a time of weakness when his mother fell ill. Believing she was going to die, their father mourned at a friend's home and the woman took advantage of his sorrow. When Morgan was born, Mother had returned to health. Father had refused to leave her to marry the other woman and she had deposited Morgan on their doorstep in order to ruin the marriage. She was rather surprised to find that Mother had actually wanted a baby, feeling her own mortality after being so ill, and convinced she could have no other, welcomed Morgan into their home. The woman had left Patras in disgrace.

It had turned out mother was right about not being able to have any more children so Morgan became the baby of the family, and he had never known a stigma or unequal treatment at the hands of Mother. It was only when Myrgen was a man that he discovered this secret. Morgan's mother had come around, trying to cash in on the scandal, and had tried to use it to threaten Myrgen's pending appointment as Kingdom Chancellor. Myrgen had disposed of her before any of his family knew she was back.

"So, what are you doing these days?"

Morgan crossed his arms. "I'm vicar of this town now."

"Vicar? That's not true. The vicar of St. Marguerite is someone named Morgan *Wolf*. I remember filling in the name on official documents regarding his appointment."

"Yes, that's me. The townsfolk gave me the moniker when I saved some children from a wolf in the woods nearby." Morgan raised his left sleeve, revealing a prominent scar in the shape of an animal bite. "The local Duchess decided to oust the man who was already here for suspected embezzlement and put me in his place."

"Ah. Well, congratulations then brother. Honestly, I'm very happy for you."

"Thank you, Myrgen. That actually means a lot to me." The two men finally embraced, and Morgan put his hand on Myrgen's shoulder. "Come, let me buy you a drink at the local tavern." The two started towards the gangplank.

Myrgen glanced at the deck before returning his eyes to his brother. "Have you heard from Tangl?"

"No. Why?"

"She's missing. She was under house arrest in Patras and she was rescued and spirited away, literally. I was hoping maybe she had contacted you."

"House arrest? Saint's Blood, Myrgen! What did you get our family into?"

"*I* didn't get our family into... Morgan, I'm not going to try and dodge my responsibility in this," Moving ahead of his brother down the gangplank, "but you know as well as I do that Tanglwyst can get herself into plenty of trouble without my help."

On the docks, Myrgen turned to look at his brother and was confused to see him still standing on the gangplank where Myrgen had passed him. Morgan frowned. "I'm sorry, brother. I swore an oath."

Two guards stepped out of the shadows of the nearby ship and grabbed Myrgen by the arms. "Myrgen de Sablonnieres, you're under arrest for high treason to the King."

Myrgen looked back at his brother. "Morgan, don't!"

Morgan descended the gangplank. "I'm sorry, Myrgen. I have no choice. I'm an appointed official of the Crown, His Majesty's representative here in St. Marguerite. It is His Will that traitors to the Crown be executed, and that execution order has not been rescinded. It is His Will that you die."

"You son of a *bitch!*"

"Don't insult our mother like that, Brother. It will be hard enough to tell her I had to do the deed myself."

"Yes! When you explain to her that you murdered her only son? Yes, that will crush her!" Myrgen struggled against the arms of the guards as they tried to pull him away.

"What? What do you mean?" Morgan held up a hand to the guards, staying their progress.

"Haven't you ever found it odd you don't look *anything like her?*"

Morgan's eyes grew wide and Myrgen watched his suspicion grow. Suddenly, he realized this was wrong, that it wouldn't save him. *Fight against the darkness. Don't give in.*

"What are you talking about, Myrgen?" Morgan stepped up and grabbed Myrgen's collar, shoving his face into his brother's. *"What are you saying!?"*

Myrgen swallowed and looked away. "Nothing."

"What do you know?"

"*Nothing!* I was playing on your fears, like I always have."

Morgan gritted his teeth and Myrgen could smell rich food on his breath. His eyes were wet and his face was a furious crimson. He pushed his brother away. Morgan saw Octavius come to the railing overlooking the dock. "Hey! What's all the yell…"

"Octavius! Tell Catriona I've been arrested!"

Morgan struck Myrgen across the jaw, silencing him. Blackness dotted his vision and he blinked, trying to shake it off. He heard more guards come up behind him. Morgan glared into his brother's eyes.

"Guards, watch this ship. No one gets on or off. If anyone tries to escape, kill them and burn the ship. And take this traitor to the holding cells. Tell the headsman he has work to do at dawn."

Forty-Two

"An iron nail will cancel the magic of an oaken
altar."
The Wise Wench's Tavern Book

Alexander opened the door to his room and gestured for
Catriona to enter. A quick scan proved they were without servants
and he kissed her shoulder, his arms on hers as he stepped in
behind her and kicked the door closed. She moaned beneath his
lips and he felt the twitch of life beneath his breeches. He had
hoped to feel her wrapped around him, but had not truly expected
it. In earnest, this was what love inspired.

Her response beneath his touch excited him even more and he
knew this time, he would go a lot longer. Her thighs were already
wet from his first go. Slipping into her would be easier than before
and even more pleasurable with full penetration. He could barely
contain himself.

"I'm not accustomed to these clothes, Alexander. They took so long to get into. I imagine they'll be just as frustrating to get out of."

Alexander chuckled. He slipped a dagger from its sheath at his wrist and smiled at the prospect before him. "Don't count on it, Kikotu." He pressed the blade against the ties holding the gown closed. "And don't move."

He moved the dagger down the ties, severing them. The bodice popped open, revealing the strings of the corset beneath, and he went to work on those as well. She inhaled in relief as the pressure to her torso was released and looked at him over her shoulder. "Thank you, my King."

He turned her to face him, eyes glistening. "Do you mean that?"

Catriona laughed. "You just freed me from the prison of that garment. I owe you my life." She started to pull herself out of the bodice, but Alexander stopped her.

"I'm serious, Catriona. I need to know. Do you mean that? Do you truly surrender to me?"

"Alex..." She touched his face and he melted like butter beneath her. "I've fought this long enough. I love you. I have for a long time and I'm no longer afraid of the road you offer. Yes, I surrender to you."

Ysabel leaned down and picked up the other towel Catriona had used. The room was still steamy from the bath water. The floor and the bath were heated under the tiles, some engineering feat she didn't understand. Still, it worked well. This room was always comfortable and she loved the smell. Catriona's own scent, what she caught of it, was rather distinctive. Not Mervol at all. Ysabel decided to ask her about it in the morning. If she could learn the components, she was sure she could reproduce it.

She walked past a potted plant next to the settee she had folded the Stâpâna's clothes upon and a small glimmer caught her eye. She looked closer and saw a small black stone key on a leather thong in the dirt. She recognized it immediately.

Damn! The lady will be angry. She was very reluctant to remove this in favor of the jewelry that came with the gown. I'd best get it to her. She walked through the halls to the room set aside for the Stâpâna and knocked. When there was no answer, she opened the door, planning on putting the necklace by the bed. Then an idea occurred to her. *This was important to her. She made sure I promised it would get back to the ship. If it got lost here, it could jeopardize the Vicar's standing with her, which could, in turn, incur the King's wrath. I don't get the feeling he was simply looking for a bed partner. This lady mattered to him.*

She put the item in her pocket and put a cloak on to ward off the light chill. It wouldn't take long to get to the docks since everything was downhill from the Vicar's mansion. As she approached them, she saw the guards hauling off some man who was screaming out someone's name, but she couldn't quite make it out. Sound often carried well on the cobblestone streets and she stopped, trying to hear what he was saying. *Octavius? The Captain? Ah well, some poor sod in trouble again, from the looks of it. Probably stealing.* She pulled the key out of her pocket so she could hand it to the first person on the ship that she came across.

The prisoner was taken past an alley and this time, she heard what he was saying. Ysabel looked up. *Catriona? He's calling for Catriona?* It was too much of a coincidence for her to be near the Stâpâna's ship and for someone to be calling for her. She ducked down the alley that had carried his calls to her and crouched in the shadows. The guards lost their grip on the man and he ran, but one of the guards thought quickly and threw his dagger at the fleeing man. The hilt caught in the back of a knee and he buckled not ten feet from her. He looked up and she saw he had stunning blue eyes. This man was wearing clothes that had a similar scent to them as the one Catriona wore.

She saw wrinkles and ink stains, like he had been sitting at a desk. His hair was not combed, but looked like he ran his fingers through it often. His clothes were well made and clean but worn, like they had been put through a lot in recent tendays. And she saw a tailor's mark she recognized. That shirt was made by Ada, the woman who had made Catriona's clothes. The rest of his garb was someone else, but she recognized the blackwork on the cuffs.

This man was not just some unruly sailor. This was Myrgen, the man under Catriona's protection. *The King wasn't interested in the Stâpâna after all. He was just distracting her while he got the Vicar to get the man off her ship and imprison him. He was probably planning to execute him before Catriona knew of his peril!* But how to get the message to the Stâpâna? She was apparently with the King at that moment. Ysabel's own life would be forfeit if she interrupted them. Then she felt a small pulse in her hand and looked down. *The key! Of course!* She could use it as an excuse to get a moment alone with the Caratian dignitary. This necklace had been very important to her. She was certain Catriona would step into the hallway in order to secure it from a servant girl. Ysabel would even make sure she had some simple clothes for the lady to wear if she needed to make a sudden getaway.

Myrgen looked into Ysabel's eyes. He glanced down and saw the key, then back to her face, panic crossing his features. She closed her hand around it and mouthed *I'll get her.* The guards ran over and she ducked back into the shadows as the Vicar came up to the men and prisoner.

"Good thinking, Spencer. Now get him inside, before he wakes the whole city. We don't need his traitorous words causing trouble."

"Come along, you."

Ysabel hazarded a peek from the shadows and caught Myrgen's eyes right before he stepped into the jailhouse. She closed her eyes and took a breath. *The Vicar said Myrgen was his brother. It must be tearing him apart to arrest him. I have to help them both.*

She turned and slipped down the alleyway towards the Manor.

"A crisis is an opportunity riding a dangerous
wind."
The Wise Wench's Tavern Book

Appendices

Appendix A: Characters of the Saintlands

Alan Moriarity: Catriona's son.

Alexander Angloume (ANG-loo-may): Prince of Mervolingia, Alexander is heir to the Throne after Charles. Alexander is also the Duke of Anjou, the family lands of the Angloume house.

Anika Heartholder: Dûcesa of Caratia and adopted mother of Catriona.

Antoinette: Cook in the mornings at the Patras Royal Palace.

Archbishop Alonzo de Patrone: Archbishop of Patras.

Armand de Mortes: Poison-maker employed by Catriona for making pest remedies for her ships. Roommate and companion of Captain Tristram Wulfschlager.

Arnold: Servant of the Royal Family in Patras.

Artemisia: Mythical name of the Moon and mother of the Sea Goddess Callista.

Alistair Hapsburg MacGlarren: Prince of York during the Soulless Wars, his debt to the Winter Queen has prolonged his life. The original Black Sparrow who trained James.

Black Sparrow: Notorious pirate who attacked the Tanglwyst Trading Company. Taken out by Catriona Moriarity.

Caiaphas de Sablonierres: Tanglwyst's younger brother.

Catriona Moriarity (CAT-tree-OH-nah MORE-ee-AR-it-tee): Stâpâna of Caratia. The Stâpâna is the Protector of the Land's

People in the country of Caratia, the second highest rank in the country. The Stâpâna is chosen through a secret ritual known only to those in Caratia.

Cecilia: Cook in the Patras Royal Palace.

Charles Maxamillian IX: King of Mervolingia, ruler and instigator of the St. Michael's Day Massacre.

Count Gabriel Plantyn: General in the Emilianite army and good friend to King Charles of Mervolingia. Murdered in the St. Michael's Day Massacre.

Dominic D'Medici (DOM-uh-nik dee MED-ee-chee): Assistant Chancellor of Mervolingia and fiancé of Gwen.

Drake Zapolya: Duce of Caratia. The ruler of Caratia can be either male or female and is chosen directly by the Land through a ritual involving several trials and finally culminating in a ceremony in the town square of Zara.

Duncan McVryce: A notable member of the Back Streets of Patras, Duncan has played a role in several events involving members of the Royal family, the Augustinian church and Tanglwyst's interests.

Evelyn: Arnold's wife.

Fallon: Princess Marie Elizabeth's nursemaid.

Father Benjamin: A priest in service to Marco Giovanni, he was killed helping Catriona escape her captivity in the breeding pans of the Giovanni estate.

Francois Angloume: Bastard son of King Charles, named after Charles' older brother.

Gomez de Santander: Head of Alexander's personal guard, Gomez began as a guard at the Giovanni estate.

Grand Guard Marcel: Head of the Gendarme police force in Patras.

Grymalkin: Prince Alexander's traveling identity.

Guillaume de la Rapiere: A big player in the Back Streets of Patras, Guillaume killed Richard de Holloway, Tanglwyst's first husband.

Gweneviere "Gwen" Douglas (GWEN-eh-veer DUG-lus): Handmaiden of Catriona, Gwen has the distinction of being her most trusted companion.

Henry of Vitus: Husband to Princess Margaret of Mervolingia and third in line for the Mervol throne. Member of the House of Guise, a financially powerful house in Mervolingia.

King Henry II: Father of Francois I, Charles, Alexander and Margaret, husband of Catherine, Deceased.

James Douglas: Brother to Gwen, Black Sparrow, the younger.

Lawrence: First shift baker at the Patras Royal Palace, Lawrence has been with the Royal family for over twenty years.

Lord of Kilmory: Yorkish landholder of the capital of Glarren, Kilmory is the trade face of Glarren on the continent side and still under the direct control of the Queen of York.

Marco Giovanni: Mandian Count and head of the Apolodorus family, Giovanni almost married his cousin to secure a large financial conglomerate but murdered his son and then committed suicide the tenday before his wedding, leaving the Apolodorus fortune to his oldest child.

Margaret - Sister to Charles and Alexander. Married to Henry of Vitus.

Marie Touchet - King Charles's mistress. Mother to Francois.

Martin - A guard in the Patras Palace

Michael - Myrgen's Nubian Slave. A very large man who is fiercely loyal to Myrgen.

Morgan Wolf - Viscount in St. Marguerite.

Myrgen "the Grey" de Sablonierres (MUR-gun dee SAB-yon-air): Chancellor of Mervolingia, he is in charge of all funding and expenses for the entire kingdom.

Nicolai Moriarity - Husband of Catriona Moriarity. A guard in the Patras Palace.

Nigel - King Charles's Castellan before Myrgen.

Octavius - First mate of the *Enigma* under Captain Catriona Moriarity.

Pierre - A guard in the Patras Palace.

Pope Gregory - Head of the Augustinian Church.

Princess Isabelle - A Mandian Princess of marrying age

Princess Marie-Elizabeth - The three year old daughter of Elizabeth and Charles.

Queen Elizabeth of Krakte - Queen of Mervolingia, married to Charles Maximilian IX. Mother of Marie-Elizabeth. A school friend of Tanglwyst's along with Adriana Capaletti

Queen-Mother Catherine D'Medici - Mother of Charles and Alexander. Married to Henry II. Is currently away from Patras on business in the Papal City.

Simon - A young Valet of Tanglwyst's.

Tanglwyst de Holloway (TANG-gul-wist dee HALL-oh-way): Owner of the Tanglwyst Trading Company and Catriona's secret partner.

Tristram Wulfschlager - Captain of the *Righteous*, one of Catriona's ships.

Urien Atredes - Husband of Tanglwyst de Holloway, a Latian Merchant who owns The Atredes Trading Company, which along with the Tanglwyst Trading Company controls 73% of the Mervol - Mandian trade.

Appendix B: The Augustinian Calendar

The world of the Saintlands has four seasons, and those are the purview of the Fae Lords. Embertwist Apocraphix, the Vernal Monarch, rules over spring, Corrigan Starshadow, the Midsummer King, rules summer, Calpurnia Allegheri, the Autumnal Sovereign, reigns over fall and Gloriana Talnig, the Midwinter Queen, rules winter.

To combat these lords, the Church originally invoked the Archangels against them. These were sufficient but as Heaven gave the Church the Saints, these former humans were invoked in addition, adding to the strength of the protections against Fae trickery. The saints were originally celebrated upon the day of their ascension and delivery by Heaven into the Rolls.

However, 300 years ago, the Church, in the aftermath of a great war, decided to write down a formal calendar, honoring saints for their purviews instead of their date of ascension. This was to battle non-church beliefs, unify the masses and establish lines of Church control.

Pope Richard I told the cardinals to which he assigned this task to begin the year prior to the apex of Gloriana's control, so as to get ahead of the rise of her power. The Cardinals discussed it and Cardinal Cosimo of Pardua offered up Genevieve, invoked against disasters, to start the year. Richard approved and the calendar was begun.

Genevary became the first month and the months were divided into 31 day sets with 10 day weeks. In the center of the month, the 16th is the Devotional Day, where all work stops for a day to pray and invoke the saints of the month. This strengthened the divinity in the realm, repelling anything not Heaven related. Although the new calendar reorganized the role of Saints during the year, many days are still known by the saint who ascended upon that day, though the Archangel's days were established during the Augustinian Calendar.

Months

1st: Named after Saint Genevieve, **Genevary** 16 honors Sebald, Martin of Tours, and Raphael the Archangel. Genevieve is invoked against disasters, which abound in the Saintlands during the winter. Sebald once burned icicles in a poor woman's home to produce heat. Martin of Tours cut his cloak in half to give to a naked beggar. Raphael brings the heat of the sun and dawn to battle freezing cold.

2nd: Named after Saint Vitus, **Vitusary** 16 honors Medard, Catald, and Barbara. Vitus is invoked against storms, but is also the Patron saint of dancers so balls abound in Vitusary. Medard is invoked against bad weather because he sheltered the beautiful queen Angelica, granddaughter of Saint Marie Angelica, when she fled the intrigues of the Mervol court during a storm. Medard gave his own tent so she would be safe and dry. An eagle sheltered him from the weather, creating an umbrella for him as he rested. Catald cured the ill and is invoked against plagues, which often abound from bad weather. Barbara was saved when lightning struck her attackers during a siege.

3rd: Named after Saint Florien, **Florias** 16 honors Vincent, Jude, & John of Nepomuk (bridges & flooding). Florien is invoked against floods, a common problem in the Saintlands the third month. Saint Vincent Ferrer is the patron saint of builders, often put to work during this time. Jude helps the hopeless. John of Nepomuk strengthens bridges during floods to save the towns.

4th: Named after Saint Elmo, **Elmos** 16 invokes Fiacre (gardeners), Phocas (market gardeners), and Uriel the Archangel. Elmos starts the sailing season, so Saint Elmo, patron saint of sailors marks this month. Fiacre and Phocas bring the first harvests from winter, began indoors or in warmer climes to feed the masses while Uriel protects the people from the lies and trickery of thieves.

5th: Named after Saint Walburga, **Walpurgisnacht** 16 invokes Valentine, Rose of Lima, & Theodore of Sykon (reconciling the unhappily married). Walpurgisnacht 1 allows the young and amorous to pursue each other unhindered and as such, this month marks the beginnings of many marriages. Valentine honors true love. Rose of Lima honors florists and flower growers. Theodore, known for his counseling skills, reconciles the unhappily married, reminding them of the way they felt their first month of marriage.

6th: Named after Saint Wilgefortis, **Vilgfort** 16 honors Felicity (women wanting sons), Monica (wives), & Marie Angelica (nun who married). Felicity is invoked by women wanting sons, usually royals, due to her miracle of delivering sons whenever she was a woman's midwife. Monica honors wives as she was Heaven's example of a perfect wife and Marie Angelica was a nun who married for the sake of the world. A vision held that Marie Angelica would have a daughter who would alter the church and though she was a nun, she was persuaded to leave her vows to fulfill this vision. Her daughter, Tanglwyst Angelica, inherited a powerful shipping company which was destined for the hands of a corrupt Church. Her sacrifice honors all women who must abandon their own dreams for the sake of a greater good.

7th: Named after Saint Maurice, **Maur** 16 honors Elizabeth (war), Clara (savior in the Soulless War) and Michael the Archangel. This is the season of war, and thus, the people invoke Saint Maurice to keep their soldiers safe while away from home while Elizabeth is invoked to find peaceful resolutions to wars. Clara was a woman whose role in the Soulless War enabled the plague to be destroyed through the spreading of soil she had walked upon, preventing the plague from crossing it. Michael fought the creatures of Hell to preserve the faithful during the great wars.

8th: Named after Saint Francis, **Franco** 16 honors Hubert (hunters), Andrew, & Sebastian. Saint Francis honors all animals and those who tend them. Hubert honors the hunters. Andrew the fishermen and Sebastian protects archers.

9th: Named after Saint Thomas Aquinas, **Aquin** 16 honors Ivo, Augustine, and Albert. The season of scholarly pursuits, Aquin honors those who devote themselves to study. Ivo honors lawyers. Augustine honors theologians and his ideals of Heaven are the basis for the Augustinian Church. Albert honors scientists and herbalists.

10th: Named after Saint Benedict, **Benedine** 16 honors Gabriel the Archangel, Giles, & Margaret. As this is a time of darkness descending upon the land and things turning cold, people were often creating tales of ghosts and fear. Those who had died in the wars of the summer or in the professions of the year were often "seen" wandering the desolate places during this month. To counter these tales of fancy, the church brought in their strongest saints against fear and superstition. Saint Benedict fought his greatest fear, being homeless, and opened his home as a shelter. As such, he is their patron saint. Giles protects against night terrors. Margaret defends against those being attacked by devils, enabling their escape. Gabriel the Archangel heralds Heaven's will, driving away doubt and fear.

11th: Named after Saint Ferdinand, **Ferdin** 16 honors All Saints (Fer 1), Eloi, and Anne. To celebrate the survival of the month of fear, All Saints Day was noted as the first Church holiday. It also honors those responsible for the greatest achievements of humanity: Ferdinand for Engineers, Eloi for jewelry and metal smithing and Anne for pregnancy.

12th: Named after Saint Brigit, **Brig** 16 honors Cosmas & Damian, Raymond, and Roch. A most notable saint, Brigit was one of the first saints ascended to Heaven after giving her life to heal others. Her blood created a fountain by which those who were ill or damaged could be restored. This fountain is in the center of the Papal Palace in the Papal City. Cosmos and Damian are conjoined twins who became doctors. Raymond honors midwives. Roch is invoked against epidemics.

Weekdays

Day 1: Honorasday: named from Honoratus, for bakers.

Day 2: Bernaday: Named after Saint Bernadette, shepherds.

Day 3: Rufinasday: Named after Saint Rufina, potters.

Day 4: Simproniday: Named after Four Crowned Martyrs, stonemasons.

Day 5: Julianusday: Named after Saint Julian, boatmen.

Day 6: Vincentsday: Named after Saint Vincent Ferrer, builders.

Day 7: Wencesday: Named after Saint Wenceslas, brewers.

Day 8: Genesday: Named after Saint Genesius, Actors & Comedians.

Day 9: Columbasday: Named after Saint Columba, poets.

Day 10: Dismasday: Named after Saint Dismas, undertakers.

Appendix C: Religions

Augustinian (AHG-us-TIN-ee-uhn)

The Augustinians believe God created the world and Heaven. God set up the ability for Man to ascend to Heaven body and soul by doing good works. If a human is good enough and helps enough people, they can become a Saint. Each Saint in the Augustinian Rolls was once a human and their name appears in the Heavenly Roster when they ascend. The Heavenly Roster is a book kept in the Papal City on the Official Altar in the center of the Cathedral under constant guard.

In the 1300s, the Church stopped acknowledging new names in the Roster after The War of the Soulless which they blamed upon the heathen religions. The reason cited for this denial was the War made it difficult to believe all the reports of ascended Saints. At the time, it was unknown by the populace about the Heavenly Roster but after the declaration and an investigation by nobles outside the church, this information was revealed to the public. Regardless, once the Pope responsible passed away and the scandal was uncovered, the new Pope acknowledged the updated Rolls and the new Saints were canonized.

The main Tenant of Faith in the Augustinian religion is the Saints are the world's connection to Heaven. It is only by praying to the Saints that one can communicate with Heaven. It is against the Laws of the Church to pray directly to God, bypassing his appointed representatives, to make requests, though one can offer praise unto Heaven without invoking a particular Saint. However, if one prays to a particular saint for guidance or assistance and they receive it, it is against the laws of the Church to not acknowledge the Saint who answered the prayer.

Emilianite (uh-MEEL-ee-uhn-ITE)

After the War of the Soulless and the Scandal of the Unacknowledged Saints, a group of followers broke away from the Church. Citing corruption in the dictations of the papacy, it was determined that apparently the Church could communicate directly to Heaven without the help of the Saints since they refused to acknowledge the Saints received in the Rolls. They called these Saints "the Abandoned Children" and called themselves Emilianites, after Emilio, the patron Saint of abandoned children.

The Emilianites believe that man cannot be trusted with the will or intent of Heaven through a conduit, for that can be hidden or destroyed. Instead, they believe man can be more assured of correct information if he prays directly to Heaven. If Heaven wants the Emilianites to pray to a Saint, they will communicate that Saint's name to all the Faithful. Until that happens, the Emilianites will pray directly to Heaven. Since the Scandal of the Unacknowledged, no Emilianite has ever noted a Saint's name being given to them. As such, they continue to offer prayers only to Heaven.

Land Worship

The Maker split in two, creating the Heavens and the Land. Both are sentient and great entities unto themselves. Heaven holds the Well of Souls and deals with all things ethereal such as dreams and thoughts, ideas and concepts. The Land deals with all things physical, be it body, plant, or liquid. If it can be held, it is the purview of the Land.

When the body dies, the Land takes it into itself and dissolves the flesh, leaving the soul. The soul is filtered and cleansed of the sins of its life. When all the sin is gone, the soul that is left is returned to the Well of Souls. The Land interacts with the people on a daily basis, feeding them, clothing them, healing them. They trust the Land and count on its gifts for life.

Callista's Call

Oceanus, Father of Waters, was alone and lonely. He wandered across the world without drive or direction. Sometimes, to relieve his boredom, he would slice through a mountain or sink an island he made but in the end, he was aimless and alone. Then, one night, he heard a stirring song. It beckoned him from across the Land and he fell upon a beach, kneeling before the singer. A beautiful maiden of silver hair and glowing pale skin sat naked on the beach, her voice filling the night. He crept up behind her. She saw him and screamed, then grabbed her clothes and fled to the sky.

Every night, he went to the beach to fall upon the shore, begging her to return. He brought her gifts from the sea and faraway lands, creatures and stones, wood and plants. Eventually she peeked from behind the curtain of night and slowly emerged, a little more each night, until she fell in love with Oceanus and they made love upon the beach. They created a daughter of rich blue skin like her father and glowing white hair like her mother. They called her Callista. The salt from their tears of joy at the sight of her soaked her, making her touch turn water into salt water.

Callista watches the sea and keeps her secrets and those of her followers. She is a fickle goddess though, and prone to fits of fury that can seem unprovoked. When she is happy or dealing with honorable people, her hair is the white of sea foam. Mermaids gather the honored dead and if a sailor is a good follower, Callista recognizes them and grants them the ability to live underwater as merfolk in her cities. Her dolphins and sea mammals guide ships through treacherous areas and are always signs of her pleasure.

But she has her primal side as well. When dealing with the dishonorable, she sends her teeth to rend them. Her hair turns bloody red and her sharks and sirens call the evildoers to their destruction. If there is an argument in ship at sea and sharks arrive on the scene, it means someone in the fight is lying. If a criminal is sentenced to death at seas, the sharks will take him, but if the criminal is remorseful, they take him to the depths where he becomes a Marked One and serves Callista for as long as they breathed air. Sirens call the unjust to the sharks' maws. The heavier the sins on their soul, the harder it is to resist them.

If a body is rendered with fire at death, Callista will know them not and shall cast their spirit out of her mouth to walk the earth forever.

The Ancient Ones
Sovereignus was a good king. He loved Magic so much, that he mated with her, and fathered the Fae. The Fae were everywhere. They were the merfolk in the sea and the harpies in the air. They

were the pixies and dryads in the trees and the white-furred talking animals in the snows. All the magical creatures, great and small, frolicked in the love of their mother and father. The Fae loved humans and played with them, guiding them to good places. They punished the lazy or wicked with their games and tricks.

But then a sickness came, one that threatened all the magical creatures. Dark men captured the Fae, torturing them to find the sources of Elemental magic. Sovereignus roared and rode to war against these dark men and felled them. In the battle, he was mortally wounded and returned home to die. He gave to his four eldest his power, divided as to their gifts.

To his youngest son Embertwist Apocraphix, he gave the powers of Spring. The Vernal Monarch is the quintessential thief and like a thief, it comes in the night, stealing the cold of winter and revealing the living things beneath her skirt. To his oldest son, Corrigan Starshadow, he gave the powers of Summer. As the Midsummer King, his paladin nature marches forthright towards the good and just.

To his oldest daughter, Calpurnia Allegheri, he gave the powers of Autumn. Calpurnia so resembled his beloved Magic, she channels the gifts of change and harvest during her reign as the Autumnal Sovereign. To his youngest daughter, Corrigan's twin, he gave the power of Winter. Gloriana Talnig, the Midwinter Queen, uses the cold to stop disease and preserve and heal, but also to punish the wicked and delay the unjust. The children split and went to different parts of the world to preserve their realms from the followers of the Dark Men, but each season, they return to Sovereignlumin, the great Tower That Watches All to transfer the power of the seasons.

Karma
Karma is all about balance. For each act, there is an equal and opposite reaction in a person's life. As they get closer to the end of their life thread, they can find themselves bound by the threads they have thrown. Negative acts cause sticky threads, positive acts throw stabilizing threads. If a soul has cast more sticky threads than stabilizing, they can be caught up in the negative and it will strangle them. Thus are many of the symbolic gods of Karma multi-limbed creatures.

The Primordial Egg

The Primordial Egg twitched and cracked. From the shell, four Dragons emerged. They opened their mouths and breathed forth the world. The Earth Dragon formed land and grass, ore and metal, wood and dale. The Water Dragon formed oceans and rivers, lakes and streams, snow and ice. The Fire Dragon breathed the sun and stars to warm the world. And the Air Dragon gave life and the moon. As all things came from magic, all creatures upon the world were magical, and all things communicated with one another in the combined tongue of the elements.

But then, a threat loomed on the face of all and it tried to conquer the magic in the world. It's flashing sword and violent means crushed all but its own belief, slaying the dragons in the world. The Elemental Dragons Rose against it, but to destroy the threat meant to destroy all they loved as well. Instead, they seized their followers and sealed them away in special places. The Earth Dragon hid the giants and Dwarves in the mountains. The Fire Dragon hid her faithful in the ash and lava. The Water Dragon took her children and gave them the ability to breathe water. And the Air Dragon took his children to the sky, to the place between life and death.

At first they spoke aloud to one another, but monsters found their hiding places, so the Dragons broke the world and spoke only in secret languages so none could find their whereabouts. The Earth Dragon spoke through entrails and omens, the Water Dragon through storms. Fire claimed its own hypnotic power and Air spoke through the dead. Together, they all keep the legends and the magic safe, making certain that only those who wish to keep magic in the world can find them.

Fang and Claw

The practice of having an animal choose to join with a person's soul to guide them is standard practice in the followers of Fang and Claw. They also believe in the consuming a part of the animal allows for that animal's superior quality to enter the consumer.

As a rite of passage, warriors of the tribes will hunt a dangerous animal with which to partner. Shaman may not be led by a dangerous animal, but by a wise one such as Snake or Owl. And those who become the Seers find themselves in the company of spiders.

Appendix D: Countries

Caratia (CUH-ray-SHEE-uh)
Capital City: Zara
Native tongue: Caratian (CUH-ray-SHEE-uhn)
Dominant Religion: Land Worship

Glarren (GLARE-uhn)
Capital City: Kilmory (kill-MORE-ee)
Native tongue: Glarren
Dominant Religion: The Ancient Ones

Krakte (KRAHK-tuh)
Capital City: Austra
Native tongue: Krakten
Dominant Religion: Augustinian, Emilianite, the Ancient Ones

Latia (LAH-tee-uh)
Capital City: Cheryb (SHARE-eeb)
Native tongue: Latian (LAH-tee-uhn)
Dominant Religion: Callista's Call

Mande (MAHND)
Capital City: Vincenzia
Other Cities: Pardua, Floren, Roma
Native tongue: Mandian (MAHN-dee-uhn)
Dominant Religion: Augustinian

Mervolingia (MER-vole-LIN-jee-uh)
Capital City: Patras
Other Cities: Rouen (ROO-en), St. Giles, St. Andrew, St. Marguerite
Native tongue: Mervol (MER-vol)
Dominant Religion: Augustinian, Emilianite

Nubia (NOO-bee-uh)
Capital City: Leeus Brul (lee-OOS bruul)
Native Tongue: Fangspek
Dominant Religion: Fang and Claw

The Papal City (PAY-puhl)
Capital City: None
Native tongue: Mervol
Dominant Religion: Augustinian Church Seat

Toledo (toe-LEED-dough)
Capital City: Tuscan
Native tongue: Toledan
Dominant Religion: Land Worship

York (YORK)
Capital City: Landen
Other cities: Canterbury, Kent, Oxford, Cambridge
Native Tongue: Yorkish
Dominant Religion: Emilianite

Yndia (YIN-dee-uh)
Capital City: Yantap (YAN-tap)
Native tongue: Yndian
Dominant Religion: Karma

Yokotama (YO-ko-TAH-mah)
Capital City: Kūki doragon
Native Tongue: Yokotaman
Dominant Religion: Dance of the Air Dragons

About the Author

Tonya Adolfson has been a member of the Society for Creative Anachronism for 23 years and has met thousands of people with very interesting personas. Many of these people have made it into these books and she is grateful to them for enriching her life.

Tonya lives in Boise, Idaho with her husband, two children, two housemates, four cats and two dogs and yet, strangely, the house is actually pretty clean.